"*In* The Cantaloupe Thief *Deb Richardson-Moore spices her perfectly paced story with just enough detail to let us see, hear, know, and feel exactly what we need and no more. And she does it with writing that's vibrant, crisp, and real — we're treated to a master storyteller showing us how it's done. Murder may be the plot that drives Richardson-Moore's yank-you-in-from-the-first-sentence yarn, but it's her supple and admirable talent that's to die for.*"

John Jeter, author of The Plunder Room

"*Prepare to read Deb Richardson-Moore's* The Cantaloupe Thief *like you're getting ready for a southern snowstorm. Run out and buy your bread and milk, stock the pantry to the brim, and cross everything off your calendar, because once reporter Branigan Powers draws you into her mystery, you'll stick fast to the couch until you turn the last page. Bravo to Deb for creating a captivating novel so full of heart, humour, and suspense. I simply loved it.*"

Becky Ramsey, author of French by Heart

"*Fantastically entertaining, this beautifully written, intelligent page-turner gets at both the prejudice and promise of the New South. Our curious heroine, Branigan Powers, has guts and heart. Deb has concocted a winner in this first installment of a great mystery series.*"

Matt Matthews, author of Mercy Creek

"*Deb brings the authenticity of her own work with the homeless and extensive background in newspapers to this terrific debut with a twist ending you'll never see coming. I can't wait to see what Branigan Powers takes on next.*"

Susan Clary Simmons, former Executive Editor,
Greenville Journal

Deb Richardson-Moore is a former journalist, and the pastor of the Triune Mercy Center in Greenville, South Carolina. Her first book, *The Weight of Mercy*, is a memoir about her work as a pastor among the homeless. She and her husband, Vince, are the parents of three grown children. To find out more about Deb, you can go to her website: www.debrichardsonmoore.com.

PROLOGUE

Alberta felt every one of her eighty years, felt them deep in the rigid muscles that supported her slender neck. Her Fourth of July party last night was exhausting in a way it hadn't been in previous years. This morning's pancake breakfast with her teenage granddaughters was raucous, at least by her standards. She loved the girls, God knew – loved them with a ferocity that surprised her. Still, their exuberance was wearing.

She eased onto the sagging den sofa, solicitous of her aching hip, and kicked off her ecru pumps. Her chihuahua Dollie hopped up beside her, head cocked, waiting for a pinch of bread crust.

"Dollie, you're my best girl," she said, giving the cinnamon-colored dog a small bite. "Though I don't think poor Amanda wants to compete."

The tête-à-tête earlier with her only daughter had been as difficult as she'd imagined, disclosing the long-held secret about her younger son, the family rogue. Alberta could tell that Amanda was shocked.

"At least that shut her up about my so-called dementia," she told Dollie.

Then the doctor's visit with her older son, the stalwart one, the one she trusted. She'd given him a hard time over the years, she knew. But he'd remained steadfast.

Now all she wanted was to curl up on the end of this worn sofa with her sandwich and potato chips and a glass of Tabitha's sweet iced tea. Her maid brewed tea better than the maids of anyone in her bridge club. Everyone said so.

This den off the kitchen was a sanctuary of shabbiness and warmth, unlike the high-gloss rooms with their hardwoods and brocade draperies and gleaming piano. She enjoyed those rooms, of course, enjoyed their cool elegance. That's where she entertained her book club and bridge club and music club. Though she'd had about enough of those music club biddies tut-tutting over the homeless man who'd shambled into her parlor last month and sat down at the piano.

"My lands, Alberta!" she mimicked in a high-pitched voice for Dollie's enjoyment. "That man could have killed you for yoah wedding silvah."

Alberta had no use for fear or flightiness.

She fed Dollie a broken chip, then punched the remote control for her soap opera, sighing at the simple pleasure of this break in her day. She took a bite of sandwich – banana and crunchy peanut butter on white bread, a combination she'd enjoyed since girlhood yet hid from those same music club friends. With them, she'd choose chicken salad. "Or cucumber, God forbid," she said aloud. "Dollie, whoever invented the cucumber sandwich should be shot. Now banana – I understand that's what Elvis ate. So don't tell anyone."

She savored the combination of peanut crunch and firm banana. She was reaching for a chip when she heard a knock on the kitchen door. Her heart sank. Probably Amanda, early for their trip to the lawyer's office. She wasn't ready to see her daughter yet.

No, wait, Amanda had a key. It wouldn't be her. The knock came again.

Sighing, Alberta rose and slipped her pumps back on. A Southern lady never answered the door, even the back door, without shoes.

Dollie followed, nails click-clicking on the linoleum. Alberta opened the door, puzzled, surprised, though not entirely displeased to see her visitor. After a few words, though, she was more than displeased. She was outraged. Dollie picked up on her fury and yapped ferociously, threatening to trip Alberta by skittering around her feet. Alberta slammed the door.

She pivoted to return to the den, to her lunch, shaken, but certain she'd settled things. That's how she lived her life: always certain, always settling things properly.

Only now she heard a crash, and turned in disbelief to see a rock land on the kitchen floor, accompanied by a rain of shattered glass. She cried out in anger – red-hot, shocked anger that turned to fear only in the last moment of her life.

CHAPTER ONE

B ranigan Powers rushed into the newsroom, its silence still disconcerting though the layoffs had been steady for years now. It was 9 a.m. and the remaining *Metro* and *Style* writers were filing into the conference room for their weekly meeting, led by Julie in a hot pink sheath, pink-tinted hose, and shoes of improbably colored pink leather.

Branigan grabbed her battered construction worker's Thermos and Christmas coffee cup, and followed. Christmas was seven months away, and the mug with its sinister elves was truly ugly to boot. But because she had a habit of breaking ceramic mugs, she carried the one she'd miss least.

Julie was already seated at the head of the table when Branigan slid into one of the many empty seats. Settling back with a steaming cup of coffee, she squeezed her eyes into a squint and let Julie's monochromatic attire blend into a Spandex bodysuit.

It always worked. With her blond ponytail, twenty-six-year-old complexion and unremitting color coordination, Julie Ames metamorphosed into the aerobics instructor from Helstrom – Helstrom being the chain that was gobbling up newspapers from Virginia to Florida and remaking them in the relentlessly cheery style favored by the attention-deficit crowd. The chain didn't have *The Grambling Rambler* yet, but its reporters knew enough about the state of the industry to know it wouldn't be long.

They were the dance band on the *Titanic,* playing feverishly to keep from thinking about the freezing water just inches away. Chirpy Julie was the publisher's way of lowering a lifeboat to see if the chain's methods had anything to offer before abandoning ship.

13

"I've been talking to Tan," Julie began with a bright smile, "and we read some interesting statistics in Sunday's paper. The story on mobile home safety said that Georgia is one of the four leading states in manufactured housing."

She looked around as if waiting for the reporters to acknowledge this fact as ground-shaking.

"Along with Texas, Florida and Alabama." Her smile lost a shade of its luster. "Sooooo... we want to incorporate those people into *Living!*"

Living! – the exclamation mark was an official part of the name – was the weekend arts/dining/recreation/decorating tabloid that had replaced the old *Trends!* section, that had replaced the old *Home!* section, that had replaced the old *Georgia Homes* section, back when two less excited words were allowed. All reporters had to contribute to the section, regardless of what actual news they might be covering.

There was a sound of choking as someone's coffee got caught mid-slurp. Marjorie, sixty-ish, raspy-voiced and very un-Helstrom, was the first to speak. "Tanenbaum Grambling IV wants us to write about trailer decor? Like he's ever been inside one!"

"Well, that's not exactly the point," said Julie, who got a little flustered when confronted by Marjorie. "The point is we've been doing a lot of rich people's homes and historic homes and renovated farmhouses. And that's fine. But those people already take the paper. We're trying to reach non-subscribers and we may find them in our... um... mobile home... ah... subdivisions.

"Now, I don't mean go out and find just any trai... mobile home," she continued hastily. "We'll want to find just the right one to show what can be done with the proper décor and color sense."

She was nodding now, trying to get agreement through sheer motion.

Lou Ann turned a saccharine smile Julie's way. "Oh, like a doublewide."

"Yes!" Julie pounced on Lou Ann with relief. "A nice spacious one that's done in lake cottage or minimalist or something else real cute. Now, who wants to do the first one?"

14

Six pairs of eyes studied the conference table. Hard.

"Harley, what about you?"

Harley, the only one at the table even close to Julie's age, looked up, startled.

"Me? Well, I wouldn't mind, but um… I'm working on that lake house and the Main Street apartment." He was rolling now. "And I figured you would want me to finish up that teen dating story."

A faint crease appeared between Julie's impeccably plucked brows. "I guess you're right."

Branigan looked at Harley in admiration. She caught his eye and raised an eyebrow in salute. He tried not to smile.

Undaunted, Julie pressed on. "Branigan, how about you?"

"Gee, decorating trends in trailers," she answered. "Good as that sounds, I'm up to my ears in a story Tan asked me to look into."

An overworked excuse, but safe. The rest of the newsroom was a black hole to Julie, and the evocation of publisher Tan's name was a bona fide "Get Out of Jail Free" card. Marjorie and Lou Ann rolled their eyes.

Julie glanced briefly at police/court/political reporter Jody Manson, then thought better of it: he was apt to get called to something more urgent at any time. Her eyes flicked to arts writer Gerald Dubois, engrossed in his latest *Art in America* magazine. Few people on the staff remembered when Gerald was Jerry Dubert from neighboring South Carolina, the unhappy oldest son of a clan of hunters and fishermen. Here, in northeast Georgia, within driving distance of Atlanta, Jerry had bloomed into an imaginative if overbearing arts critic. And if, as Gerald Dubois, he had reinvented his identity, few people knew. Or cared.

Certainly not Julie, brought in eight months before by Tan-4, as the staff called him behind his back, to see if a shake-up in the newsroom might staunch the bleeding in his family-owned newspaper. It was a route traveled by all the chains as they squeezed American papers for profits. Readers had neither the time nor the attention spans for long, in-depth articles, or so the reasoning went. Give them short. Give them lively. Give them perky.

It was enough to make Branigan wish she were sixty-five and at the end of her career. Instead, she was forty-one, and had some decisions to make.

Julie started to talk trailers to the perfectly coiffed Gerald, then retreated. She clamped her lips into a hot pink line.

"Very well," she said tightly. "You all think it over and I'll expect a volunteer by next Monday."

Marjorie caught Branigan in the bathroom moments later, her heavy-lidded eyes meeting Branigan's vivid green ones in the mirror. Without a word, the women burst into laughter.

"Friggin' trailers!" Marjorie growled. "Maybe we'll start with mine!"

Branigan laughed harder. Marjorie's mobile home was a firetrap. Books and papers and magazines were piled from the tiny kitchenette at one end to the single bedroom at the other. Her nod to decorating was one poster of Tommy Lee Jones and another of Harrison Ford, a kind of geriatric dorm motif.

Marjorie was not the kind of writer newspaper chains would hire today. She was decidedly un-perky, rude to callers, and downright contemptuous of editors. But she could ferret out information and she could write – two skills that even a management fighting for its life had to respect. She represented the best of old-time newspapering. Marjorie and reporters like her were the reason the folks of Grambling had fought the trends and stuck with their *Rambler* when every other newspaper in the country was in freefall. To a point, at least. Young readers were not signing on, of course. Delivery men could bring them a newspaper and coffee in bed, and they wouldn't read it. They got their news from TV or the internet like their counterparts nationwide.

But older readers hadn't deserted *The Rambler* as they had many other papers in the South. The Grambling family, for whom the town was named, knew those readers would die out eventually. But they clung to a vision of integrity and purpose – with the occasional toe in the water that was behind Julie's hiring.

The upshot was that Marjorie was pretty much left alone.

"So how is the 'story for Tan' going?"

"Actually, I wasn't making that up," Branigan said, flipping her honey blond hair behind her ears. "He wants a ten-year anniversary piece on the Alberta Resnick murder. It's the only unsolved murder in the city."

"Ah, good story. Anything new on it?"

"Not exactly. But I had an idea I mentioned to him. He bit."

"And it was...?"

"You remember Liam Delaney who used to work here?"

"Sure."

"He's pastor of a homeless mission. Homeless guys. Transients." Branigan waited for the light to dawn in Marjorie's eyes.

"Oh, my gosh, yes. Why didn't we think of that before?"

Branigan washed her hands and didn't answer. She didn't want to go into the reason the homeless were never far from her mind.

CHAPTER TWO

S he was jolted awake by a mouse scurrying over her foot, its sharp-clawed feet piercing her thin sock, its naked tail flicking at a bare spot below her pant leg.

In another time, another life, she would have screamed. Now she merely grunted, flipped her foot feebly. What was a furry rodent compared to last night? Three men, two of them paying enough for four rocks of crack, one paying with a punch to the head. She raised her head gingerly and felt the left side with dirty fingers. Yeah, there was a bump. She hadn't dreamed it. Damon. No, Damien. No, Demetrius, that was it. Demetrius.

"Wha's a white boy doin' wi' a name like De-ME-trius?" she'd slurred, sliding her malt liquor bottle under her backpack, away from his greedy hands. Come to think of it, the question was what had brought on the fist.

He'd talked non-stop during the act. She wasn't expecting love – that hope was long dead – but it didn't even feel like sex, really. More like meanness. He'd talked about leaving the *hos-pi-tality* of South Carolina for Hot 'Lanta. But the fool didn't make it to Atlanta. Got off the Greyhound about five towns too early.

Too bad for her.

She sat up, head aching, and peered at the empty bottle of King Cobra. For a moment, she couldn't figure out where she was. Then the light piercing the leaves of a river birch sank into her alcohol-sodden brain. The coolness of the packed red mud registered beneath her aching body. She glanced around at the familiar tents. Those snores belonged to Slim, Malachi and Pete.

She risked a protest from her head by looking up at the girders rising steeply to a slim ledge under the bridge. That's where her paying customers were sleeping off their crack. She had slept where she fell, on the hardened clay beside the railroad track, a new low even for her. She sobbed once, but it was hoarse and dry. She had no tears left.

No tears, no dignity, no life.

If only she could end it without pain.

If only she could tell what she knew. Maybe someone would pay for that information.

And then as some want, some need, some primal longing stirred deep inside her brain – the *rep-til-ian* part of her brain, an addiction counselor once told her – her thoughts shifted. If only, if only … if only, she could find one more rock. One more glorious high, then she would quit.

Once she quit, she would tell everything.

CHAPTER THREE

Malachi Ezekiel Martin finished the grits, scrambled eggs, toast and sausage at St James African Methodist Episcopal Church, a stately brick building on the block behind the *Rambler* offices. He threw his paper plate and empty coffee cup into a fifty-gallon rubber can. Then, without being asked, he tied up the full trash bag and carried it to the parking lot dumpster.

He returned to the church dining hall, grabbed a broom and began sweeping as other homeless men shrugged into their backpacks and walked out. They were engrossed in their own problems, but it was a point of pride for Malachi to "pay" for his meal by cleaning up afterward.

This morning's breakfast manager, a solemn-faced black man with a limp, nodded his thanks. When all the chairs were turned upside down on the tables and the linoleum floor swept and mopped, Malachi shouldered his knapsack and walked into the early June sunshine.

Within moments, he was in front of *The Grambling Rambler*'s three-story brick and glass building facing South Main Street. He rounded the building and walked through a side alley to the loading dock. A barrel held newspapers discarded because of a bad print – too faint, bleeding colors, shadowy pictures. He could almost always find the day's edition, and sure enough, there it was: Monday, June 1.

He looked around to make sure no one was watching. The papers were discarded, but still... A man unloading a truck glanced at Malachi, then continued his work, uninterested in what was going on at the recycling barrel.

Malachi wanted to see if the paper had anything further on the hit-and-run of his friend, Vesuvius, five nights before. He'd heard talk in the encampment under the bridge, plenty of talk. *Vesuvius was drunk. Vesuvius had angered some teenagers who tried to roll him.* And his personal favorite: *Some artists in Atlanta were afraid Vesuvius was encroaching on their territory.*

Malachi shook his head. You had to be careful what you believed out here. More than once he'd heard that one of Grambling's street dudes was dead, only to see him walk into St James for breakfast a week later. Malachi seriously doubted a resurrection had occurred.

For all the drug-fueled silliness that went on out here, there was an undercurrent of violence too. *Casual violence*, Pastor Liam at Jericho Road called it. *Casual death*, Malachi silently added.

The newspaper had run three inches the day after Vesuvius's death. Three measly paragraphs. Malachi had seen nothing since. Nothing about an arrest. Nothing about an investigation.

A story that would've made the front page if an upstanding citizen had been the victim was banished to the inside when the victim was a homeless man. Even if, as Malachi suspected, it was something more than Vesuvius being drunk, Vesuvius angering teenagers.

He folded the paper carefully under his arm and walked back up the alley, looking forward to an hour on a shaded bench, keeping to himself, keeping informed.

CHAPTER FOUR

B ranigan punched the familiar number into her desk phone, smiling as he answered.

"Is this Liam Delaney, the pope of Jaw-ja?" she asked.

"Brani G! Haven't seen you in awhile."

"I need two things. One, a lunch to catch up. And two, a time to talk to you about a story I'm working on."

"The hit-and-run?"

"What hit-and-run?"

"One of our homeless men was killed at the corner of Oakley and Anders five nights ago," Liam said. "That's not what you wanted?"

"Sorry, but this is the first I'm hearing about it. I'm working on a tenth anniversary piece on the Alberta Resnick murder."

"Come on over and we'll negotiate. I can make time this afternoon."

"Ah, you remember deadlines. I'll be there at two if that's all right."

"See you then."

Branigan left the office at 1:30, giving herself time to run by Bea's Bakery to grab bagels and coffee. She figured Liam wouldn't have taken time to eat. The Main Street bakery smelled deliciously of yeasty, sugary treats and Bea's to-die-for biscuits, but she virtuously selected two wholegrain bagels, no cream cheese. She didn't let Bea slice them, convinced that slicing kick-started a slide into staleness.

She pulled into Liam's parking lot with five minutes to spare. She saw his eight-year-old SUV, apparently a requirement for dads of soccer players. Liam was carpool dad times two, with his children Charlie and Chan finishing their senior year at Grambling High East.

Branigan smiled at the names, as she did every time she thought of Liam's striking offspring. Liam and his wife Liz had no intention of naming their children after the fictional Chinese detective. They named the girl Charlotte after Liam's great-grandmother, the boy Chandler after a family name they discovered in Liz's ancestral tree. Leave it to seventh-graders to get Charlie and Chan out of that. So that's who they'd been since middle school. Charlie and Chan, the Delaney twins. That's what most people thought anyway.

But a few family friends knew they weren't twins at all, but first cousins. Liz was twenty-four and pregnant with Charlie when Liam's teenage sister, well on her way to becoming a heroin addict, turned up pregnant. Shauna Delaney refused to name the father, and threatened to have an abortion. Liam's parents begged her to reconsider, promising they would care for their grandchild. But it was Liz who finally persuaded the fragile young girl. She and Liam offered to raise the baby as a sibling to their own. Shauna, who worshiped her older brother, consented. Hours after the birth, she relinquished the baby and disappeared from the hospital. Liam's family hadn't seen her since.

Since Chan was just six months younger than Charlie, they were in the same grade at school, and most people assumed they were twins. Liam and Liz certainly treated them the same, and so did Liam's grateful parents. It was not until Chan turned a gangly twelve and began to develop the long muscular legs that would serve him so well running a soccer defense that Branigan had the first inkling of who his father might be. For she had known his father when he was twelve.

The homeless shelter showed signs of Liam's five years on the job. It was a Big Box, a sprawling, high-ceilinged, one-level former grocery store. The city had been delighted to get the food store twenty years earlier. But after seven years and profits much lower than its suburban stores, the chain abruptly pulled out, leaving an empty shell and city council members appalled that their predecessors hadn't ensured an exit penalty.

For six years, the building sat empty, an eyesore and graffiti magnet. Well, empty if you didn't count its homeless residents who broke in and built fires and left trash piles heavy on whiskey bottles and malt liquor cans. All told, it was a mess that defied the mayor's efforts to attract developers to its promising location six blocks west of Main Street.

A suburban church interested in inner-city ministry ultimately sought it out as a satellite campus. Such a use wasn't the city's first choice, but council members figured it was better than an empty storefront. Unfortunately, the newcomers understood little about the lives of the homeless and mentally ill and addicted who lived in proximity to the satellite campus. They went through three pastors in quick succession.

Liam was the fourth, a former *Rambler* reporter and seminary grad, his only experience a single stint as youth minister. He took the struggling mission church as a last-ditch effort by the mother church; the missions committee made it clear they were leaning toward closing it within eighteen months.

As Liam told the story, he didn't know enough to understand what would and wouldn't work. He began by looking at the property as a homeowner, wanting to create a more visually welcoming space by breaking up its monotonous asphalt and concrete. He recruited students from his and Branigan's alma mater, Grambling High East, to perform student service hours; they dug up dead grass and planted trees and flower beds. Liam wheedled them to use Student Council funds to buy river birches and roses, tulip bulbs and verbena, geraniums and day lilies. Soon the students and the mission church had an easy partnership that served both well.

Inside, the teenagers painted an entire interior wall with a colorful mural, peopled with Bible characters. From what Branigan could tell, Adam and Eve were sharing an apple with Daniel as he fought off lions, one of which was saddled and ridden by Joshua entering the land of Canaan, which was populated by multiple Goliaths fighting off sling-wielding Davids. Liam smiled wryly the first time he showed Branigan the mural. "Exhibit No. 1 on why we need Bible study," he said.

Within a few months, the homeless people who ate breakfast and dinner in the church's soup kitchen and attended its sparse worship services began showing up to garden and clean. Liam was surprised, but instinctively realized their participation was a positive step.

Other churches took note and began sending teams over to learn about homeless ministry. When Liam's eighteen-month trial period was up, the mission church had its partner high school, eleven partner churches, and had opened the back of the grocery store as an eighteen-bed homeless shelter for men. Liam contemplated housing women as well, but a trip to a women's shelter in North Carolina convinced him that both genders couldn't be housed in the same building. For now, the shelter remained for men only, though women were welcome for its hot meals.

Branigan shook her head admiringly as she walked past the results the students and homeless men had wrought – the beginnings of dappled shade, ruby roses and pink geraniums, deep yellow day lilies and golden marigolds. Raised vegetable beds flourished in the field beside the building.

She knew that Liam wasn't everyone's idea of a proper minister. He drank beer at the city's outdoor festivals. He dealt with the homeless with brusque expectations rather than sympathy. He welcomed gays with an outspokenness that didn't always play well in conservative Grambling. But the Delaneys' roots in Grambling ran deep, and city leaders couldn't argue with Liam's success. He had his admirers as well.

Branigan reached the former grocer's electric doors, which slid open silently. She passed under the sign proclaiming "Jericho Road". To the side was a folk art painting of multiracial diners sharing a meal. In calligraphy across the bottom were the words "Where the elite eat – with Jesus".

A man she vaguely recognized greeted her from a desk behind an open receptionist's window, a huge smile splitting his face.

"Miz Branigan? You hasn't visit us in awhile."

She searched her mind frantically for a name. Dan? Don? Darren? Liam had taught her the importance of using names.

"Dontegan!" she said triumphantly, a moment before her hesitation would have been obvious. She could see the pleased look on his face and was glad she'd made the effort. "I'm here to see Liam."

"Pastuh told me you was coming," he said. "Go right in."

Liam's office was a boldly colored space, painted lime green and sporting canvases from Jericho's art room. He stood to greet his old friend, his red hair unruly, his face breaking into a welcoming grin.

"Hey there!" he said, pulling her into his skinny six-foot frame and grabbing the Bea's Bakery bag. Though Branigan was taller than average – five-feet-six in flats – she reached only his shoulder. "I've missed you!" he said. "And I've missed lunch."

He rooted around in the bag. "Are you kidding me? Naked bagels? No cream cheese? What's wrong with you, girl?"

"Think of it as an appetizer." She plopped her bagel and coffee on the coffee table that sat between two rocking chairs. He took the rocker with navy cushions, motioning her to take the softer, green-upholstered rocker she loved.

"Despite your unwillingness to feed me adequately, I'm glad you're here," he said. "These guys think no one cares when one of them dies."

Branigan was embarrassed. She hadn't been aware until this morning that one of them *had* died, and reluctantly told Liam so.

"You can make it up to me," he said. "I'll help if I can with your murder story, and you write something on the hit-and-run."

"Deal." She took a sip of coffee. "You know what I've always remembered you saying? Early on you said a man told you the worst part of being homeless wasn't being cold or wet or hungry. The worst part was being 'looked right through'."

Liam nodded. "And we try to look. I say that in every speech."

"That sticks with people. Anyway, tell me about your guy. After I talked to you, I looked it up. All we ran was three inches. I missed it entirely."

"Well," he said, "Vesuvius Hightower was killed on his bike where Oakley crosses Anders, there at the library. The driver didn't stop." The intersection was three blocks away, between the church shelter and Main Street. "I have no idea what he was doing there. Obviously, he missed our 9 o'clock curfew, so he was going to have to sleep outside. But he had done that before. No big deal.

"Vesuvius was a sweetheart when he was on his meds," Liam continued. "Very gentle. Childlike. I'm pretty sure he was MR in addition to bipolar."

Branigan scribbled "mentally retarded", which was still the official diagnosis, though not the politically correct one. "Mentally challenged" or "mentally disabled" were the terms *The Rambler* used.

"He lived here for eight months," Liam went on. "Our mental health worker was making progress with him. He was on his meds and about to get permanent housing. But the reason I thought it was a story for you is that his father died the same way five years ago."

"You're kidding."

Liam picked up his phone and punched in three numbers. "Dontegan, can you come to my office for a minute?" He turned back to Branigan. "Dontegan told me about Vesuvius's father on the morning we got word about V. It must have happened just weeks before I got here, because I didn't know."

Dontegan walked through Liam's open door.

"Don-T, can you tell Branigan what you told me about V's father?"

"V used to ride his bike with his ol' man," Dontegan said. "Ever'where. You ain't never see one 'thout the other. They come to church here way before Pastuh Liam, when nobody else hardly came. They stay in that neighborhood 'cross Garner Bridge. One night the ol' man got on his bike, way late in the middle of the night. They think he was headed to the grocery. He got hit crossin' the bridge. Car kilt him."

"Another hit-and-run?" Branigan was amazed at the careless violence this population faced.

"Nah, the woman, she stop," Dontegan said. "She was all cryin'."

"Was she charged?"

He shrugged.

"Then how do you know she was crying?"

"Just what I heard."

She nodded. Armed with Vesuvius Hightower's last name, she could search the paper's archives for confirmation.

Liam took up the story. "A lot of times our guys don't have any family to organize a funeral service. But Vesuvius did. He had aunts, uncles, brothers and sisters. We held his service yesterday. They had honestly tried to help him, I think, but he'd worn them out. That happens a lot with the mentally ill and mentally challenged. Their families don't have resources for the basics, much less mental health care."

Branigan knew this was why Liam had been so determined to hire a mental health counselor as soon as he could raise the money.

"Damn," she said, then repeated a question she'd asked him a dozen times. "Doesn't this work break your heart?"

Liam shrugged, held his palms up. "It probably should. But this stuff comes so fast and so often, it mostly washes right over you." He smiled apologetically. "But I did think the angle of father and son dying the same way was a story that cried out for the Brani G touch. You can talk to Dontegan more if you need to. And anybody else." He finished his bagel and tossed the wax paper into a trashcan as Dontegan left. "V was well liked," Liam added. "He ran the laundry room most weekends."

"Okay," she said, "I'll try to flesh it out with your men and the Hightower family, and have it ready to run Sunday."

Liam picked up his coffee. "Now, how can I help you?"

"You remember the Resnick murder?"

"Sure." The entire newsroom had been called in on the first few days of the notorious case in July, nearly ten years ago. Alberta Elliott Grambling Resnick, a cousin of Tan's father, had been stabbed to death in the kitchen of her lovely shaded mansion, two blocks off North Main Street. The case was strange, start to finish.

Mrs Resnick was an elderly widow with two sons and a daughter, all of them well known in historic Grambling. Because the murder occurred over a long July 4 weekend, all the children and grandchildren had been gathered. And given Mrs Resnick's wealth, all were suspects.

July 4 fell on a Thursday, and the family threw its lavish annual holiday party, followed by the city's fireworks display, easily seen from the front yard. Around 11 p.m., the party broke up. The older son, the daughter and two thirteen-year-old granddaughters spent the night.

The next day, July 5, there was still plenty of activity at Mrs Resnick's house. The family members who'd spent the night had breakfast together. The son then took his mother to a doctor's appointment. The daughter dropped the two teens, her nieces, at the Peach Orchard Country Club pool, then returned to the hotel where her husband and sons were staying.

The son dropped Mrs Resnick at home after her doctor's appointment. She assured him she could fix her own lunch, so he went home. The granddaughters walked back to their grandmother's house in late afternoon, to find her lying on the kitchen floor, stabbed seven times.

Hysterical, the teens ran next door and flagged down a neighbor who was cutting grass. When he could make out the girls' disjointed story, he yelled for his wife to call the police, sent the girls inside his house, and headed over to Mrs Resnick's. He stayed until the police arrived, blue lights spinning, four minutes later.

Because of Mrs Resnick's standing in the community, because she was a Grambling and because she had a large family, the house filled quickly. Police, the coroner, and city council members rushed to the scene. Detectives feared the crime scene was being contaminated, but it was hard for officers to keep out their bosses. Only when the police chief arrived three hours later – summoned from a theme park with his family – did he crack down on unnecessary personnel and send his bosses home. By then it was too late. Detectives were sure their crime scene had been polluted.

Meanwhile, officers herded family members onto a back porch for interviews. Neighbors brought plates of cookies, and coolers filled with soft drinks. One detective Branigan interviewed called it "Southern hospitality run amok".

The Rambler's cop reporter, Jody Manson, was one of the first on the scene, but police kept him and the rest of the media at bay in Mrs Resnick's driveway. It wasn't a bad vantage point to see family members arriving in twos and threes, some granite-faced, some crumpled and wailing. Jody and two other reporters gathered information at the crime scene while Branigan and the rest of the staff worked from the newsroom, preparing a front-page story about Mrs Resnick's life and charitable contributions, and another in which Grambling society talked about the loss to the community.

That was day one.

In the confusion of the murder, no one noticed that Mrs Resnick's car was missing from a detached garage. So the lead story on day two was that the murderer had apparently stolen Mrs Resnick's 1980 Thunderbird from her garage and abandoned it a mile away in the parking lot of a vacant grocery store – the very lot where Branigan's Honda Civic was now parked outside Jericho Road. Inside the store, three homeless people, squatters, lived without running water or electricity. Police interviewed them repeatedly, but they seemed genuinely bewildered by the whole thing.

On day three, *The Rambler* had another blockbuster: a witness had seen Mrs Resnick's distinctive gray-green T-bird streaking by early on the afternoon of July 5. The young man laughingly told friends later that day, "She'll have fun, fun, fun 'til her children take the T-bird away." The comment made its way back to neighbors, who told police, who brought the young man in for questioning. He'd been on a bicycle and didn't get a look at the driver, he said. That was why he assumed it was Mrs Resnick. Police assured him she was dead by then.

For a week, a month, three months, police chased leads, interviewed and reinterviewed family members and neighbors and service providers. Mrs Resnick's neighbors were understandably nervous and eager to speak with officers. The net was cast broad and wide, for Mrs Resnick's sons had hired numerous workmen at her home in the weeks preceding the July 4 party. So workers from a fence repair company were interviewed, painters, landscapers.

People who were visiting neighbors came under suspicion. In a city with no unsolved murders, this over-the-top stabbing in broad daylight stymied police.

Now, as the tenth anniversary neared, the case was on Tan's mind. Which meant it was on Branigan's.

"Tan-4 has asked me to do a piece on Mrs Resnick's murder," she explained, "looking at the investigation and how it could have gone unsolved this long."

Liam nodded. "There's still a lot of interest. But how can I help?"

"Well, you remember how every lead fell through on the family members, the workmen she'd had in, the neighbors?"

Liam looked thoughtful for a moment. "Yeah, and remember that stranger living in her pool house? And then coming inside her house and playing her piano? Looking back, I'm sure he was mentally ill. At the time, we didn't know what was going on."

"Exactly. Once every logical suspect fell through, the police wondered if it wasn't some transient who killed her, hopped on a train, then left."

"Okay."

"Who would know better about that population than you?"

Liam's eyes widened. "Now I see where you're going."

"Could you ask around? None of us knew these folks ten years ago. But now you do."

"I guess so," Liam said slowly. "But there's no reason to believe a transient would have returned."

"I know. It's a long shot. But I've been at the police station for a week, looking through boxes and boxes of files. Believe me, Liam, these guys were committed. They eliminated everyone who had the remotest connection to Alberta Resnick. I'll be spending most of my time looking over their shoulders and interviewing family members. But what if it *was* a stranger? Someone with no reason – no *sane* reason – to kill her? Someone who just stumbled in during that window of time between her son leaving and her granddaughters returning?"

"We always thought that was a possibility," Liam said. "Especially with her car left here where homeless people were sneaking in and out. Man, I haven't thought of that case in years. Probably since I left the paper. That was the last story I worked on."

"It was?"

"Yeah. I left that August for seminary."

"Anyway, that's what I'll be doing between now and July 5. If any of your guys have memories that go back that far, please ask 'em."

"Can't hurt."

As Branigan rose to leave, her eye fell on a slim table half hidden behind Liam's desk. He had a new picture of the family – himself tall and freckled, Liz, tiny and olive-skinned beside him. Charlie was her father's daughter, tall and fair-skinned, with long, red-gold hair caught in a ponytail, blue eyes laughing in a way dear and familiar. But it was Chan, almost Liam's height but looking nothing like him, who made Branigan nearly stop breathing. With his sandy blond hair and tanned skin, the boy looked like neither of his parents. In fact, Chan looked far more like her.

"Have you seen him?" she asked, her voice strained.

"Who?" Liam started idly, then saw where her gaze had landed. "Oh. No. Of course I'd tell you if I had, Brani."

She nodded, blinking rapidly to clear her vision. "Great picture of Charlie and Chan," she said.

She closed the door quietly behind her.

CHAPTER FIVE

Amanda Resnick turned her powder blue Mercedes off North Main, cutting her speed automatically, watching for children to dart into the street. She'd played on these streets as a child and knew how one could lose all sense of danger when chasing a ball or a cat.

She passed a giant magnolia tree, and her mother's elegant, three-story stone house came into view. Her mother's house – that's how she always thought of it, though she'd lived in it herself for twenty-one years. She and her brothers Ramsey and Heath had built forts under that magnolia, caves really. No sunlight could penetrate its huge branches and flat, glossy leaves.

The spacious front yard was nicely trimmed, she could see, grass low, shrubbery squared off. Thank goodness. Amanda knew what a chore it'd been for Ramsey and Heath to get Mother's permission to let landscapers prepare for this party, to get the iron fence on the side repaired, to have the front porch painted. Or the *ver-an-dah*, as her mother throatily intoned. She also knew they'd had no such luck with the back yard and pool area. Mother had put her foot down, accusing them of trying to sell the house out from under her.

What an old bat.

She turned the Mercedes into the driveway, arching oaks overhead making it a dim tunnel. The car purred to the back of the house, where the driveway widened into a slate expanse large enough to hold six cars. On one side was a detached three-car garage, wooden, painted white. On the other side of the parking area was the house itself, with a simple white door breaking up its flat stone face, wood on the bottom, six glass panes on top.

Beyond the parking surface, the path to the pool was barely visible through the wildly growing hedge. Little had changed since she last lived here, twenty-four years before.

Amanda sighed, and rummaged in her bag for the key she used once a year.

"Mother," she called, knocking and turning the key simultaneously. Dollie, her mother's chihuahua, walked to the door and yipped twice. Seeing it was Amanda, she turned and waddled back to her pillow in the laundry room. Amanda stepped into the kitchen, dim like the driveway, and dated, its yellow and brown wallpaper hideous. The cupboards, once gleaming white, were faded and yellowed. Depressing, Amanda thought, and unnecessary. The house was once a showhouse, and could be again if Mother would let go of a few dollars.

At least it was clean, she could tell, sniffing pine-scented floor cleaner. Tabitha had seen to that.

She walked through the kitchen into the spacious dining room, set up for tonight's party. Through an arch was the living room – or *par-lah*, according to her mother – with its handsome hardwood floors, cabbage rose rug and gleaming black grand piano. The formal rooms, at least, retained their grandeur. She found her mother, seated at the silent piano.

"Hello, Mother," she said formally.

Alberta Resnick, regal even in gray slacks, paisley blouse and black ballet flats, raised her head with a start. "Amanda. I didn't hear you come in."

Amanda came forward and hugged her mother stiffly.

"Where are your boys?"

"By the hotel pool by now, I imagine."

"But they'll be here tonight?"

"Of course."

"I... I... need to tell you something, Amanda. Before everyone arrives."

"Okay." She settled into an armchair. "We've got hours before the party."

"You heard about that man who came in the house last month, the one I caught playing the piano?"

Amanda laughed. Her brother had shared the bizarre story about a mentally ill homeless man who had set up residence in the pool house, then had dared come into the main house. "Ramsey said you gave him what for."

Alberta Resnick didn't join in her daughter's laughter. In fact, she looked at her a long moment.

Finally, Amanda said, "I'm sorry, Mother. It wasn't funny. It was sad, or even scary, I suppose. But it was so like you. Eighty years old and not afraid of a stranger in your house."

"And I'm not afraid now," her mother continued. "I'm... wary, I guess you could say." Then abruptly, "I think Heath was behind it."

"Behind what?" asked Amanda, bewildered by her mother's sudden shift.

Alberta gazed at her steadily.

"Behind the crazy man playing your piano?"

Her mother nodded.

"Mother, that makes no sense. Ramsey said the guy was mentally ill and thought he lived in your pool house. What could Heath possibly have to do with that?"

"Heath wants me to sell the house," Alberta said stubbornly. "He's been after me to cut the shrubbery and list the house. When nothing was working, I think he tried to scare me out."

Amanda's lips parted, but no words came. She stared at her mother. Finally, she got her thoughts together. "Heath? Mother? Do you hear yourself? No offense, but you're eighty years old. Heath has money of his own. What possible reason could he have for wanting to sell your dam... to sell your house a few years early?"

"He does," Alberta said with finality. "And I want to cut him out of my will. Tomorrow. I want you to take me to my attorney's office tomorrow."

Amanda breathed out noisily, already exasperated after just two minutes with her mother. Why couldn't the old lady go quietly?

"Mother, I don't think this is right. I'm going to have to think about it."

"Think about it, and let me know tonight," her mother said, effectively dismissing her.

Amanda sat for another moment, but it was clear she had lost her mother's attention. As always. She rose with a silent shake of her head and walked toward the kitchen, heels ticking on the hardwood, then less stridently on the linoleum. She let herself out of the kitchen door, checking to make sure she had locked it behind her. She was puzzling over her mother's request, but puzzling too over something else. Something she couldn't quite put her finger on. Her mother was as aggravating as ever, but something was a little off.

Amanda didn't want to get in the middle of her mother's war with her younger brother. She'd distanced herself from her family, and that's how she liked it. She'd made a life with Bennett and their sons, and now she wanted nothing more than to find her husband and get his take on her mother's request. He would know what to do.

She was so engrossed in her thoughts, in finding Bennett and sharing this latest weirdness in her family, that she didn't glance toward the hedges that blocked the pool.

Even if she had, she wouldn't have seen someone crouching, watching, so thick was the tangle.

CHAPTER SIX

She was hungry. When was the last time she ate? She searched her mind, but couldn't come up with an answer. She squinted from the shade of the bridge to an abandoned warehouse. The trees in between were casting almost no shadows, so it must be midday. Lunch time. She'd had no breakfast, obviously. No supper last night. Come to think of it, no lunch yesterday either.

Her mind couldn't go back further than that. Maybe she'd had breakfast yesterday at that ol' mission church that looked like a grocery store, where they let men live but not women. What the heck was up with that? Everybody would tell you the streets were harder on a woman.

Maybe she'd go back there. There were all kinds of do-gooders around that place who would give you crackers, or canned goods with ring-tabs, if it wasn't time for a meal. Specially if you could find a time that Pastor Liam wasn't around. He'd want to talk about *re-hab*. You'd think *re-hab* was the gospel itself to hear that freckled freak go on about it.

She sat up and unzipped the dirty backpack she was using for a pillow. Was there a little something in there to get her going? Her hands grasped a bottle, but when she pulled it out, it was empty. And worse: a brown spider came with it and went scurrying up her arm. She flailed wildly, a screech erupting from her parched throat.

A head popped through the flap of the tent closest to her. "You all right, hon?" asked a heavyset woman, her head wrapped in a blue kerchief.

She nodded mutely, suddenly scared that she might be heard by Demetrius. She wanted to stay as far away from his swatting hands as she could get. She glanced around the campsite, but no one else was paying attention. At the far end of the shaded area, a small fire was going, with a grill rack propped on rocks, and a battered coffee pot on top. Two men, one black, one white, were avoiding its heat, trying to bring days-old coffee to a boil.

Her neighbor was chatty. "Elise and Slick got arrested last night," she said, with a nod up the concrete incline to the plywood shack under the bridge's girders. Perched on no more than four feet of concrete ledge, it was tucked directly beneath the roadway. She blearily wondered how the builder had gotten the large plyboards up the incline without tumbling off.

"I bet you could use it while they's gone."

Now her neighbor had her attention. "You think?" she said.

"Ain't no one else up there."

She thought for a moment. The shack had a door she could peer out of, and even a roughly cut window, covered in plastic. From high atop this tent city, she could see Demetrius coming. Or the steep incline might keep him away altogether.

"I thank you," she told her neighbor formally. She grabbed her backpack and her grimy tennis shoes, and made her way, crab-like, up the concrete to her new home.

Maybe she'd get even luckier. Maybe old Elise and Slick had squirreled away a rock she could fire up.

CHAPTER SEVEN

It was getting close to 5 o'clock by the time Branigan finished talking to Dontegan and a few other men about Vesuvius Hightower. That was more difficult than it sounded: many of the shelter residents knew little about the deceased man. Until Branigan told them, they didn't know his last name. Some didn't know his first name. When she explained that she was writing a story on the homeless man who had been run over, their faces cleared. "Oh, you mean V," one said.

Liam had told her that everyone on the street had two names – sometimes a real one and a street name, sometimes a middle name used interchangeably with a first, sometimes, inexplicably, two completely different names. Liam suspected they were aliases designed to throw off the authorities, but even he wasn't sure. He had settled on one discerning question: "What does your mother call you?"

That worked fine for him, but Branigan needed more precision.

When she and the men agreed on whom they were talking about, she learned that Vesuvius/V was "not all there", as the men put it, tapping their temples, but he was gentle and gracious. He was proud of his job running the laundry room, and strict about enforcing Pastor Liam's rule: *No chore, no laundry*. If someone refused to do a chore in exchange for having his laundry washed, Vesuvius would bring the sign-up sheet to Dontegan and point to the offender's signature. Then he would hang over Dontegan's shoulder until he was sure Dontegan had informed the offender of his transgression.

Branigan was pleased to be able to write a story about someone the news staff, and indeed the community, "looked right through". As she clicked off her recorder, she asked the question with which she always ended: "Anything else you can think of that I didn't ask?"

Dontegan furrowed his brow. "Nothin' I know," he said. "But you might wanna talk to Malachi. He let V stay in his cat hole a time or two."

"Cat hole?"

"You know – a place you stay. Away from the po-lice."

Branigan wasn't sure she did know, but she let it go for the moment. "What's Malachi's last name?"

"Don't know. But he be here tonight for supper."

"Does he have a room here?"

"Naw. He stay up under the bridge."

Branigan assumed he was talking about the Michael Garner Memorial Bridge. It was within walking distance of the mission, and Liam and Dontegan led their church partners on educational trips to see the settlement under it. She'd accompanied them more than once.

"Okay, I'll find Malachi soon."

Since it was only Monday, she had plenty of time. As she pulled out of Jericho Road's parking lot, she turned away from the *Rambler* office and headed for home. There was more work waiting for her there than in the office: she had filled two boxes with copies of police reports on the Resnick murder and had them at the farmhouse. That's how she'd be spending her evening.

As usual, the fifteen-minute drive from downtown Grambling to her farm helped soothe away the puzzles of the day.

Her farm.

She loved the sound of that, even if it wasn't exactly true. Everyone else in the family still called it Gran and Pa's farm, and that was fine with her. Technically, she supposed, it wasn't a farm any more at all.

It was 200 acres of rolling pasture and lakes and woods that were once home to a hundred head of her grandparents' cattle. Gran and Pa Rickman were raised in huge farm families right here in northeast Georgia. They'd quit school in the eighth grade, and married not too many years afterward.

Like most farming sons, Pa had done his time in the textile mills that surrounded Grambling. But even in the town's textile heyday, he was too ambitious to work for any mill owner long. He saved his money, opened a machine shop, and invested in land. And when the time was right, he sold everything and bought his 200 acres of red Georgia clay.

Branigan and her twin brother Davison were four the year Pa had built a modern ranch house that made Gran the envy of her six sisters. The twins lived with their parents in town, two streets over from Mrs Resnick, in a smaller, two-story colonial that enjoyed the same leafy canopy as her loftier address. The children loved their neighborhood, with its sidewalk-cracking oaks and maples, and neighbors who waved as they rode their bikes. But the farm, Branigan thought, ran in their blood.

Gran and Pa were certainly part of the draw. Gran pampered them shamelessly, rolling out homemade biscuits and letting them select from a half-dozen jam jars at every meal. At night she and Davison would contemplate where to sleep. Branigan preferred the guest bedroom where she could open the window and hear the lonesome drone of long-haul trucks on US 29 a half-mile away. Headed past other farms where other little girls slept, they sounded as desolate as train whistles. She still heard those trucks in her dreams.

Davison preferred the fold-out couch in the den, because it meant Gran would serve them cinnamon toast and hot chocolate in bed the next morning; she didn't want them to miss a single minute of cartoons.

In the afternoons, Pa would take the twins to watch the cows, stunned by the heat of a Georgia summer and wading into lukewarm pasture lakes. Next stop was the barn, where bats hung like furry winter slippers from the rafters. Then on to the chicken houses, nearly empty when Pa introduced the yellow baby chicks, and full to bursting when the white adult chickens were ready to be shipped out.

The children's first paid labor came from picking Pa's cotton – an excruciating half-hour's work that netted them a dime each. Years later, Davison told Branigan it was Pa's way of making sure they chose college over manual labor. It worked. The memory of her hands, splintered and bleeding from the prickly cotton husks, sweat trickling down her itchy back, made an air-conditioned school room look positively inviting.

Still, the farm inhabited her reveries. It was home for a daughter of the South in a way no city street or suburb could ever be.

It took her decades to realize it. The summer she turned fifteen, she joined a youth group from First Baptist Church of Grambling for a two-week bus tour of the Southwest. They woke at six each morning to get on a charter bus for another day of riding through the treeless taupe of Texas and Oklahoma, headed for a church camp in the foothills of New Mexico. They visited the "must-sees" – the Gateway Arch in St Louis, outdoor dramas, the Alamo – but Branigan was quietly miserable. She thought she was homesick – for her mom and dad, certainly, and for Davison, who ducked the trip at the last minute. But as the trip wound down, and the bus sped through the Atlanta bypasses and reached the stretch of Interstate 85 where rolling green hills ran up to meet the asphalt, she began to cry.

She had no idea why, but the relief at being back on familiar soil, at seeing woods so dense and green and inviting after the arid landscape of the Southwest, was palpable. *Bizarre,* she told herself. *You live on a city street, for goodness' sake.*

She didn't get it. And she didn't get it years later, when long after graduating from the University of Georgia and feeling stifled at *The Grambling Rambler* she accepted a job at the *Detroit Free Press*.

Of course, she hated Detroit. She hated the cold. She hated the violence. She hated flying home for her cousins' weddings, then Pa's funeral, then Gran's. She hated not being there for her family, with her family. And no matter how much she denied it, she hated that she'd turned thirty-five then thirty-eight and wasn't married.

But surely all that wasn't Detroit's fault. So she dug in, and became very good at her job. She had so little else.

Then one night in April three years ago, she had been talking to her mother on the phone. They'd covered the weather – frigid in Michigan, balmy in Georgia – then a cousin's new baby, a merger at her dad's bank. "And oh, did I mention we accepted an offer on Pa's farm?" her mother said.

Branigan's hand froze on the receiver, and the wind whipping around her apartment building was suddenly the most forlorn sound she'd ever heard.

"Honey? Did you hear me?"

"You're selling the farm?" she asked.

"Yes, we got a very good offer from Mr Bronson. You remember him. He owns the adjoining pastures."

"How much, Mom?"

"Now, Branigan." Her mother's Southern breeding often battled her accountant's head for business. Branigan could almost hear the voices: *You don't tell your children about family finances!* one hissed. *You want your daughter to grow up helpless?* scoffed the other. She knew which one would prevail.

"How much, Mom?"

"Oh, all right. Nearly $700,000."

"Wow. That's pretty good, isn't it?"

"Yes, it is. We're pleased. Rock and Bobby said that's more than they thought it would bring, and I agree." Rock and Bobby were her mom's younger brothers and had inherited the farm along with her.

"Mom, don't sell it." The words were out of Branigan's mouth before she had consciously thought them. "I want to live there."

Branigan could already hear what her mother was going to say next. *Why, Branigan? You live 800 miles away!*

Only she didn't. What she said was, "Would you really?"

Branigan confronted the truth of the statement with a jolt. "Yeah. I'm ready to come home, Mom."

"Then you will," Mrs Powers said quietly, and Branigan realized that selling the farm had not been an easy decision for her either.

"What about Uncle Rock and Uncle Bobby?"

"Don't worry about them," her mother said briskly, and Branigan could tell her mind was already working to embrace this new order, to find a way to get around her brothers, to back out of the deal with Mr Bronson, to do whatever was necessary to get her daughter home.

Three years later, Branigan still marveled whenever she entered the oh-so-familiar house that she rented from its new owners: her mother and her Uncle Bobby. They had bought out her Uncle Rock's share and were glad to hold on to the farm for awhile.

As Branigan pulled into the driveway, her German shepherd Cleo bounded from the cotton field to meet her. She laughed to see a tuft of the purest white cotton on the dog's nose. "Could you get any goofier?" she asked, brushing the white wisps from the shepherd's regal black head. Branigan patted Cleo, and said "Walk?", a word the dog understood. Cleo leaped happily up the brick steps, knowing Branigan would go inside first.

"Let me change clothes," she verified. "Be right back."

She yanked her flowered dress over her head as she walked through the den and adjoining kitchen, then to the bedroom where she kicked her sandals into the closet. Pulling off her rings, watch and earrings was a highlight of a work day.

She tugged on her most comfortable pair of blue and white striped running shorts, a sleeveless gray tank top, gray socks and well-worn Nikes. Her arms and legs were muscled and lean, and already tanned from an early spring. She caught her shoulder-length blond hair into a ponytail holder that Charlie had left on her last visit.

Cleo was sitting patiently as Branigan let the screen door slam, not bothering to close the wooden door behind it. She knew it wasn't the smartest thing in the world, but did it almost perversely, as a way of saying, "See why I left you, Detroit?"

She detoured into the back yard to check on her cantaloupes. She'd planted them in the center of a flower patch, beneath the kitchen window. She thought one might be ripe for supper, and sure enough, a pale yellow-orange melon, smelling both fruity and earthy, looked perfect.

But that's not what caught her attention. To one side of the tough vine that connected different sized melons was a crushed branch of lantana. And a step closer to the window, a footprint – from the look of it, made by a rather large tennis shoe. Branigan cast her mind back to the last rain. Friday night, she thought. A drenching one. So someone had been outside her kitchen window sometime Saturday or Sunday or today.

She looked thoughtfully at Cleo. The dog stayed outside during the day, inside at night. "I would expect to find body parts," Branigan told her. "Either you're falling down on the job or someone was here at night."

Despite her attempt at nonchalance, a chill settled over her as her eyes swept the cotton patch, barn and pastures in the distance. She hurried back to the side stoop and locked the door, pocketing the key. Then she and Cleo walked the much trampled path through the cotton field that abutted the yard. Cotton hadn't been harvested here since the 1990s, but occasionally a plant still yielded the brown pods with their puffs of raw cotton.

The pair rounded the barn, the empty chicken houses, then rolled under barbed wire to enter the pasture, Branigan's mind puzzling over possibilities. Cable guy? Power guy? Uncle Bobby was her landlord and lived on the next farm over. Could he have been looking over the property?

Branigan started across the pasture at a lope, watching for cow patties. Uncle Bobby kept a few cows here, so the grass was low and good for running, aside from the obvious drawback. She crossed the first broad swath before following the fence line past the lake, then a stand of trees, then a second lake. Plum trees and aged oaks reached like scraggly crones over the fence, scratching her arms if Cleo nudged her too close. But Cleo didn't stay with her long. The dog's strong leg muscles needed far more exercise than Branigan's pace could give her, and soon she was sprinting ahead to take a drink at the lake, then backtracking to lap her mistress before taking off again. *Who would mess with me as long as Cleo's around?* Branigan thought.

There was more of a breeze here than there had been at the house, and slowly Branigan's unease evaporated. The trees whispered the promise of evening. At this time of early June, the entire South smelled like honeysuckle, and the pasture fence was awash with the trumpet-shaped flowers. The green of the grass, the gray-brown of the tree trunks, the azure of the sky, and the silent blue-green of the lakes were so rich and clear that her breath caught.

This… this land, this vividness, this startling clarity was what she had come home for, what she had come home to. She breathed deeply, knowing as certainly as she had ever known anything that her decision to return had been right.

It had taken her until nearly forty to find out. But she was ahead of the game. Some people never did.

Back at the house, Branigan showered, pulled on pajama pants and a sleeveless T-shirt, and fed Cleo, convincing herself that the footprint outside her kitchen window belonged to a power company employee. She cut up a bowl of strawberries, and added pieces of her garden's first cantaloupe. She toasted a wheat bagel, mounded it high with shredded cheddar and set it all on the glass-topped table beside the couch. Cleo settled at her feet and they watched an episode of *Law and Order: SVU* as they ate.

Branigan resisted the temptation to watch another recorded episode when it was finished. "Back to work," she told Cleo. "Real life 'Law and Order'."

She dragged the cardboard box of copied police files from her home office to the more comfortable den, and settled back to read.

Liam had reminded her of one of the more intriguing aspects of the Resnick murder: "Remember that stranger living in her pool house?" She flipped to the first day's investigation, because this lead had surfaced early.

Mrs Resnick's property held not only her regal three-story home, but a pool and pool house in the back yard. Despite her children hiring landscapers and despite the landscapers' entreaties, Mrs Resnick wouldn't allow them to prune the trees or shrubs behind the house. As a result, you could hardly walk from the main house to the pool house. Oak limbs and prickly holly scratched and clawed even if you followed the path.

The March before the murder, Branigan read, Mrs Resnick sent Tabitha, her maid of forty years, to clean the pool house, untouched since the previous summer. Tabitha pushed her way through the tangle of shrubbery and bumped open the unlocked door to the one-level structure made of stone and cedar shingles.

In the living area sat a heavily built white man. He was talking to himself.

Tabitha screamed, and the stranger stopped abruptly.

"Who are you?" demanded the elderly black housekeeper.

"Billy," he answered.

Tabitha backed out of the secluded pool house and stumbled up the overgrown path to call Mrs Resnick's older son, Ramsey. By the time Ramsey and the police arrived, Billy was gone.

On May 2, two months after his first appearance, Tabitha looked out of a window and saw Billy in the back yard, heading down the path to the pool. She called Ramsey.

An amazing sight met Ramsey when he entered his mother's pool house. Furniture was rearranged, frozen hamburger was thawing on the kitchen counter, cigarettes were lying about, and the remains of a fire littered the fireplace. Ramsey settled in to wait.

Thirty minutes later, Billy walked up the driveway, carrying a bulky television. He was moving in. According to Ramsey's statement to police, he thought he lived there.

Ramsey called the police, who identified Billy as a mentally ill resident of Forest Lawn, a mill village on Grambling's west side. They impounded his TV, clothes, the sheets he'd slept on, even the cigarette butts from the ashtrays. But because he'd simply jiggled the pool house lock to get in, they could charge him only with unlawful occupancy, not the more serious breaking and entering. A judge placed him on trespass notice.

On June 15, continued the reports, Tabitha answered a knock at the front door of the main house. There stood Billy. He told Tabitha he wanted to get a T-shirt he'd left in the pool house.

Tabitha hurried upstairs to get Mrs Resnick. When the women came down, Billy was seated on the piano bench in the formal living room. Mrs Resnick, all 115 pounds of her, faced the burly six-foot-two man.

"She asked him what in the world he was doing in her house," the report quoted Tabitha. "I don't know what he told her, but I slipped to the phone and called Mr Ramsey."

Tabitha heard Mrs Resnick's raised voice speak sharply to Billy. Mrs Resnick then hustled him outside to wait for Ramsey and the police, who arrested him for trespassing. Ramsey wasn't surprised at his mother's cool. "Mother wasn't scared of the devil," he told officers.

But when his mother was murdered just twenty days later, he feared her sharp tongue had triggered a disturbed man's anger.

Branigan paused from reading the incident reports on Billy that Grambling police had dutifully attached to the voluminous interviews from that first day. It hadn't taken long for the news to spread among downtown neighbors about the man living on Mrs Resnick's property. Branigan remembered her mom and dad shaking their heads at the thought of Billy living in the pool house that was a three-minute walk from their house; her dad had quietly installed bolt locks on their exterior doors.

On the day of the murder, police officers made the connection almost immediately.

By 5:23 p.m. – just forty-four minutes after the neighbor's first call to the police – a patrol car with two uniformed officers was sitting outside Billy's grandmother's house in the crumbling mill village of Forest Lawn. Billy was there.

The officers escorted him to the Grambling Law Enforcement Center, a squat building behind the more gracious courthouse, and handed him over to detectives. Throughout the evening, detectives called and asked the officers to pick up friends whom Billy named as companions during the afternoon.

Branigan shuffled through other incident reports that were clipped to the investigative time line. Nine months before the murder, Billy had spent time in the Gainesville jail, forty-five minutes from Grambling. The charge was domestic violence for attacking a girlfriend, plus simple assault on the first officer who tried to subdue him. It took five officers and a stun gun to wrestle him into a cell.

Since returning home from Gainesville, Billy had been haunted by hallucinations, said family members. He saw black flies swarming from his belly button and planes zooming over his house. The grandmother blamed his condition on the stun gun, but it sounded more like full-blown schizophrenia to Branigan – and to the psychiatrist whose report was attached to the file.

Flipping forward to the July 5 incident report, she read the police department's conclusion. Because Mrs Resnick had last been seen alive at 12:40 p.m., because police had Billy in custody by 5:23 p.m., and because he'd been in the continuous company of Forest Lawn neighbors in between, it was apparent he did not commit the murder. Detectives would question Billy further in ensuing days, but their obvious suspect – the stranger who had moved into Mrs Resnick's pool house, the man she had angrily removed from her piano bench – was not her killer.

The problem was that Billy had looked so promising that clues leading to someone else might have been overlooked. This tidbit didn't come from the police file, but from a later interview conducted by Jody. Branigan reached for the notebook he'd given her when she took the assignment. It took only a moment to find the quote he'd transcribed from a homicide detective who was one of the first responders.

"My thinking was clouded by it," the detective admitted. "I was completely focused on this guy Billy at the time."

Branigan remembered those first few days after the murder. Billy made such a logical suspect. Who wouldn't focus on him? She idly wondered if Billy still lived with his grandmother, if she was even alive. Or did he hang out now at Jericho Road, with so many of those who faced similar demons?

The phone rang as she put down the last report on Billy. Its words were blurring, and she knew her focus was waning. She rolled her neck while reaching for the receiver.

"Brani G, I've found him," came Liam's voice.

She was momentarily confused, thinking of Billy, then of Vesuvius's hit-and-run driver. His next words yanked her to lucidity.

"I've found Davison."

CHAPTER EIGHT

B ranigan quickly changed from pajama pants into jeans, leaving on her sleeveless T-shirt, and grabbing her keys and purse. Cleo skidded to the door, and looked up hopefully.

"Yeah," she told the dog. "I might need you."

Cleo barked and followed Branigan to the car, hopping into the passenger seat. Branigan didn't bother with the sheet she usually placed beneath the dog.

Driving fast, she soon pulled into the convenience store parking lot Liam had named. It was in a shabby former mill village less than a mile from Jericho Road. Grambling was dotted with these mill villages, remnants of vibrant communities in the early twentieth century that were now collapsed and drug-infested. A few unbroken streetlights made a half-hearted effort, but the area beyond the lot was in deepest shadow. This parking lot was the city's single most active spot for prostitution and drugs, Jody had once told her. For rapes and murders, too, when things went wrong.

She nervously pulled alongside Liam's SUV, her stomach in a knot. Liam emerged as soon as he saw her Honda.

"He's under the bridge," he said.

"Is he strung out?"

"No. I smelled alcohol, but he's coherent."

She smiled tightly. "Did you tell him you were calling me?"

"Yeah. He knows. Get in the back, Miss Cleo," Liam commanded. "I'll ride with you."

Cleo obediently leaped over the seat back as Liam climbed in. Branigan knew where they were headed – the Michael Garner Memorial Bridge, named for a police officer gunned down in this neighborhood fifteen years before. When the bridge was built some years later, Grambling's police chief lobbied for naming rights. Had she been part of Michael Garner's family, she wasn't sure she'd want his name connected to a site so close to his murder. But they considered it an honor, and the bridge now bore his name. It also sheltered dozens of the city's homeless.

Liam knew the bridge community. He and his staff frequently visited, inviting residents to Jericho Road for drug rehab, mental health counseling and worship. But even he never came here after dark. With the blackness impenetrable, suffocating, Branigan felt her heart thumping. She was about to face the man she loved above all others.

Her twin brother, Davison.

They parked in the pitted lot of a storage facility 200 feet from the bridge. It was as close as they could get in a car. Liam had wisely brought a flashlight that helped illumine a path through the weeds. Cleo ran ahead, and Branigan heard her excited bark before they reached the bridge.

Then she heard the voice so like her dad's, so like Chan's.

"Well, what a pretty girl! You must be one of Gran's."

Branigan stumbled forward. There, sitting on a cement block, was her brother. Even with Liam's dim light, she could see that his blond hair was shoulder-length and matted. A week's stubble grew along his jaw line. His jeans looked too large. But she could see the glitter of his familiar emerald eyes, identical to hers and shining like a cat's in the dark. The slow smile that emerged when he saw her was one she remembered well.

"Brani G," he said through cracked lips, using the childhood nickname Liam had adopted. "Hey, Sis."

The bridge soared at least fifty feet above them, devoid of traffic at this hour, and invisible. Branigan peered into the darkness, but could see nothing past Davison in Liam's little circle of light. Still, she'd never known this site to be vacant and sensed people listening from nearby tents staked into the hard red mud, and from the girders forty-five feet up an incline.

Davison stood to hug her, and she walked into his arms silently, awkwardly. She steeled herself against the smell of dried sweat, dirt and grime, and he sensed it.

"Sorry. I haven't bathed in awhile," he apologized, pulling away. "Liam says I can shower tomorrow at the shelter."

Branigan nodded, not trusting herself to speak. Then clearing her throat, she fought the urge to scream a hundred questions and instead said quietly, "Tell me how you've been."

He shrugged. "Not much to tell."

The siblings had never been ones for chitchat. So she asked what was foremost in her mind: "Are you clean?"

He hesitated, knowing how badly she wanted him to say yes, and she presumed, wanting pretty badly for it to be true.

"No," he said.

She exhaled and slumped, not realizing how tightly she'd been holding on to this hope until it was whisked away.

"Crack?" she asked.

He nodded. "And beer. Some meth."

She glanced at Liam. It didn't get much worse than crystal methamphetamine, he'd once told her. The rotting teeth, the skeletal face, the aging skin. Five years and Davison would be unrecognizable.

Branigan took a shuddering breath, stopped the cries of *Why?* before they flew from her mouth. But it was as if he heard them anyway. He shrugged again, turning inward.

"I'm glad to see you," she managed. "So glad to know you're okay."

He gave her a sad smile.

"*Are* you okay?"

He gave a sideways wag of his head, meaning yes and no.

"I thought it was time to come and see Chan, now that he's heading to college." She heard Liam draw a sharp breath. "But I'm having second thoughts," he said to Liam. "I don't want him to see me like this."

"I agree," Liam said. "Telling him is one thing. Having him see you strung out is another."

Branigan cringed. Liam didn't mince words. Chan knew he was adopted, had known since he was old enough to know the word. But Liam and Liz had never shared the part about his biological parents being drug addicts.

Davison hung his head. "So here's what I'm thinking. I'd like to go to rehab, then tell Chan before he leaves for Furman."

Liam and Branigan looked at each other. She didn't know what surprised her more – rehab or that he knew where Chan was going to college.

"I need to tell him he has a royal screw-up for a father. So he can do everything in his power to be different."

"All right," she whispered, gripping her twin's shoulder. "Sounds like a plan."

In the glow of the flashlight, Liam's face was expressionless. Branigan knew him well enough to know he wasn't happy.

Davison had been younger than Chan was now, sixteen and a junior at Grambling East, when he had his first drink. Branigan saw it happen, saw the light dawn in his eyes. She just didn't know what she was looking at.

Gran and Pa had taken their RV to visit Gran's sister in Texas. They were going to be gone for two weeks, maybe more. Pa had timed the visit to coincide with the selling of chickens, so the chicken houses were empty. Uncle Bobby would take the cattle into his adjoining pastures. That left only the dogs – Cleo's grandmother and great-uncle, to be precise.

After driving out to the farm every afternoon after school to feed and play with the German shepherds, Davison and Branigan casually told their parents it would be easier to spend the weekend there. Mrs Powers, who ran an accounting business from their house, was in the middle of tax season. She welcomed the break in cooking. "As long as you call us every morning and every night," she said.

The twins didn't go wild, but they did invite their best friends to the farm on Friday night. Davison's swim team buddies, Brandon and Liam, brought beer, and Branigan's softball cohorts, Sandy and Alissa, sweet white Zinfandel. After sunset, they plugged in a CD player on the back porch and let their friends introduce them to alcohol.

Branigan quickly got giddy, then silly, then sick on the candy-colored wine. She was asleep by eleven, leaving the party in full swing. When their friends left around noon on Saturday, they couldn't take the alcohol back to their houses, so they left it. Branigan could no more have touched another glass of wine than she could have eaten the dead mouse Gran's shepherd proudly dumped on the porch. But Davison could hardly wait to get back to the beer.

In mid-afternoon, he pulled one from the refrigerator, popped it with a satisfying spurt and licked the foam from the can. He then settled onto the porch and began talking excitedly about his plans for senior year, then college, then law school. Her normally reticent brother talked excitedly, non-stop. In fact, he pretty near babbled.

She watched, puzzled, as he drank four beers in a row, then stretched out on Gran's couch and fell asleep.

Five years later, he mentioned that afternoon once. Just once.

It was the night he came to her dorm room to tell her he was dropping out of college. Certainly she'd heard the rumors; heard about Davison's reputation for being the hardest drinking frat man at the University of Georgia – which was saying something.

She had watched him uneasily the preceding summer, when he stayed overnight at friends' houses more often than he came home. She had heard whispered conversations between her parents, and much louder confrontations between them and Davison. She had walked into his bedroom and been stunned by the boozy smell.

But she wasn't prepared for what he was saying that fall evening in her dorm. He wasn't fully sober, though it was just past dusk. He had failed every mid-term, he said. He was giving up.

"But what about law school?" she cried, honestly bewildered.

He laughed bitterly. "No law school's going to take me."

"But Davison, why? You're throwing away three years of school."

He waved her words aside as if they were mosquitoes. "Do you remember the weekend we spent at Gran and Pa's that spring they went to Texas?"

She nodded.

"And you remember that was the first time I tasted a beer?"

She nodded again.

"Well, something happened that night. It was the first time I felt normal. It was the first time I felt what other people feel like all the time."

"What are you talking about? You're not making sense."

He sighed. "Anyway, Brani, I just wanted you to know. Mom and Dad don't get it and never will. But I'm not like you. I'm not like other people."

He got up to leave then, even as she was attempting to argue him out of this rash plan. He quietly closed the door while she was in the middle of a sentence.

It would be two years before she saw her brother again.

CHAPTER NINE

Branigan's first stop the next morning was the house she had grown up in, two blocks from the stately Resnick home. She wanted to catch her folks before her dad left for work.

Her father was eating cereal, and her mother was drinking a glass of cranberry juice when she arrived. Her mother hugged her, and poured coffee into a mug without asking. Her dad remained seated at the breakfast table, but pulled her in for a quick hug.

"What brings you out so early?" he asked.

"I need to tell you both something."

They glanced at each other.

"It's good. It's Davison."

Her mom's eyes widened, and her dad's jaw tightened. Davison had caused them so much pain.

"He's back?" breathed her mom. "Davison's back?"

She nodded. "Apparently he wants to go to rehab. He got in touch with the treatment counselor at Jericho Road. Liam called me."

"Well, I guess that *is* good," said Mrs Powers. She'd been down this road before, knew not to get too excited. Branigan's dad only cleared his throat.

"There's one more thing," Branigan said. "He wants to tell Chan."

"Why?" asked her dad.

"Something about Chan going off to college. So he'll know his gene pool regarding addiction."

"That may not be a bad thing."

"It'll be good for you guys too," she said. "To finally let Chan know you're his grandparents."

56

As friends of the Delaneys, they knew Chan – knew him well. But with Liam and Liz's decision to keep Chan's junkie parents a secret, they hadn't known his parentage until Chan grew into his tall and loose-limbed physique. Branigan had come to them with her suspicions and they realized instantly that she must be right. But they respected the Delaneys' decision and said nothing to anyone outside the family.

Now her mom nodded, sitting down to take in this new development. She blew out a slow breath. "Tell Liz and Liam to call us when they're ready."

Branigan's second stop was Jericho Road. She wanted to see if Malachi, the homeless man Dontegan had recommended she speak to, was there for breakfast.

Three of the shelter residents were cooking grits, bacon and eggs as she walked in. Two of them ducked their heads, but Dontegan waved a greeting.

"You have a plate, woncha?" he called.

"Sure, if you have enough." She helped herself to a cup of steaming coffee from a battered urn, ignoring the packages of artificial sweetener. Liam once told her it was impossible to keep real sugar, because alcoholics poured entire bowls into their coffee, trying to get a mini-high.

Dontegan passed her a generously filled plate through the cafeteria window. She asked him if Malachi was around, and he pointed to a man of medium build sitting alone at the farthest table. Malachi's skin was dark black, possibly the darkest Branigan had ever seen in Georgia, a shade she associated with beleaguered Nigerians or Sudanese in the news. His cornrow braids dangled a few inches below his camouflage baseball cap. His clothes were so worn as to be colorless – threadbare shades of khaki and green.

She set her plate on his table, leaving an empty space between them.

"I'm Branigan Powers," she said. "Is it okay if I sit here?"

He nodded politely. "You can sit anywhere," he offered, showing no surprise at her skirt and heels.

"Are you Malachi?"

He nodded again. Branigan explained the story she was doing on Vesuvius's death, and he arched his eyebrows. "*The Rambler* doin' a story on a homeless dude?"

"Yeah, I know. Do you believe his death was an accident?"

"He sure wouldna been the first to get run over," he said. "It happens prob'ly six times a year."

"Really?"

"Sure. Walker versus car. Bicycle versus car. Moped versus car. Not much of a fight."

She thought about the two- to four-inch stories the newspaper combined in a column down an inside page. Sometimes they were about a cyclist getting hit by a car. If it happened on Mrs Resnick's street, it'd be a full-length story. But west of town? Probably not.

"But Vesuvius," she persisted. "Accidental?"

Malachi lifted his shoulders. "No way of knowin'. V wasn't all there, you know? Nice guy, but …" Malachi tapped his head sadly.

She stabbed her eggs. "That's what I hear."

Malachi's gaze snagged on something on the far wall. Branigan glanced over, but saw only paintings from Jericho's celebrated art room.

"There was one thin' though," he said.

She waited.

"I let V stay with me one night when he missed curfew." He nodded down the hallway that led to the men's rooms. "If you come in after nine at night, Pastor Liam won't let you in. V liked his room and didn' miss curfew much. But this night he had money."

"That was unusual?"

"Oh, yeah. He said he sol' a paintin'. Like that one."

She looked at the glowing moonscape Malachi was looking at. It depicted woods at night, moonlight streaking through tree branches but never reaching the forest floor. It was beautiful. In the lower right hand corner, she could see a large black V. So Vesuvius had been one of the Jericho Road artists.

"What's unusual about that? I thought your artists were always selling work out of here."

"Yeah, but V said this paintin' had been bought by another dude. Someone who live on the street. But when I asked him what dude be buyin' a paintin', he clammed up. Wouldn' tell me."

Branigan couldn't see a connection between Vesuvius selling art and getting hit on his bike, but the fact that the homeless man had been a talented artist was a good detail. She'd send a photographer to get a picture to accompany her story. She thanked Malachi and got up to leave.

"Oh, and Malachi? I need your full name."

"Malachi Ezekiel Martin."

"Is that your real name?"

"Yeah."

"I mean, is it your only name?"

A smile played at Malachi's lips. "Do I need more 'n one?"

"No," she stumbled, flustered. "I just meant that a lot of the guys seem to have more than one, or a nickname or whatever."

"Nope. Malachi Ezekiel Martin. It's all I got."

Now he was openly smirking, so she thanked him hastily, threw her paper plate in the trash, and left for the newsroom.

CHAPTER TEN

"**C**razy white woman." Malachi shook his head and went for more coffee. He lingered a half-hour over two more cups and a year-old *Sports Illustrated* from the dining hall's rack. There were more articles he wanted to read, so he slid the magazine into his faded backpack. Pastor Liam didn't mind, so long as you brought it back.

He slipped his arms into the backpack's straps. He was traveling light today, having left his bedroll, duffle bag and canned food in his tent under the bridge. He wasn't sure they'd be there when he returned.

It was a warm June morning, as good a day to live outside as Georgia offered. The flower beds flanking Jericho Road were filled with day lilies and verbena, as well as blooms on the roses. He liked to weed and water the beds, but today they needed neither.

He shifted his pack to better balance the weight between his shoulders, then set out for the Grambling courthouse. It wasn't the courthouse he wanted – not by a long shot. He'd seen the inside of municipal court more times than he could count. Vagrancy. Loitering. Trespassing. Urinating in public. Being homeless wasn't illegal, but being a human and doing human things outside was.

One thing he was proud of: no panhandling charges. Fourteen years on the streets, and he'd not panhandled once. He'd gone hungry, Lord knows. Hungry and wet and cold and chafed and sick and hot and mosquito-bitten and lice-infested and weary – as weary as a man could be. He'd eaten free meals at every church, restaurant, hospital room and jail cell that offered. But it was always by invitation, never because he went begging. The distinction was important to him.

Still, the grassy square that surrounded the courthouse was shady and well stocked with benches. It was his favorite place to read on days as fine as this one.

He covered the six blocks to Main Street easily. Most days, he walked eleven miles, he'd once calculated. Since it wasn't yet 10 a.m., the benches were deserted except for other homeless people. Malachi recognized everyone except a tall and beefy white dude, mid-thirties, his work pants streaked with red mud, his hooded, brown eyes darting restlessly over the square. Was he vaguely familiar? No, maybe not.

Malachi hoped he was just passing through. Clearly bad news. He ducked out of the white dude's line of sight and found a bench under a massive oak.

He was engrossed in a story about soccer in the slums of South America when a professionally dressed man, maybe thirty-five, walked over and sat on a bench three feet away. The man was on his cell phone, and he looked right at Malachi.

"Oh, babe, you know what'd happen. She'd take the house and the kids. Her old man has so much clout I'd lose my job too. You have to be patient, and we have to be careful."

So careful you're letting a perfect stranger hear you're cheating on your wife, Malachi thought. I mean, the man was looking right at him.

It wasn't the first time. He'd told Pastor Liam about it – "The worst thing about being homeless is being looked right through." Pastor Liam was something of a crazy white guy himself. But he got it. He told Malachi he quoted him every time he gave a speech.

The man finished his conversation and jammed his phone into a holster on his belt. Muttering to himself, he got up and walked back into the courthouse.

Malachi wondered if he had stabbed someone as the man was talking, stabbed someone right here in the open, would Mr Cheating Cell Phone Guy be able to describe him to the police?

CHAPTER ELEVEN

Tanenbaum Grambling caught Branigan as soon as she stepped off the elevator. "What've you got?" he growled.

She followed him to his office, the largest in the building, with a quartet of windows facing Main Street. He eschewed the gargantuan desk that fit his six-foot-four bulk and joined her in his seating area, furnished for eight. Trouble was, there were rarely eight people in the newsroom any more. Between layoffs and reporters filing remotely, the staff was seldom in the newsroom together. Branigan missed the camaraderie of her early years.

She took a burgundy leather chair while Tan settled with snorts and sighs on a couch facing her. Tan-4 didn't do anything quietly.

"What?" he barked.

There was a time she would've jumped. Now she barely registered his tone. Neither did he.

"When I went to see Liam about the homeless angle on the Resnick murder, I stumbled onto a good story," she began. "It's about a homeless cyclist killed last week in a hit-and-run whose father was killed almost the same way five years ago. The father wasn't homeless, just poor. In fact, it was the father's death that threw the son into homelessness.

"But the point is, these people are invisible, you know? I think we should start covering the whole homeless issue more aggressively."

"What the hell are the police doing?"

"I still have to check with them. But it's bigger than that. This happens all the time with these people. They're disposable."

Tan looked pensive. "I'm hearing squawking from Main Street businessmen about the homeless," he said. "Of course, they're bitchin' about panhandlers. Write your story for 1A, then we'll decide where to go."

She nodded. "Then on Mrs Resnick. Whew! There's so much to go through."

He looked unsympathetic. "And?"

"And I'm revisiting some of the major players to see if they remember something or realized something later. I've got Liam Delaney questioning the homeless guys about rumors that may have gone around ten years ago. Also, I want to see if that man who moved into Mrs Resnick's pool house is still around. Remember that?"

"Oh, yeah," Tan said. "I'd nearly forgotten. So strange – then Alberta throwing him out of her living room for playing her piano. Which was no surprise. *Nobody* touched that piano but her."

"Alberta Resnick's two sons still live here," Branigan continued, "including Ramsey, the one who stayed at her house the night before she died. What's he – your second cousin?"

Tan waved away her question. "Whatever. I am well acquainted with Ramsey."

"Well, I've got an interview set up with him. And I'll get to his brother. But their sister – the one who spent the night of July 4 in the house – lives at Lake Hartwell. And the two granddaughters are living on the coast of South Carolina."

He nodded. "Sounds right."

"One granddaughter in Edisto, the other, who apparently married well, on the Isle of Palms. So I was wondering…"

"If you can have an all-expenses-paid trip to the Grand Strand?"

She laughed. "Actually, those beaches are south of the Grand Strand. Mom and Dad still have their place, so I wouldn't need a hotel. Just mileage and meals."

"Go ahead," he said, dismissing her. "Keep it cheap."

Branigan sat down at her desk. The room was cool and quiet; more like a morgue, she thought morosely, than a newsroom.

The Rambler had started in the early 1900s as a Monday-Wednesday-Friday newspaper, founded by Tanenbaum Grambling Sr. His son, Junior, added a Sunday edition. But Tanenbaum III didn't want anything to do with the family business, so the newspaper fell to his younger brother, Josiah.

Josiah turned out to be the savviest newspaperman of them all, taking the paper to a daily, and building a state-of-the-art printing press and offices to anchor the south end of Main Street. At every leap, there were discussions about whether to change the name *Rambler* to something more sophisticated. But the people of Grambling loved vestiges of their small-town roots even as they were outgrowing them. The name remained.

In *The Rambler*'s heyday, the newsroom had held sixty-five desks populated by editors, reporters, columnists, copyeditors, artists, designers, clerks, interns and secretaries. Now, under Tanenbaum IV, who'd taken on the dual roles of publisher and executive editor, the staff was down to a third of that number. No one blamed Tan-4. The whole industry was in seismic upheaval.

Branigan slipped on the ugly maroon sweater she kept on her chair to ward off the chilly air conditioning, and opened her email. Not too bad. She worked through it for an hour, then stood, stretched and poured a cup of coffee from her Thermos. The few reporters around were busily working, heads down, so she didn't interrupt.

She sat again, and called the police for an update on the hit-and-run that killed Vesuvius Hightower. They had nothing. She pulled out her notebook, recorder and earphones. There were a few quotes from the Hightowers, Dontegan and other men at the shelter that she wanted verbatim. *Rambler* policy dictated that she clean up their pronunciation, but she wanted their verbiage intact.

Fortunately, she had enough background from Liam on homelessness in Grambling that she was able to weave the narrative of the Hightowers' deaths seamlessly into a larger fabric. She wrote about Vesuvius's artistic talent and about how he and his father were inseparable, using quotes from the younger man's siblings.

By the time she had finished, it was 1:30, and her stomach was protesting the passing of the lunch hour. She saved the story to give it a final read-through before handing it over to Julie. When not up against a deadline, she liked to revisit a story after twenty-four hours and see what glaring holes or inappropriate wording struck her.

She told Julie she was heading out for the afternoon for interviews on the Resnick story. Julie nodded distractedly, as she did when editing one of Gerald's arts stories. If he turned in a story without at least four words an editor didn't know, he considered it a personal failure. Branigan peeled off her sweater, glad to escape the building.

Outside the sunshine and heat felt welcoming. She walked the six blocks up Main Street to Bea's, passing black iron lampposts hung with baskets of geraniums and petunias. Grambling worked hard to retain its small-town flourishes while courting banking and industry headquarters. Cranky old-timers like Branigan worried that new money would eventually trump old charm.

She ordered an uncut rye bagel and an iced tea, then took them to a sidewalk table. She opened the morning's *Rambler* and for the next half-hour caught up on stories she'd missed. Harley had the annual preview of bathing suits, poor guy. Gerald had a yawner about an art exhibition in an obscure Atlanta gallery. Not sure how that got in. But Marjorie had an exceptional piece on a woman in nearby South Carolina who'd researched her family land, including a graveyard that was covered when the mountain lake Jocassee filled in those secluded valleys. The writing was sparse, and got across the point of terrible loss without being syrupy. Branigan silently applauded Marjorie.

She chucked her trash into Bea's bin, and walked back to her taupe Civic, parallel parked outside the *Rambler* building. Her interview with Ramsey Resnick wasn't until three, so she planned to drive to the Forest Lawn community. She wanted to see if Billy's grandmother knew where he was.

The grandmother's address was on the incident reports, so she got to the dilapidated mill village with no trouble. But finding the house was another matter. Few of the houses were numbered any longer. Many of the old mill houses – distinctive four-room structures with sloping roofs to cover a shallow rear porch – were boarded up. Branigan knew from Liam that the homeless were likely to be inside, having pried boards from windows then replacing them to hide their presence.

The ones occupied by owners or renters looked scarcely better. Broken-down cars littered the streets and alleyways between houses. Rusted fences guarded yards of knee-high weeds and the occasional chained pit bull. Sporadically, there was evidence of someone trying to infuse a little beauty with a petunia or zinnia in a coffee can.

Billy's grandmother had given up even that attempt. The steps leading to her rickety porch were missing. A cement block had been placed as a substitute; it required some athleticism to reach the porch. Once Branigan did, she tiptoed across, afraid her foot would rip through the rotting wood at any moment.

She knocked on a door that wasn't latched. Her knock sent it swinging into a dark interior.

"Is that my lunch?" The voice sounded ancient, scratchy.

"No, ma'am. I'm Branigan Powers from *The Grambling Rambler*."

She heard shuffling. Moments went by, but finally an elderly woman, maybe seventy, maybe one hundred and ten, stood before her. "You Mobile Meals?" the woman asked, examining Branigan hopefully.

"No, ma'am. Did they not come today?"

"They did not."

"Well, I can bring you something to eat. May I ask you a few questions first?"

The woman turned, leaving the door open, so Branigan followed her inside.

"Are you Mrs Shepherd – Billy Shepherd's grandmother?"

"Sure am," she said, smacking her lips. She took Branigan's arm and escorted her to a long, slender table that took up almost an entire wall of the living room. It was covered with photos – babies, school pictures, wedding pictures, church directory photos – all in cheap metal frames. "This here's him."

She plucked one of a large teenager, his laughing eyes squinting at the camera. "And then here": another photo of a young man, possibly mid-twenties, standing over a car engine, caught unawares.

"Here's the last one I have. It was took after them po-lice hit him with that stunned gun in Gainesville. Made him crazy."

Branigan recalled the incident report saying it took five officers to subdue Billy.

"Came home talkin' 'bout flies and airplanes, all crazy," his grandmother said disgustedly.

The man in the picture did look like a different person: bulkier, face transfigured, all but snarling at the photographer.

"When did you last see Billy?" Branigan asked.

"When he went off to prison in South Car-lina," she replied, plopping onto a faded sofa that answered with a screech. "Damn near three years ago. Guess he still there."

"What was his sentence?"

"Don't remember."

"Do you remember ten years ago when he moved into the pool house of Mrs Alberta Resnick?"

The old woman broke into an amused cackle. "I shore do, honey. I thought he was stayin' in my back bedroom and come to find out he was spendin' half his time in that old lady's pool house." She laughed again.

"Do you remember Mrs Resnick getting killed about that same time?"

"Do I? Whatta you think? Them po-lice was here for months questionin' my Billy. But it warn't him. He was here with me all day."

Branigan made a note to check with the South Carolina Department of Corrections, and asked a few more questions about Billy. Learning nothing that wasn't already in the police reports, she thanked Billy's grandmother and told her she'd return shortly with lunch.

There was a McDonald's within three miles of the house, so Branigan kept her word. As she tiptoed gingerly across the porch once more, she saw a shadow pass before the window. But when the old woman met her at the door, reaching eagerly for the fragrant sack of cheeseburgers, fries, apple pie and sweet tea, the living room behind her was empty.

Branigan asked to borrow the most recent picture of Billy. His grandmother shrugged and nodded, her hands occupied with the McDonald's sack. Branigan walked once more to the table with its montage of a mill village family. She slipped Billy's photo out of its frame, careful not to bend the picture of the menacing young man.

CHAPTER TWELVE

Amanda and Bennett entered her mother's house by the same back door Amanda had exited hours earlier. Bennett Jr and Drew, dressed in khakis and nearly identical blue dress shirts, trailed behind. As they entered, Ben Jr dutifully took off his baseball cap and shoved it in a back pocket. Amanda shot her older son a grateful look. They could hear chatter from the dining room, glasses clinking, laughter.

Tabitha was in the kitchen, pulling a cookie sheet of hors d'oeuvres from the oven. "Hello, Miz Amanda, Mr Ben," she said, setting them down and nodding at the boys.

"Anything I can help you with?" asked Amanda, not particularly eager to join the party.

"No, Miz Amanda. You a guest tonight."

Amanda gave the elderly housekeeper a quick hug, squared her shoulders and entered the dining room.

"Ah, Bennett. Amanda. Boys." Ramsey grabbed his sister in a bear hug. "How are you, old man?"

Bennett smiled, showing no trace of his distaste for his brother-in-law. The nephews shook hands formally with Ramsey. Seeing him only once a year, they had none of the easy familiarity they had with their dad's family in Atlanta.

"Want to get a plate and go out to the *ver-an-dah*?" Ramsey whispered.

Amanda burst into laughter. She picked up a glass of pinot grigio and turned to Bennett and her sons.

"You guys get something to eat. I'll mingle out front."

She saw Ben Jr edging toward the bar, and started to say something. She stopped herself. *He's twenty-one. Let it go.*

She hooked her arm into Ramsey's and they strolled toward the front door. "Where are Mother and Heath?" she asked.

"Not sure," Ramsey said, looking over the crowded room. "I saw them earlier."

"I need to talk to you about her afternoon craziness," Amanda whispered.

"As opposed to her morning or evening craziness?"

She snorted. "Right. But sometime tonight, I do need to tell you about it."

They reached the sprawling wraparound porch, which had another open bar and buffet set into the curve. Amanda saw the Powers couple from two blocks over. "Bank president, right?" she mouthed to Ramsey.

He nodded. "And accountant."

Amanda glided over to speak to them, her wide-legged black pants swirling like a long skirt.

"Paul, Eileen, hello."

"Amanda, it's good to see you," said Eileen Powers. "Are your boys here? I want to see them."

"You can't miss them," said Amanda. "They're dressed like Twiddledee and Twiddledum."

Eileen laughed. "I should be able to find them, then."

"And your twins? Are they in town?"

"Yes. Branigan works for *The Rambler*. She's working tonight, in fact."

There was a pause, heavy with the absence of the unremarked-upon twin. Amanda thought she remembered something about a scandal with the son, but she couldn't quite recall what it was. So she just stood there, feeling like an idiot. *These small Southern towns are minefields*, she thought.

The silence stretched on, uncomfortable. Finally, not knowing what else to say, Amanda ventured: "And your son? Is he here?"

Eileen smiled sadly. "We aren't in touch with Davison. We miss him terribly."

Amanda placed a hand on the woman's arm. "I'm sorry," she said. "Families are hard, aren't they?"

"Yes, yes, they are," said Eileen, with a knowing look at the younger woman. "You know that as well as anyone."

At that moment, Alberta Resnick, dressed in a navy dress of as yet unwrinkled linen, appeared at Eileen's side.

"Eileen, dear, might I borrow my daughter?"

"Certainly, Alberta. Lovely party."

"Amanda," her mother asked, drawing her away from Eileen. "Can you spend the night?"

"Yes, we have the hotel for the night, as always."

"No, I mean here. In the house."

"Whatever for?"

"I'd just like for you to. Ramsey is staying. And Caroline and Ashley," she added, referring to Ramsey and Heath's teenage daughters. When Amanda still looked uncomprehending, her mother said, "I don't ask you for much. Can you do this one thing?"

"Well, okay. I guess I can find something to sleep in."

"Very good," said her mother. "Thank you, Amanda. I need to get something straightened out."

Ben Jr got a bourbon on the rocks from the bartender in the dining room. Twenty minutes later, he got one from the bartender on the front porch. Then the dining room. Then the porch. Within an hour, he had four under his belt.

He looked around for some good-looking girls in this overgrown Mayberry, but apparently that was too much to ask. The only young girls he saw were his cousins. Carlisle was chatting up the adults, bootlicker that she was. Then there were flighty Caroline and Ashley, in their "rat stage", as he thought of thirteen. Flat chests. Curly hair. Skinned knees. He could hardly tell them apart.

He stumbled slightly as he navigated the steps from the front porch to the yard. *A swim. Maybe that's what's called for. Yes, a swim.*

The old lady – he never thought of her as "Grandmother", though that was what she insisted upon being called – kept swim trunks in the pool house. Though who knew what was in there after the famous episode of the re-tard living in it? Maybe he took the swim trunks when he left.

As Ben walked round the back, he pulled his crunched baseball cap from his back pocket. He smoothed it out, gazing reverently at the NYU Law logo. This was his ticket out of Atlanta, out of the South, to the big time. *NYU Law, here I come.*

He fitted the cap snugly over his brown curls and swaggered into the dimness created by his grandmother's trees. Six cars filled the space between the detached garage and kitchen entrance. Ben bumped a few of them as he made his way to the hedge.

Good grief, you can barely get through the hedge and onto the path. What's wrong with the old lady? Is it really that hard to hire a landscaper? He'd heard his mom tell his dad that his grandmother had a thing against keeping the grounds trimmed. Something about Uncle Ramsey and Uncle Heath wanting her out of the house. Sheesh. Re-tards were running the place.

He pushed his way along the path, shrubbery and low-hanging branches crowding in. A splintered branch stabbed him in the forearm; he yelped and dropped glass number five. It landed on soft ground, but most of its precious amber liquid spilled. Ben let loose a string of curses.

He finally reached the pool, which didn't look that inviting. Certainly not the clear blue he remembered. But it wasn't filthy either. He could see the bottom, at least, through the bottle-green water.

Ben walked to the pool house. He knew Uncle Ramsey had installed a new lock after throwing the homeless guy out. Sure enough, the door was bolted. But Ben knew about a window at the back that didn't lock. He circled the house, pushing through dense undergrowth and gathering a few more scratches, until he came to the bathroom window. He pulled out a credit card to flip the screen tabs. He removed the screen, then shoved upward on the glass pane. The window screeched, just as he remembered, but opened. Ben boosted himself over the sill and plopped head first onto the closed toilet seat. He slid to the floor, and lay there a moment, the room spinning.

He heaved himself to his feet and went in search of swim trunks. He found the bedroom chest of drawers all right, but the drawer he pulled open held something unexpected – a makeshift crack pipe and a small cloth pouch. He upended the pouch, and several yellowish, irregularly shaped rocks tumbled into his palm. Powdered cocaine was Ben's drug of choice, but he'd seen someone smoke one of these.

Clearly the police hadn't searched this room when expelling the vagrant. He laughed out loud to think of the old lady getting arrested on a drug possession charge.

He opened the second drawer long enough to see the swim trunks he'd been looking for. But now, his curiosity aroused, he opened the third drawer as well. A dozen paperbacks were stacked neatly inside. Ben flipped through them: *The Old Man and the Sea, Requiem for a Dream, Ironweed, One Flew Over the Cuckoo's Nest, The Shipping News, Invisible Man.* And that high school staple all over Georgia, *Cold Sassy Tree.*

What the heck? Ben knew these books hadn't been here before. And he knew as well as he knew anything they weren't his grandmother's. But the man living in her pool house had been a retard. Surely he didn't bring these.

Ben's mind was fuzzy, but he was coherent enough to reach an obvious conclusion. Had two people been living in the pool house this spring?

Ben was startled by a sharp knock on the front door. He dropped *Cold Sassy Tree.*

He wobbled through the recreation room that took up most of the pool house, the giant trees rendering it darker than the time would suggest. He saw a man's outline through the sidelight, and hesitated.

What if someone was still living here?

The knock came again, then his name. "Ben. Open up."

He peeked through the window and relaxed. He flipped the new bolt, and opened the door to his Uncle Heath.

"What are you doing in here, Ben?" his uncle asked sternly.

"Looking for my swim trunks."

His uncle frowned. "You're going in that dirty water?"

"Sure am."

Heath's glance darted all around the cavernous room. "How did you get in?"

"A window that we kids know about."

"Window, huh? I guess we better lock it too, if we don't want any more homeless guys moving in. You heard about that, I guess."

"Yep."

"Well, be careful in that pool. You might be joined by some slimy friends."

"Don't say that about your kids, Uncle Heath."

Heath chuckled. "Okay, wise-ass, don't call me if you get bit by a water snake." His uncle playfully pulled the cap from Ben's head and plopped it on his own.

"NYU Law, huh? Not too shabby, kid."

Ben reached for the hat, but his uncle stepped away.

"You don't want to get it wet," he said. "I'll keep it safe for you."

Chapter Thirteen

Grambling's downtown consisted mostly of Main Street, a long, straight stretch anchored by the courthouse on the north end and *The Rambler* on the south. The street-front stores were a mix of New South and Old Dixie – five trendy restaurants in addition to Bea's and a diner called Marshall's. A hardware store stood side by side with a vintage clothing store, which resided next to a state-of-the-art fitness center favored by young professionals. Two banks, three bars, a drugstore, a florist, two men's clothing stores, a stationery store, and several women's specialty shops filled the rest of the spaces. On the shady courthouse lawn soared a Confederate monument: a twelve-foot Johnny Rebel, musket in hand.

Johnny was covered in toilet paper every time Grambling High East played Grambling High West in football; no matter how the game went, the winners celebrated by rolling the statue. Johnny was also the subject of frequent letter-writing campaigns to pull him down. So far Old Dixie had won that battle.

Branigan headed to Resnick Drugs, the domain of Ramsey Resnick. Ramsey's designer wife had created the feel of an old-fashioned drugstore, without the grime. Ramsey Resnick worked the store, but he was landlord of another four businesses on Main.

As Branigan pushed the door open, cords of dangling bells announced her entrance.

"Hi, Mr Resnick. I take it 3 o'clock is your slow time?"

"Sure is. Come on into my office. I can hear those door bells from there."

He took a glass bottle of Coca Cola from an antique ice chest and offered it to Branigan.

"I sure can't turn that down," she said reverently, inserting the bottle's metal cap into the opener on the side of the chest. It popped with a satisfying burp, and she tasted the ice-cold sweetness. Heavenly.

"So you want to talk about Mother's murder?" he prompted.

"Yes," she said. "As you probably know, it's the only unsolved murder in Grambling. The police covered every logical angle. With it going unsolved this long, we at the paper always suspected it might be a transient with no real connection to your mother. So I've asked Liam Delaney at Jericho Road to check with any of the homeless men who might know something."

"Interesting."

"Meanwhile, is there anything that's occurred to you since that day? Anything that seems odd in retrospect?"

Ramsey Resnick looked skeptical. "Do you think I haven't gone over this every day for ten years? There's nothing."

"Let's go over the day of July 5," she suggested. "Start when you woke up."

He sighed. "I got up around eight. Mother had that yappie chihuahua, Dollie. She woke me up. I took Mother to see Dr Arnott for her high blood pressure. He was having a hard time getting it under control."

"Go back a minute," she said when he paused. "What about breakfast? Did you see your sister Amanda and the girls – let's see, your daughter and your niece – before you left?"

He nodded. "Tabitha, Mother's housekeeper, made her special blueberry pancakes, and Amanda cut up some grapefruit or apples or something. I remember Ashley and Caroline loved Tabitha's pancakes and asked her to make faces with the blueberries, though they were really too old for that." He looked bemused. "Surprised I remember that."

Branigan nodded encouragingly. "What did you talk about?"

"Not much. Mother's doctor's appointment. Ashley and

Caroline's plan to go to the club to swim. I wouldn't remember at all if I hadn't gone over it so many times with the po…"

They were interrupted by the loud jangle of bells, then a strident, "Ramsey!"

"That's my brother," he said, then raising his voice, "Heath?"

"There's a woman down here robbing you blind!" the disembodied voice called. Ramsey Resnick started out of his office door.

Heath Resnick had a raggedy woman by the collar, holding her distastefully, as if she might infect him. She was dirty and wrinkled, her skin sunburned. She wriggled to get free of his grasp, her snarled mouth opening to reveal one third of the teeth she should have. Branigan was ten feet away and could smell the competing odors of liquor and urine. Two packs of feminine pads lay at the woman's feet.

"Rita," Ramsey murmured. "Not again."

Branigan looked away, embarrassed for the woman. She appeared too old to need the pads, but as Branigan got closer, she realized she was younger than she looked. Her blue eyes were filmy and unfocused; the wrinkled skin could be the result of long years exposed to the sun. The backpack gave her away: she was homeless.

Heath Resnick finally let her go with a disgusted harrumph, and she sagged to the floor. "You know her?" he asked his brother incredulously. Ramsey and Branigan each took an elbow and helped her up.

"Rita sometimes eats at Marshall's," Ramsey said with a nod toward the diner next door.

Heath continued to look disbelieving. "From Marshall's dumpster, you mean?"

"Okay, Heath, that's enough," said his brother. "Rita, you need to go now. Take one of these packages with you." He propelled her toward the door. Rita never said a word.

When she was outside, there was a tense silence between the brothers. Branigan took her cue to leave. "I'll get back to you," she murmured, eager to escape.

She met Rita on the sidewalk, where she was stuffing the sanitary pads into her backpack. "Are you all right?" Branigan asked. "Can I get you something?"

"Sure, lady. Five dolla be fine."

"I'm sorry, but I don't give money," Branigan said, parroting the words Liam had taught her. "But I'll be glad to buy you a hamburger or take you to Jericho Road."

"Well, ain't you just the fines' ol' church lady?" Rita slurred. "Y'might wanna stop stickin' your nose where it don't b'long."

She straightened, settling the backpack between her shoulder blades, and lurched down the sidewalk.

Branigan wondered how Rita had managed to open the front door without ringing the dangling bells. And she wondered how much of her conversation with Ramsey the woman had overheard.

Her interview cut short, Branigan decided to see if Davison had made any progress on getting into a rehab facility. She left Main Street heading west and drove the short distance to the dilapidated mill village that surrounded the Michael Garner Bridge. The bridge bisected Randall Mill, once known as "the jewel in Grambling's textile crown". Each mill village once sported its own baseball and basketball teams, with good players recruited to work cushy jobs. Each village developed its own personality, and Randall was known as the finest of them all – the most athletic, the most stable, the most affluent.

Years before, Branigan had written a story conjecturing that Grambling's growing Eastside owed homage to its Westside, this crescent of dilapidated mill villages that had been the modern city's start. *The Rambler* wrote so many stories about the newer area that "Grambling's Growing Eastside" became shorthand for Chamber-of-Commerce-friendly stories. Reporters, always a snarky bunch, called it GGE. As in "I gotta do another friggin' GGE story".

The *Style* section, especially, was a cheerleader for Grambling's Growing Eastside, its malls, its soccer teams, its book clubs, its cheerleading camps, its innovative kiddie parties, its prom seasons, its monied subdivisions rising endlessly from former cow pastures. Lord knows, Branigan had done her share. But the Westside was where the real stories were, as far as she was concerned. There was dignity to the farmer who grew eggplant and zinnias within a stone's throw of train tracks; to the lifelong millworkers who told shocking tales of the murderous Textile Strike of 1934; to the foster mother who defied the odds on losing children when crack moved in.

And boy, did crack move in. And heroin. And alcohol. And to some extent crystal meth, though the close quarters of these mill houses made brewing the noxious mix almost certain to grab the attention of neighbors – and police. Far more often, the meth lab busts occurred in the countryside south of Grambling, where a house might not have a neighbor for half a mile or more.

Randall Mill, once queen of the crescent, was now as bad as it got. Whereas some of Grambling's old manufacturing mills had become hot condominium properties – including a few owned by Heath Resnick – the Randall plant had burned. All that remained was a single blackened smokestack, surrounded by a massive swath of cracked concrete. Local skateboarders had built makeshift wooden ramps, but plans to make it a more commercial establishment failed repeatedly. Seems skateboarders weren't the most able businessmen.

Now Randall was broken, defeated, weary. The original residents had died, in many cases leaving their properties to children who no longer lived in Grambling. The mill houses with their distinctive four-room floor plans might be rented, or they might be abandoned. Crack dealers moved freely through both. Power and running water were optional. Boarded-up windows and signs announcing "condemned" were no guarantee that a house was empty.

It was depressing. Or it was, until Branigan entered the path toward the Garner Bridge that she and Liam had walked last night. Then "depressing" took on a whole new meaning.

She walked past a garbage heap, jumping back when she heard a hiss from its depths. A snake? A possum? She didn't wait to find out.

Hurrying past in unsuitable sandals, she reached the leafy river birch that made a feeble attempt to conceal the opening to this city under the bridge. Once she rounded the tree, the view opened – numerous tents, open fire pits, another garbage pile and a stack of firewood left over from winter. A pit bull the exact color of the packed red mud was chained to a wooden doghouse. That house always raised the eyebrows of Liam's visitors: *So the dog has a house, but his owners don't?* The dog opened one eye in the afternoon heat, but decided Branigan wasn't worth a bark. He closed it again.

She was already inside the camp when she realized she didn't know what she was doing. Did these people know Davison? She peered over a tent and saw three men sitting in rusting beach chairs around a cold fire pit. To her relief, she recognized Malachi.

She walked over, speaking softly, aware she was entering someone's home.

"Mr Martin? I'm Branigan? From breakfast at Jericho Road?"

Malachi looked up and gave, if not a smile, at least an acknowledgment. "Yes, ma'am. I remember. *Gramblin' Rambler.*"

"I'm here looking for my brother. Davison Powers?"

If the men were surprised, they didn't show it.

"Skinny white dude? Look kinda like you?"

"Yes. Do you know where he is?"

"Rita let him stay in her place," Malachi said, swiveling to point to a rickety plyboard structure at the top of the incline. "Guess he's still asleep."

She looked at her watch: 3:45 p.m. Sheesh. And Rita? Could there be more than one homeless Rita?

"Um, how do I get up there?" Branigan asked, eyeing the incline.

"Well, not in those shoes," said one of Malachi's buddies.

She laughed along with them. "Clearly you gentlemen haven't heard of Ginger Rogers. She did everything Fred Astaire did, but in high heels and backwards." To her relief, the men laughed again. All but Malachi, who sat with a bemused expression.

Branigan kicked off her sandals. She wanted to leave her purse as well, but thought it unwise. Gripping it under one arm, she started to creep up the concrete incline sideways, the way Liam had indicated that residents reached the ledge.

The men watched, snickering. Finally Malachi stood. "Ma'am, that's gon' take you all day. Lemme get 'im."

Branigan was only a quarter of the way up, and looked at Malachi gratefully. He wore rubber-soled athletic shoes, and passed her quickly, his feet crossing and recrossing. If he'd been on level ground, he would have been line dancing.

He arrived at the structure with its cut-out window covered in plastic, and knocked gently on the door. "Dude," he said, "your sister want you."

The door opened almost immediately, and Davison's stubbled face appeared, slack with sleep. "Branigan?"

He took in Malachi, then his sister, barefoot, thirty feet below, and laughed. "I'll meet you down there," he said, ducking back inside.

Two minutes later, Davison joined her on the ground, a worn, military knapsack slung over one shoulder. "What's up?" he said. She could smell alcohol, not on his breath, but through his pores. He hadn't been drinking today, she surmised, but had been drinking heavily in the days preceding.

"I want to hear about rehab," she said.

"The gospel mission can take me Monday. They start a new group every week."

It was only Tuesday. "Where are you going to stay 'til then?"

"You're lookin' at it. Liam didn't have an open bed."

At that moment, the woman from Ramsey Resnick's drugstore stepped past the birch and into the shade provided by the bridge. She looked from Davison to Branigan. "Wha's ol' church lady doin' here?"

"Church lady? Branigan?" Davison looked bewildered. "Rita, this is my sister, Branigan. She's a reporter."

Branigan closed her eyes, feeling physical revulsion at the thought of her brother and this woman.

"Yo' sistah?" she cackled. "Damn. She don't wanna stay with us too, does she?"

"No," Branigan said emphatically. "You don't have to worry about that."

"Liam says I have to be detoxed by Monday, or the mission won't let me in," Davison said.

She looked at him, looked beneath the matted hair and the dirt-streaked face, looked past the stale scent of alcohol emanating from his pores, looked at the brother who, for so many years, had been her shadow self. Clearly he hadn't taken up Liam on his offer of a shower.

"Can you do that here?"

"I can try."

She didn't know she was going to say it until the words came out. "Why don't you come back to the farm with me? We'll keep you sober 'til Monday."

Davison and Rita had a whispered conversation before he left. She didn't look happy that he was leaving. She thrust a dirty finger at his chest several times, her face contorted angrily as she whispered and pointed to her shack. He finally shrugged and walked away.

Branigan needed to get back to work, so she dropped Davison at an outdoor table at Bea's with enough money for a sandwich and coffee. She dreaded telling her mom and dad what she was doing. After Davison dropped out of college, they had taken him in countless times. They paid $40,000 for a four-month rehab ranch in Utah, $60,000 for a six-month stay in New Mexico. After each, he moved in with them – and began using.

Finally, on a Saturday morning twelve years ago, they'd had enough of the heartbreak. "We will support you in recovery," they told him in the language they'd all learned so well. "But we will no longer support your addiction. You cannot live here."

He had gone to Branigan's apartment before hitting the road. She gave him all the cash she had on hand – $35 – but had little hope it would be used for anything other than beer or crack. After closing the door in his face, she went to her bedroom and cried off and on for twenty-four hours.

For weeks afterward, her chest felt tight, as if there were a vise squeezing her lungs. Or more likely, her heart. She refused her parents' invitations to dinner, regretful that she was adding to their hurt but unable to face her co-conspirators in this awful decision. The only time she didn't feel like crying was when she was working.

So she worked.

She got back to the newsroom and glanced at the large desk calendar she kept as a backup to her iPad. Only then did she realize what she'd done: the word BEACH was written in large capital letters across Friday, June 5. She wasn't even going to be at the farm this weekend.

"Oh, no!" she said, laying her head on her desk. "Now what am I gonna do?"

Could she leave Davison at the farm alone? No. To his mind the place was full of great drunken memories. Could she take him with her? She didn't want to. But maybe he and Cleo could stay at the beach house while she conducted interviews. It wasn't perfect, but it was better than leaving him under the bridge where the crack and alcohol flowed freely.

She updated an online story about a fundraiser for the public library. She answered email, confirming interviews with Mrs Resnick's daughter at nearby Lake Hartwell, then her granddaughters in Edisto and Isle of Palms.

She called the South Carolina Department of Corrections, and left a message for the public information officer, asking if Billy Shepherd was still in prison. Then she called Liam to ask if he'd gotten any leads on the Resnick case.

"Yes and no," he said. "I brought it up at this morning's meeting. Sixteen of our guys were there – which is rare. More are usually working third shift and I don't ask them to wake up. Anyway, only six remotely knew what I was talking about. Four remembered the story from news accounts back then. But two – Dontegan and Jess – said they'd heard vague rumors over the years. Let me get my notes." Branigan heard scratching as Liam searched his desk, then a yelp and a curse.

"Why, Saint Liam, what did you do?"

"Knocked my coffee over."

"Sorry."

"I do that at least once a day. Okay, here you go. Jess said that a man named Max Brody – he's a bad alcoholic – got drunk one night and was babbling that 'this evening's drunk is courtesy of an old lady who had the good taste to get stabbed'."

"Those were his exact words?" She began scribbling. "'This evening's drunk is courtesy of an old lady who had the good taste to get stabbed'?"

"Yeah, as well as Jess could remember, anyway."

"When was this?"

"Don't know."

"Okay, I'll need to talk to Jess and this Max Brody. What did Dontegan say?"

"Dontegan said he'd heard a woman talking about a lady who got murdered downtown, but the woman was drunk and he couldn't make much sense of it. I pressed him, and he said it was a homeless woman who eats here a lot. Rita."

Rita again?

"Can you describe her?" Branigan asked.

"Tiny. In her forties, but looks sixty. White, horribly sun-damaged and wrinkled. Washed-out blond hair. She's a prostitute and a bad alcoholic and, from the look of her teeth, a meth addict. She's been impossible for us to reach out to."

"I've met her."

"How?"

"I ran into her on Main Street. Pretty drunk. And Davison stayed in her shack under the bridge last night."

"Not good. No telling what kind of diseases she has."

"I know. I'm taking him to the farm then the beach with me until he can get into the mission on Monday."

"Hmm. Are you sure, Brani G?"

"No, not at all."

He laughed. "As Mom would say, 'Bless your heart.'"

"Yes, it needs blessing," she agreed.

* * *

She worked for another hour. Before heading to Bea's to pick up Davison, she drove to the Grambling Farmers' Market, an open-air, tin-roofed series of stalls located several blocks off South Main. Operating daily nine months a year, it was the spot to get fresh flowers and vegetables, as well as home-baked breads, jams, milk, eggs, cheese and other goodies from local farmers.

Branigan loved the smell of the place, due primarily to the aromatic cantaloupes in a giant bin next to the watermelons. One August in Detroit, she'd stumbled into a farmers' market. Walking down its concrete-floored aisle, she was suddenly transported to Gran and Pa's farmhouse. Her heart swelled, and she looked around to see what had brought on the wave of homesickness. Sure enough, it was cantaloupes, their heady scent mimicking the smell of Gran's kitchen. After that, she spent many a Saturday wandering the aisles of the giant market, always starting and ending by the melons. More than once, she went back to her apartment and booked a flight home.

Now she enjoyed a sniff, but she had arranged for the same smell to waft through her kitchen window. She selected half a pound of green beans to cook for Davison, then picked up some strawberries as well. She handed a ten-dollar bill to the clerk, a woman with a tight brown perm and fat arms straining at a sleeveless blouse. The woman took the bill, glancing behind Branigan. She felt an unfamiliar prickle on the back of her neck.

She turned, but no one was there.

Turning back to the woman for change, Branigan saw her eyes dart behind her again.

"What?" she asked.

"Them homeless," the clerk muttered.

Branigan glanced back and saw a couple standing in the shade just inside the shed, telltale knapsacks on their backs. The woman caught Branigan's eye and smiled. Branigan saw the man edge away from his partner, toward the parking lot.

"They gonna ask you for money," the clerk said. "Can't keep 'em away."

"I thought you provided leftover produce at the end of the day."

"We do. They's a crate over there we fill with stuff too ripe to sell. It can get pretty full around 6 o'clock."

"Maybe that's what they're waiting for."

The clerk looked at Branigan skeptically. "Yeah, you come tell me that after you get to your car."

Branigan gathered her produce and purse. She didn't feel like being panhandled, so she walked down the shed's interior, pretending to look at the marigolds and petunias. When she could see her Civic through the open side, she veered and made straight for it.

As she pressed her remote entry button, the homeless woman stepped from the shade, startling her. Branigan looked around for the woman's partner, but didn't see him. She wondered if he was behind her, but she didn't want the woman to catch her looking.

The woman was short, with thin legs and a protruding stomach. She wore a yellow kerchief over dyed black hair. Tattoos ran up both arms. She smiled, revealing a missing eyetooth.

She started right in. "Ma'am, my husband and I just arrived in town for construction jobs, but my cousin, who was supposed to hire us, never picked us up from the bus station, and now we're stranded. Could you give us a few dollars for a motel room tonight? Tomorrow, we'll work day labor and get a room and bus tickets home."

Branigan listened politely, dread settling in her stomach. It would be easy to give the woman a few dollars, but Liam had convinced her it was the wrong thing to do. Panhandling was the method for getting drugs and alcohol, he said, almost never meals and shelter.

"Have you been to the Salvation Army or the Rescue Mission?" she asked. "They have women's shelters."

"You have to wait in line," the woman said smoothly, "and we couldn't, because we were trying to find work."

"I'm sorry, but no," Branigan said. "I give to the Rescue Mission and Jericho Road. They're set up to help."

"We'll go there tomorrow," the woman said, a whine creeping into her voice, "but we need enough money to eat and get a motel room tonight."

"Jericho Road is serving dinner," Branigan said, getting into the Civic and feeling terrible. She shut the car door, but the woman didn't stop talking. Since the window was down an inch, she could hear her continuing monologue.

"We're not asking you to pay the whole $39 for a room, just $5 or $10." The smile remained fixed on her face, but it was looking more like a grimace. The woman's partner suddenly loomed in Branigan's rearview mirror, blocking her exit. She wanted to lock her doors, but was embarrassed for them to hear the click. "You never know when you might need help yourself."

Branigan looked up sharply to see the woman's dark eyes boring into hers. *Did she really say that?* Her discomfort rising, she glanced to see if anyone else was around.

At that moment, a farmer came out of the market, carrying a load of unsold corn that he placed in his truck bed. He looked silently from the woman to the man. Without a word, they turned and hurried across the parking lot. The farmer met Branigan's eyes, gave an almost imperceptible nod, and walked back into the market.

Unsettled by the encounter, Branigan drove quickly to Bea's, unsure if she was feeling guilt or menace. She wanted to help people, but didn't want to play into their scams.

She found Davison where she'd left him, at an outdoor table with an iced tea and a *Rambler*. "Ready to go?"

"Ready," he said, standing to stretch.

"How are you set for clothes?"

"I'd love to chuck everything in this backpack."

"Want to run by Dad's and get some things?"

"No, I don't think I'm ready for that. Could we go to the Salvation Army store? I have a little money."

"Where'd you get it?"

"Day labor."

She drove to the thrift store located a few blocks from Jericho Road. The Salvation Army kept it clean and well ordered so that customers from the Eastside sought it out. Charlie and Chan had put together Halloween costumes here. Davison and Branigan entered the cavernous space. He headed to the men's clothes racks, and she found a table stacked with paperbacks. She rummaged idly until she found a novel by Anita Shreve she hadn't read, and seized it for a dollar. She was searching for another when she heard her name. She jumped, and looked up to see Malachi Martin on the other side of the table. He had come up so quietly she hadn't heard him.

"You still workin' on a story about that hit-and-run?" he asked.

She nodded.

"You know the pitcher I was talkin' about that Vesuvius sold? I found it buried in a trash pile under the bridge."

"I don't understand."

"I told you V sol' a paintin' with that black V in the corner, right?" he explained patiently. "He said he sol' it to a homeless dude. This afternoon, I thought I saw a bottle with somethin' still in it stickin' out the trash pile. So I went to pull it out. And under it was that paintin' V sold. I remembered, 'cause it hung in Pastor Liam's lunchroom a long time."

At that moment, Davison walked up, a pile of shorts, pants and shirts folded over one arm. Malachi eyed the clothes and narrowed his eyes, but didn't speak.

Davison broke the silence. "I'm moving in with my sister for a few nights."

Malachi simply nodded and walked off.

"Thanks, Malachi," Branigan called, not knowing what else to say. *What does Vesuvius selling a painting have to do with anything?* she wondered. Still, it was nice of Malachi to tell her. She supposed he wanted to amplify the portrait of Vesuvius as an artist.

Davison paid for his clothes and they left.

Back at the farm, Davison emptied his knapsack into the trash bin in Branigan's garage, then carried his new clothes into the guest bedroom. "I'm going to open that window and listen for the long-haul trucks tonight," he said with a grin.

"I discovered I can hear them from Gran's bedroom too," she said. "I listen every night."

Her brother looked at her oddly. She thought he might be fighting back tears, but it was hard to tell. She didn't really know him any more. "I'd hug you," he said, "but you might prefer if I get a shower first."

"Sure thing. You remember where the towels are. My casa is your casa."

While Davison was showering, Branigan gathered the unopened bottles of Malbec and pinot noir and cabernet sauvignon from her kitchen wine rack and the half-full bottles of vodka and rum from the armoire in the living room. Placing the bottles in two cardboard boxes, she loaded them into the Civic trunk and drove to her closest neighbors.

Uncle Bobby and Aunt Jeanie's farmland was similar to Pa's, but their house was far grander, more coastal antebellum than upcountry farmhouse, thanks to Jeanie's upbringing. Its massive central portion rose two stories, with four giant columns marching across the front of a wide, brick-floored porch. Six whitewashed rocking chairs softened the formality and provided a welcoming touch. To each side of the porch, one-story additions sprawled. On the far side was a sumptuous sunroom; on the driveway side where Branigan pulled in, a large kitchen. A three-car garage was hidden at the back.

The family marveled that Jeanie let roughneck Uncle Bobby inside such a place.

Jeanie had been a beauty queen in her day, a Miss Savannah, but was now "fat and sassy", as she put it. "Ain't nothing uglier than a skinny old woman," she'd say when piling her plate at family gatherings.

She came to her kitchen door as her niece drove up, wiping her hands on a dish towel and grabbing Branigan in a fierce hug. "Hey there, stranger," she said into her hair. "For a next-door neighbor, we sure don't see much of you."

"And now I'm here to ask a favor. I'm a pretty sorry niece."

"Name it," Jeanie said.

Branigan took a deep breath. "Davison is staying with me for a few days. I wanted to get all the alcohol out of the house. Can I leave it with you?"

Jeanie's brown eyes softened. "Of course you can, sweetie. When did this happen?"

"He got to town yesterday, and is going to rehab at the Grambling Rescue Mission. But they can't take him 'til Monday."

"Good for him."

"Yeah, I told Mom and Dad this morning."

She eyed Branigan sympathetically. "Honey, you want to come in and open one of those bottles?"

Branigan laughed. "I'd love to, but I'd better get back. I guess I'm going to be on the wagon this week too."

"All right, but when you get that one straightened out, you and I can have a girls' night." She winked, and took one of the boxes from the trunk. Branigan followed with the other and they stashed them in Jeanie's laundry room, which was the size of Branigan's entire kitchen.

She returned home to find Davison dressed in his newly purchased khakis and T-shirt. He had shaved and was toweling his thick hair dry.

"Tomorrow, a barber," he announced. "Brani G, you didn't have to get rid of your wine. I'm going to have to learn to be around people who drink."

"Yeah, but you don't have to learn the first week you're trying to get clean."

He shrugged.

"I'm going to bake some chicken breasts and potatoes and cook some fresh beans from the farmers' market. Sound good?"

"Got any biscuits?"

"Frozen ones. They aren't quite as good as Gran's, but close."

"That'll do." He smiled and she got a glimpse of the brother she used to know. He walked over to the refrigerator and rummaged around. "Got any tea?"

"No, but lots of Diet Pepsi and Diet Dr Pepper."

"What have you got against sugar?" he complained, grabbing a can nonetheless.

As she banged around and found pans she'd not used since winter, he perched on a high stool at the center island. It felt funny not to offer him a drink. She'd never had a guest who *didn't* drink wine or beer at the island while she cooked. Branigan thought, not for the first time, how many hours must yawn before a recovering alcoholic. *What do you do with all that time you previously spent drinking?*

"I'm really glad you're here," she told him, putting water on to boil for the potatoes. "Last night I found a footprint in the flower bed just outside that window." She pointed to the window over the sink.

Davison put his soda can down. "You're kidding. Do you have an alarm system?"

"Cleo."

"Brani G, I don't like this. You're out in the middle of nowhere." He strode across the den, slamming the screen door. She raised the window so she could hear him. His head soon appeared. "It's a tennis shoe like mine," he said, stepping over the lantana and cantaloupes to fit his shoe in the print. "But a size or two larger."

"I figured it might be the electricity meter reader or the cable guy or Uncle Bobby," she said through the screen.

"When have you seen Uncle Bobby without work boots?"

Moments later, he came back in. "It's fine as long as I'm here," he said. "But you need to get an alarm system. Bobby and Jeanie's house is – what? – a quarter mile away?"

"Or more."

"Seriously. Please do that."

"All right, all right."

"So catch me up," Davison said, sipping his Diet Dr Pepper. "Tell me about Mom and Dad and Chan and Charlie and Liz and Liam."

She told him about the merger at their dad's bank and the scare with his heart that turned out to be indigestion. She told him about their mom's growing accountancy business and her election as a deacon at First Baptist. She told him about Liam's mission church and Liz's interior design business and Charlie's plans to attend the

University of Georgia. But mostly she told him about Chan – every detail she could remember of her nephew's high school career. She told him about the soccer game against Grambling West, in which Chan's goalkeeper got lured out of the box, and Chan darted behind him to save the goal. She told him about the college scouts who had called from Division 2 schools, but how Chan had decided on Division 1 Furman because of its academics. She told Davison how handsome he looked in his prom tuxedo back in April.

"He's a wonderful young man," she told her brother honestly. "Liz and Liam have done a great job. They have always treated him and Charlie alike."

He nodded. "I knew they would."

"Have you been in touch with Shauna?"

"Nah. She's not been back here, has she?"

Branigan shook her head. "It's like she fell off the face of the earth."

"I wonder if Chan would be better off if we both had."

She looked at him silently. She didn't want to jump in with a cheery dismissal of his behavior. But she didn't think that was true either – that Chan would be better off never knowing his real parents.

"I don't think so," she said slowly. "I think it's always better to know the truth. And I especially think you're right that he needs to know his genetics. He's at a huge risk for addiction."

Davison nodded. "That's what I wanted to come back to tell him. I don't want him to live like I have. I've messed up so badly."

"Yeah, you have. But you're only forty-one. You've got lots of time left if you want to change."

"I don't know about that," he said, finishing his soda and crumpling the can. "Brani G, would it hurt your feelings if I ate this dinner tomorrow? I can't tell you the last time I slept in a bed, and Gran's mattress is calling my name."

"Sure, that's fine."

An hour later, she and Cleo ate alone, as they did most nights.

CHAPTER FOURTEEN

Malachi slid a fragrant cantaloupe from his backpack. Supper.
Sitting on an upright section of cut log, he took out his pocket knife and sliced through the taut rind and into the soft, orange fruit. Down South, the variety was actually a mushmelon, he'd once read. A true cantaloupe had a thicker rind or something like that. But he preferred the word cantaloupe. Such a colorful word. A word his grandmother had liked.

This particular cantaloupe had rolled off a truck backed up to the Grambling farmers' market. Well, *rolled off* might be a stretch. Rolled off, with a little help.

The small Martin farm in the sometimes dusty, sometimes lush countryside beyond Hartwell had produced fine cantaloupes – and tomatoes, corn, okra, squash, string beans, and watermelons. Malachi and his grandmother had sold them at a vegetable stand at the end of their dirt driveway every Friday and Saturday. Malachi urged her to sell on Sundays too, but she harrumphed and didn't bother to answer. Sunday was the Lord's Day, and Granny wasn't about to sell on the Lord's Day. Malachi suspected she didn't want her reading time interrupted, but he kept that opinion to himself.

As he got older, somewhere in his early teens, Granny left him on his own at the vegetable stand so she could help his grandpa with the chores around the farm – feeding the chickens, slopping the hogs, picking and carrying more fruits and vegetables from the garden patch to the stand.

That's how he came to be the only witness to the original cantaloupe thief.

The first time Malachi saw him, the man was driving a black station wagon with South Carolina license plates, water skis tied securely on top, car laden with cold drinks – and children. It was the Saturday before the Fourth of July, and the family was plainly headed to Lake Hartwell.

The car passed Malachi's stand and cruised on for another 100 yards, past a gentle curve in the road. If Malachi's stand hadn't been perched on the highest point around, if his grandfather's pecan trees had been nearer the road, he wouldn't have seen what happened next. The car stopped, two doors flew open, and two boys of around seven or eight ran with the precision of a mini-SWAT team to the edge of the Martin melon patch. Before Malachi could yell or even get off his stool, really, they had plucked what looked to be two cantaloupes; laughing and squealing, they dived back into the car, which took off in a burst of ditch dust.

Malachi sat with his jaw dropping. Did that white family just steal cantaloupes out of his grandpa's melon patch? A part of him was indignant and couldn't wait to tell his grandparents. Another part of him was tickled. After all, the hogs got more than their share of mushy cantaloupes, the fruits ripening too fast for the family to eat or sell them all. In the end, he didn't tell.

The next year, the Fourth of July fell on a Monday. The Saturday before, Malachi was minding the stand. He saw the black station wagon as it slowly passed, the driver a handsome, laughing man, his wife smiling, at least four children and a large collie bouncing between a back seat and a rear-facing third seat.

Bemused, Malachi watched them re-enact the scene from the year before, only this time, sending out a boy and a tiny girl, no more than five, to steal the cantaloupes. The girl struggled to carry her fruit from the patch, and another boy, maybe ten, jumped out to help. Then with squeals and laughter, they hurled themselves into the back seat, and the car sped off.

Malachi shook his head in amazement. *Is this a white family's idea of bad-ass?* he wondered?

The next year, on the Saturday before the Fourth, he was on the lookout for the family, but they didn't return. Malachi found himself watching for them all day, wondering what had happened. Had they taken another route to the lake, stealing from some other melon patch? Had they gone to the beach instead, helping themselves from a farmer's sandy field in Horry County? Strangely, he missed seeing the family, so full of excitement at their tiny larceny.

More than thirty years later, Malachi held to a strict moral code – with a few exceptions. Taking – he never thought of it as *stealing* – was allowed in a few instances. Ketchup and mayonnaise and sugar packets from fast-food restaurants. Cups and plastic knives and salt and pepper packets from Jericho Road. Margarine and soap and toilet paper from St James African Methodist Episcopal Church. And cantaloupes – as many sweet, delicious cantaloupes as he could eat – from the farmers' market or roadside stands or farmers' fields.

The way he figured it, he saw that family take cantaloupes from his family's patch twice. But who knew how many people stopped how many times during the good years of the Martin farm, helping themselves to a watermelon here, a tomato there, a cantaloupe?

The way he figured it, sometimes justice had to be snatched.

CHAPTER FIFTEEN

The first full day Davison stayed at the farm, Branigan made it a point to get home early. It wasn't even 6 o'clock when she pulled into the driveway.

Davison and Cleo were piled on the sofa, watching TV news. Davison's straggly locks were gone, replaced by a near-buzz that accentuated his strong jaw line. The two of them followed her into the kitchen, where she put on water to boil for tea. She asked Davison what he'd done all day, and he smiled broadly.

"Mostly ate," he said, lifting his shirt to show that his sunken stomach was already showing signs of changing shape. "You'll know when you go into your fridge."

"That's all?" she asked, laughing.

"Well, Cleo and I walked through the pastures and scared Uncle Bobby's cows. We threw rocks in the lake. We drowned some worms, but caught squat. And we slept. Cleo's always up for a nap."

"Sounds like the life."

"Oh, and I took a ride on your girlie bike."

"So that's how you got your hair cut. You're a better man than I to ride on these roads."

"It wasn't too bad. I stopped at that barber shop at the crossroads, so I didn't have to go all the way into Grambling.

"I can't tell you how great it is to be back here," he continued, waving his arm around Gran's kitchen. "Do you know, I can smell cantaloupes even when they're not here?"

She laughed. "They are here! Right outside the window. Didn't you see them when you went out there last night?"

"Oh, you can smell them through the screen," he said. "Duh. Glad to know I'm not going crazy. I always heard that the sense of smell is the best trigger to memory. Guess it's true." After a moment he added, "But how do you like living this far out of town?"

"It's worth it," she said. "After those years in Detroit, I never want to live in a city again. And I couldn't keep Cleo in an apartment. This is perfect for me."

He looked around the kitchen and the connecting, light-filled den that Pa had renovated from a garage. Branigan had kept its practical tile floor, but now it sported her cotton-upholstered pieces in old-fashioned green and rose – florals for the couch and two-seater, stripes for a pair of armchairs, a solid mint green for the antique lounge chair she'd been given by their Powers grandmother.

She'd painted the walls too, in mint green, and hung them with paintings she'd collected, mostly watercolors, mostly landscapes, all the work of artists she'd met, including one from Jericho Road. Down a hallway, her office – with its sliding glass door onto the back porch – allowed her to look out over the cotton field and see the barn and one corner of a chicken house in the distance. In winter, when the trees were bare, she could make out the first lake, blackberry bushes crowding its shoreline, winter sun glinting off its surface.

"You've done a good job with it," Davison said. "Got rid of Gran's kitsch without losing the farmhouse feel. It's like before, only better."

"Well, it's as much yours as it is mine," she said. "I'm just renting it from Mom and Uncle Bobby."

"That reminds me," he said. "I can't wait to see the beach house. It's been – what? – twelve years since I was there. I'm surprised Mom and Dad still have it."

"Yeah, Mom keeps crunching the numbers and saying they aren't losing money on it. Yet. I've got one stop to make at the lake on Friday, then we'll head straight there."

On Thursday Branigan felt comfortable enough about Davison to work late. She was leaving the newsroom around 6:30 when Jody waved her over.

He was still on the phone, so she waited by his desk as he scribbled something on a legal pad.

Colonial Inn, she read upside down. *8 p.m. Augusta Room.*

He hung up. "You're not going to believe this."

"What?"

"Do you remember that psychic the police brought in for the Resnick murder?"

As with any murder investigation, the publicity had brought out the crazies. At least seven so-called psychics had contacted the Grambling police, offering help. Nine months into the investigation, a desperate Chief Marcus Warren had finally invited one in – Marla Demarnier from New Mexico. Mrs Demarnier came highly recommended by the Albuquerque Police Department. They claimed she had led them to three burials in the desert they would not have otherwise discovered.

Jody and Branigan had talked to Mrs Demarnier when she visited the spring following Mrs Resnick's murder. They'd been impressed with her – not because she presented any new information, but because she wasn't a publicity seeker. Marla Demarnier was a reserved and attractive woman in her mid-sixties. The reporters got the impression she would have much preferred to stay on her family's ranch outside Albuquerque, but she was plagued by visions and dreams. The Albuquerque police had developed a respect for her insight. They were quick to tell Chief Warren that her work wasn't always helpful, but she'd had enough offbeat successes that they didn't dismiss her.

Mrs Demarnier came to Grambling after dreaming for three consecutive nights about a stabbing in the deep South. She contacted her friends on the Albuquerque force, who ran a check and discovered the Resnick case. They called Chief Warren, who, by that point, welcomed her.

Mrs Demarnier spent two days in Grambling, walking through the Resnick house, grounds and pool house. "It was someone she knew," she told detectives. "But I can't see him – or her. All I can see is the old woman, looking up in such surprise. She is so surprised at the attack. The feeling I get is not fear, not fear of a stranger. Just shock that this could be happening right here in her kitchen."

"Sure, I remember," Branigan now told Jody.

"Well, Marla Demarnier didn't have any answers. But now the Southeastern Association of Psychics wants a crack at it."

"What do you mean?"

"Apparently, we aren't the only ones interested in the tenth anniversary. This regional psychic group is holding their annual gathering tonight at the Colonial Inn. They've gotten Heath and Ramsey Resnick to give them some of their mother's personal items to try to get vibes from."

"You're kidding."

"Nope," he said, tearing the page from his legal pad. "That was the group's president, asking for coverage. I'm not going to do a live story. You want it?"

"You bet," she said, grabbing the paper.

Branigan made a quick call to Davison to let him know she'd be late. Then she called Liam and asked if he wanted to accompany her. She'd heard him reference the TV show *Medium* in a sermon, so she knew he was familiar with the idea of psychics and police work.

He agreed to meet her at the Colonial Inn, an unpretentious motel a mile from downtown where numerous Grambling civic organizations held meetings.

"It's really okay for you to come?" she asked. "Spooks and spirits not of the holy persuasion?"

"Wouldn't miss it."

"What if your congregation finds out?"

He chuckled. "If I worried about what every Christian in this town thought, I wouldn't drink a beer, let gays in the church, or sleep with Liz. I'll be there by eight."

Branigan arrived at the motel fifteen minutes early and quickly ran through the rooms in use: Albany had an engagement party. Macon had Veterans of Foreign Wars. Athens had optometrists. Valdosta had... well, it was hard to tell what was going on in there, but it had something to do with sci-fi enthusiasts. Sure enough, Augusta had the Southeastern Association of Psychics.

Branigan wasn't sure what she was expecting – perhaps women in gauzy fabrics and headscarves, crystal balls in hand. But it was nothing like that. This crowd could have been the optometrists. Two dozen men and women, remarkable only for looking so unremarkable, sat at one long table in the center of the wallpapered room. At the room's far end, a table was filled with soft drinks and ice. Beside it, another table held bowls of nuts, an urn of coffee and the inn's specialty cranberry muffins.

She waited for a lull in the conversation, then asked for the association president. A thin woman with stylishly cut gray hair and matching coral lipstick and pants suit stood and introduced herself. "You must be from *The Rambler*," she said. "We're glad you could make it on such short notice. We got our signals mixed on alerting the media. I'm Ethel Manchester."

"I'm Branigan Powers. I'm working on a tenth anniversary story on Alberta Resnick's murder. Can you tell me what you're doing tonight?"

"Certainly." Ms Manchester picked up a scarf, framed photo and clip-on earrings from the end of the table. The scarf was silky, navy and green paisley, obviously expensive. The silver-framed photo was of Alberta Resnick in her later years, perhaps for a church directory, her white hair perfectly coiffed, her blue eyes steely. The earrings contained faux rubies. At least, Branigan assumed they were fake. Maybe not.

"The Resnick family provided us with these personal items from their mother. We'll pass them around and see if any of our members register any heat from them."

"No offense," Branigan said, "but I'm a little surprised the Resnicks would do that."

Ms Manchester smiled. "I seriously doubt they are believers," she agreed, "but they saw no harm in our trying. After all, the poor woman's murder has gone unsolved for ten years."

"You're right about that."

Liam walked in at that moment, and Branigan introduced him to Ms Manchester. She didn't ask if Liam worked for *The Rambler*, so the two didn't volunteer further information. He made a beeline for the food table, wolfing down half a muffin before he sat.

"I can't take you anywhere," Branigan murmured as he slouched in the chair next to her.

Promptly at eight, Ms Manchester called the meeting to order. She introduced Branigan and Liam as newspaper reporters who had worked on the Resnick story ten years earlier. The men and women nodded politely.

She then invited reports from members' work. For the next hour and a half, members told how they had offered assistance in various unsolved cases around the country. Only one sounded as if the psychic had provided information that led to an arrest. The others seemed to think so too, because they plied the woman with questions.

It was past 9:30 and Liam was yawning when Ethel Manchester picked up the scarf that had belonged to Alberta Resnick. "Now for the important work of the evening," she said. She gave a brief and accurate summary of Mrs Resnick's murder, then turned to Branigan and Liam. "Have I left anything out?"

The two shook their heads.

"All right, then," Ms Manchester said briskly. "You've all done this before. You know how it works. Feel free to speak out if you get an impression, or save it until all the items have gone around. Either way is fine."

"Aren't they going to turn off the lights?" Liam whispered.

"Guess not."

"They're missing out on the creep factor."

The scarf started around the table, followed by the photo, then the earrings. As individuals took the items, they closed their eyes and held them in both hands. After handling all three, a plump young woman in jeans and black T-shirt grabbed a notepad and pencil from the center of the table and began drawing furiously. Branigan peered surreptitiously over her shoulder and saw a cabin taking shape, surrounded by cedar trees.

The items continued around the table. A man halfway down the far side took the earrings in his palm, and closed his eyes. A moment later, his eyes flew open and he threw the earrings down as if they had burned him. He looked frantically at the woman next to him, who had handed him the baubles. "Did you feel that?" he demanded, rising abruptly from the table. "Did anybody feel that?"

The others looked at him with interest.

"What'd you get, Abe?" asked a man across the table.

"He thought he'd got away with it," Abe said. "All these years, he thought he'd got away with it. Now he knows he didn't."

He turned abruptly to Branigan and Liam. "He knows," he repeated. "And you're in danger."

Branigan looked at Liam. He was struggling to keep a straight face.

The woman with the drawing spun around and looked at the visitors, then addressed the president. "This is where he's been living," she said, shoving her pad toward Ethel Manchester. "He's been holed away, isolated. But I think this cabin is empty now."

Ms Manchester passed the drawing to Branigan. It showed a long, low cabin, with trees closing in on it. An Adirondack chair was turned upside down on the grass out front. Indeed, the place looked abandoned and desolate.

"Take it," said the young woman, looking from Branigan to Liam. "Maybe it'll help."

They stayed for another half-hour, but none of the other psychics professed sensations from Mrs Resnick's possessions. Branigan pressed the artist and Abe as to whether the killer was male for sure.

"Not necessarily," said the artist. "I know I said 'he'. But that's just because a loner in a cabin seems to indicate a man. But I didn't feel anything that said definitely male."

Abe agreed. "I guess I said 'he' because the threat seemed so strong, and I can't imagine a woman being that threatening. But that's my prejudice talking, not my sixth sense."

Branigan made another run at Abe, but he could add nothing to his original statement. "All I can tell you is this guy has been feeling safe," he said. "And my sense is that's over."

At 10:45, Liam and Branigan thanked the group and left them trading more stories in the brightly lit room.

They stood for a moment in the motel parking lot. "This sounds stupid," Branigan said, "but I guess I haven't thought about the danger before. What if we stir up something and bring this guy into our lives?"

"You don't believe this stuff, do you?" Liam said. "I thought you just wanted color for your story."

"You're the *Medium* fan," she protested. "And yeah, I do think some people are sensitive to these things. If police departments ask them for help, there has to be something to it. Did you see that guy when he touched those earrings? He wasn't faking."

"No," Liam said slowly. "Not faking exactly. I think they just work themselves into a furor."

"Maybe. Or maybe Abe's right: the killer thought he'd got away with something, and now we've reawakened him."

Branigan's skin began to crawl as she drove back to the farm. The country road was deserted this time of night, and she found herself glad that both Davison and Cleo were waiting at home.

She'd been thinking of this story as a puzzle, a juicy read. Now she realized that it represented a threat to someone. Chances are the "someone" wasn't even around. But what if they were? What if someone had been watching her through her kitchen window because she'd brought the police files home?

What if her blind slapping at the hornet's nest stirred up more than she could handle?

She saw red eyes in her headlights and screamed.

The opossum turned and fled into the roadside vegetation.

Damn, she thought, easing her foot off the gas. *Get a grip!*

It was past eleven when she pulled into the driveway. Davison had left the side porch light on. Still, she exited the Civic nervously, peering into the inky cotton patch and knowing full well she wouldn't be able to see if someone was hidden there.

She walked swiftly to the door, jamming her key into the deadbolt and stepping inside. Cleo, sleeping on the rug and waiting for her, stood and whined a welcome. She hugged the shepherd's neck and felt herself relax. Only then did she realize how tense she'd been.

CHAPTER SIXTEEN

I t was Friday, so St James was serving breakfast. Malachi had been making his rounds for so long he hardly had to think about where the meals were. He was a source of information to Greyhound-riding newcomers from Florida or the Carolinas, or, especially in winter, from points north.

In any decent-sized Southern city, folks didn't want you to go hungry. They might not have jobs or health clinics or mental health care or much of anything else, but they wouldn't let you go hungry.

The dining hall's tables were half filled with Grambling's homeless, along with a smattering of folks from St James. Everyone knew Malachi, and nodded or grunted a greeting. But he had something on his mind, so he took his plate of sausage and eggs and grits, and walked to the only empty table at the far side of the room. He took a seat facing the door.

This Demetrius fellow had been in town all week, and the word under the bridge was that he was a powder keg waiting to blow. Two women, including that crazy Rita sitting two tables over, claimed he'd raped them. Course they were prostitutes, so that could mean he'd refused to pay. Hard to know.

Still, something wasn't right about the guy. Sure enough, ten minutes later, Demetrius slumped through the doorway. As far as Malachi could tell, he wore the same mud-spattered work pants, T-shirt and hoodie he'd come to town in, looking the worse for a week's wear. That meant he wasn't asking for clothes, because the gospel mission, Trinity Episcopal, First Baptist, and even St James had free closets.

Demetrius walked to the cafeteria window and took his plate, eyes locked at floor level, ignoring the server's smiling attempt at conversation. He grabbed a coffee, then raised his eyes long enough to survey the room. Several tables had only two or three people, but he chose the one with just one diner. Malachi's eyes darted to Rita to see if she'd seen Demetrius. Apparently, she had. She was cringing so far down in her seat that her head had all but disappeared. Malachi could see the St James folks on either side of her exchanging baffled glances.

But he couldn't worry about Rita right now. Demetrius was headed his way.

The huge man pulled out a chair at Malachi's table, as far away as he could get. He sat without a word. He crouched over his food as if fearful Malachi might snatch it, and voraciously stuffed the scrambled eggs into his mouth.

"Mornin'," Malachi ventured.

Demetrius flicked his eyes to Malachi's face but said nothing.

"Where you from?"

"Goin' to 'Lanta," Demetrius mumbled.

"Spen' time there myself. Izzat home?"

"Goin' to 'Lanta," he repeated.

He'd been locked up awhile, Malachi would bet on it. But that wasn't the kind of thing you asked, especially not of someone like Demetrius.

"Okay, man," Malachi said, rising to get a refill of his coffee. "Good luck wit' that."

Demetrius couldn't leave for 'Lanta fast enough as far as Malachi was concerned.

CHAPTER SEVENTEEN

Early on Friday morning Branigan roused Davison – and Cleo – from a sound sleep.

She put on a pot of coffee and packed a small suitcase and Cleo's leash and dog food. Davison came out of his room with his Salvation Army clothes in the same plastic bag he'd brought them home in. For some reason, that wrinkled grocery bag brought the ache back to Branigan's chest. She grabbed a soft-sided overnight bag in a Burberry plaid from the guest room closet, and tossed it to him.

"Dad keeps swim trunks at the beach house," she told him. "And sunscreen."

He nodded. He'd been asleep when she left each morning, so she hadn't seen him like this. He seemed subdued, a little shaky. He poured himself a cup of coffee, and dumped in four teaspoons of sugar. Then he put two Pop-tarts in the toaster.

He noticed her noticing, and grimaced. "I know. Why don't I just hook up the sugar IV?" He shrugged. "It helps. A little."

"Whatever," she said. "I want one of those Pop-tarts too."

They ate silently at the kitchen island, passing sections of *The Rambler* back and forth. Fridays meant entertainment, so Gerald and Lou Ann had the *Style* front with stories on the opening of *Les Mis* at the Grambling Little Theatre and the start of a bluegrass series that brought classic bands down from the mountains of north Georgia and Tennessee.

"A bad weekend to leave town," she said.

"No such thing as a bad weekend to leave Grambling," Davison muttered.

"You really think that?"

"I know that."

107

"Why?"

"Brani G, look at me. You're the star. Everything you've touched has turned to gold. Everything I've touched has turned to crap."

She didn't respond for a moment, just looked into his tortured green eyes. "You don't think I've had disappointments? You think I really wanted to be past forty and single?"

He looked surprised. "That bothers you?"

"Sure it does. I see Liam with Liz and Charlie and Chan. I always wanted that. And it's too late."

"I figured you wanted to be single," he said slowly. "Because of your work."

She shrugged. "The work's fine. It really is. But I see Chan, and I know how much I've missed."

Davison looked stricken. "I know how much I've missed too. I'd give anything for another chance. We're quite a pair, aren't we?"

She smiled ruefully, came around the island and gave his shoulder a quick squeeze. "Yes, we are."

They placed their skimpy luggage into the trunk and invited Cleo to jump onto the sheet-shrouded back seat. As they pulled out of the driveway onto the empty country road fronting Pa and Gran's house, Davison said, "I know where we're going. But I don't know why."

"I didn't tell you about my story?"

"Nope."

"Sorry. It's the Resnick murder."

Branigan glanced over and saw the surprise on his face. "That's *your* story? I heard some street guys talking about it. Liam had a meeting and asked if anybody knew anything."

"Did you even know she'd been killed?" she asked. "You were gone then."

"Yeah, I did hear, but not 'til much later. Why are you doing an old story like that?"

She explained about the tenth anniversary of the murder and Tan's impatience with the police investigation. She told him how they'd never dismissed the possibility that the killer was a transient who had skipped town immediately afterward.

"A transient? How would you ever prove that?"

"That's just it," she admitted. "We probably can't. But we got Liam to ask among the homeless community. Ten years ago, we didn't know anything about those people. Now he does."

"I'm not sure I get it. What are you asking Liam to do?"

"To ask around among people on the street. Ask them if they heard anything at the time or since. I know it's a long shot, but it's the only thing we've got. At the time, Jody – he's our cop reporter – was convinced it was a family member. But I think the police would have found that out. And I sure don't believe the other family members would have covered it up."

Davison was silent for a moment. "That sounds pretty far-fetched. Has Liam found out anything?"

Branigan told him about Liam's call earlier in the week – that a man named Jess remembered Max Brody's statement that "this evening's drunk was courtesy of an old lady who had the good taste to get stabbed".

"And so you're going to talk to this Jess?" Davison asked.

"And I hope Max."

Davison shook his head. "Brani G, you really do have an interesting job."

"There was another man who lives at Jericho who mentioned a drunk woman talking about an old lady who got murdered. In fact, I think it's your drunk woman."

"*My* drunk woman? *What?*"

"You know, that Rita, with the shack under the bridge."

Branigan turned to find Davison staring at her, horrified. She burst into laughter.

"Believe me, Rita isn't 'my woman'." He shuddered. "I didn't touch her. I'd be afraid to. Do you know how many men she's been with?"

"Then why were you in her shack?"

"It had two beds – if you could call them that – and I slept in one. It's not even Rita's place. It was built by someone who's in jail now. I went up there and fell asleep and she didn't even come in 'til the middle of the night. And believe me, she doesn't give sex for free. I was safe."

"I have to say, I'm happy to hear that. I was worried about your... um... health."

Davison shook his head again. "Sheesh. Please don't share your overactive imagination with Mom."

Branigan took the back roads to gargantuan Lake Hartwell, the reservoir playground shared by Georgia and South Carolina. It was only a forty-minute ride from Grambling to the cove where Amanda Resnick Brissey had a second home.

Of the Resnick family, she knew Amanda least. Amanda had been in college by the time Branigan entered kindergarten. She married right out of school – a private one, according to Jody's notes – and then moved with her husband to Atlanta. Branigan knew from her parents that the couple traveled a great deal, had two children quickly, and Amanda, at least, spent half her time at their Lake Hartwell home. According to Branigan's mom, Mrs Resnick and Amanda had a tense relationship. After her father's death, Amanda came home only once a year – for the Fourth of July party. Branigan wouldn't know her if she passed her on the street.

A couple of minutes outside Grambling, the two were in the countryside. Zoning was unheard of outside the city limits, so they passed lovely farms with decrepit trailers next door. They passed peach orchards and wildflower fields and shacks with high-flying Rebel flags. News of the Confederacy's demise hadn't reached every household in Georgia.

They crossed expanses of the sprawling lake twice. Davison and Branigan – and just about everyone who grew up in Grambling – were raised with boats and water skis, so the terrain was familiar.

Following the directions Amanda Brissey had emailed, Branigan pulled onto a bumpy road lined with pine trees, cedars and underbrush on one side and wooded lake lots on the other. Grand houses of stone and stucco sat beside fishing shacks with lavish sundecks. But there was no mistaking the only house on the cove owned by a Grambling heiress.

The Brissey house was three stories, with a circular driveway and fountain. Brick steps, twenty feet wide at the bottom, swept up to a second-floor entrance, where double oak doors were framed by windows of leaded glass. Whereas even the rich neighbors had used stone and stucco and vinyl siding, the Brisseys had chosen a reddish-purple brick. If this is what faced the humdrum road, Branigan couldn't wait to see the house's lake-facing side.

Davison agreed to walk Cleo while Branigan interviewed Amanda. The two of them started out on the rural road the way they had come, while she vigorously shook Cleo's hair off her navy summer blazer. She pulled it over her cream-colored slacks and red-and-white-striped top. She had driven barefoot, so she stepped into her off-white mules. Straightened and ready, she slung a slouchy red purse over her shoulder and climbed the steps feeling like a character in a movie.

According to her *Rambler* buddy Jody, this was the daughter who had killed Mrs Resnick.

Amanda Brissey had to be fifty-five, but looked fifteen years younger. She answered the door in jeans that had a slight rip in one knee, a white tunic and black flip-flops. Her hair was a tousled auburn, cropped short: there wasn't a trace of gray. She greeted Branigan warmly, handing over a mug of coffee without asking.

"So you're the Powerses' daughter," she said. "Where did you get those stunning eyes? I don't think I've ever seen that shade of green."

Branigan heard such comments frequently, and never knew how to answer. "Thank you," she said weakly.

Amanda stepped aside to let Branigan enter. "I can't believe we've never met."

"From what Mom told me, you've been traveling a lot."

"Yes, and now I'm ready to sit tight for awhile," she said with an airy wave to indicate her choice for sitting tight. She led Branigan into a lakeside sunroom that ran the width of the house. The sofas, chairs and valences sported vibrant fabrics in blue, white and yellow, but it was the view that caught Branigan's breath. An impressive lawn sloped to the water's edge. A double-armed dock stretched far into the water, with a pontoon boat moored in the middle, and a speedboat tied to one side. The lake was peaceful and smooth this time of the morning, with none of the weekend boat traffic that would churn it up tomorrow.

"The boys are grown," she continued, "and Bennett can get up here only on weekends." She reached for an ornately framed photo on a side table. Bennett Brissey was older than Amanda, Branigan could see at once. Or at least his silver hair made him look it. He had one arm around her. The couple were flanked by two handsome sons in their early thirties.

"That's Bennett Jr," she said, pointing to one. "He practices in New York. And that's Drew. He works with Bennett Sr's firm in Atlanta. All attorneys, all the time."

She drew in a breath, as if bracing herself. "So. Mother?"

Branigan gave her practiced speech, never sure if family members would welcome this story or find it an intrusive reminder of a horrible time.

"As you may know," she began, "this is the only unsolved murder in the city of Grambling – if you don't count the recent hit-and-run of a homeless man. The newspaper wants to explore how it could have gone unsolved this long."

Amanda looked skeptical, so Branigan dialed the rhetoric down a notch. "There's a lot of interest in this," she said more frankly. "I grew up two blocks away. My brother Davison and I really liked your mother."

Amanda Brissey nodded. "How can I help you?"

"Let's go over that July 4. Tell me about the entire day, and I'll interrupt if I don't understand something."

"Father and Mother always had a Fourth of July party – since before I was born. When Father died – that was eight years before Mother – we children persuaded her to carry it on." She looked thoughtful for a moment. "I don't know how much you know about my mother's later years, Branigan. But she had… problems."

Branigan kept quiet, but looked up attentively.

"She was depressed about my father's death. Nothing odd about that. But then she developed symptoms of paranoia. We couldn't tell if it was due to the anti-depressants she was taking or if it was something else. Did you know she wouldn't let Ramsey and Heath do any pruning or cutting back in her yard?"

Branigan nodded. "I did know that."

"She said the landscapers were in cahoots with a realtor who wanted to get her house. They wanted to butcher the landscaping so she'd be forced to sell."

"That doesn't make sense."

"Tell me about it. It was that kind of stuff all the time. People were listening to her phone conversations. People were walking through her property at all hours. People were sneaking into her house and garage while she was at church." Amanda raised her shoulders in an exaggerated shrug.

"I had no idea," Branigan said. "Poor Mrs Resnick."

"Poor Mrs Resnick nothing," Amanda said vehemently. "Poor Ramsey. He was the one who had to listen to that. And Heath, to some extent." She laughed suddenly. "But I have to admit – we were wrong about the guy in the pool house. At first, we assumed it was more of Mother's imaginings. When Ramsey found that man actually living in her pool house, you could've knocked me over."

"Did you ever see him?"

Branigan pulled the photo of Billy from her purse. Amanda studied it closely.

"No," she said, handing it back. "The police showed me a picture too, but I'd never seen him. I came to Grambling only once a year after Father died. I'm not proud of that. But I… I… my mother and I weren't close. She was…." She closed her eyes, searching for a word. "Imperial," she said finally. "Do you know what I mean?"

Branigan had a sudden memory of a sultry summer day when she and Davison were nine. They were riding bikes in front of Mrs Resnick's house, and Branigan hit a piece of raised sidewalk where an ancient oak had buckled it. She pitched over her handlebars, dragging her right arm across the sidewalk, ripping skin, before landing in Mrs Resnick's hostas. A wail rose to her throat.

Mrs Resnick was getting into her car, dressed in a yellow summer suit, white gloves, and straw hat.

"My lands, child!" she said. Branigan waited for her to bend down and comfort her, as her mom or gran would have done. Instead, she turned on her heel and called, "Tabitha!"

Tabitha came running, and she and Davison helped carry Branigan, still bawling, to the front porch. There Tabitha bathed her arm in warm soapy water, then applied antiseptic and a large gauze bandage, murmuring gently the whole time. Mrs Resnick got into her car and drove away. Branigan could imagine her lunch companions tsk-tsking about the inconsiderate child who had almost made her late.

She smiled now at Amanda. "Yes, I do know what you mean."

Branigan prompted Amanda to continue with details from July 4.

She ticked off the family members who had come for the party – Ramsey, his wife Dale, his grown son Armand, and teenage daughters Carlisle and Ashley; Heath, his wife Serena, and their thirteen-year-old daughter Caroline; herself, Bennett, Bennett Jr and Drew. "Twelve of us, plus Mother."

"And the guests?"

"Oh, my Lord! Who knows? I'm sure the police had a guest list. There were probably fifty or sixty people – neighbors, Father's old business partners, other mill owners, Mother's bridge ladies. In the old days, we had pool parties, but the pool area wasn't nice enough for that any more – even without Billy," she added with a laugh.

"How late did the party go on?"

"Not terribly late. So many of the guests were older. We all went outside to watch fireworks around 9:30. A lot of people left after that. Some of the grandkids' friends stayed late and braved the pool. I remember Drew telling me later that they found a snake in it."

"Yikes. But the whole family didn't stay overnight?"

"Oh, no. Bennett would never stay there. We had two hotel rooms, one for us and one for the boys. But I did end up spending the night at Mother's. She asked me to."

"May I ask why?" Branigan knew this was the point that had stuck in Jody's mind.

Amanda didn't hesitate. "She wanted to talk about her will."

"What about it?"

"Well, she had been going on about making a new will. She first told me on the afternoon of July 4. I guess I didn't respond quickly enough because she asked me to stay overnight and had another run at me the next morning. She said she was eighty, her heart was weakened, and she knew she didn't have much time left. And she wanted to cut Heath out."

Jody had told Branigan this much, though the information didn't make the stories that *The Rambler* printed. "Did she say why?"

"She did, but I thought it was more of her paranoia. She said Heath was trying to get her to sell the house and move her into a nursing home. She accused him of everything from trying to ruin her landscaping to wanting to develop her two acres as an apartment complex – as if the city would allow that."

"What did you say?"

"I told her I didn't think she should do it. And if she did, she didn't need me. Her lawyer was right there in Grambling. To be honest with you, I thought I was seeing signs of dementia."

To be honest with you. The words of Branigan's first editor came back to her. They'd been sitting over beers on a long-ago election night. Someone had already uttered the well worn, "How can you tell when a politician is lying? [Pause.] His lips are moving."

Over the laughter and groans that followed, her editor leaned in. "Seriously," he said, "watch it when someone looks you in the eye and says, 'To be honest with you. To be honest with you, Branigan, I did not sleep with that woman.'"

She paused now, thinking maybe Jody was on to something. This was the first statement that didn't ring true. She couldn't picture Amanda Brissey brutally stabbing her mother to death. But why would she lie about a suspicion of dementia? That was innocent enough. Wasn't it?

"So what happened next?"

"Nothing, really. Ramsey took her to the doctor. I ran by that store on South Main that sells crafts made by women in Third World countries. Mother asked me to pick out earrings for Caroline and Ashley. I did and left them there to be wrapped and held for pick-up."

Branigan had read in the files that police had indeed found the gifts at the store, purchased by Amanda at 2:10 p.m. on July 5. Officers had followed her timeline carefully.

"Was it the girls' birthdays?"

"No, they had spent the night, and Mother liked to give them little treats. To be honest with you, they were her favorites. It was fine. The other grandchildren were old enough not to mind."

There it was again. *To be honest with you.*

Amanda continued. "Then I got the boys from the hotel and we drove home to Atlanta. Bennett Sr stayed to play golf with some clients. He had barely left Grambling when I reached him on his cell to tell him to turn around and meet me at Mother's. We'd gotten word of her... death."

"When did you tell Heath about your mother's plan to cut him out of her will?"

"Late, late, late on the night of the murder. I tried to reach him right after I talked to the police. I wanted to tell him myself before they questioned him. But they whisked him away. In retrospect, I'm sure it was on purpose. They wanted to see his reaction."

They talked for another thirty minutes. As Branigan suspected, she wasn't getting new information so much as a feel for the players before writing her story. Amanda had "reluctantly", according to one detective, shared her mother's comments about Heath, which made the younger brother a prime suspect for a few days. Officers had investigated the finances of all three Resnick children. Alone among them, Heath's fortunes had been up and down. Being cut from his mother's will would have been a blow. But Heath swore he had no idea his mother intended to disinherit him, and Ramsey and Amanda backed him up.

Branigan was no detective, but it was hard for her to picture Jody's scenario. He contended that the police had only Amanda's word that Mrs Resnick intended to cut Heath from her will. What if Mrs Resnick really confided that she was cutting Amanda out of the will? That left Amanda – not to mention Bennett, Bennett Jr or Drew – in town to stab Mrs Resnick before she had the chance to do so.

Branigan knew that Jody had floated his theory to the police, who had looked into the Brissey family finances. But Bennett Brissey, an Atlanta attorney, wasn't having money troubles. The family seemed quite comfortable even without inheriting the Resnick fortune.

Of course, she thought, you can't measure greed. How much is enough? That varies from person to person. Heaven knows she'd heard Liam preach that message often enough. Bennett Jr and Drew had been in college, headed to law school, a decade earlier. Their grandmother's early death meant graduating debt-free and living a non-student-like lifestyle. And from everything she'd heard, Ben Jr was quite the party guy.

She took one more look at the photo of Amanda's handsome family, and repacked her purse. As Amanda showed her out, she asked her parting question. "Anything else that I forgot to ask?"

"I was surprised," Amanda said promptly, "that police suspected the family. You know that from books and movies, but it honestly shocked me that anyone could think that."

"Who do you think killed your mother?"

"Some kind of hobo," she answered. "It had to be."

Davison was leaning against the car as Cleo nosed around the Brisseys' front yard.

"How'd it go?" he asked. "Catch your murderer?"

"I'd be very surprised," Branigan said, kicking off her heels and removing her jacket for the ride to the beach. "But something's up with her."

CHAPTER EIGHTEEN

M alachi gazed at the painting he had tugged from the trash pile underneath the bridge. There were a few coffee grounds on it, but they wiped off easily.

He had liked Vesuvius, and he liked this painting – oil on a piece of thin plywood. He propped it against the fabric wall of his tent. Its colors were muted, realistic. The brooding landscape showed a pond at night, the moon lighting its surface to a creamy yellow, encircling trees in shades of darkest green and brown and black.

Malachi knew V had a gift for painting, despite his mental disabilities. Heck, maybe because of his mental disabilities. Maybe part of his brain was on fire because of something missing in another part.

Malachi had first seen this particular piece in the dining hall of Jericho Road. He saw it again during a Sunday morning service, when Pastor Liam leaned it on an easel beside the pulpit. He was always doing that: calling out the artists and having them stand and accept applause.

He'd even gotten him, Malachi, to lead the responsive reading once. Malachi surprised the pastor with his easy mastery of the words, he could tell. Pastor Liam clapped him on the shoulder as he left, and mouthed, "Well done." Malachi knew what he was up to, but it made him feel good just the same.

What puzzled him was the journey this painting had taken from Jericho Road to the trash pile beneath the bridge. It didn't make sense. Pastor Liam worked hard to publicize the artwork of the homeless, whether they were shelter residents or not. Malachi attended every art show held at Jericho Road – not to buy art, of course, but for the food and hot coffee. Once he stood behind the table where volunteers were taking money, and he saw what the paintings went for: $30 to $50 mostly, but some as high as $400. Two of V's eerie nightscapes topped $200.

So what was this one doing at the bottom of a trash heap?

He thought back to the conversation with V, the one he'd tried to tell that Branigan woman about at breakfast. He could tell she had no idea what he was talking about. But she wanted information about V's life and death, and this particular piece didn't fit.

It was early last week, and Malachi had been sitting hunched on a bench at the courthouse, after dark. V rode past on his bicycle, coming from the direction of Jericho Road, where he stayed. "Why you not at Jericho?" Malachi called out.

V stopped and came closer. "I missed lock-up," he said. "You know that's one rule Pastuh Liam don't be messin' with. Nobody get in past 9 o'clock."

"Where you gonna stay?"

V shrugged. "Don' know. I got me some money. Thinkin' about a mo-tel."

"Good for you."

"Malachi? Would you look at my money and see if I gots enough for a bottle and a mo-tel?"

"Sure," Malachi said. V handed him a wad of cash. Malachi walked over to a streetlight and counted out $130. "Whoo-eee! Where'd you get all this money? You got enough for a mo-tel room and the fines' bottle they make."

"Then I might have some to share." V grinned, his remaining teeth flashing under the streetlight. "Come wit' me."

"Okay," said Malachi. "I be glad to share yo' bottle. But don' waste yo' money on no mo-tel. You be back in Jericho tomorrow. You can stay in my cat hole tonigh'."

V pushed his bike as the two walked to a bootlegger's house in Randall Mill. They asked the man who answered the door for a bottle of his "finest likker" and paid $45 for a $25 bottle of bourbon. Then they made their way to Malachi's two-man tent under the Garner Bridge.

"Where'd you get you a tent?" V asked.

"Mexican had it, and got put in jail. Shame to let it go to waste."

Malachi produced Styrofoam coffee cups borrowed from Jericho Road and poured each of them a hefty splash of bourbon. "V, you need to be careful with that money," he said. "Don't be flashin' it 'round. Where'd you get it, anyway?"

V gave him a sly smile. "Sold a paintin' I done. Sold it to a dude who saw it at Jericho. I asked Pastuh Liam and he took it right off the wall."

"What kinda dude be having $130 for a pitcher?"

"Can' tell. I promised I wouldn' tell."

Malachi didn't pry. But two nights later his friend had been killed crossing Oakley Street. And now the painting he'd sold had turned up in the trash pile under the Garner Bridge.

Malachi wished he had pried.

CHAPTER NINETEEN

The new guy didn't know her. That much was obvious.

Actually, no one in this town did. Even the ones she'd known in her other life; even the ones who knew her parents. Sometimes that bothered Rita, how far she'd fallen. Most times, it suited her fine. Kept down the questions: *Oh, how could you let this happen? Do your parents know where you are? Blah, blah, blah.* She didn't need to hear it.

Some days she could hardly believe she'd ever had a comfortable bed behind a locked door, taking for granted that no one was going to assault her body, steal her booze, leave her with diseases. Could hardly believe she'd ever woken to an alarm clock, climbed into a car, gone to work.

That was the thing about being homeless. *We know how other people live because we've lived it. But they haven't lived like us.*

So really, when you thought about it, the homeless had a much wider world view. They knew more. They'd seen more. So where did the others get off being so disrespectful? Being so dismissive? Being so downright superior?

Yeah, I know big words, she felt like saying to those social workers who spoke to her as if she was eight years old. *I graduated high school.*

Even the folks at St James and Jericho Road who fed you – those meals didn't come without strings. They all talked about helping the homeless; Lord, did they talk. But what they meant was they wanted to help you not be homeless. They came right out and said it. No one wanted to help you get what you really needed. Which was basically oblivion.

The only people who understood were other people who needed oblivion. It looked like the new guy needed it.

He knew his way around a homeless encampment, the way he'd invited himself into her shack. She'd been nervous at first that he'd recognize her from the mall. But if there was anyone as invisible as a homeless person, it was a retail clerk. She didn't want to think what a decade of crack and meth had done to her appearance, how it might have made her unrecognizable even to her parents.

No, that didn't merit thinking about. That was the kind of thinking that brought on the need for the curtain, the need for oblivion.

That was why she'd let the new guy stay. He'd had a little money, enough to buy some oblivion.

Too bad his uppity sister had swooped in and taken him away.

CHAPTER TWENTY

From the Brisseys' cove on Lake Hartwell, Branigan had to drive only six miles of winding country road until hitting I-85 North toward the South Carolina line. About the time she crossed over, making her third pass over the lake, she received a call on her cell phone. She fumbled in her purse to catch it before it went to voice mail. It was the public information officer at the South Carolina Department of Corrections: Billy Shepherd had been released on May 10.

She did a quick calculation – not quite four weeks ago. She wondered if he was making his way home to Grambling.

Davison and Branigan stopped for lunch at a fast-food café overlooking the final finger of Lake Hartwell. They ate at an outdoor picnic table so Cleo could have the run of the place. Branigan wanted her to get plenty of exercise so she'd sleep on the long ride to the coast. Davison ate ravenously, downing a hamburger, cheeseburger, French fries and ice cream in the time it took his sister to eat a grilled chicken sandwich.

He looked sheepish. "There's not a single minute I don't want a drink," he confessed. "I guess putting anything in my mouth is better than nothing."

Branigan was glad he had never taken up cigarette smoking. From what Liam said, nicotine withdrawal was the hardest of all of the addictions to overcome. She didn't mention it, because she didn't want to give Davison ideas.

She tried to think of things to talk about that dodged the mines. But she didn't know what the mines were. So she was relieved when after lunch Davison slept – slept through the back roads to bypass Greenville, slept through the merging with I-385 north of Clinton, slept through most of I-26 that linked upstate South Carolina to Charleston and the Isle of Palms.

As she drove, she thought of the abuse Davison had visited upon his body in the past twenty-five years. He'd been doing drugs and alcohol longer than he hadn't. It was a wonder he was still alive.

She looked over at the passenger seat, where he lay, face slack against a pillow he had brought from the house. In sleep, his face looked no older than his forty-one years, and Branigan allowed herself to wonder what his life might have been like. Law school after college. Practicing, maybe in Atlanta or some other big city, but like her, ultimately returning to Grambling. Marrying. Raising Chan. Being a family of four-plus with Mom and Dad, rather than the sad threesome they had become.

When he woke sixty miles outside the Isle of Palms, she couldn't wait any longer.

"I've been trying not to ask too many questions," she said with a sideways glance as he stretched and yawned. "But I really want to know how you've been living."

"Okay. What do you wanna know?"

"Have you been living on the streets?"

"Sometimes."

"When and where?"

"That's hard to answer. Sometimes I'd have a job for a year or more and get an apartment. Sometimes I'd stay with friends. Sometimes I'd work day labor and pay upfront for a motel room for a week or more. But the money always ran out, and I'd end up on the street."

"Literally?"

"Well, yeah. In Columbia once, I had a nice tent in the woods for nearly a year. In Atlanta, I stayed in a shelter. One winter in Myrtle Beach, I slept in a campground bathhouse. In Asheville, a boarding house that charged $40 a week. I was pretty flush then. Oh, and once I joined a carnival that looped from Florida to Texas. They put us up in travel trailers."

"You're kidding. What do you know about carnivals?"

"You don't have to know anything to put up tents and pull 'em down. And I actually ran a game booth one season."

"What game?"

"The one where you throw plastic rings over big soda bottles. On one swing into Texas, we crossed over the border into Mexico. That's where I really saw poverty. We don't have it too bad up here."

Branigan turned to look at him for so long that he motioned for her to return her eyes to the road.

"That's hard to picture," she said.

"You get used to it." He yawned again.

"But why would you want to?"

"It's not a question of *wanting* to. I went to rehab twice that Mom and Dad don't know about – a Salvation Army in Texas, and a gospel mission in St Louis. Then I'd get out, have all this time on my hands, meet some guys, and the next thing I knew someone was offering me a free smoke. That's no excuse, I know. But that's what happened."

That made four times he'd tried rehab. Branigan's chest pinched as she realized how hard he'd tried.

"I don't quite know how to ask this…"

"Go ahead," he prompted. "You're on a roll."

"Well, you seem to be doing well this week. You've had – what? – four days clean now?"

"Branigan, I've had nine months clean before. But sooner or later, I go back. I always go back."

"One last question and I'll stop. For now. Have you ever been homeless in Grambling before this week?"

She held her breath. The thought of Davison living in woods or under bridges or in abandoned houses in Grambling was somehow more horrifying than knowing he was homeless in another city. He was silent for so long she didn't think he was going to answer.

"No," he finally said. "I was afraid of running into people I knew. Embarrassing you and Mom and Dad and the rest of the family."

She nodded past the lump in her throat. They continued in silence for the next fifteen miles.

Then he spoke softly. "Brani G, you don't have to feel bad. There's nothing you could've done. Nothing anybody could've done. It's me. It's my problem, my sin, my weakness, whatever you want to call it. But it's all mine."

"I know," she said. "I guess I just wish you cared about yourself as much as we care about you."

He didn't say anything.

She tried again. "When you're part of a family, your choices affect everyone – not just you. I wish you cared enough about us – about Chan and Mom and Dad and me – to get sober."

He said something she didn't catch. "What?" she asked.

He sighed. "It's not about choice."

As soon as they crossed over Highway 17 onto the Isle of Palms, they stopped at a grocery store. Branigan bought grapes, strawberries, blueberries, cheese, crackers, soft drinks and paper towels. Davison added Oreos and a half gallon of chocolate chip ice cream.

"We're only going to be here two days," she protested.

"It'll be gone."

She rolled her eyes.

"Not going to make daiquiris?" he teased, reading her mind.

"Not this trip."

He didn't argue. As they rolled over the bridge spanning the inland waterway, they hit their window buttons at the same instant. Branigan threw back her head and laughed as the brackish wind poured in. The wind whipped her hair into her eyes. This moment was one of the best of any beach trip.

"Oh, man!" Davison shouted. "It's been a long time since I smelled that."

The bridge to the Isle of Palms dumped them abruptly at the town's main intersection. To the left, the road passed between two nicely landscaped shopping strips, then curved in front of a white clapboard Methodist church before becoming the beachfront drive. It passed a mile or more of private homes before veering into Wild Dunes, a private golf enclave.

Branigan turned right instead, zig-zagging to the block-long downtown with its condos, beachfront bars, and stores featuring ice cream and beachwear. She drove slowly on the street that was divided by a palm-lined median. They quickly passed through the downtown and entered the two-lane oceanfront boulevard. Beach houses on stilts lined both sides of the road.

The Isle of Palms didn't look like other South Carolina beaches, which were a mix of 1950s shabby and post-2000 *nouveau riche*. The Isle of Palms looked newer, sleeker, more consistently wealthy. That was because it had been hit a direct blow by Hurricane Hugo in 1989. The Category 4 storm had uprooted the namesake palms and destroyed many of the houses – spinning some into the middle of the street they were now traveling. A few underwent renovation, but many homeowners couldn't afford to rebuild. Prices skyrocketed. New buyers came in, razed the debris and built seafront mansions.

One of the few exceptions was the Powers house. Somehow their modest beachfront cottage, snuggled into a tangle of vegetation, had survived. Located halfway between the tiny downtown and the inlet that separates Isle of Palms and Sullivan's Island, the sturdy house on stilts was all but hidden by wind-bent scrubby post oaks, palmettos and palms. Branigan suspected the neighbors had added more trees to screen the house from their view.

She pulled into the unpaved driveway. Crushed oyster shells crunched beneath the Civic's tires. Cleo began to bark excitedly as Branigan maneuvered under the trees that grew right up against the house.

She and Davison saw the weathered sign at the same time, and laughed. Their dad had replanted the trees uprooted by Hugo, and now a twenty-five-year-old pair of palms flanked the roadside porch, straight and tall.

The name with its silly double meaning endured: *Twin Palms*.

CHAPTER TWENTY-ONE

F riday night was pizza night at Jericho Road. St Mary's Catholic
Church brought it in, and the church's youth group served soft
drinks and sweet tea. Pizza was popular, and the dinner crowd swelled
far past the shelter's eighteen residents to seventy-five homeless and
community residents. Because Liam was adamant about making
Jericho Road mealtimes a fellowship of the entire community, the
Catholic youths also sat self-consciously to eat. Charlie and Chan,
far more accustomed to dining at the shelter, joined Dontegan and
Liam and Liz before heading out to a pool party.

"Don-T!" Chan greeted Dontegan with a fist bump. Dontegan
grinned a response. As his wife and children talked soccer with
Dontegan, Liam quietly slid his plate next to Rita, seated on the
other side of the round table. Chairs on either side of her remained
empty, due to Rita's sharp tongue and sharper smell. Liam gave up
momentarily on his pepperoni pizza and took a gulp of tea.

"Rita? I'd like to ask you something."

Rita grunted. Liam took it for assent.

"Ten years ago, a woman was murdered in her home downtown.
Stabbed to death in her kitchen. Mrs Alberta Grambling Resnick.
Were you living here then?"

Liam thought he saw a cunning gleam enter Rita's watery eyes.
"Yeah."

"Did you hear anything about it back then?"

"What if I did?"

"Well, the newspaper is working on a tenth anniversary story
because it's still unsolved. My friend Branigan is talking to people
who might know something. People the police wouldn't think knew
anything."

Rita wiped her mouth with a grimy sleeve. The powerful smell of urine washed over Liam, turning his stomach. He breathed through his mouth and tried not to flinch.

Malachi came up quietly on the other side of Rita, sat down and began eating with gusto.

Rita bent over her pizza, and for a moment Liam feared she was going to pass out in her plate. Then she spoke so quietly Liam had to lean in. "Don't know nothin' 'bout no ol' lady gettin' stabbed."

Liam persisted. "But I heard you had been talking about a lady who was murdered downtown."

"Who said that?"

Liam didn't want to get Dontegan into trouble with Rita. "I can't remember."

"Well, maybe the ol' lady asked for it. Maybe she all stuck up and wouldn' share the wealth." She cackled.

Liam sighed. "That's no reason for murder, Rita, and you know it."

Rita stood abruptly. "If a person can't eat in peace, ain't no use stayin'," she said, leaving her plate and cup on the table. She lurched away. "Damn nosybody do-gooders."

Liam's eyes followed her departure, watched her stiffen as a newcomer entered. She put her head down and scuttled toward the side door. Liam stood to greet the newcomer, who was heavily built, wearing mud-streaked work pants and a dirty T-shirt. Liam offered his hand.

"Welcome to Jericho Road. I'm Liam. Can I get you some pizza?"

"Yeah," the stranger muttered.

"Are you new in town?" Liam asked, as he signaled the St Mary's teens for a plate and drink. Something about the man was familiar, but he muttered only another "yeah". Liam indicated a vacant spot at his table, asking, "What's your name, friend?"

The stranger ignored the invitation, walking instead to an empty table. "'Metrius," he said over his shoulder, then hunched over his pizza, clearly wanting to be left alone.

Liam met his son's eyes across the table and gave a shrug.

"Did you make Rita mad?" Chan asked.

"I guess I did."

"It don't take much," Malachi said. "She take offense quite easily."

Liam laughed. Malachi cracked him up, the way he mixed formal English with street slang. He liked Malachi, had repeatedly offered him a room at Jericho Road. But apparently the long-time homeless man had no use for sleeping inside.

"Your daddy didn't do nothin' to that woman," Malachi told Chan. "Somethin' bad got a-hold of her. Ain't nothin' Pastor Liam done."

Chan frowned, took a bite of his pizza.

Malachi turned to Liam. "She ain't telling the truth either. I heard her say the same thing you was asking her 'bout. V and I were under the bridge last winter. She came in our tent, drunk and babblin' 'bout she might get rich if she told what she knew 'bout some ol' lady gettin' stabbed. Said the rich-ass family would pay to keep it quiet. Then she passed out, so V and I didn't pay no mind."

"Did she mean the Resnick family?" Liam asked. "Is that who would pay to keep it quiet?"

"Don't know. She just called 'em rich."

Liam stood, and whispered to Liz that he had to make a quick phone call from his office. He wanted to tell Branigan what he'd heard before his friend walked into any more of the Resnicks' homes.

CHAPTER TWENTY-TWO

Cleo bounded out of the car. Branigan knew she'd stay on the property, so she didn't bother with the leash. She carried an overnight bag in one hand, a bag of groceries in the other and climbed the steps to the small front porch. Her parents didn't want to waste money on this side of the house. It was the beach side that had the expansive, multilevel decking.

Her mom rented the house out occasionally during the winter, so it no longer had that closed-up, musty smell it'd had during their childhood. Her mother had been down herself a few weeks earlier, so everything was clean.

She and Davison stepped into the kitchen, and put the groceries on the new granite-topped island, added during a 2010 upgrade. "Wow!" he said. "Nice."

The house's pine-paneled living room – the decorating choice of every beach house built in the 1950s and 60s – remained. Branigan knew their mother had considered painting it, but sentimentality got the better of her. Except for its modern kitchen and ever-expanding decks, the look of the house had changed little since the family bought it.

Two bedrooms and a bathroom opened off each side of the main room. Branigan went directly to her old room, still sporting its coral paint. Davison looked lost, so she prompted him. "Want your room? Or Mom and Dad's king bed?"

He swallowed and crossed the main room, taking neither. He threw his Burberry bag into the guest room, streetside and pine paneled. "This one will do," he said.

Normally at this point, Branigan would have located the blender and mixed up an icy pina colada to carry onto the beach. Instead, she popped open a Diet Pepsi and offered him one. "Want to take a walk?"

"Sure."

They called Cleo and set off down the weathered gray walkway, through a gazebo, then onto the beach, hours past high tide and luxuriously wide.

"Boy, does this bring back memories," Davison said.

"Tell me."

"Well, let's see. Pa, who never walked on the beach in less than long pants, socks and shoes."

She laughed.

"Aunt Isabel and her brownies," he continued. "Uncle Rock fishing until dark and making us eat what he caught. The time we brought Liam and Alissa, and stayed at Coconut Joe's past curfew. Not to mention getting in there with fake IDs to begin with. Watching Mom and Dad dance at that beach bar I can never remember the name of."

"You do have a memory." She bumped his shoulder, and he put an arm around her.

"And," he said, "I remember you meeting some Marine on leave when you were seventeen. Mom had a fit."

She laughed again. "Uh-huh, I remember him *well*."

He squeezed her shoulder. "Thanks for bringing me back."

"My pleasure."

Branigan's cell phone buzzed and she stopped walking to take the call. It was Liam.

"I'm glad I caught you," he said. "I heard something at supper I wanted to warn you about."

"I'm listening."

"It's Rita again. At dinner just now, she wouldn't tell me anything. But Malachi Martin, one of our guys…"

"Yeah, I know Malachi," she interrupted.

"Well, I wrote down what he said so I could remember it for you. He said he and Vesuvius were in his tent under the bridge last winter. Rita came in drunk, talking about how she might get rich if she told what she knew about some old lady getting stabbed. She said the rich-ass family would pay to keep it quiet. But then Malachi said she passed out, and he and Vesuvius didn't think any more about it."

"If she knew someone rich did it, that doesn't fit our theory," Branigan said. "How would Rita know something like that?"

"I have no idea. I just wanted to warn you, as you're going into Resnick territory."

"Yeah, they certainly fit the rich part, don't they?"

"And Branigan? One more thing. Do you remember that Billy fellow who was living in Mrs Resnick's pool house?"

"Of course."

"I think he came to Jericho Road tonight."

"What?!"

"I could be wrong. He said his name was Demetrius. I saw Billy just once when the police were interviewing him. But I think it's the same guy."

"Billy Shepherd was released from prison four weeks ago," she said.

"He wasn't talkative," Liam added. "He had that missing-a-beat rhythm people get when their meds aren't quite right. From the look of him, he's on the street."

"Try to find out where he's staying, and I'll talk to him next week."

"Will do. Meantime, you be careful. Like our voodoo friends said, you may be poking someone who thought he was safe."

She clicked off. Davison was watching her.

"Did you hear that?" she asked.

"Enough. Brani, I didn't realize this story was dangerous. I'm going to these interviews with you."

"You can't do that. I'd feel like I was bringing a babysitter."

"Well, that's exactly what you'll be doing. You are *not* going into these people's houses alone. That's all there is to it."

She looked at him quizzically. "The girls I'm interviewing were thirteen when their grandmother was killed. I seriously doubt it was them."

"Still. Look, I know I haven't been much of a brother, but I'm here now, and you are not going to see these people alone."

She shrugged. "Whatever."

The next morning Branigan got up quietly, showered and dressed in her favorite taupe fitted slacks and a sleeveless teal blouse. She had intended to leave before Davison woke, but she emerged from her bedroom to find him sitting at the island, drinking coffee.

"I was afraid to drink it on the deck," he said, holding up his mug. "Afraid you'd sneak past me."

"All right. All right. Let me have some fruit and we'll go."

She washed some blueberries and grapes, and cut up strawberries, placing them in a bowl the color of orange sherbet. She poured coffee into a tall mug sporting a cartoon skyline of Grambling.

She took her breakfast to the covered deck. The ocean was striped in blues, greens and grays, calm with mini-waves breaking far down the beach. Low tide. A perfect beach day. She was sorry she had real-life interviews on a murder instead of a paperback mystery and a comfortable beach chair. She promised herself she would get back here as soon as she had wrapped up this story.

They left Cleo in the house and drove the short distance to the home of Caroline Resnick Mason, the only child of Heath and Serena Resnick. Caroline, Branigan had discovered, had married during her senior year at the University of South Carolina. Her husband was somewhat older – *but not old enough to have bought this house,* she thought as they pulled in. It was across Palm Boulevard from the beach, a peach-colored mansion that rose four stories with an infinity pool on the second. If twenty-somethings were living here, it must be family money.

"Now do you see why I came?" Davison's voice brought her out of her momentary envy.

"What?"

He nodded at the black Range Rover parked in front, Georgia license plates clearly visible.

"Uh-oh," she said. "I wonder if Mama Bear Serena is visiting."

But it wasn't Serena who loomed over Caroline's shoulder when she answered the door. It was her father, Heath.

Caroline wore a sundress of lavender and navy plaid, with matching flat sandals of lavender. Her auburn hair hung thick and shiny over her shoulders.

She greeted Branigan politely. "Miss Powers? I'm sure you know my father, Heath Resnick. He wanted to sit in."

"Of course," she said. "I wasn't expecting you, Mr Resnick."

"I know," Heath said heartily. "But I had some business on the coast and decided to drop by and see if you or Caroline needed any help." He looked at Davison and held out his hand. "And this is?"

"My brother Davison."

A wary look came over Heath's face. "Of course. Davison. It's been a long time since I've seen you, son."

Davison reached back into his teens and called up the manners their dad had instilled. He shook Heath's hand firmly. "It's good to see you, sir."

Caroline ushered them into a large, rather formal living room, with a wool rug and upholstered furniture and plantation shutters, topped by upholstered valences. It wasn't Branigan's idea of a beach house. *But this isn't a beach house,* she reminded herself. *It's her full-time residence.*

A coffee tray held three delicate cups, a silver urn, creamer and sugar bowl. Caroline poured the three cups and handed them around, not taking one herself. Davison's presence had muddled her careful staging.

"So?" Caroline asked. "You said on the phone you're doing a story on Grandmother's murder? Do you really think you can solve it after all this time?"

"I don't know about solving it," Branigan admitted. "It's more looking at how it could have gone *unsolved* for ten years. But sometimes when you shake things, people remember something they hadn't before. Or alliances have shifted. The police say there is no such thing as an unsolvable case. There is always someone who knows something. Always." She looked squarely at Heath Resnick, whose tanned face remained composed.

"Okay, then," Caroline said. "Ask whatever you need to."

Branigan heard once more about Tabitha's blueberry pancakes with faces. She heard about Aunt Amanda dropping Caroline and cousin Ashley at the country club pool.

"Can you tell me anything about your Aunt Amanda's demeanor that morning? Did she and your grandmother talk at breakfast?"

Heath leaned forward, and Davison tensed in response to his interest.

Caroline didn't seem to notice. "Yes, but they weren't saying much. You know that feeling you get when adults aren't saying things until you leave the room? It felt like that. Not that Ashley and I cared very much. But Grandmother took Aunt Amanda to her bedroom while we got ready for the pool."

"No idea what she wanted to talk about?"

Caroline looked at her guilelessly. "No."

Branigan couldn't help but wonder if her father had coached her before their arrival. "Go on."

"Well, Ashley and I were ready and waiting for a good while before Aunt Amanda came down. I remember because we were fooling around on the piano. I was the only one Grandmother let play her piano because Mom made me take lessons. I was showing Ashley the lame song I'd been practicing." She glanced at Heath. "Also, Uncle Ramsey was stomping around a good bit. He said Grandmother was going to be late for her doctor's appointment."

Branigan knew the police had checked out the appointment, confirming that Mrs Resnick and Ramsey had been in the doctor's office from 11 a.m. until 12:25 p.m.

Caroline tucked her hair behind an ear and continued. "We didn't even get to the club until nearly lunchtime and stayed a long time. It was Friday of a holiday weekend, so it was crowded. By 4 or 4:15, we were starving. We'd skipped lunch because of those pancakes. So we tied our towels around our waists and walked to Grandmother's."

The police had walked the distance from Peach Orchard Country Club to Mrs Resnick's house, and the girls' twenty-minute walk checked out.

Caroline hesitated a moment, her confidence wavering. Branigan looked up, but didn't speak.

Heath spoke first. "You have to realize, Branigan, that Caroline – and Ashley too – were quite traumatized by what they saw. We had the girls in therapy for some time afterward. They had nightmares, maybe even PTSD."

"I'm really sorry to bring it up again," Branigan said.

Caroline barely nodded. "It was just so awful."

"Can you tell me about the kitchen door?"

Heath and Davison looked at her.

"The top panes were broken," Caroline said promptly. "We noticed it right away, but didn't really think about a break-in, you know? Ashley and I talked later about why we weren't scared at that point. But we just weren't thinking along those lines.

"We pushed the door open because it was unlocked. Unlatched even. There was shattered glass and a rock on the kitchen floor. And there was Grandmother, with Dollie sitting beside her, whining. And blood. So much blood." She drew in a fractured breath.

"Ashley screamed. And we both just turned and ran. Mr Carnes was cutting his grass next door. You know how Grandmother's front yard was. . . exposed at the street, but secluded on the sides and back. But we could hear the lawn-mower through the hedges. We ran into the street, then into his yard.

"We'd seen Mr Carnes the night before – at the party. We both jumped all over him, climbing up his body just about. He hustled us in his side door, practically shoving us at his wife. And he ran to Grandmother's."

"When you say you noticed the broken panes right away," Branigan said, "was there glass on the outside? Or only the inside?"

Caroline closed her eyes, as if recreating the scene in her mind. "Outside too," she said. "I remember my flip-flops crunching on some before we ever pushed the door."

"Why do you ask that?" said Heath.

Branigan stared at him evenly. "Because a rock thrown from outside would leave glass only inside. Glass on the outside could mean the crime scene was staged to look like a break-in."

Heath's mouth tightened, but Caroline's widened in horror. "But... but... that would mean..."

"It would mean that your grandmother was killed by someone she knew."

Heath's eyes narrowed. "Are we through, Branigan?"

"Did you want to talk here?" she asked. "Or make an appointment back in Grambling?"

He glanced at his daughter. "Call my office," he said. "I think Caroline has had enough for one day."

Davison and Branigan said awkward goodbyes. Davison remained silent until they rounded the curve at the Methodist church.

"I'm sure he wouldn't have done anything in front of his daughter," he said finally. "But I'm still glad I went with you. I don't trust Heath Resnick."

"You may be right." She filled him in on Amanda's story about her mother's plan to change her will to eliminate Heath.

"My goodness, Branigan! There's your motive right there."

"Except he and Amanda and Ramsey claim their mother was killed before he knew about it."

"Hmm. Maybe. Or maybe he's connected enough in that town to have heard some other way."

CHAPTER TWENTY-THREE

Branigan's internet search showed it was sixty-three miles from the Isle of Palms on a zig-zagging path southward to Edisto Beach. A crow could've flown a lot quicker, but she and Davison had to find roads across the mass of inlets and inland waterways.

Highway 174 into Edisto was one of the most picturesque on the coast. Spanish moss hung from every colossal oak, cloaking the road in shadows on the sunniest day. They passed signs of poverty – shacks and beer joints and small farms cut off from the immense wealth that had flooded this coastline.

Apparently, Davison was thinking the same thing. "Looks like they need our buddy Liam down here."

"Every place needs a Liam," she agreed.

Ashley Resnick was single, Branigan had learned, and living with roommates in a house on the tidal creek, a few rows off the beach. She was a teacher in the island's only elementary school. Branigan wondered what had led her and Caroline, once fast friends as well as cousins, down such different paths.

Highway 174 deposited them into Edisto's "downtown", which made Isle of Palm's half-mile stretch look positively New York-ish. An oceanfront state park with a campground turned off to the left; a grocery store sat on the right. That was about it.

Edisto retained its shabby island feel, with decrepit houses sharing pristine beachfront with gleaming newcomers. They took a side street to the back row, soon finding themselves on sand rather than asphalt.

Ashley's rental stood on stilts like its neighbors, but there was a single suite at ground level. Maid's quarters, folks once called such lodging. Now Branigan assumed it held one of Ashley's roommates.

Five bikes with sand-encrusted tires were parked in the shade under the house, none of them locked. Towering trees crowded in on either side, and Branigan could see a wooden walkway and aged gazebo on the tidal creek out back. The sunsets were bound to be spectacular.

A young woman, blond-streaked and barefoot, bounded down the steps, a black Labrador retriever at her side. "Right on time!" she called. "You must be Branigan!" Then she saw Davison unfolding himself from the Civic and stopped short. "Whoa!" she said, looking from one to the other. "You've got to be related."

Branigan offered her hand to shake. "This is my twin brother Davison. He was visiting Grambling and decided at the last minute to come with me."

"Cool," she said. "Do you like hot tea? Or is it too hot for that?"

"No, it's fine," they answered at the same time.

Branigan and Davison followed Ashley and the silent dog up the steps, through a screened-in porch and into a spacious kitchen/living area that showed signs of multiple occupants. Books and magazines, CDs and beach towels were strewn everywhere. The kitchen sink was half full of dirty dishes and the dishwasher stood open. Branigan suspected they had interrupted Ashley as she tried to clean before their arrival.

"Forgive the mess," she said. "With five of us, it's a losing battle." She busied herself placing teabags into three mismatched mugs, and rummaging in a drawer for packets of sweetener.

"No problem at all," Branigan said. "We appreciate you being willing to see us on your day off. Where is everybody? I hope we didn't run them off."

"No. They're at the beach" – she waved toward the front door – "or fishing" – she waved at the back. "It's just me and Bandit." At his name, the black Lab gave his first bark. "Please make yourselves at home." Again, the wave.

Branigan moved a *People* magazine and perched on a wicker chair, placing her recorder, notebook and pen on a round, glass-topped table. Davison moved towels and settled on the floral chintz-covered couch, picking up a magazine. Ashley delivered the mugs, then joined Branigan at the table.

"We've come from talking to Caroline and your Uncle Heath," she began.

"Uncle Heath was there? That's weird."

"Well, yeah. Please tell me everything you can remember about the July 4 party and the next day. I'll interrupt if I have questions."

Ashley's first words were a surprise. "I remember my cousin Ben was drunk as a skunk," she started. "Caroline and our cousin Drew and two of our friends and I decided to go swimming right after the fireworks. We found Ben by the pool, passed out on a lounge chair. Drew woke him up. He wanted to make sure Aunt Amanda didn't see him like that.

"Caroline went into the pool house and turned on the pool lights. The water was pretty gross, but we dared each other to dive in. We swam for a few minutes, but then Drew found a snake. He held it up, and Caroline and I screamed and screamed." She laughed at the memory. "He threw it into the bushes, but that was it for us. We got out."

"How did Caroline get into the pool house to turn the lights on?"

"Ben had already unlocked the door. He had even found swim trunks. That reminded us that we'd left suits there too. Our friends swam in their underwear."

"Do you know how Ben got in? I understood that your father had installed a new bolt lock."

"Yeah. After Ben woke up, he threw up in the bushes, then came into the pool with us. I guess that sobered him up a little. He showed us how he'd broken in through a window in the bathroom. He always thought he was too good – or maybe just too *mature* – to talk to me and Caroline. But I heard him telling Drew that 'someone else' had been living in the pool house. I knew all about that man Billy because I'd heard Dad yelling about it so much. So I was kind of listening. Ben said, 'I think there were two people living here.'"

Branigan stared at Ashley. "That's the first I've heard of that. Did you tell the police?"

"No. All they asked about was the afternoon we found Grandmother's body. They didn't ask about anything else. I didn't figure it was important, because even if Billy had a friend with him or whatever, they were gone by then. Believe me, my dad was on the warpath about getting him out of there." She hesitated. "*Was* it important?"

"I have no idea. It's just that it wasn't in the police file and they were pretty meticulous. Go on." Branigan flicked her eyes to see what Davison was doing, but he was engrossed in another *People*. Bandit had settled at his feet.

"Let's see. Our friends went on home with their parents. Caroline and I stayed in the blue guest room we liked. It had twin beds. We always kidded that we were Grandmother's favorites, because she'd gotten those twin beds for us. All the other cousins rolled their eyes. Being Grandmother's favorites was hardly something to brag about."

"Why was that?"

"Oh, I don't know. She was kind of… distant, I guess you'd say. Frosty. My other grandma, for instance, lived out in the country. We called her Grandma – or G'ma during my gangsta stage." Ashley grinned, and Branigan could see the impish thirteen-year-old she must have been. "She kept my brother and sister and me a lot. She grew watermelons and cantaloupes for us. She played cards with us. Just different, you know?"

Branigan nodded. "Sounds like my gran."

"Anyway, *Grandmother* was in bed by the time we came in from the pool. We checked in with Dad and Aunt Amanda. Dad told us to shower, because there was no telling what kinds of bacteria were in that pool. We did and went to bed."

"And the next morning?"

"We slept late, then Tabitha made us pancakes. Chocolate chip, maybe? I remember some kind of faces on them. Then Aunt Amanda took us to the club."

"Did you overhear your aunt and your grandmother talking, by any chance?"

"No."

"Caroline said your aunt kept you waiting quite awhile."

"I guess so," Ashley said slowly. "It seemed like Dad was getting impatient, now that you mention it. But it didn't occur to me to care what they were talking about."

"Okay. So coming home from the country club?"

Ashley's demeanor shifted visibly. She cast her eyes around the room. "Come here, Bandit." The big dog woke up and walked over, nuzzling the girl. She gripped his neck in a hug.

"We walked home in our bathing suits. I remember we were starving and talked about ordering pizza or Chinese. We walked around to the back door, the way we always did." Ashley stopped, and hugged the dog again. Branigan waited. "Then we saw the back door, with the panes busted out. I don't know why, but it didn't register. We walked right in."

"Do you remember if there was glass on the outside?"

"I have no idea. I do remember that I had Grandmother's door key already out, but we didn't have to use it. Caroline pushed the door open. And we saw Grandmother with her little chihuahua, Dollie. That was the thing that got me: that little dog just sitting there. I don't remember screaming, but I know I did because my throat was sore later. We both turned around and ran."

"Did you see a murder weapon?"

She shook her head. "Just blood," she said, echoing her cousin. "So much blood."

Branigan knew the police had never recovered a murder weapon. A steak knife was missing from a matched set in Mrs Resnick's kitchen. Forensics had matched the stab wounds to the serrated blades of those remaining in the wooden block, but the murder weapon itself was never found.

"And then?"

"We ran next door to Mr Carnes' house. Mrs Carnes took us in and kept trying to feed us. But we weren't hungry any more."

"Ashley, I'm sorry if this is upsetting for you. But is there anything else you think might be important that the police never asked about? Like Ben saying there was a second person living in the pool house. Anything else like that?"

"Just that dog, you know? The fact that Dollie must have seen everything. Mom and Dad let me take her home, and she lived another two years. But she always seemed sad to me."

"That is horrible," Branigan agreed.

There was a silence and Branigan couldn't think of anything else to ask. She met Davison's glance and he raised an eyebrow.

They told Ashley goodbye and drove away. The last thing they saw was Bandit standing guard beside his mistress.

Dollie the chihuahua was a good angle for the story. As was the glass outside Mrs Resnick's door. As was the late-night swim and the snake. Branigan would need to call Bennett Brissey Jr, however, to follow up on his assertion that two people were living in the pool house. That theory was not on the police radar.

But that could wait until Monday. Branigan was ready for a seafood dinner and a day at the beach tomorrow.

It was late afternoon by the time she and Davison arrived back at the Isle of Palms. She took Cleo for a walk along the beach, then joined Davison on the deck for soft drinks and cheese and crackers. He was working on a mixing-bowl-size serving of ice cream.

"Where do you want to eat dinner?" she asked. "Shem Creek? Sullivan's Island? The marina?" Then with a pointed look at his bowl, "Or will you want dinner at all?"

"Oh yeah. I'll be hungry again by seven."

"Well, I'm going to take a quick nap, then we can shower and go."

She slept longer than she intended, so it was 7:45 before they left the house, choosing the Isle of Palms marina because of its proximity. They sat on the restaurant's upper deck, enjoying the cool breeze and the flamboyant orange sunset, watching the occasional pontoon and luxury fishing boat puttering in for the evening. Branigan wanted a glass of pinot noir, but didn't order one, thinking, not for the first time, that she'd hate to be the one going permanently alcohol-free.

She wore a simple white sundress and flat sandals. Davison wore the island uniform: faded khaki Bermudas, navy golf shirt and flip-flops. Branigan recognized the entire outfit from his Salvation Army trip, but it looked good on him. She saw several women looking him over as they sat at a table for two along the railing.

He held up his iced tea for a toast. "To the Resnicks," he said. "They brought me to this fabulous place I'd nearly forgotten."

The siblings ordered platters of fried shrimp and flounder, with French fries, coleslaw and hush puppies.

"Yep, tonight we even fry the bread," Branigan said, closing her eyes and biting into a crispy brown hush puppy. "We have no shame."

Hush puppies could taste like cornbread or they could taste like cake. These had the sweet flavor that signaled the chef had mixed sugar into the batter. They were delicious. All six of them.

Davison snatched the last one before she could get to it. "Brani G, do you remember the time Uncle Bobby, Dad and I got boiled shrimp, and you ladies tried to make hush puppies at the beach house? We ended up driving over here to get these."

"I know. Just couldn't get them to taste the same. It's harder than it looks."

"And remember the time Mom took us on a float in the inland waterway and we came out in the inlet between the islands? That current scared us to death."

"I think it scared Mom too, but she didn't want to let on," Branigan said. "What I always remember is coming down with the Harrisons and Barnhills, and all the teenagers throwing the parents' beer out the window and burying them in the sand for later. Which meant drinking hot beer."

"Dad and Mr Harrison and Mr Barnhill each thought the others were drinking up a storm," Davison added, laughing. "Not to mention we drained part of their rum and vodka bottles and refilled them with water."

Branigan tried to smile but it came out twisted. "I'm so sorry you can't have a drink or two and stop," she said. "The bad luck of brain chemistry."

"Don't I know it."

They stayed at the rooftop restaurant after the meal, comfortably stuffed, listening to an acoustic guitarist singing an eclectic mix of Jimmy Buffet, the Tams and Johnny Cash. When the singer was joined by a keyboardist who blasted out the brass section for "Be Young, Be Foolish, Be Happy", Branigan pulled Davison from his chair.

"On your feet, big man."

He laughed. "I can't dance without a six pack in me."

"Mom taught you to dance before you started drinking," she said, kicking off her shoes. "Come on."

It took only a moment for muscle memory to take over, and Davison twirled her non-stop through the laid-back moves of the shag, an East Coast dance that resembled a slow jitterbug. The point was to make it look effortless, their mom used to say, teaching them to keep up a 1-2-3 shuffle from the waist down while pretzeling their arms in intricate maneuvers. Davison had learned well, and he led Branigan expertly. When they had finished, the other patrons applauded.

They grinned, gave mock bows and sat back down. They left when the musicians took a break at 11 p.m., but when they arrived at the house, Branigan wasn't sleepy.

"Guess it was the nap," she said. "I'm going to sit on the deck and listen to the ocean." She wrapped herself in a blanket, because the wind coming off the water was cool. Davison popped open a Sprite and joined her. The moon was at three-quarters and lit a sparkling stripe across the gently heaving water. With no porch lights, the stars seemed touchable.

"Ah, this is what I remember," Branigan said dreamily. "Being out here with all the Harrison and Barnhill kids while the adults played cards. Did you know Pete Barnhill is a judge in Gainesville?"

"I heard. Scary."

"How'd you hear?"

"I go on Facebook sometimes in public libraries. That's the one place in most towns where street people are welcome."

Branigan was silent. She had heard Liam say the same thing. Somehow it was worse hearing it first-hand from Davison.

"You know, you're only forty-one," she said tentatively. "Do you ever wonder how you might like to spend the second half of your life?"

He was quiet for a long time. She looked over, and the moonlight showed his jaw was taut. She knew that look.

"Yeah," he said huskily. "I think maybe I'd like to train as a paralegal. I'd like to build a little fishing cabin on Lake Hartwell – nothing fancy. A place where Chan could come visit from college. A place where we could go out in the early morning and fish like I did with Pa and Dad. A place where I could get to know him." He paused. "How about you?"

"How about me what?"

"Second half of *your* life?"

"Oh. Well, I guess… Actually, that's a good question. The way journalism is going, I'm not sure I'll have a job in five years. Or two. I sure don't want to get into that fifty-five to sixty-three age bracket and get laid off. I've seen too much of that."

"I didn't mean career-wise," her brother said. "What about personally? You said the other night you didn't want to be single."

This conversation had gotten way too personal way too fast.

"Any near misses?" he pressed. "Are you dating anyone?"

"Yes and no. Two near misses. Right guy, wrong time. Wrong guy, right time. I'm not dating anyone right now, or you'd be sitting in his lap."

"Who was the 'right guy'?"

"A reporter named Jason Hornay, who came to Grambling from Birmingham. We were sort of getting serious when I got the offer in Detroit. He couldn't find a job there, so we went our separate ways. In retrospect, I'm not sure it was the right decision."

"Nah. You wouldn't want to hear 'Branigan is Horn-ay' the rest of your life."

She gave him her best withering look. "Since I don't hang around eleven-year-olds, I doubt I would."

"One of my addiction counselors – who were legion, by the way – told me that an addict is often emotionally arrested at the time of addiction. That makes me sixteen."

"With your clean time, maybe you matured to nineteen or twenty."

"Okay, smart-ass. One more question. We all know I've messed up my life as much as a human being can. Has your life turned out like you wanted?"

There it was. The vise was squeezing her chest.

"No," she said softly. "I feel guilty even saying it because I've been blessed in so many ways. Mom and Dad. Gran and Pa. The farm. Work. Financially. Even Liam and Liz. But I wanted this." She swept an arm to indicate the ocean, the beach, the house. "I wanted to fill it up with a husband and children and friends like the Harrisons and the Barnhills. I wanted a family. I wanted to be the mom in a family like we had."

"Before I blew it up."

"Well, partly. But you didn't keep me from having my own. I managed that all by myself."

"I wonder," he said. "Or did I cast a stain so wide you were afraid to try?"

She was genuinely startled. "I never laid that on you."

"No. But what you said on the way down, about my choices affecting you and Mom and Dad and Chan: I never thought about that. I knew I'd hurt you. I knew you missed me. But I'd never really thought that I might have changed the course of your lives. I guess I thought you'd gone right on without me."

She murmured a response.

"What?"

"Fat chance," she repeated.

CHAPTER TWENTY-FOUR

JULY 4, TEN YEARS AGO

Rita Mae Jones watched Bennett Brissey Jr and his fast drinking. He was a quick drunk, but he looked to be the most promising male here. Plus, he was a Grambling heir. Nothing shabby there.

Rita Mae's dad and Mr Resnick had been work colleagues, so the Joneses were charter members of the July 4 guest list. The elder Joneses had since moved to Atlanta to help Rita Mae's sister, but in a town like Grambling, you didn't get kicked off the list unless you did something heinous. The fact that Alberta Resnick considered Rita Mae cheap wasn't enough to get her disinvited.

Rita Mae counted Ben Jr's trips to the bars, matching him drink for drink. But four hardly affected her; at thirty-two she had built up considerably more tolerance.

When Ben took drink number five and stumbled down the porch steps, she followed, around the side yard, across the parking area and onto the overgrown path leading to the pool. She heard him drop his drink and curse. She covered her mouth to stifle a giggle.

She remained in the shadows while Ben Jr crashed through a bathroom window in the rear of the pool house, giggling again at his ungainly head-first entrance while his butt and legs dangled outside. Through the open window, she could hear him opening and shutting drawers, bumping into furniture, mumbling to himself. Then she was startled by a sharp rap on the front door. Though she was far out of sight behind the pool house, she crouched instinctively.

She couldn't make out the conversation between Ben and another man, but it didn't last long. The other man left. Rita Mae sidled around the house to find Ben stretched out on a lounge chair at the pool's edge.

"Hi," she said brightly. He didn't even startle, but opened one eye lazily. "Well, hi," he said, openly taking in her tight capris, halter top and tanned shoulders. "Were you – are you – at the party?" he asked, sitting up.

"Sure thing."

"Well, things are looking up," he said. "I'm Ben."

"And I'm Rita Mae. You got anything stronger than your grandma's bourbon?"

He blinked. "As a matter of fact, I do. You ever smoke crack?"

"No-o-o," she said slowly. "I prefer powder."

"I saw something," he said, and stood. She followed him through the dim interior of a recreation room and into a bedroom. He pulled open a bureau drawer and extracted a crack pipe and a cloth bag. She had never tried cocaine in crack form, but she'd seen it smoked a few times.

"Got a lighter?" she asked. Ben scrambled further in the drawer and found a cheap one, encased in blue plastic. He thrust his hand into the far corner and came up with a tarnished spoon.

"Well, you've got everything we need," she said, gathering the paraphernalia and walking back to the pool, her hips swinging a little more than necessary. She placed a rock in the spoon and lit a flame under it. "Get ready to fly, big boy."

The high was incredible, intense and warm and multicolored. It was the best twenty minutes of Rita Mae's life. When she came down, dreamy and satisfied, she saw that Ben Jr had fallen asleep on the lounger.

Big party man, indeed. There are more rocks in that drawer, I do believe, she thought, so she walked back through the pool house and opened the bureau. She placed the cloth bag in her pocket for later, took out a single rock and fired up again.

This time she didn't bother going back to the pool, but simply lay back on the bed. Perhaps this one was a bit short of the first high, but it was still darned good. She closed her eyes and drifted away.

***

Ben woke with a start, his brother Drew shaking him, and his rat cousins Caroline and Ashley dancing around like idiots. Two more kids he'd never seen were with them. "Ben's drunk!" they squealed, laughing uproariously.

Drew was hardly better. "Get up, man. You don't want Mom's wrath tonight."

The rat cousins and their friends leaped into the pool, screeching madly. Drew jumped in right behind them, calling for Ben. He got to his feet. Wait a minute. Where was that woman? He'd better hide any evidence of the crack before his loud-mouthed cousins saw it.

He walked back into the pool house, seeing more clearly because the lights were on. "Rita Mae?" he whispered. In the bedroom, he could see that the old chenille spread was wrinkled. There was a lump where the spread met the floor. He lifted it to find Rita Mae's strappy sandals. She must have left barefoot. He opened the drawer and saw immediately that she'd taken everything else – the pipe, the cloth bag, even the damn lighter.

All that was left was the tarnished spoon.

Ben walked back outside, but made it no further than the flower bed beside the front door before a wave of nausea hit. He threw up a good bit of the evening's bourbon.

After five minutes, he felt better and cannonballed into the pool, setting off a cacophony of squeals among the young teens. He hadn't been in there two minutes when Drew held a brown snake above his head and flung it into the bushes. The ensuing screams from the rat cousins were ear-splitting; that was pretty much it for any further swimming.

As Ben toweled off and dressed, he peered into the jungle that was his grandmother's back yard. Where had the lovely and adventurous Rita Mae gone? Was she watching him still?

CHAPTER TWENTY-FIVE

PRESENT DAY

At the farmhouse on Monday morning, Branigan woke before the alarm went off. Cleo wasn't on her pillow beside the bed.

She padded into the den in bare feet. Davison was dressed and sitting on the couch, the Burberry bag packed on the floor at his feet. Cleo sat with her head in his lap.

Branigan's heart pinched, as it had so often over the weekend. He looked like a little boy, anxious about camp.

"Couldn't sleep?" she asked.

He smiled nervously. "Just ready to get this over with."

"We can't check in until eight," she said, putting on the coffee. "Want to watch cartoons?"

That got a laugh out of him.

She stirred up a pot of grits, which they shared along with coffee, toast and the newspaper. When it was time to leave, he buried his face in Cleo's neck. Branigan thought he might be crying, but when he raised his face it was dry.

"Let's go," he said.

They drove in silence to the Grambling Rescue Mission. He didn't want her to come inside, so when they pulled into the parking lot, he kissed her on the cheek.

"Wish me luck," he said shakily.

On impulse, she said, "What would you think if I prayed for you? Too weird?"

He looked at her oddly. "You've been around Liam too long."

"I know. But it's something I want to do." He shrugged, so she started. "God, please watch over my brother. That's all I ask. Amen."

"Don't quit your day job," Davison said, but he was smiling. He tossed the Burberry bag over one shoulder and walked into the mission.

Branigan drove to the newspaper office feeling unsettled. From long experience, she knew work would help. As soon as she sat down, she placed two calls – one to Ben Brissey Jr in New York City, and one to Liam. She left a message for Ben Jr that she needed a phone interview to follow up on something his cousin Ashley had told her. Liam answered his phone.

"Just calling to confirm lunch," she said. After hearing Liam's assent, she paused. "I dropped Davison at the mission this morning. I found him sitting on the couch at sunrise with his clothes all packed. I don't think he slept at all."

"How was it?"

"Sad. I enjoyed having him at the farm all week. And then the beach trip was good. A little deep at times, but good."

"You're doing the right thing," Liam said. "Those guys at the mission know what they're doing. You know what I always say."

"I know. I know. 'If Charlie or Chan were on drugs, that's where I'd put them.' I do listen to you, you know."

"Doesn't make it any easier. He's out of touch for awhile, right?"

"Right. No visits the first week. But they do allow cell phone calls one hour each night, so we'll be able to talk. I've got my fingers crossed."

"It's the best thing," Liam repeated. "Want to come here at noon?"

"Sure." Flipping her notebook open, she added, "I need to talk to Jess, Max Brody, Dontegan, Malachi, Rita and Demetrius. Will they be around?"

"Maybe Jess and Dontegan. The others don't live here. I can give you a schedule of the week's meals where you might find them."

"Okay. See you in awhile."

Branigan spent much of the morning answering phone calls and emails about the story on Vesuvius and his father that had run

Sunday. Tanenbaum Grambling stopped by her desk to tell her it was Sunday's most-read story, and that *The Rambler*'s website had logged forty-two comments.

"That answers our question about interest in homelessness," he said. "Pitch me your ideas for where you want to head next."

She left the office at 11:15, hoping to catch Jess and Dontegan before meeting Liam for lunch. She was surprised to find the Jericho Road parking lot filled, then remembered that Monday morning was the mission's grocery distribution day. Liam had arranged pick-ups of dented and otherwise unsalable canned goods from three grocery chains. Families, urban and rural, could come once a month and shop in the free "grocery store" set up on one long wall behind the dining room. Many of Liam's homeless residents volunteered to serve coffee and load car trunks. But many of these cars belonged to community volunteers who wanted to be part of the ministry as well. Liam's staff had trained them as intake workers, shopping assistants, prayer counselors, and appointment takers for the nurses and attorneys who volunteered their time. In addition, Jericho Road's mental health worker and social worker took walk-ins on Monday mornings.

"People come for groceries," she'd heard Liam say in speeches. "But they're met with transformational help."

She spotted Dontegan as soon as she parked; he rolled two boxes of groceries in a red metal wagon, then hoisted them into the trunk of a rusting car with no hubcaps. Two Hispanic women and at least six children piled into the car.

Sometimes, she supposed, groceries were enough.

Dontegan greeted her with a wave. "Pastuh told me to take a break when you come," he said, wiping sweat from his face. "Gotta say I'm glad you here."

Dontegan led her through the dining hall, where she was surprised to see Ramsey Resnick seated at one of the tables along the back wall.

"Is Mr Resnick a volunteer?" she asked.

Dontegan followed her gaze. "Oh, yeah, Mr Ramsey. He teach a finance class. And he pray with people."

Dontegan ushered her into a small office furnished with two armchairs and a battered end table. He waited expectantly.

"I think Pastor Liam already mentioned the story I'm working on," she started. "It's about an old woman who was stabbed to death in her home, downtown, ten years ago this summer. As you know, very few murders in Grambling go unsolved. But this one has flat-out stumped the police. So much so that Chief Warren didn't even mind us looking into it – which is saying something."

Dontegan gave every sign of listening intently.

"Of course, we covered the investigation for months at the time," she continued. "The police were thorough. They interviewed every family member, every service worker, every neighbor, every conceivable person who had a connection to Alberta Resnick. That was the lady's name. But there was one detail that never made sense. The killer took Mrs Resnick's car and abandoned it right outside in your parking lot."

Dontegan's eyes widened. "Our church parkin' lot?"

"Yes, but it wasn't a church back then. It was an empty building. But if you remember, there were homeless people living in it."

"Oh, yeah. I slept here sometimes."

"You did? Did the police question you?"

He shook his head.

"Must have been a different time frame then. The police always thought there was a possibility that the crime was random, a burglary gone wrong. And they thought it possible that it was committed by a transient who left Grambling immediately. They looked hard at the three homeless people they found camping in here. But there was nothing as far as evidence, nothing at all. And the killer would have been blood-spattered. Plus, those three passed lie detector tests. Police speculated that if it was a transient, he left the car, hopped on a bus or train, and never went back inside the building."

Dontegan was nodding. "But Miz Branigan, they's another way to look at that car business."

"And what's that?"

"That someone *wanted* the po-lice to think it was a homeless dude."

She paused for a minute. "You're right. That is one possibility. But what I wanted to ask you is what you told Pastor Liam about a woman named Rita. Could you tell me that story?"

"You know Rita?" he asked.

She nodded.

"Well, she a mean one. Real bad temper. Always yellin' about why no womens sleep here. I know bein' on the streets is hard on womens, harder than on mens even, but it's not like I can change the rules and give her a bed." He spread his hands apologetically.

"Of course not."

"Anyway, before Pastuh opened beds at Jericho Road, I had me a tent under the bridge where I stay. Late one night, Rita came under there, all staggerin' and cryin'. I felt bad for her, so I told her she could stay in my tent and I'd move my sleepin' bag outside."

"That was nice of you."

"It was a warm night," he said, grinning. "Cooler outside the tent than in it. Anyway, she say okay, but she kept cryin' and kinda crashin' around inside the tent. I be a little scared she gonna knock it down.

"Then she came out with a can of malt likker and sat out where I be tryin' to sleep. Finally she kinda run down and was mutterin' before she pass out. That's when she say it."

Branigan waited.

"She say, 'I don' need your stinkin' tent. I could be rich if I wanna be.' I kinda laughed. That made her mad enough to wake up. She say, 'I tell about Ol' High and Mighty gettin' her nasty self stab, I be off these streets and on Easy Street.'"

"That's a colorful way of putting it," Branigan said.

"Yes, ma'am. I think that's why I remember it so long."

"When was this, Dontegan? Do you remember?"

"Nah. I know it was a year or two before Pastuh opened Jericho. I was the first one to move in. I helped with all the work."

She nodded, preoccupied with the thought that Rita might actually know something. She needed to find her. Today.

* * *

Dontegan and Branigan walked back into the dining hall, where grocery boxes were dwindling. Only a few stragglers were left, waiting for their names to be called to see an intake worker.

Branigan asked Dontegan to point out Jess. He pointed to a neatly dressed white man who was wheeling a large coffee urn into the kitchen. She'd mistaken him for one of the partner church volunteers. She introduced herself and asked Jess if she could ask him questions while he worked.

"Sure," he said, closing the kitchen door to give them privacy. "Pastor Liam told me you were coming."

"First, if you don't mind my asking, do you live here in the shelter?"

"You're thinking I don't look like it?" he said, smiling.

"Or sound like it."

"Believe me, Miss Powers, addiction is no respecter of race or education or anything else. I grew up in Oklahoma. Had a good family. Went to college. But when I insisted on smoking marijuana instead of going to class, my father stopped paying. I don't blame him."

"Smoking marijuana in college is a long way from living in a homeless shelter."

He shrugged. "Not as long as you might think. Once I dropped out, I started working in restaurants and hanging out with people who were doing harder stuff. Coke. Heroin. Then when I got laid off, some of the cheaper stuff. Crack mostly. It doesn't take long to start smoking up the rent money."

"What brought you to Georgia?"

"Work. Everything dried up in the Midwest during the recession, so I joined a carnival. First night we pulled into Grambling, I was helping put up a tent. My buddy dropped one of those huge poles on my foot. Broke eight bones. I couldn't work, the carnival moved on, and I was stuck. I'm trying to get disability."

"From what I've heard about Max Brody, you don't sound like you'd be hanging around him."

Jess laughed. "You got that right. We're *not* friends. But I still have a beer from time to time. I'm trying to stay away from the hard stuff, but I can handle my alcohol."

She knew Liam disagreed with this line of thinking, but she wasn't Jess's counselor. Or his pastor. She remained silent.

"Anyway, this was on the first night of that Thursday outdoor music series last month. You know what I'm talking about?"

She nodded. The city closed off half of Main Street on Thursdays, starting in mid-May. Bands played on a stage set up in front of the courthouse, and beer vendors sold beer and wine from trucks.

"I'd worked day labor that day, so I had fifty bucks in my pocket. That beer truck was calling my name. Apparently, Max saw me pay for one, and he came over, already drunk. I thought, 'Uh-oh, he's going to ask for money.' But instead, he pulled out a pretty thick wad of cash and bought his own.

"I didn't know anybody else there, so we sort of stood together, listening to the band. Max got another beer, then another one. I wasn't sure how long he could stay upright. I was still working on my first one when he got his third. He held it up, as if he were toasting, and said something like, 'This evening's drunk is courtesy of an ol' lady who had the good sense to get stabbed.' Or 'good taste to get stabbed'. Something like that."

"What did you say?"

"Nothing. Or maybe, 'What?' But he didn't say anything else; just kind of swayed, then plopped down on the curb. He was wasted. I honestly didn't think any more about it until Pastor Liam told us about that unsolved murder. When he said 'old lady' and 'stabbing', I was like 'Whoa! What are the odds that could be a coincidence?'"

"Where can I find Max Brody?"

Jess shrugged. "Your guess is as good as mine. Here when we're serving breakfast or dinner. St James during breakfast. Covenant Methodist sometimes at dinner. Library. Bridge. Main Street. Day labor places."

"If you see him, will you tell him I'm looking for him?"

"Sure thing."

Liam needed to make a pickup after lunch, so he and Branigan planned to take the Jericho Road van to Marshall's, the diner beside Resnick Drugs on Main Street. As they got in the old van, Branigan smelled the distinctive odor of bleach.

"Do you bleach the inside after you bring in groceries?" she asked.

"Heck no," Liam said. "What *is* that? My eyes are watering."

He climbed out and walked in a circle around the van. "The smell is stronger up here around the front bumper. It's got some more dings in it too. I guess one of the staff hit something and was trying to fix it before I saw it."

"But why would they bleach it?" she asked. "That's weird."

"Haven't a clue."

They opened the windows for the short ride to Marshall's. After they were seated and had Marshall's meat loaf, macaroni and cheese, green beans and fried squash in front of them, they compared notes. Malachi and Dontegan's nearly identical stories of a drunken Rita talking about a rich lady who was murdered were promising. So was Jess's story about Max Brody saying something very similar.

"I gotta tell you," Branigan said, "I thought this whole idea of a transient killing Mrs Resnick was a shot in the dark. Now I'm almost wondering if Rita could've killed her."

Liam was startled enough to stop mid-bite. "Not really?"

"Well, she certainly sounds familiar with everything, doesn't she? Maybe she did it, and the guilt drove her crazy. Or maybe she's doing drugs to ease the guilt."

"I think you're veering into fiction," Liam said.

"Either way, I've *got* to find her this afternoon. I'll try the bridge and the library. If she's not at one of those, Covenant Methodist has supper at 5 o'clock. Right?"

"Plus, you could try the bus station," Liam suggested. "Sometimes she panhandles there. But if you really suspect her, Brani G, you need to make sure you talk to her out in the open."

"Nah, I don't really. The police said the stab wounds were made by a person taller than Mrs Resnick. She was at least five seven. So little Rita couldn't have done it unless she was standing on a stool."

Liam drank from his sweet tea. "There's something else that's bothering me," he said. "What you said about Max having a wad of cash. Where did that come from?"

"Day labor?"

"That would never be a 'wad' unless it was in dollar bills. And who pays in dollar bills? What if it wasn't a transient who did the murder? What if it was a transient who *saw* the murder?"

She mused. "And someone else, someone with money, is trying to buy silence?"

They thought for a few minutes.

"You know," she said, "now that you mention it, there was another story about money showing up unexpectedly. Malachi told me that Vesuvius had a little windfall from selling a painting. But then the same painting showed up in a trash pile under the bridge. And Vesuvius ended up dead."

"You're confusing me," Liam said. "Back to Rita. There are two ways to look at what she said. She could think she'd 'get rich' or live 'on Easy Street' by solving the case. You know, get a reward from the Resnicks. The other way is to blackmail them. How did Malachi put it? She thought the 'rich-ass family would pay to keep it quiet'."

"That puts us back to square one. The family."

"Could be. Let's see what the lovely Rita has to say. I want to go with you."

"I thought you'd never ask," she said.

CHAPTER TWENTY-SIX

M alachi Martin didn't know it, but people on the street looked up to him. They marveled at his calm, his kindness, his dignity. He managed to live without lying, without hustling, without stealing – well, if you didn't count the occasional sugar packets and cantaloupes. And he'd been out here longer than any of them.

Sometimes, when they were "flying a sign" – holding up a handwritten sign that said "Homeless. Please help!" at an intersection – or when they were spinning a story about getting to Florida for their mother's funeral (her sixth), Malachi would slip, unbidden, to mind. Malachi was famous for refusing to panhandle. Ever.

Malachi didn't know this either, but it was his acceptance of Pastor Liam that enabled the inexperienced minister to turn Jericho Road around so quickly. The church's previous three pastors had tried to build a traditional church and bend a homeless congregation to fit it. The red-headed former reporter came in like a... well, like a reporter. He admitted he knew nothing of homelessness and wanted to learn all he could. He spent time asking questions. Lord, could the man ask questions. But when you answered, he listened.

He didn't try to impose *his* ideas so much as listen to yours. So when Malachi told him the homeless had a hard time keeping their clothes clean, Pastor Liam found funding to build two showers and a laundry room. But then he required the homeless folks to run them. They took responsibility or they didn't use the facilities.

Dontegan, for one, was so dependable that he worked himself into a paying job.

Malachi could probably do that too. Pastor Liam sure asked him enough times if he wanted a room at Jericho Road. He knew lots of folks would kill for a steady job and a room with running water and heat and air. But that wasn't him.

Still, he liked Pastor Liam. Respected him. And so when someone from the street joined him on a bench in front of the courthouse or passed a bottle under the bridge late at night and asked what he thought of that very white, freckle-faced preacher, Malachi said he thought he was just fine. People listened, and began attending Sunday worship, talking to the church's counselors, helping around the shelter.

On this late Monday morning, it was growing too hot to be on the courthouse lawn. Malachi relinquished his bench and headed for the cool of the Cannon County Public Library. At this time of day, he was able to claim an entire table. He selected a current *Sports Illustrated* and settled in to read.

"Hi, Mr Malachi."

He looked up to see Pastor Liam's son Chan, wearing a T-shirt with the sleeves torn out, baggy shorts and a backward baseball cap. Under his arm was a bike helmet.

"What you doin' here on summer vacation?" he asked the young man.

"My mom sent me to see if I could find my college reading list before we hit a bookstore. Okay if I sit for a minute?"

Malachi nodded. "You in that Volkswagen I heard your daddy talkin' about?"

Chan smiled. "Nah, it's not ready yet. Not sure it ever will be. But we're trying. Charlie and I share an old Jeep, and it's her day. I'm on my bike."

"That's nice – you and your daddy fixin' up a car. You lucky to have a daddy like that."

A shadow passed over Chan's usually open face. "Did you know your dad, Mr Malachi?"

"No. But I knew my granddaddy. He and my grandma raised me. We had a farm outside Hartwell. Raised hogs. Chickens. Vegetables we sold at a stand ever' Friday and Saturday."

Chan asked tentatively, "You didn't want to go on living there?"

"Wasn't a question of 'want'. They was rentin' the property. They died while I was in service. I got back and the farm was gone, rented to somebody else."

"Is that when you became homeless?"

Malachi shrugged. How to explain to this young white boy all the threads that made up that tangle? Most days, Malachi wasn't sure he understood it himself.

"No, not right away. I had some military pay that lasted awhile. I moved to Atlanta, worked construction. Drank a little too much. Worked some in Hartwell. None of them jobs lasted. I finally ran out of money. In Hartwell, we always heard about the construction goin' on in Gramblin'. So I took the Greyhound and here I am."

"And did you work construction here?"

Malachi paused. Chan was a nice kid. But he wasn't about to get into the nightmares and the panic attacks and the long nights in the woods when the only sleep he got came from a bottle of Jim Beam. So all he said was, "Nah, didn't work out."

Chan looked embarrassed. "I'm heading to college in August – Furman, in South Carolina."

"Your daddy done told us that in church. He's mighty proud. Proud of your sister too."

"It's just that my dad…" Chan paused, looked away. Then he stopped, apparently coming to a decision. "You're right," he said, standing. "I am lucky. Or, as he would say, blessed."

CHAPTER TWENTY-SEVEN

JULY 5, TEN YEARS AGO

Amanda woke with a strange sense of déjà vu. It was her old bedroom all right, but she hadn't spent a night in it in twenty-four years. In fact, she didn't know why she'd spent last night in it. It was the first five minutes of the day, and she was already irritated at her mother.

She sighed, and dressed in the solid colors she favored – black capris, black sandals with a half-inch wedge, and a sleeveless yellow top. She dampened her auburn hair and re-blew it dry. Her expensive cut settled into its deliberately tousled shape.

She paused for a moment at her mother's bedroom door, but hearing nothing walked downstairs. There she found Ramsey in the dining room, already on his second cup of coffee, and Tabitha in the kitchen, making blueberry pancakes.

"I'm sorry. Did I keep everyone waiting?"

"Not at all," Ramsey said. "The girls asked for Tabitha's famous 'face' pancakes, so she made them with blueberries. We haven't seen Mother yet. Ashley, do you want to run up and make sure she's awake?"

Ashley scampered up the central staircase. They heard her pounding on Alberta's door and shouting, "Grandmother? Are you up?"

"You're a braver woman than I," Amanda murmured. She drifted into the kitchen to cut up a pineapple, strawberries and cantaloupe.

"Ashley, that's quite enough." The regal voice wafted downstairs.

Alberta soon joined them, dressed for her doctor's appointment in a short-sleeved pink dress, belted at the waist, hose and ecru-colored pumps. "Ramsey, we need to leave the house at 10:45," she said. "Amanda, I'd like to talk to you before we leave."

"Fine. Do you want to give me a hint?"

"Little pitchers," Alberta said, with the faintest of nods toward Ashley and Caroline.

"Big ears, maybe, but little interest," said Ramsey.

Amanda turned to her nieces. "Did I hear I'm to take you to the country club?"

"Yes," Caroline fairly shouted. "We're old enough to stay there by ourselves this summer."

"You have to be thirteen," Ashley explained, looking up from a pancake with a line of blueberries that formed an exaggerated smile.

"Look, I made mine frown," Caroline said, moving the berries around the face.

For goodness' sake, aren't they a little old for this? Amanda gave what she hoped was an indulgent smile for Ramsey's benefit. She hadn't been all that fond of Ben Jr and Drew at this age, much less other people's adolescents. Her nieces were all kinky hair and knobby knees and screechy volume.

She looked up to find her mother's eyes on her. "When you've finished, Amanda, please join me in my sitting room."

"I can come now," said Amanda, ready to get this morning over.

She took her coffee with her, and followed her mother's straight spine up the spiraling staircase to the second-floor bedrooms. Her mother's master bedroom suite included a smallish bathroom – the house was built in a time before luxurious baths became a selling point. But the attached sitting room with its matching floral chaise lounge, wing chairs and ottomans was lovely. Amanda took a wing chair, and waited. She wasn't prepared for where her mother started.

"I always tried to be equal with you children. I spent the same on your birthdays, Christmas, back-to-school clothes."

"I've heard you say that," Amanda agreed.

"But when it came to Heath, your father didn't always agree."

Amanda cocked her head, interested now.

"You and Ramsey were away at college, and your father, to my mind, indulged Heath more than he should have."

"That Mustang?" Amanda laughed. She and Ramsey had had plenty to say about Heath getting a brand new Ford Mustang at sixteen when they had inherited their dad's used sedans. It had been a source of kidding, but she – and, she presumed, Ramsey – had not really minded. They were out of the house by then and not terribly concerned if their younger brother got a few extra perks.

"That was the first manifestation, yes," said Mrs Resnick. "But hardly the last. Heath got into some trouble as a teenager. I thought he needed to make restitution, but your father took care of things."

This was the first Amanda had heard of it. "What kind of trouble?"

"He was a lifeguard at a community pool on the Eastside. There were accusations that he stole from a lockbox."

"You're kidding!"

"Then there was an accusation by a young woman that he had… been inappropriate." Mrs Resnick's vocabulary faltered as she forced herself through this most unpleasant conversation.

"Sexual assault?" Amanda asked.

"Yes, something like that." Her mother looked acutely uncomfortable.

"Mother! How did we not know this?"

"Your father," her mother said again. "He took care of everything. He didn't want Heath's future ruined over what he called 'youthful indiscretions'. And for awhile, I have to admit, Heath seemed to straighten out. He graduated from college, married Serena and moved back here. Then he began buying those mills for renovation."

"And did great," Amanda inserted.

"Yes and no," said her mother. "The last two did well, I believe. They were close enough to downtown to benefit from its cachet. But there were another three on the Westside you probably never heard about. Your father loaned – or as he said 'invested' – a great deal of money in them. They went bankrupt."

"Does Ramsey know all this?"

"I'm sure he knows that Heath had some failures. He doesn't know of your father's involvement."

"Is Heath broke?" Amanda asked. "Or is he okay now with those new mill condos?"

"I really don't know. And that isn't my concern in telling you this now." Alberta Resnick paused. "I'm telling you because I sensed you didn't believe me yesterday. The reason I want to cut Heath out of my will is not maliciousness on my part. Or dementia, as you seemed to think."

Amanda reddened slightly.

"The fact is that your father already gave Heath his portion of the inheritance in all those loans that were never repaid. So I want to change my will simply to reflect what has occurred."

Amanda blew out a long sigh. "Mother, I'm sorry. I had no idea. But you were talking yesterday about Heath wanting to sell your house and sending in a crazed piano player to help him do it."

"Actually, that's true as well," said Alberta. "He's pushing hard for me to sell this house. That makes me wonder how well those mill condos are doing. I think he may be trying to get the estate into a more liquid form before I die. But that doesn't change the fact that he has already been through his portion of the inheritance." She looked at her daughter. "So will you drive me to my attorney's office this afternoon?"

Amanda gazed at her mother for the first time with empathetic eyes. "Certainly," she answered slowly. "You and Ramsey and I probably need to discuss whether we want to tell Heath. But we can decide that later."

Her mother stood. "Yes. I should be back from the doctor's office around 12:30 or 1 o'clock. Give me time to eat lunch. Can you come back at, say, 1:45? My appointment with the lawyer is at 2 o'clock."

Amanda nodded absently. "I'll arrange for a late check-out at the hotel."

***

Rita Mae Jones realized her mistake the minute she awoke. She wasn't sure which hurt more: her head or her feet.

She rolled over to look at her clock, and saw it was past 10:30. She threw back her lightweight duvet and crooked her knee so she could look at the bottom of her feet. Yep, scratches and bruises. They looked as bad as they felt.

Why the heck had she left her shoes at the party? Come to think of it, where the heck had she left her shoes? And did she drive home barefoot?

She padded on bruised soles to the bathroom, brushed her teeth and tried to remember. She'd not had that much to drink – five bourbons on the rocks, but that wasn't unusual. And then she'd followed Ben Brissey Jr to the pool house and they'd... *Oh my gosh, the high. The best high ever.*

She forgot her feet for the moment, forgot the beer she'd intended to open. Was there any of that crack left? This was a holiday weekend, and she had no commitments today. What was wrong with firing up one of those babies?

The cotton sack wasn't on her bedside table. Nor was it on her faux granite kitchen counters. Her pockets. That was it. Rita Mae found last night's capris tossed over the footboard of her bed. She reached into the pocket and pulled out the little sack. One rock left. *Ah.*

What the heck is she doing? Ramsey Resnick wandered from room to room of his mother's house. Caroline and Ashley were banging on her piano in the living room. He let them continue, though the noise jangled his nerves. If that didn't get her down here, nothing would. She didn't allow anyone on that piano who hadn't had *mus-i-cal in-struc-tion.*

When he'd seen Amanda accompany their mother to her bedroom, he figured it'd be a short meeting. Amanda could never spend more than five minutes with Mother without exploding.

He looked at his watch: 10:45.

"Mother!" he called. "I thought you wanted to leave at 10:45!"

Tabitha chuckled behind him. "She can't hear you, Mr Ramsey. You wan' me to tell her?"

"No, you go up and down those stairs enough. If she's late to her doctor's appointment, she's just late, I guess."

At that moment, he heard his mother's bedroom door open. "Ramsey, I am ready to go," she said. "Did I not say we would leave at 10:45?"

He sighed. "Yes, Mother."

In the driveway, he held open the passenger door to his BMW. Even at eighty, his mother seated herself sideways, then primly swung both legs into the car's interior. He mentally rolled his eyes, remembering poor Amanda undergoing etiquette lessons: How a Young Lady Properly Enters an Automobile. There were worse things than being Alberta Resnick's son. Namely, being her daughter.

He slammed the door shut, then hopped into the driver's seat. "Dr Arnott's, I presume?"

His mother nodded.

"So what were you and Amanda talking about?" he asked as he backed out of the driveway.

"Just a little legal matter." His mother sighed, as if exhausted. "I would prefer not to go into it."

"Your call." He said it lightly, but inwardly he seethed. *Why does she do this? Play one child against the other?* "Do you want to tell me what the doctor is seeing you for?"

"He has not been able to control my blood pressure to his satisfaction. He seems to think I'm at risk for a stroke."

"Then he's right, Mother. Blood pressure is nothing to play around with."

The drive to Dr Baxter Arnott's office in a converted house near St Joseph Medical Center took only a few minutes. If his mother had been able to find a doctor still practicing in his eighties, she would have done so. As it was, Dr Arnott, who had to be past seventy, was the closest she could find. He'd been her physician for twenty years.

Ramsey settled himself in the waiting room with a *Field & Stream*. When a nurse called his mother, she surprised him by beckoning him to accompany her. Bewildered, he joined her in one of the doctor's homey examination rooms, where she took a seat, wordlessly, in a wing chair. A nurse took her blood pressure, and moments later Dr Arnott entered.

"Your blood pressure is still higher than I'd like, Alberta," he said. "I recommend that we try another medication."

"Very well," she said. "I'll do whatever you think best. But the reason I brought Ramsey is there's something I want both of you to hear. As you know, Ramsey holds my health care power of attorney. For years, it has contained a Do Not Resuscitate order. I would like to revoke that."

Ramsey looked up in confusion. If Dr Arnott was surprised, he didn't show it.

"But Mother, you've always talked about not wanting to be hooked up to breathing machines or feeding tubes or anything like that."

She shrugged her pink-clad shoulders.

"As you get older, Ramsey, you begin to think a little differently. Should anything happen to me, I want you, and only you, to make the decision about withdrawing life support. I want you to satisfy yourself that I have no chance of coming back to my senses. Then it will be fine to end things. But perhaps that DNR order was a little hasty."

"Fine, Mother. We will certainly do whatever you wish."

That's what Ramsey was saying aloud at least. Inwardly, he wondered what had changed his mother's mind. And did it have anything to do with the legal matter Amanda was handling?

On the drive home, Ramsey attempted to learn more about his mother's abrupt change of mind, but he got nowhere. She did, however, seem more relaxed than he'd seen her since before yesterday's party.

"Ramsey, you needn't come in," she said, as his car glided to the back door. "Thank you for driving me." She opened her door, swung her legs in tandem to the driveway. "And Ramsey," she added, giving him a rare and hesitant smile, "I hope you know that I trust you. And love you."

Ramsey nodded, dumbstruck. He hadn't heard those words from his mother in three decades.

Alberta Resnick opened her back door and stepped into her kitchen. Amanda was always on at her to update it, but the faded wallpaper and clunky appliances were fine with her. What the younger generation didn't appreciate, she found, was the comfort of familiar things. That's why she lived the way she did – in this much-too-large house, with a maid of forty years and a twenty-five-year-old Thunderbird. If she had her way, those decades-old shrubs out back would stay the same too. But she'd gotten tired of her sons' muttering about snakes and rodents. Didn't snakes keep the rodents out anyway? She supposed she'd allow them to be pruned come fall.

Her chihuahua Dollie came trotting out of the den, eyes blinking.

"You were on my couch, weren't you?" Alberta greeted her. She checked the dog's water and food bowls, and saw that Tabitha had fed her before leaving.

She opened the pantry, took out peanut butter and white bread. She searched in the refrigerator for a banana, and prepared her guilty-pleasure lunch: a peanut butter and banana sandwich, a triple helping of potato chips, and a glass of Tabitha's sweet tea over ice. She carried the meal into her den, a comfortably shabby room off the kitchen and out of sight of the formal parlor and dining room. She kicked off her pumps with a sigh, and settled on one end of the sofa to watch her soap opera.

She pinched off a piece of bread crust and gave it to Dollie. She took a bite out of the sandwich, the crunchy peanut butter, ripe banana and fresh bread making a tasty combination. And then in the midst of this simple enjoyment, an annoyance: a knock on her kitchen door.

CHAPTER TWENTY-EIGHT

PRESENT DAY

"I'm a little surprised you can take off in the middle of the day," Branigan said to Liam as they climbed back into the Jericho Road van outside Marshall's.

"My boss seldom messes with my schedule," he said. "Unless you count funerals and hospital visitation, in which case He messes quite a bit."

"Well, I'm glad you can help me find Rita. I'm sure you'll have better luck than I would."

Their first stop was the main branch of the library, located at the corner of Oakley and Anders streets – the intersection where Vesuvius Hightower and his mangled bike were found. The library was a sleek building of glass and brick, with none of the homey warmth of the library on South Main that Branigan remembered from her youth. Inside, everything was hard surfaces, leather and vinyl and wood seating, gun-metal gray tile and carpeting. She wondered for the first time if the décor had been chosen with the homeless in mind. Liam once told her he'd had to remove fabric chairs and sofas from all the public areas of Jericho Road; they'd been soaked in grime, sweat, urine – and worse.

Several years earlier, she'd written a story on the removal of a public phone from the library's front desk. The director had explained that homeless people stood in a never-ending line to use it. Conversations grew heated. Fights broke out. *The Rambler* didn't usually cover the library's sleepy board meetings, but for awhile, taxpaying citizens were roaring for a fix and homeless rights advocates were pushing back.

Now the homeless were welcome in this public place, but there was no phone for them to use. From the entrance, Liam and Branigan recognized many of his churchgoers, some at the computers, others at desks along the room's perimeter, still others – did they have money? – at the smattering of round lunch tables in the Book It Café.

Liam began walking the perimeter. At every table, Branigan saw people greeting him with a smile, a word, a hug. He bent to talk to each one, presumably asking for Rita's whereabouts, because she saw a lot of shaking heads.

He next made his way to the audio-visual wing, where two lines of computer stations, ten per line, allowed free internet access. Even on a Monday afternoon, the room was nearly full, with only three stations not in use. It was impossible to tell with certainty who was homeless and who wasn't, but Liam knew many by sight. He moved easily among five people engrossed in their screens, then returned to where Branigan stood.

"No one saw Rita under the bridge this morning or at St James for breakfast," he reported. "Or they don't *remember* seeing her. Most of them said she could have been there. They just weren't looking."

"Let's drive around town a little, then head to the bridge," Branigan suggested. "I guess she could still be asleep."

They circled to the far north end of Main Street, beyond the courthouse, then cruised down the center of town. "Just like high school, baby," said Liam, "except for the whole driving in a church van thing."

"It's as good as that old Beetle you drove."

"Hey, don't mock. I'm restoring that for Chan."

"You're kidding."

"No, Charlie won't touch it, but Chan thinks it's cool. Or reverse cool. Or so uncool it's cool. Or something like that."

"Drive slower," she commanded.

"More slowly, newspaper lady."

Branigan scoured both sides of the street for Rita. At this time of day, not a whole lot of people were out, so she was confident she hadn't missed her.

After they passed *The Rambler*, they drove another eight blocks south, past a used car lot, seedy bars and light industrial sites. Branigan doubted that Rita would be out this far.

"Let's try the bridge," Liam said, turning west.

Trash had increased along the path to the bridge. Mildewed clothes and discarded beer bottles made up the bulk of it, but there were also watermelon rinds rotting in the sun, covered with black flies.

"Whoever brought that watermelon is probably not too popular about now," Liam said.

They walked hurriedly along the hard-baked path and into the welcome shade of the river birch. There wasn't a breath of breeze beneath the bridge, and no one was visible – just empty tents, fire pits and the pit bull she'd learned was named Bruno.

"That's her place," Branigan said, pointing to the outermost plywood structure forty-five feet up the concrete incline.

"Rita!" Liam called. Then again, "Rita!"

He looked at Branigan's shoes. "Guess we're going to hike," he said.

She shed her open-toed sandals and purse, and started barefoot up the steep incline. Liam, in rubber-soled work boots, followed.

"After all this time, I've never been up here," he said, criss-crossing his feet the way Malachi had. "I always wondered how hard it was."

Branigan didn't speak, concentrating on placing one foot across the other so she didn't tip over and roll down the incline.

Liam matched his pace to hers, holding his arms out occasionally when he feared she was about to slip. They made it to the rudimentary door of the plywood shack, and knocked. Liam called Rita's name again. No answer.

He reached past Branigan to push open the door. They could see immediately there was no one inside. But Liam was fascinated.

"Wow! This is some set-up." Slender bunk beds, held together by two-by-fours, anchored the inside wall. Studs on the outer wall were used as simple shelves, which were lined with cans of food.

A row of bottled waters filled the bottom rung. "Here's our stuff," he said, picking up a bottle with his church's blue and white label: "God loves you. And so does Jericho Road." The entire structure was seven feet long and four feet deep. "I wouldn't want our middle-schoolers to see this. They'd think it was a great way to camp. I wonder who built this."

Branigan wasn't nearly as interested in the engineering as she was in Rita's absence.

"I guess I'll head back to the office, then try the Methodist church at 5 o'clock," she said. "I don't know what else to do."

Branigan arrived at Covenant Methodist at 4:45 p.m., and found a crowd milling in the parking lot. She roamed around, looking for Rita, but didn't see her. Promptly at 5 p.m., church volunteers opened the doors, calling out for people to please line up single file.

Branigan didn't get in line, but instead chose a seat near the door so she could see everyone who entered. A woman serving tea brought her a large cup.

At 5:15, the tables were full and she still hadn't seen Rita. Where in the world was she? Branigan's cell phone rang, and she stepped outside to take the call.

"Branigan!" Liam fairly shouted. "I've found Rita!"

"Where?"

"St Joe's ER. Meet me there." He hung up.

She stood for a moment, confused. Why was Rita at the hospital?

Chapter Twenty-Nine

July 5, ten years ago

It was not quite noon when Rita Mae came down from her high. That was the good thing about crack, she thought. It didn't take much of your day.

Now, to get her favorite shoes back. She remembered the discomfort of walking through Alberta Resnick's back yard, so she must have left them in the pool house. She didn't want to face the old lady – didn't want to tell her she'd been in the pool house with her grandson who was a decade younger. She'd just slip in and out. It was so overgrown back there no one in the main house would see her.

Rita Mae's parents had moved to the suburbs of Atlanta to help Rita Mae's sister care for her children. Rita Mae now lived on Grambling's Eastside, in an apartment complex with fourteen identical buildings and decently cared for grounds and pool. She put on dark-colored long pants and long sleeves, for protection against shrubbery, then socks and tennis shoes to cushion her sore feet. She found her faded Chevy Tahoe parked in its normal spot, and with a sigh of relief set out to retrace her route of the previous evening.

She parked the Tahoe in the parking lot of the Methodist church on North Main Street. There were enough cars there so it wouldn't draw attention. She set out for Mrs Resnick's house two blocks away.

The day was sticky with humidity, and when she turned onto Conestee Avenue, no one was stirring in the mid-day heat. Rita Mae walked unnoticed along the buckled sidewalks that occasionally reared up four inches or more from the persistent push of oak roots. She circled the block, not wanting to approach the Resnick property from the front. Fortunately, it looked as if the neighbors to the rear were gone for the holiday weekend.

Rita Mae walked up their empty driveway, then through the jumble of woods that separated their back yard from Mrs Resnick's. The underbrush snagged and yanked at her pants, and she was glad she hadn't worn shorts. She emerged on the far side of Mrs Resnick's pool, directly across from the pool house. She walked around the pool, thinking to try the front door before resorting to the bathroom window. She was in luck again. Ben hadn't bolted the door; the knob turned at her touch.

She tiptoed through the recreation room and into the bedroom where they'd been the night before. She didn't see her shoes at first, and wondered if she'd lost them later. But then she saw the slight bump of the chenille spread and flipped it back to reveal her colorfully striped sandals.

Grabbing them, she quickly exited the pool house without a sound. She was almost to the place where she intended to enter the woods when she heard voices and a dog barking; the sounds came from the main house.

She wavered for a moment. Nobody had seen her, and if she cut straight through the neighbor's yard, in all probability no one would.

Mrs Resnick's voice rang out, commanding as always, but with an unaccustomed shrillness. Rita Mae was surprised at how well she could hear, but then she realized the house's back door was only thirty feet from where she stood. The density of the shrubbery and trees made it seem further.

She heard another voice, but it was pitched lower. She couldn't make out the words, partly because the dog's yapping was growing increasingly frenzied.

Mrs Resnick's voice came again, shriller still. Something wasn't right. Rita Mae's curiosity overrode her caution. She crept behind the tree line, and inched toward the main house. She hid behind a massive magnolia, confident that no one could see her. The tree's heavy leaves obscured the detached garage, and much of the parking area. But she could see Mrs Resnick standing in her kitchen doorway in a pink dress, one hand on her hip, giving somebody what-for. An obnoxious chihuahua danced at her feet, yipping in a continuous blast.

The other person's back was to Rita Mae, so she couldn't hear any words. But apparently Mrs Resnick could, and didn't like what she heard. She abruptly slammed her kitchen door with such force its window panes rattled.

Who is that? Rita Mae stared intently at the person's back, unable to tell by the jeans and T-shirt if it was a man or woman. *A family member?*

Then again, she had heard the stories, whispered at last night's party, about a man living in Mrs Resnick's pool house this spring. Was that him? From Mrs Resnick's anger, it seemed likely. If so, she was probably calling the police right now. Rita Mae had best get going.

Before she could creep from beneath the magnolia's embrace, however, the person leaned over into the flower bed that flanked the parking area, chose a river rock the size of a softball, reared back and hurled it through the window pane.

Rita Mae stifled a cry, too shocked to run. She heard Mrs Resnick's scream of rage from inside, heard the dog's bark rising in hysteria. Before thrusting a hand inside the broken pane, knocking shards both inside and out, the rock-thrower whipped around to look at the nearest neighbor's house, then at the deep foliage where Rita Mae hid.

In that moment, Rita Mae recognized the face.

CHAPTER THIRTY

It took Branigan nearly ten minutes to drive through 5 o'clock traffic to St Joseph Medical Center, a mile and a half from downtown. She turned off the radio so she could think, and her mind ran perversely to Detroit. *What if I were facing real 5 o'clock traffic?* she thought crazily.

She parked in a lot beside the emergency room, then ran as fast as her heels would allow up its circular drive. A metal detector took another two minutes. "If you want to keep your cell," said the security guard, "you need to turn it off." She tapped it off without looking.

Two volunteers sat at the information desk. "Rita…" she said, then stopped short at their blank faces. She didn't know Rita's last name.

Branigan looked around wildly, hoping Liam was waiting for her. She turned back to the volunteers. "'Rita' is all I know. She's homeless."

"Oh, you're clergy," one volunteer said. "Your colleague is already here." Branigan didn't correct her. "Your lady is in Trauma Bay 4."

Branigan nodded her thanks and ran to the door they indicated. She followed some rather confusing signage until she saw cubicles marked with numbers, encircling a large nurse's station. In the fourth cubicle, she saw Liam pressed against a wall, white-faced, trying to leave enough room for the doctor and two nurses bending over the bed. If Rita was in the bed, Branigan couldn't see her.

A young woman holding a Bible turned. *Chaplain*, Branigan read on her nametag.

180

"May I help you?" she asked.

"Time of death, 5:33 p.m.," said the doctor.

Abruptly, Branigan's adrenaline was gone, and she sagged into a chair in the hallway. Liam conferred for awhile with the chaplain, then motioned for Branigan to accompany him. "Let's get some coffee," he said, leading her on a byzantine pathway to the hospital cafeteria. They poured coffee and paid in silence, then chose a small table well away from the early diners.

"Tell me," she said.

"Rita had the chaplain call the church," Liam said. "She told her she was a member at Jericho and wanted to speak to me. She wasn't, but that doesn't matter. The chaplain didn't think she would last long, so I called you and drove right over."

"But what happened?"

"Hit-and-run."

"Oh no! Again? When? Where?"

"Around midnight. On Conestee Avenue."

"Mrs Resnick's street? How did I not know?" She grabbed her phone from her purse and sure enough saw two missed calls from Jody. But they were received well after 5 o'clock that afternoon.

"I guess because it wasn't a fatality at first?" Liam hazarded. "Your police reporter isn't looking at all traffic accidents."

"Yeah, but to think we were running around all day trying to find her and she was right here. My story on Vesuvius's hit-and-run ran *yesterday*! They couldn't let me know there was another one? I gotta get back to the newsroom."

Liam wasn't listening to her hissy fit. He looked pensive, stricken even.

"Sorry," she said. "Did she say anything to you? Rita, I mean."

"Not really. She was rambling. They had started morphine."

"But what did she call you for? To talk about God? Or hell? What?"

"Yeah."

"What did she want to know?"

"The usual. Did I believe in heaven and hell? Did I think God could forgive her?"

Branigan stared at Liam. He wouldn't meet her eyes. Why was he being strange about this? Did he think she wouldn't understand the pastoral part of his job?

She waited him out.

"I read her the twenty-third psalm," he said finally. "There's nothing better for someone who's dying."

She tried one more time. "But nothing about an old lady getting stabbed or her getting rich or anything like that?"

"No, nothing like that. I promise I'd tell you anything like that, Brani G."

Maybe so. But there sure is something you're not telling me.

CHAPTER THIRTY-ONE

Liam trotted from the hospital, ducking the huge raindrops that a thunderstorm had blown in. Some weeks, especially as it got hotter and more humid, there'd be one of these every afternoon. It was as if the air got so suffocating that it reached a tipping point. Black clouds rolled in, thunder crashed, lightning bolted, and the temperature plunged twenty degrees. Then came fat drops of welcome rain.

There were other kinds of summer, summers of drought, when the endless sunshine went on and on, unbroken, unabated. Lakes shrank. Crops shriveled. Cows languished. So it was an unspoken rule: no one besides Little League coaches complained of afternoon rain.

But today, Liam hardly noticed the cool, heavy drops. He hopped into his SUV and drove to the church. He left it in the Jericho Road parking lot, and splashed through the sliding doors. He turned right for the receptionist's office, locked for the evening. Shelter curfew was monitored out of the staff lounge down the hall. He fumbled for his office key and unlocked the receptionist's door, slid open the top drawer of the desk and found a ring with a single key on it. The key to the cargo van.

Liam locked up and headed back into the rain. Then he did something he'd never done before. He jumped into the bulky cargo van and drove it home.

The Delaneys lived in a downtown neighborhood in the process of regentrification. Liam and Liz had bought the two-story red brick house as newlyweds nineteen years before, when they had two steady, if small, salaries. At that time, the neighborhood along

183

the western end of Oakley was wavering, with half rentals and half homeowners. It wasn't at all certain which way these blocks would go. But Liz's eye was unerring, and soon the Delaney property was alive with roses and geraniums and lantana in the sun, and in the shade of towering hardwoods, azaleas and blue hostas as big as tires. The rental next door was purchased and refurbished by new owners who moved in; then, like dominos, the next was purchased, and the next. Now, the neighborhood was almost entirely owner-occupied, and the value of the Delaney house had tripled.

Liam pulled the van into his cracked driveway, seeing Liz's car and the twins' Jeep parked ahead of him. That didn't mean both Charlie and Chan were home. They split their car time, and rode bikes on alternate days.

Liam ducked under the car port, entering the house through the unlocked kitchen door. Liz stood at the refrigerator, pulling out salad ingredients. "Hi, hon. Dinner in half an hour?"

"That's fine. Is Chan home?"

"Upstairs."

Liam dashed off in search of his son, taking the stairs two at a time.

He rapped on Chan's bedroom door, scarcely waiting for a reply before pushing it open. He closed it behind him, so he didn't see Charlie creep up to listen through the crack.

"Hi, Dad. What's up?"

"I drove the church van home," Liam said.

Chan kept his face straight, but Liam glimpsed a nervous swallow. "Yeah?"

"I know you've sometimes 'borrowed' it when it was Charlie's turn in the Jeep. Did you borrow it last night?"

"No. Yesterday was my turn for the Jeep."

Liam thought for a moment. He did remember seeing Charlie come in on her bike shortly after he returned home from evening service. For the first time in the last hour, he allowed his shoulders to relax. He blew out a breath, and laughed.

Chan looked at him oddly.

"Okay, so where were you last night?"

"Well," said Chan, "you saw me at the 6 o'clock service, right?" Liam nodded.

"Then Winston and Mark and I went for burgers, then swimming at Mark's club." Liam knew Mark's parents were members of Peach Orchard Country Club. "The pool was open 'til eleven 'cause it was opening weekend. Then I came home. Why?"

Liam was so relieved, he saw no harm in answering Chan's question.

"Kind of a long story. But there was a hit-and-run of one of our homeless women last night. Rita."

"Oh, no. Dad, I'm sorry."

"Anyway, she wasn't killed instantly. She asked to see me at the hospital before she died this afternoon. And when I got there, what she wanted to tell me…" Liam hesitated, not sure whether to burden his son with this.

"You have to tell me now, Dad."

"What she wanted to tell me was… it was our church van."

Chan looked as if someone had sucker-punched him. He swallowed again. "The church van ran her over?"

"I think that's what she was saying. This morning, Branigan and I noticed a strong smell of bleach on the front bumper. So you can see why I was scared when I thought you had borrowed it."

"Jeez, Dad."

"I'm not saying you'd deliberately hit someone and leave the scene. With Rita being so little, the driver might not have realized he hit a person."

"But the bleach?" Chan said. "That says he knew."

"Yeah. Now I have to ask the staff. And the volunteers. Even the shelter residents could have sneaked that key." Liam stood up. "I'm just glad it wasn't you." He grabbed his son in a fierce hug, giving the top of his blond head a "noogie", as Chan had called the headlock when he was five. Then he turned and left the room, unaware of the gentle closing of his daughter's door across the hallway.

He leaned against the wall. His reporter instincts were not just kicking in: they were kicking and screaming. Chan was telling the truth about not driving the cargo van yesterday.

But he wasn't telling the truth about everything.

Chapter Thirty-Two

A nother friggin' hit-and-run of a homeless person and the newsroom hadn't called her? What the heck was going on over there?

Branigan parked her Civic with a screech, and ran into the pouring rain. She dashed past the newspaper's security desk, and bounded up the stairs, too angry to wait for the elevator. Tan saw her first and barked, "Help Jody with a 1A for tomorrow's edition. He's already got something online."

Jody met her next, his hands held up in surrender. "We didn't know, Branigan. We didn't figure out it was a homeless woman until after 5 o'clock. I started calling you, but it went to voice mail."

"How could you not know?"

"It wasn't on the police scanner last night. All they had was a traffic injury on Conestee. No fatality. I was tied up in court all day, and didn't get to the police station until five. That's when I saw the report that said the victim was possibly homeless. We started calling the hospital, you, Jericho Road, the gospel mission, anyplace else we could think of."

For the second time in an hour, she sagged. "It's my fault," she admitted. "I haven't been working with the police on this story. If I had been, maybe they would've called me."

"For now, can you pull together some quotes from your sources and I'll feed you the new stuff? We don't have much."

"She died, you know. At 5:33."

"Yeah. I got that already."

"Okay." Branigan went to work.

By the time she looked up again it was 8:55. The gospel mission's phone privileges extended only from eight to nine. She punched in Davison's cell phone number, and was relieved when he picked up.

"Brani G! I was afraid you'd forgotten me."

"No way," she said. "It's just been a busy day. How are you?"

"Truthfully? Shaky. Not so much physically as the other stuff."

"Are they feeding you well?"

"Sure."

"What did you do all day?"

"Got assigned a counselor. Met in a group. Mandatory chapel. Bible study."

"They don't waste any time."

"Idle hands and all that."

"I guess so." She didn't want to tell him about Rita. If the mission subscribed to the newspaper, he'd find out in the morning, but she didn't want to share the news over the phone. So instead she said, "Davison? There are a lot of people pulling for you."

"I know. Thanks for calling. Love you." He hung up.

She went back to work. So far, her frantic pace had allowed her to keep a creeping question at bay: was she responsible for Rita's death? Had her poking around unloosed the killer the psychics warned her about?

Jody and Branigan merged their two stories into what they hoped was a seamless narrative. Branigan called the director of the gospel mission and the president of the Grambling Homeless Coalition, a collection of public and non-profit agencies that served the homeless. She pulled liberally from Sunday's story on Vesuvius and his dad.

Jody worked the police investigation. Apparently no one on Conestee Avenue had been awake at midnight on Sunday. Asleep in their air-conditioned houses, the neighbors had heard nothing, seen nothing.

But there was plenty of consternation inside the police department, Jody said, because of the previously unsolved hit-and-run. Chief Warren personally responded to Jody's call rather than sending him to the public information officer. And Jody did get one vital piece of information Branigan had missed – Rita's last name: Jones.

After they'd filed the story online and for the next morning's edition, Tan, Jody and Branigan met in Tan's office. She brought her notebook.

"Obviously," Tan began, "this changes things. We're moving homeless stories to the front burner. Two hit-and-runs in two weeks? What the hell is going on?"

"There's more," Branigan said. "We couldn't put this in tonight's story because nothing is nailed down yet." She hesitated.

"Spit it out, Powers," Tan growled.

"These homeless deaths could be connected to Mrs Resnick's murder."

Tan sat back in his chair, clearly startled. Jody's eyes widened. He was the first to speak.

"I knew you were looking at transients. It panned out?"

"I... I... don't know yet." She laid out what she'd learned as coherently as she could, starting with Rita.

She told them Dontegan's story first, because it had taken place more than five years earlier. He reported a drunken Rita saying – she flipped through the notebook to get it exactly – "I could be rich if I wanna be. I tell about Ol' High and Mighty gettin' her nasty self stabbed, I be off these streets and on Easy Street."

She told them of Malachi's assertion to Liam that Rita said she "might get rich" if she told what she knew "about some old lady getting murdered" and that a "rich-ass family would pay to keep it quiet". Branigan admitted that she didn't know when the conversation took place, but that Malachi and Vesuvius heard it. And Vesuvius was dead.

Then she told about Jess's account of Max Brody's wad of money and his comment: "'This evening's drunk is courtesy of an old lady who had the good sense to get stabbed.' Or maybe 'the good taste to get stabbed'.

"I'm still trying to find Max Brody," she added.

She told them that the man who'd lived in Mrs Resnick's

pool house, Billy Shepherd, alias Demetrius, might be back in town, though she hadn't confirmed it. And that Mrs Resnick's granddaughter, Ashley, overheard her cousin Ben Brissey Jr say on the night of July 4 that a second person had been living in Mrs Resnick's pool house.

"And to top it all off, Ramsey Resnick volunteers at Jericho Road."

"Good Lord!" Tan-4 exploded.

"I'm not saying I understand it yet," Branigan said. "Any of it. But there seems to be some strong links between the Resnicks and the homeless."

"Okay, here's what we're going to do." Tan rubbed his meaty hands together. "Branigan, I want you to continue on the Resnick murder anniversary. But I want it moved up to run this Sunday.

"Jody, you stay on the Rita Jones death, with updates online and a new story daily. And the hit-and-run of the guy whose name sounds like a volcano. See if they're connected. Who would you like to help pull together an overall piece on homelessness in Grambling?"

"Marjorie," the reporters answered in unison.

"Okay. Send her home with background reading tonight. Anything else?"

Branigan asked, "Should I share my information with the police?"

Tan thought for a moment. "Not yet. They may leak it to TV. Anyway, they've had their turn at this. For ten damn years. Now go get some sleep."

Branigan wasn't sure that was going to be possible.

Chapter Thirty-Three

Branigan was back in the newsroom before eight on Tuesday morning. Unable to sleep the night before, wondering if her digging into the Resnick murder had prompted Rita's death, she'd finally gotten out of bed and made a list.

Number 1: Talk to Ben Brissey Jr about why he thought a second person was living in his grandmother's pool house.

Number 2: See if the police had any information on why Rita Jones was on Conestee Avenue Sunday night. Could she have been living in the pool house, either recently or ten years ago?

Number 3: Look through the pool house.

Ben Jr hadn't returned Branigan's call from yesterday, so she phoned him again at his New York office. She got his voice mail. Then she called his mother at the lake house. Amanda gave her his cell phone number.

Branigan called that number and he picked up. "I'm so sorry I didn't get back to you, Miss Powers," he apologized. "I had you on my list for today. How can I help you?"

His tone was a pleasant surprise.

"As your mother may have told you, we are looking into your grandmother's murder. It's been ten years next month and it's the only unsolved homicide in Grambling." That last part wasn't technically true any more, but Ben Jr wouldn't put the hit-and-runs of homeless people into the same category – even if he was aware of them.

"Yes, Mom did tell me."

"On the night of the July 4 party, your cousin Ashley said several of you went swimming."

"That's right."

191

"She also said she overheard you say that someone else was living in the pool house. I assume you meant someone besides Billy Shepherd?"

"You're taxing my memory, Miss Powers. Billy Shepherd – is that the name of the man Uncle Ramsey found living in the pool house? And who tried to play Grandmother's piano?"

"Yes, it is."

"Okay. I remember now. But first, let me explain something. I was a douche bag in those days."

Branigan choked back a laugh. "Um, okay."

"I've been in AA for two years. I don't know how much you know about AA, but we do a lot of looking back, a lot of soul searching. I'm not proud of who I was then."

"I'm familiar with Alcoholics Anonymous."

"At any rate, I was drinking that night. Pretty heavily. I went into the pool house to get some swim trunks. Broke in, in fact." He chuckled. "The police asked me plenty about that. Anyway, when I was looking in the bedroom for my trunks, I found stacks of books that I knew weren't Grandmother's."

"How did you know that?"

"Well, for one thing, they'd not been there all the other times I'd been in the pool house. And for another, there's no way she'd be reading them. They weren't Dickens or Tolstoy or Hardy, and they weren't her typical book club material. More like first-rate modern fiction."

"And so you thought...?"

"And so I thought someone besides a mentally deficient fellow must have been there too."

"Did you tell the police? I didn't see anything about a second person in their files."

"I honestly don't remember. But I doubt it. They were asking me about my relationship with my parents and my grandmother, and if Drew or I had gambling debts, stuff like that. Since we were from Atlanta, they weren't asking us anything to do with Grambling."

That made sense.

She asked Ben a few more questions about his time at the pool, and heard a repeat of what Caroline and Ashley had said. She was uttering a few last-minute pleasantries on autopilot when, almost without thinking, she posed her standard final question: "Is there anything else you can think of that I haven't asked?"

"Well, at the time, I sure wasn't mentioning this to the police," said Ben. "But the statute of limitations has run out." He laughed. "We found and smoked some crack that night in the pool house."

That stopped Branigan short. "Crack? Was it Billy's?"

"Probably. Or whoever else was in there. I'm assuming it wasn't Grandmother's." Ben chuckled again.

"You said 'we' smoked crack. You and Drew?"

"Oh, no, I had enough decency not to pull Drew into my craziness. It was me and an older woman at the party. Rena. No, that's not right. Resa. No, Rita. That's it. Rita Mae."

Branigan clinched the phone more tightly.

"There was a Rita Mae at the Fourth of July party?" Even to her own ears, her voice sounded squeaky. "What was her last name?"

"I don't think she ever told me."

Branigan's mind was racing. How could this be?

"Can you describe her?" she asked. "I mean, was she... homeless?"

"Homeless?" Ben said. "No. I mean, she sure didn't look homeless. She looked like everybody else at the party."

"And she was at the party?" Branigan knew she was repeating herself.

"Sure."

"Describe her to me, please."

"She was short – petite, I guess you'd say. Blond hair. Nice tan. Good-looking. Wearing one of those summer tops that are bare at the shoulder. Halter tops, I think they're called. Maybe thirty to thirty-five, somewhere in that range."

"Was she a neighbor? Did she live nearby?"

"I have no idea. I'd never met her before. And as I said, I was pretty drunk. We didn't talk much before we fired up a rock. Then she disappeared."

"Did she bring drugs to the party?"

"No, we found them in the pool house. Actually, I found them before she got there. She asked if Grandmother had something stronger than bourbon. I guess I was trying to impress her, so I showed her. We smoked. I must have fallen asleep, 'cause when I woke up she was gone and so was the rest of the crack."

"She stole your crack?"

"Well, yeah. She stole somebody's crack."

This was sounding a little more like Rita. Movement in Branigan's peripheral vision caught her attention, and she looked up. Jody was waving excitedly from his desk. She thanked Ben and told him she'd call back if she needed anything else.

Jody was beside her desk by the time she put the phone down.

"The police tracked down Rita Mae Jones," he said. "She wasn't a transient at all. Grew up right here in Grambling. Graduated from Montclair High on the Eastside. Worked awhile at the Eastside Mall in one of the department stores. Arrested for stealing from the store. Then went off the grid. She was arrested more recently for drugs and prostitution. Her parents live in Atlanta. They're on their way to ID the body."

"I'll go one better," Branigan said. "She was at Mrs Resnick's Fourth of July party."

CHAPTER THIRTY-FOUR

Tuesday was Liam's sermon writing day, but no writing was getting done.

He was torn. He thought it likely that the cargo van from Jericho Road had run over Rita. Her dying accusation and the fact that the front bumper had been cleaned with bleach were pretty damning.

He thought it unlikely that Chan had been the driver: Chan had the Jeep and no need to borrow the van, even should he want to sneak out and drink and do whatever else eighteen-year-old boys did. So that concern was lifted.

So why not report it to the police? He was leaning that way.

But he was hesitating. Why? He searched his conscience for an answer, and wasn't quite sure.

The church was a sanctuary – he certainly believed that. He didn't worry about the vows of the confessional, as the Catholics did. But there had to be something that set the church apart from the world.

He remembered the transient from last summer who was so belligerent that Liam banned him from the dining hall for a month. The man then ran up on the stage and flung himself across Liam's pulpit. "Religious asylum!" he shrieked. "I'm seeking religious asylum!"

Liam chuckled at the memory. No, he wasn't confusing silliness with theology. There was something else niggling at his brain.

He leaned back in his desk chair and closed his eyes. Rita was killed on Conestee Avenue, the most prestigious address in Grambling. Mrs Resnick's street, in fact. What was she doing there?

Police hadn't solved Vesuvius's death, perhaps hadn't even tried very hard, given the victim. What if – Liam bolted upright at the thought – what if he was killed by the church van as well?

Oh God, what if someone connected to the church had killed two of its homeless parishioners? The place might close down. All his hard work would be for naught if people thought it was a harbor for murderers.

Liam stood and paced his office. He looked at its artwork — two canvases depicting Jesus' crucifixion, an intricate Celtic cross purchased during a trip to Scotland, a crucifix given by a grateful job-seeker. He sat heavily in the green-upholstered rocker, put his head in his hands, and prayed to the God who'd hung on a cross.

He started for the prayer room down the hall. He often got more clarity in that quiet and sacred space. But before he could leave his office, the phone rang.

Chapter Thirty-Five

"Liam?" Branigan asked. "Can you come to Mrs Resnick's? Everything points back to the pool house, so Jody and I are going through it again. We'd love to have your eye."

He hesitated for a moment, but assented. Branigan ended the call.

Marjorie was at the Grambling Rescue Mission, getting a crash course in homelessness – lack of affordable housing, medical crises, mental health issues, addiction, unemployment, day labor, and the lingering effects of a felony or sex offense on one's record.

Jody and Branigan stood on Conestee Avenue, in front of Mrs Resnick's gracious old house, its front porch invitingly shady. It was quiet this mid-morning, and Branigan was beginning to think of the house itself as a *grande dame*. A *grande dame* with secrets.

"What do you know, Old Girl?" she whispered.

Branigan knew from her parents that the Resnick heirs had been unable to sell it. The murder was too publicized, too gory, too distasteful for the kind of people who would otherwise treasure such a house. Instead, Heath and Ramsey Resnick rented it to high-level executives who moved in and out of Grambling's diversifying industries with some regularity.

She and Jody had discussed sneaking onto the property and asking forgiveness later. But they gambled that if they asked Ramsey to let them look around, he would. They were right.

The police, meantime, were working the same street, canvassing neighbors, measuring tire marks, trying to get something, anything, on the incident that had killed Rita. *The Rambler*'s online letters to the editor reflected outrage at the casual dispatching of the city's homeless. The irony that their deaths inspired indignation in a way their lives hadn't wasn't lost on the reporters.

Ramsey had told them no one was home, so they walked up the driveway and around the back without knocking. The hedge separating the parking area from the back yard was neatly trimmed – and standing half as high as Branigan remembered from a decade before. They stepped onto the pathway and found it unencumbered by shrubbery or tree limbs.

"Apparently, they let landscapers in after Mrs Resnick died," Jody said.

"They probably couldn't rent it otherwise."

The maintenance stopped with the yard, however. The pool was empty, covered by an electric blue tarp. The pool house looked abandoned. A pile of outdoor furniture under another blue tarp was partially protected by the roof's overhang.

Jody had Ramsey's front door key. It took some wrestling, but finally the bolt slid open with a thump, and he and Branigan entered the recreation room. As well as they could remember, it was unchanged.

They walked to the bedroom. Branigan went straight to the bureau Ben Jr had described, and pulled open the top drawer. Empty except for a blackened spoon. Odd. The second drawer revealed faded bathing suits, women's and men's. In the third, she found the paperbacks – not cheap or lurid, but high quality.

She flipped through the covers: *Ironweed*, *Requiem for a Dream*, *Cold Sassy Tree*, *One Flew Over the Cuckoo's Nest*, *The Old Man and the Sea*, *The Shipping News*. She reached to the very bottom: *Invisible Man*. She agreed with Ben's assessment – first rate.

"Branigan!" They heard a shout from outside. "Jody!"

"Back here, Liam!" Jody called.

The men shook hands, did some kind of guy-thing shoulder bump. "Good to see you, buddy," Jody said. "How's the gospel game?"

"It has its moments."

Branigan brought Liam up to date on what they had learned about Rita Mae Jones, and what Ben Brissey Jr had said about her presence at the Fourth of July party.

"I didn't even know her last name," Liam admitted, rifling through the bureau drawers. "You say they did crack in here? That explains the spoon."

"That's why we needed you," she said. "So the spoon was used to heat crack."

The three split up and walked silently from room to room. Branigan thought about the police files she'd read and tried to imagine where Billy Shepherd had slept. Everything mentioned in the files – his blankets, food, cigarettes – had been found in the main recreation room. Had someone else been in the back bedroom? If so, did Billy know? Was it a girlfriend? Another homeless man?

And Rita? She'd been in these very rooms on the night of the party. But she wasn't homeless then. She was a party guest – a guest attractive enough to catch the eye of young Ben Brissey Jr.

Did she return the next day and kill Mrs Resnick? Did the guilt drive her into addiction? *God help me*, Branigan thought, *but I hope she did. That's better than me getting an innocent woman killed.*

Unfortunately, the downward angle of the stab wounds suggested not. So did she see something that got her killed? And if so, why ten years later?

Branigan was getting a headache. She trailed after Liam and Jody as they walked outside. Liam circled the pool house once, then began a second lap. He had a puzzled look on his face.

In a moment, he called from the rear, "Brani G, come look at this!"

The landscapers' pruning had not extended to the back of the pool house. It was much wilder back there, with only a few feet of stone pavers before the woods encroached. Liam took her by the shoulders and marched her to the far corner of the property where a mighty cedar stretched its floppy branches toward the building.

"Look at the pool house from this angle," he commanded. She stood for a moment, uncomprehending, gazing at the towering trees and undergrowth crowding the house. Then she gasped, and took off running for the pool side of the house, toward the jumble of covered furniture. She yanked the tarp off. And there beside a stack of plastic-strapped lounge chairs was what she was looking for: two Adirondack chairs, up-ended.

Jody was staring, mystified, from Branigan to Liam.

"The psychics," she told him. "This is the house a psychic drew. She said Mrs Resnick's killer hid out here."

CHAPTER THIRTY-SIX

Alberta Resnick answered the back door, brushing crumbs from her hands. She took one look and opened the door without hesitation, a quizzical look, maybe even a half-smile, on her face.

That was before the request for money. Then her face closed, contemptuously it seemed. The question didn't come again. It was a demand the second time. She slammed the door.

Her yelling began when the rock shattered the window panes. Then it had to stop, didn't it? All that noise had to stop before someone heard.

It didn't take a lot. Four, maybe six, thrusts of the knife snatched from a wooden block on her kitchen counter. It wasn't intentional. Not really. There had been a genuine fondness between them once. But the angry, accusatory screams had to stop.

She could have prevented this. All it would have taken was money, and she had plenty. But she wasn't afraid; she complained about her interrupted lunch. That was a little surprising, her lack of fear. Even her screaming wasn't fear. That was rage, pure rage.

The same cold rage she'd directed at Billy, when Billy wanted to live in her pool house, when he inexplicably wanted to play her piano.

Now the rage had seeped out along with her blood, puddling, trailing from her thin contorted body. But the noise continued from her yapping dog. It sounded loud, but surely no one outside the house could hear it. A half-hearted kick to the chihuahua sent it skidding across the linoleum.

Now for the money. She used to call it her "ice cream money", and kept it in the freezer. Decades ago, when her husband was still alive, she'd give Ramsey or Amanda or Heath a few dollars to buy treats from the ice cream truck for the grandchildren or neighborhood children.

Mrs Resnick didn't like things to change, so chances were she still kept money in her freezer. A yank of the top door of the ancient appliance revealed an aluminum-foil-wrapped package the length of a brick, but slimmer. It slid easily inside a shirt pocket.

That's when the visitor saw the blood. Not the blood on the floor – its pools were pristine, untouched. But her blood had spattered all over the visitor's shirt and, yes, the pants as well.

The visitor glanced around, suddenly frantic. Were there fingerprints? Straddling her body, again being careful not to step in the blood, tugging the steak knife from her chest. In that moment, the sickness hit.

The visitor looked around wildly, spotted the old woman's car keys hanging from a wooden peg beside the wall phone, and grabbed them, not thinking clearly, not thinking at all really, just obeying an almost primitive instinct to get far, far from this place.

Wiping off the door knob with a shirt tail, the visitor darted out for a quick look. No one was around. Across the parking area and through the side door into the detached garage. The old woman's quarter-century-old Thunderbird was crowded by a wheelbarrow, dirt-encrusted flower pots, tools, half-empty bags of fertilizer, potting soil, mulch – the detritus of a once-avid gardener, long sidelined. But hanging from rusty hooks were ragged gardening clothes, men's clothes, so worn and dirty they looked like they might fall apart at a touch.

The visitor grabbed a pair of jeans and a long-sleeved work shirt, thankful that Mr Resnick had been a big man, pulling the clothes over blood-spattered ones and hiding the one thing that might scare someone, might make someone notice an otherwise unnoticeable person.

Lifting the garage door manually, the visitor backed the T-bird out, then had the presence of mind to exit the car, pull the door back down and wipe the surfaces. Back in the car, heart accelerating, the visitor's body boomeranged in and out of panic. The heart flutter hit again backing down the driveway, going too fast, squealing into the street, stopping abruptly, then consciously keeping a steady foot to drive down Conestee. Passing a teenager on a bicycle, the visitor was careful to turn away.

What now? Back to Atlanta?

An idea came. Billy. Weren't the police already looking at Billy? The poor guy – he might as well live in prison. He wouldn't know any difference, most likely.

Billy was probably in some homeless encampment, maybe even that abandoned grocery store.

This could work. Of course, the old woman's car would have to be ditched. It had been handy for getting out of the neighborhood unseen. But it was too recognizable. There ahead was the sprawling grocery store, windows broken, baking in the mid-day sun. Pulling in, the visitor left the T-bird, checking that the knife was in Mr Resnick's pants, pocketing the keys to dispose of later, wiping the steering wheel clean of sweat.

Then the visitor glanced around and began walking. Should anyone see these shabby clothes they'd make a quick assessment: homeless. Then they'd look away. That's what people usually did.

CHAPTER THIRTY-SEVEN

Chan came up behind Malachi in the Jericho Road dining hall. When his mom was working late, he liked to come down and eat at the church, then help the men clean up. The shelter residents and the homeless people who ate here were always pleasant to him: he was, after all, Pastor Liam's son. But he wanted something more. He wanted to understand their lives. He wanted to forge relationships apart from his dad.

Malachi was his favorite. The two often worked side by side, not necessarily speaking, but moving in tandem, one sweeping, one holding the dustbin, one lifting the trash bag, one tying it off to prevent leaks.

Chan returned from a trash run to the parking lot to help Malachi stack the chairs on the tables, the last step before mopping.

"You 'bout ready for college?" Malachi asked.

"Nah, I've got two months before orientation. Lots to get into before then."

They lifted a few more chairs, placing them upside down on the long tables.

"Did you go to college, Malachi? Or straight into the military?"

"Directly into the US Army. Desert Storm."

"Were your dad and granddad Army too?"

Malachi looked at Chan. What was it with all the questions about his family, back at the library and now?

"No, just me."

"My dad went to Georgia. That's where Charlie's going."

"Uh-huh."

"I wanted something different, you know? Nobody in our family has gone to Furman. I won't run into my whole high school class there either."

"Uh-huh."

"Nobody will care who my family is."

Malachi stacked a few more chairs. "Mr Chan, you got a problem with your fam'ly?"

Chan took a long moment to answer. "Not a problem," he said slowly. "But do you ever worry if who they are determines who you are?"

Malachi had no idea what the young man was getting at. But he seemed to have a problem with Pastor Liam, and quite frankly that aggravated Malachi.

"No, Mr Chan. I got plenty to worry 'bout besides that. None of my fam'ly is livin'. Maybe you best count your blessings like your daddy say."

Chan looked at him, stung. Malachi was right. He shouldn't be complaining, least of all to someone like Malachi, who lived alone on the street, without family, without a dad in the picture at all.

But Malachi wasn't finished. "You afraid of endin' up a good man, a man who helps people, a minister of God?"

Chan shook his head. He didn't answer, but no, that wasn't his fear at all.

CHAPTER THIRTY-EIGHT

Liam, Jody and Branigan walked down Conestee Avenue to the site of Sunday night's hit-and-run that killed Rita. Jody knew most of the policemen and pointed Liam to the senior ranking officer.

"I think I may have the vehicle responsible," he told the policeman.

Thirty minutes later, Liam and Branigan were sitting in Chief Warren's office, along with Chester Scovoy, the detective in charge, and three other officers. Per Tan's instructions, Branigan didn't intend to tell them all of her suspicions about the pool house and Rita's attendance at the Fourth of July party. But Liam was right: they couldn't withhold Rita's deathbed charge that the church van had run her over, a charge that still had Branigan shaking her head in disbelief. And now that the police had the van in custody, they could smell the bleach.

"You know we had another hit-and-run in late May," Liam said. "Will you be able to tell if our van hit Vesuvius Hightower too?"

Detective Scovoy looked startled. "Why would you think that?"

Liam shrugged. "I don't, exactly. But I couldn't have imagined our van hitting Rita either. Since V's death hasn't been solved..." He trailed off.

"We'll get everything we can from the bumper," Scovoy said. "But between the bleach and the rain and the time elapsed, I'm not hopeful." He stopped for a moment, looking at Liam. "Are we looking for someone inside your organization who has a vendetta against the homeless?"

Liam looked miserable. He held up his palms. "Believe me, I'm as confused as you are."

"Well," said Scovoy briskly, "I'll need a list of everyone who has access to the van key. We'll start questioning your staff this afternoon. And then volunteers and whoever else has access."

"Branigan," said Chief Warren, "I know you were looking into the Alberta Resnick murder. You told me you were going to be looking at the possibility of a homeless person with no real motive. Now a homeless woman turns up dead on the same street. Any connection?"

"I wish I knew, Chief," she said. "I'm talking to Mrs Resnick's family and Liam's guys at Jericho Road, and trying to track down gossip. Something somebody overheard. Something somebody remembered. But I don't have anything nailed down."

He and Scovoy looked at her intently. She braced for a scolding about withholding information. But the chief surprised her.

"In my experience, Branigan, it's not when things get nailed down that they become dangerous. It's when they are shaken loose. I would caution you to keep Detective Scovoy in the loop. This is not about who gets the credit. I like to think we're bigger than that. This is about safety. Your safety. And from the looks of things, maybe the safety of our homeless citizens."

Branigan let Liam answer the questions about the van and the key. He explained that Jericho Road's reception office was open seven days a week, with staff, volunteers and even shelter residents coming and going freely. Dontegan was in charge of the sign-out sheet, but the van hadn't been signed out on the nights of Vesuvius's or Rita's death. No surprise there.

Branigan had no choice but to leave that angle to the police. Her focus needed to be on the Resnick murder story scheduled to run on the upcoming weekend.

But she had heard Chief Warren loud and clear. Things got dangerous when they were shaken loose. That was pretty much what the psychics had said: someone thought he got away with murder. Now he – or she – wasn't so sure.

Chapter Thirty-Nine

C hester Scovoy wasn't a native of Grambling. He'd started out as a police officer in Charleston, South Carolina, and had proved quite adept. After he made detective, he moved on to Atlanta, the murder capital in the most violent country in the world, to his mind. Oh, the FBI would tell you that Baltimore, Detroit, Cleveland, St Louis, Kansas City, Newark, Oakland, Philadelphia and New Orleans – especially post-Katrina New Orleans – were worse. But if you were going to live in the *real* South and work homicide, you wanted Atlanta. Or Memphis.

After eight years, however, Chester decided that wasn't what he wanted any longer. He was losing the stomach for the senseless gang-style shootings, the drug-related killings, the grim domestic abuse that underlay so many of his cases.

He counted it one of the great misfortunes of his life that he'd reported to his new job in Grambling the week *after* the Fourth of July ten years previously. He entered the Grambling Police Department at a time of upheaval. He liked – more importantly, he respected – the man who'd hired him, Chief Marcus Warren. At the time, Warren himself had been on the job only a year, brought in to professionalize the growing city's force. It wasn't a bad group of men and women, and there was no corruption, as far as Chester could tell. It was simply that Grambling was changing from a small town to a mid-size city. The New South, as people liked to call it, was a reality. Money was moving in. Retirees. Bank headquarters. All sorts of industry alternatives to the textiles that had ruled this town through the middle of the twentieth century.

It was a measure of Chief Warren's and Detective Scovoy's competence that every ensuing homicide on Scovoy's nearly ten-year watch had been cleared. He'd have to look it up to make sure, but he thought the number was approaching forty.

And so the murder he'd missed by days was all the more galling. He'd worked it, of course. There was no getting around it as an incoming homicide cop. But he'd always chafed at the sloppy work at the crime scene, the overly deferential treatment of the family, the allowing of refreshments, for Pete's sake, during the initial questioning. He never got traction on the case; he was always playing catch-up.

But to be fair, the crime scene might have been unnavigable in any event. Mrs Resnick's kitchen had been the site of a holiday party just hours before, with four overnight guests and another sixty partygoers. It would have been a challenge for a top-flight forensics team, much less Grambling's undertrained investigators of a decade ago.

The upshot was that Chester Scovoy, at forty-six, had nothing to prove, no turf to defend. Would he like to solve the Alberta Resnick murder? Damn straight. But he had never had the time nor the resources to handle it the way he'd like. Like now, for example. He had to turn his mind to these hit-and-runs, apparently committed by a church van, no less.

So he minded the intrusion of Branigan Powers into the Resnick case less than she'd suspect. After all, it'd been ten years. There was nothing she could do to hurt anything.

Well, except maybe herself.

CHAPTER FORTY

It was still light outside when Branigan headed home, badly needing a run to clear her head. She had no illusions of solving Mrs Resnick's murder by Sunday, but now there were so many holes in the story that she couldn't write a decent narrative. She thought Rita's hit-and-run was connected, but what if it wasn't? She would so muddy the waters that no reader could follow the story.

She still needed to talk to Malachi and Demetrius, Heath and Ramsey. Oh, and Max Brody. She had to make headway on them tomorrow. Meanwhile, she went over some of the things that were needling her.

Why did Amanda Resnick seem disingenuous when talking about her mother's possible dementia and sending Amanda to buy gifts for her "favorite" grandchildren? Such silly things to lie about. And yet her "to be honest with you's" rang false.

Why had Heath Resnick gone to the Isle of Palms to sit in on daughter Caroline's interview? An overly protective father? Or something more? Did he know his mother had intended to cut him from the will, even though his brother and sister insisted he didn't?

Why was Ramsey Resnick volunteering at Jericho Road?

And what about Ben Jr's connection to Rita Mae Jones? Was it a coincidence that the one person who almost certainly saw something the day of the murder was Ben's drug buddy at the party? Wouldn't he be the family member she'd most likely approach with a blackmail scheme?

Lastly, who was the mysterious reader living in the pool house? Did the psychic sense the killer living there at the time of the murder? Or more recently?

Branigan had to admit that recognizing the back of Mrs

Resnick's pool house in the psychic's drawing had unnerved her. For one thing, it was awfully close to her parents' house. For another, it meant the killer had spent some time in Grambling.

She'd been working under the assumption that Mrs Resnick's murderer was in and out – and long gone. To think that someone had been living in the victim's pool house, perhaps blending in with Grambling's populace, was disturbing. And of course there was the more obvious conclusion: that the psychic's intuition, or whatever it was, was based on a family member who didn't *live* in the pool house at all, but came and went freely.

As Branigan neared the farmhouse, she badly wished that Davison was there to meet her. Which reminded her: it was check-in time. She rummaged, one-handed, in her purse for her phone, and called his number. When he answered, she began singing Amy Winehouse's "Rehab" in a sultry snarl.

Davison laughed. "Don't quit your day job, Miss Winehouse."

"I'm about ready to. This Resnick story is kicking my butt."

"What's up with it?"

"It's too complicated to go into. You'll read all about it Sunday morning. Tan-4's pushed it up."

"Can you make that deadline?"

"I have to. It may not be complete, but it's going to run. But enough of that. How are you doing?"

"Not bad. My head's clearer every day. I forget how my brain starts to function better. My body, that's another story."

"Got the shakes?"

"More like the volcanoes. But it's not like I ain't been at this rodeo before."

"I'm sorry. Hey, is it okay for me to come for visitation this weekend?"

"I can do better than that. I have a twelve-hour pass on Saturday."

"Really? That surprises me."

"Well, it's only if I'm with a reputable family member."

"That counts you out. You don't have a reputable family member."

"Ha ha. I'd like to come to the farm."

"That *is* better! Want me to invite Mom and Dad?"

He was silent for a moment. "Let's wait on that a bit. I'd hate to get their hopes up again, you know?"

"No, I don't know. You are going to make it this time. But I won't say anything to them until you give me the go-ahead."

"Thanks, Brani G. See you soon."

"Love you, Davison," she said, but he'd already hung up.

The conversation with her brother calmed her down a bit. But her anxiety returned when she pulled into her driveway and saw a vehicle. *No, wait a minute, that's Charlie's Jeep Cherokee.* Then she saw the girl, leaning up against it, dressed in khaki shorts and a brown-striped rugby shirt, her red-gold hair streaming down her back. Cleo sat beside her, tail pounding the driveway. Charlie raised a hand.

"You didn't forget I was bringing dinner, did you?" she called, as Branigan pulled the Civic alongside her.

"Yikes, I did! But that's okay. You're a welcome sight! What you got?"

"Tacos," she said. "Yummy, messy tacos."

Charlie and Branigan tried to have a girls' night every other month. Branigan must have said yes to this evening then promptly forgotten it. It would do her good to turn her mind to something else, she thought. She'd get back to work when Charlie left.

Cleo followed the women up the steps, and Charlie unpacked dinner from a cooler. "Tacos are ready when you are," she said.

"Get the plates and I'll change clothes," Branigan said. "You know where everything is."

She was back in minutes, her skirt and heels exchanged for a tank top and shorts. Charlie had the places set at the kitchen island, ice in the glasses.

"Tea or water or juice or Diet Pepsi?" she asked. "You're pretty well stocked."

Branigan chose water, and settled in to eat the fragrant tacos the girl had laid out, with chips and salsa on the side.

"Tell me what's going on with you," she said after a few bites. "Getting ready for UGA country?"

"Yeah, Mom and I are shopping for curtains and bedspreads and rugs to match my roommate's. Chan's making fun of us. Apparently guys don't do that."

Branigan laughed. "I imagine not."

"Speaking of Chan…" she said, none too subtly.

Branigan waited for her to continue, but she didn't. "What?" she asked.

"I'm wondering if you can tell me what's going on."

"Going on with what?"

"Everybody in our house is acting weird. At first I thought it was Impending Empty Nest."

Charlie always made Branigan laugh, and she did so now.

"But it's not that. Chan is all moody and secretive, and Mom and Dad are holed up behind closed doors."

Branigan thought she did know what was going on. "Are the three of them meeting in private?"

"No. Chan is hardly speaking to Dad at all. Mom looks worried. I've asked all three of them what's wrong and nobody will tell me. So I thought I'd ask you." She looked at Branigan expectantly.

Branigan knew Davison hadn't spoken to Chan yet. But did the young man suspect something? She could see why Liam and Liz were worried. For Chan to find out that both his biological parents were junkies was a pretty big bomb to drop as he was headed to college.

"Charlie, I've always been honest with you, right?"

The girl nodded.

"But honey, this isn't my news to tell."

"You're kidding."

"No, and I'm so sorry. You're going to have to ask your mom and dad."

"So you *do* know what's going on?"

"I have an idea."

"And you really won't tell me?"

"I can't. This is a private matter for your family."

"Okay," Charlie said, clearly confounded.

"Have you talked to Chan?"

"He's always down at the church."

"Really? What's he doing there?"

"Volunteering. Eating. Who knows? We just hand over the car keys. It's not how I pictured our last summer as a family, you know?"

She looked so forlorn that Branigan went around the island and hugged her. "I have a feeling that everything will be cleared up soon," she told her. "Long before your summer is over."

CHAPTER FORTY-ONE

M alachi Ezekiel Martin was a reader. People might not suspect it from where he'd ended up, but he'd never stopped reading. He got it from his grandmother, a Genesis-to-Revelation Bible reader – hence the Malachi and the Ezekiel. Besides the biblical writers, his granny loved one author above all others: Agatha Christie.

Every night in their northeast Georgia farmhouse, she read the English murder mysteries to young Malachi. Jane Marple, Hercule Poirot, and Tommy and Tuppence Beresford were as familiar to him as Abraham, Isaac and Jacob.

It wasn't until he was identified for his high school gifted readers' program and started studying the likes of Langston Hughes and Zora Neal Hurston and Ralph Ellison that he realized how unusual her tastes were.

"Granny," he'd told her, "you have to be the only black woman in America readin' Agatha Christie."

But she said she'd *lived* what Langston Hughes and Zora Neal Hurston and Ralph Ellison wrote, and she sure didn't need to go over it again. No, she wanted to read about murder in gossipy English villages that had vicars instead of Baptist preachers.

And so Malachi had been pleased when that *Rambler* reporter asked about the death of his friend Vesuvius. He had wondered why V had been out on his bike in the middle of the night. Now he was "employing the little grey cells", as Hercule Poirot put it, about other oddities surrounding his friend's death.

For if there was one thing the Belgian detective with the egg-shaped head had taught Malachi, it was this: look for what was out of character, out of sequence, out of the norm.

V's breaking curfew was the first thing. He had a safe bed at

Jericho Road, and he seemed content to sleep in it. What was he doing three blocks away at the corner of Oakley and Anders?

The other thing was the sale of a painting to a homeless dude. In all the time that Jericho Road's art room had been flourishing, in all the time it had hosted art sales that attracted businessmen and city councilwomen and even gallery owners, Malachi had never known a homeless artist to sell to a fellow homeless person.

V had $130 in cash when he slept in Malachi's tent the week of his death. His small mental disability payment came on a debit card. So someone – a "dude", in V's words – paid at least $130 for V's plyboard painting. Maybe more, if V had already spent some of it. And even more peculiar, the buyer then threw the painting away.

Malachi looked at it now, a gorgeously haunting moonscape reflected on a pond, the large black V in the corner fading into the grasses that surrounded the water. Why would someone pay for a painting, then discard it?

Because he didn't want the painting, said Malachi's little grey cells. *He wanted something else.*

But what? What else did V have? He was mentally disabled. Sweet-natured but not all there.

Malachi tried to recreate their conversation in his head. He asked V where he'd gotten the money. V had responded, "Sold a paintin' I done. Sold it to a dude who saw it at Jericho. I asked Pastuh Liam and he took it off the wall and gave it to me."

Did V mean that Pastor Liam had been standing there when he made the sale? Would the pastor know who bought it? Or did V simply mean he'd asked Pastor Liam at a later time for his artwork?

It was worth a visit to Jericho Road to find out.

CHAPTER FORTY-TWO

C harlie left too late for Branigan to get in a run. With no streetlights, it wasn't like living in the city. Once it got dark in the countryside, it was *dark*.

Branigan curled up on the den sofa with a pad and pen. She needed a handwritten to-do list, something to hold. Sometimes a computer screen didn't cut it.

At the top of one page, she wrote "Demetrius". At the top of another, "Max Brody". Then she tried to think of everything she knew about them.

For Demetrius, it wasn't much. Probably schizophrenic. Potentially violent, as evidenced by the charges in Gainesville. As Billy Shepherd, he had lived for awhile in Mrs Resnick's pool house before Tabitha and Ramsey discovered him. Was there someone else with him? Could that someone have murdered Mrs Resnick? Or alternately, could that someone have seen who did?

Rita had been in the pool house with Ben Brissey Jr. Did she recognize someone there, and did that knowledge get her killed?

Most interesting was the timing: Vesuvius and Rita were killed *after* Billy/Demetrius was released from prison. Could the providers of his original alibi in Forest Lawn have lied, making him Mrs Resnick's killer after all? If that were true, the Grambling police were in for a nightmare – maybe lawsuits for incompetence.

Branigan had only a picture of Billy/Demetrius. Unlike Liam, she hadn't seen police questioning him a decade earlier.

But she had seen Max Brody, at a church service in early May. Jericho Road held its Sunday morning services in the dining hall. The men moved the tables out and set up rows of chairs in front of a raised stage. When Liam started as pastor, twenty chairs would do. Now they needed two hundred.

Branigan was a member at First Baptist Church of Grambling, where she sat with her mom and dad most Sundays. But she tried to get to Jericho Road's lively alternative every month or so. When she was there in May, a man had lurched past the gospel singers, stumbling into a woman and causing her to drop her hymnal, before slamming out of the door in mid-service. Liam told her afterward that it was Max Brody, already drunk at 11 a.m.

She asked Liam last Monday to inquire if any homeless people had heard rumors about Mrs Resnick's stabbing. Jess came forward immediately to tell about Max Brody's comments at an outdoor concert in mid-May.

She flipped open her notebook to yesterday's interview with Jess: Max was a mean drunk. Max had a wad of cash. Max said, "This evening's drunk is courtesy of an old lady who had the good sense [or the good taste] to get stabbed."

Presumably that meant his beer money was related to an old woman's stabbing. But how? What did Max know? Was he being paid for his silence? That was kind of wacky. Who could trust a drunk to be silent?

She needed to talk to this guy.

She reached for her phone and called Liam at home. When he answered, she said, "It's me. I hate to keep bothering you, but can you help me locate Demetrius and Max Brody tomorrow?"

"Sorry, but I'll be writing Rita's memorial service. Want me to call you when I finish?"

"Yes, please. Meanwhile, I guess I'll try the usual spots."

"Brani G, that might not be a good idea. Something is seriously wrong with Demetrius. And Max can be violent. Can you wait 'til I'm free? Or maybe get the police to go with you?"

"We'll see," she said. "Just call when you break free. And thanks."

Under Max's name, she wrote: library; bridge; Main Street; St James; Covenant Methodist; Jericho. But she'd been in those places frequently over the past two weeks and had never seen him.

Not like Malachi, whom she saw everywhere.

Hey, maybe Malachi could help. He'd be the next best thing to Liam.

Or even better.

With her mind set on a course of action, Branigan went to bed, knowing she had a long day ahead. She fell asleep instantly, and was still soundly out when Cleo ripped the night silence with a furious, high-pitched barking. Branigan shot up, heart pounding, fear and anger sparring for pre-eminence.

She followed Cleo to the sliding glass door in her office, which faced the cotton patch, barn and pastures. The moon was behind clouds, and she could see nothing. Cleo stood on two legs, clawing at the glass door and yowling at a hysterical pitch. Branigan's anger at being awakened turned to uneasiness.

"What is it, girl?" she whispered, holding on to the dog's neck. "What's out there?"

Heaven knew, it could be so many things. Coyote. Raccoon. 'Possum. *Human.*

Cleo wanted out badly, but Branigan wasn't about to be left alone. For the first time, she wished she had accepted her mom's offer of a security system for the farmhouse. She'd said no, pointing out that Pa and Gran had never, not once, had a break-in in all their years here. And furthermore, what security system was better than Cleo? She was proving that right now. But if Branigan were really in trouble, Cleo couldn't alert the county sheriff.

Cleo continued to growl, but returned to all fours. She trotted to the den, barked out of its window, then returned to the office. She was beginning to calm down. So was Branigan.

They went back to their bedroom, where Branigan was startled to see it was after 5 a.m. Cleo went right to sleep on her pillow, but her mistress couldn't. She tossed until the blackness gave way to gray.

"Come on, girl," she said, throwing the covers off. "Let's get that run."

Minutes later, they were rolling under the barbed wire and into the pasture. The morning was refreshingly cool and already alive with birds singing. They ran into the breeze and lapped the first pasture twice. Branigan felt her unease dissipate. *This place is alive with critters,* she thought. *It'd be unusual* not *to have nocturnal creatures running around.*

After thirty minutes, they started their cool-down walk back to the house. Branigan heard a moo from the barn. She hadn't realized Uncle Bobby had put cows in there, so they went to take a look. Sure enough, five docile black Angus were in stalls.

Branigan walked through the barn, speaking softly and petting each. Cleo, born and raised on a farm, knew not to spook them.

There were three empty stalls in addition to the occupied ones, each holding a pile of hay. But the last one had something else, something out of place. Branigan stared for a moment at the blue and white wrapper, then opened the slatted gate and retrieved it – a water bottle with a custom label affixed. "God loves you," it read, "and so does Jericho Road."

She looked around nervously. Who had left this here? Cleo was standing quietly, so the person wasn't still around.

Had someone slept here last night? Why had he – or she – left this bottle in plain sight? As a warning?

Branigan was shaken by the discovery in the barn, but didn't know whether to report it to Detective Scovoy or Chief Warren or to the Cannon County Sheriff's Office, which had jurisdiction over the farm. Or maybe to no one. She couldn't imagine a responding deputy getting too excited over a water bottle left in her barn.

She put it out of her mind, at least for the present. She showered and dressed rapidly, pulling on long pants, a long-sleeved shirt and flat boat shoes, figuring her search for Billy/Demetrius and Max Brody would take her far from her air-conditioned office and into tick-infested woods. She started at Jericho Road, where Peace in the Valley Baptist Church was serving a breakfast of pancakes and bacon.

She spotted Malachi, bent over a magazine as he ate. She grabbed a cup of coffee and slid into the seat next to him.

"Me again," she said. "I hope I'm not disturbing you."

"No, ma'am, Miz Branigan." He folded his magazine. "That was a good story you wrote on V and his daddy."

"Thanks. Have you heard Pastor Liam talking about the other story I'm working on?"

"I heard some of the mens talkin'. 'Bout that old lady who got murdered long time ago."

"Right," she said. "The police always thought it was possible it was a transient who was in and out of Grambling very quickly. I'm working on a ten-year anniversary story on how it's gone unsolved for so long. Today I need to find Demetrius. . . Shepherd, I guess his last name is, and Max Brody. Do you have any idea where they might be?"

"Why you want them? That might not be a good idea."

"Why?"

Malachi shrugged. "They're... unpredictable."

She laughed. Sometimes Malachi sounded like a precocious twelve-year-old, veering from street rhythms to English teacher. She had listened to him enough to realize that he adapted his speech to mirror whomever he was talking to.

"I still need to talk to them. For my story."

Malachi eyed her quietly for some moments.

"Maybe you could come with me?" she suggested.

"That might be a good idea," he agreed.

"Do we drive or walk?" she asked as they emerged into the bright sunlight after breakfast.

"Let's drive. Lemme make sure my bike's locked up."

"I didn't know you had a bike."

"I don't use it much. Pastor Liam lets me store it in a room with the shelter bikes."

She waited until Malachi joined her at the Civic, tossing his backpack onto the rear seat. He directed her to the courthouse lawn, and sure enough, she saw the man in the picture she'd borrowed from the Forest Lawn mill house.

"Wow," she said. "You're the best guide ever."

Demetrius was sitting on a black iron bench, one leg crossed over the other, foot pumping furiously. His head jerked as his eyes followed people passing on the Main Street sidewalk or entering the courthouse. He hopped up and circled the Johnny Reb statue, then sat back down, talking to himself. This manic energy was not what Branigan had expected, and she asked Malachi about it as they watched from the car.

"I never seen 'im like this either," he said. "Maybe his meds ran out."

"What kind of meds?"

"I don't know, but Pastor Liam's counselor been tryin' to meet with 'im. And he's been all slow and groggy like. Now look at 'im."

"Well, we're in a public place," she said. "What can go wrong approaching a bi-polar schizophrenic just out of prison?"

Malachi snorted. She realized she'd not heard him laugh before.

They exited the car and approached Demetrius quietly. Branigan slid onto the far end of his bench, while Malachi stood under a nearby maple, close enough for Demetrius to see him. Branigan had seen Liam and Dontegan do the same with their female social worker, letting a client know they were nearby.

She knew enough to approach him gently, to speak softly. But she didn't get the chance. Demetrius turned to her and launched into what must have been streaming through his head. He batted the air in front of him.

"Didja-see-those-flies-they're-everywhere-they're-bitin'-me-an'-they're-gon-bite-you-an'-they're-gon-bite-that-man-over-there-an'-that-woman-an'-that-baby-those-people-gon-into-court-takin'-them-black-flies-in-the-courthouse-my-granny-said-don't-let-flies-in-her-house..." He was rocking now, then abruptly got up and circled Johnny Reb again and sat back down. He continued to murmur.

"Demetrius?" She made eye contact. "I'm Branigan Powers from *The Grambling Rambler*."

He looked at her. "Hey-Branigan-Powers-are-those-flies-botherin'-you-they're-sure-botherin'-me…"

"There are no flies, Demetrius. No flies."

He continued swatting, his huge hands coming dangerously close to her face. Malachi took a step forward.

"I'd like to talk to you about Alberta Resnick's pool house," she said.

"I-can't-go-swimmin'-ain't-got-no-swimmin'-trunks."

"But do you remember when you lived in that house beside the swimming pool?"

"Granny-ain't-got-no-swimmin'-pool-but-'Lanta-does-I'll-go-swimmin'-when-I-get-to-'Lanta-got-to-get-a-Greyhound-ticket."

"But one time you lived in a pool house, didn't you?"

"South-Car-lina-DOC-don'-have-no-pool-but-'Lanta-will-I'll-go-swimmin'-when-I-get-to-'Lanta-on-the-Greyhound-bus-Greyhound-don'-have-no-pool-but-my-house-in-'Lanta-will."

Branigan looked at Malachi, who shrugged. She tried one more time.

"Billy?"

He swung around and looked at her, cocking his head.

"When your name was Billy, you moved into a house beside a pool, didn't you?"

For the first time, he didn't respond with a stream of words, but instead searched her face.

"Did someone live there with you, Billy?"

"*One Flew Over the Cuckoo's Nest*," he said.

"Yes! Someone read that book."

Billy wrapped his arms around himself, and rocked until Branigan felt the bench move beneath them.

"*Invisible Man*," he said, then turned abruptly to Malachi. "You're-the-invisible-man."

"Because he's black? Because Malachi is black?"

"*Cold Sassy Tree*."

"That's exactly right, Billy," she said quietly. "All those books were in the pool house. Who was reading them? Were you?"

"Oh-no-not-me-she-reads-to-me-she-reads-to-me."

"Who, Billy? Who reads to you?"

"My-granny-reads-to-me-See-Spot-run-the-cat-in-the-hat-eats-green-eggs-an'-ham." He laughed loudly.

"But the pool house, Billy," she pleaded. "Who read in the pool house?"

"*Invisible Man*. Invisible-man-eats-yellow-eggs-and-bacon-not-green-eggs-and-ham." He emitted a shrill giggle.

Before Branigan realized what he was doing, Demetrius stood abruptly and seized the iron bench. He flipped it over and sent her flying. The hard landing knocked the breath out of her, and she lay on her back, gasping. Out of the corner of her eye, she saw Demetrius lumbering away, his gait hitching.

Malachi bent over her, his cornrow braids swinging below his faded green cap. "Breathe, Miz Branigan. Nice and slow. Breathe."

Moments later she sat up, air making its ragged way into her lungs. She flexed her back gently. Luckily, she'd landed on a patch of grass rather than the exposed tree roots that could've caused some damage.

"You want to go home?" Malachi asked. "Or to your office?"

"Heck, no. Let me catch my breath and we'll go find Max."

"You sure, Miz Branigan? That was some tumble you took."

"I'm fine. Just curious about all that *Invisible Man* stuff. Do you think he meant the other person in the pool house was black?"

"Could be," Malachi said. "Or homeless. Or both."

"Like you."

Malachi didn't respond.

Max Brody wasn't nearly as easy to find. Malachi and Branigan drove to several places she'd not been previously: a low bridge behind the city's riverside amphitheater, where they saw sleeping bags and discarded tennis shoes. Another riverside park, where they found two tents hidden in dense foliage. An encampment in the woods behind a popular chain restaurant, way out on an Eastside artery. There were plenty of signs of homeless people, but no Max.

"I don't get this," she told Malachi as they walked behind the Eastside restaurant. "Why would homeless people live this far away from Jericho Road and the Rescue Mission and all those downtown services?"

"Lots of reasons," Malachi said. "Maybe they don't like bein' 'round people. It's good money flyin' a sign at these red lights. And that restaurant gives out leftovers at the end of the night."

"Did you ever live out here?"

He shrugged. She couldn't tell if it was a yes or a no.

"No, I'm interested, if you don't mind saying," she pressed. "Did you live out here?"

"Not here, but in places like this. When I got out the Army, I didn't want to live 'round anybody. Lotta vets are like that."

"So you're a veteran. Where did you serve?"

"Desert Storm. Kuwait and Iraq."

This was the first information she'd gotten on Malachi's background. She wanted more, but didn't want to scare him off.

"I got one more idea," he said. "Let's try Garner Bridge."

"But isn't that where you live?"

"Yeah, but there are other places 'cross the railroad tracks where that bridge touches down. Every place it covers, there are more tents."

"I had no idea."

"Most people don't," he said. "The other places are harder to get to."

Malachi directed her back to town, through Randall Mill, past the convenience store where she and Liam had met before finding Davison. Was it only last week? But instead of turning onto the dead-end road that led to Malachi's encampment, he had her continue another half-mile. The mill houses ended, and woods crowded to the edge of the road.

"Pull over here," he said.

"Where?" She could see no entrance.

"Just right in here." He pointed to a patch of weeds and dirt where the tree line broke for about the width of a car.

"If you had a four-wheel, we'd go through the woods," he said. "But we best not try in your Honda."

She eased the car off the uneven asphalt and into the shade. She was careful not to block the rudimentary dirt road in case someone wanted in or out.

"Now we walk," Malachi announced.

Branigan's slacks and long sleeves offered protection from biting insects and scratching underbrush, and her boat shoes made for easy walking on the rutted ground. She and Malachi walked a quarter-mile or more beneath a heavy canopy of trees.

As they walked, Malachi pointed to a few isolated tents off to the right, down a slight ravine. "Those people don't want to be close together," he said. "I used to sleep way back in those woods." He pointed to a dense thicket. Even within the city limits, these Southern woods were engulfing. He seemed to read her mind. "You go so deep in there, you don't hear no traffic."

At the end of the road, the trees ended abruptly, and Branigan looked up to see the Garner Bridge soaring above them. To their left rose an embankment topped by railroad tracks. Across those tracks, she knew, was the camp where Malachi lived. And where Rita's empty shack remained.

Directly ahead was another camp, much smaller. Three tents were grouped together, seemingly vacant this time of morning. Several sleeping bags were scattered in the open. Forty yards away – as far as you could get without re-entering the woods on the other side of the clearing – was a single tent of dullest green.

"That's where Max used to stay," said Malachi, indicating the farthest tent. "But he got drunk one night and picked a fight with the wrong dude. Dude took his tent and kicked Max out. But that dude's in prison now, so maybe Max came back."

Branigan's experience with camping was confined to Lake Hartwell and state parks at the beach. Camping meant a little sand in your eggs, sure, and maybe some sunburn. If it rained, she packed up and came home. It was nothing like this hard-baked ground with no picnic tables, grills, bathrooms or showers.

"Where do they go to the bathroom?" she asked, feeling intrusive.

"Anywhere they can." He pointed behind Max's tent. "Woods. Jericho Road. Library."

"How about at night?"

"Definitely the woods."

"Don't they..." She stopped, realizing who she was talking to. "Aren't you afraid of snakes? Or poison ivy?"

"We got all that," Malachi said. "And spiders. In the summer, you see a lot of swollen wrists and ankles and arms from spider bites. Lot of 'em get infected, and people go see the nurse at Jericho or the ER."

"Is it harder in summer or winter?"

"It's harder when it rains. The hardest thing is keepin' dry. Winter or summer, the rain comes through here in rivers." He kicked at a long, deep rut in the clay. "Everythin' in your tent gets wet. That's why they so many clothes thrown out on our side. They mildewed before we could dry 'em out."

Their voices had gotten quieter in response to the ghostly silence of the camp. As they stopped talking, Branigan became aware of a buzzing. She looked around to the woods they'd just exited. Her mind flashed to the back porch where Gran had cut a watermelon every summer afternoon. Davison and she had to take turns standing with a fly swatter in order to eat the crunchy red fruit. The sweet juice ran in streams down their arms and legs and onto the concrete porch. Black flies must have put the word out all over the farm, because they came in hordes, lighting on the fruit, the porch, Gran's metal rockers, the twins. The buzzing was an irritating wave of noise, interspersed by the slap, slap, slap of the plastic swatter.

That buzz was growing now, as they approached Max's tent. Branigan slapped at a black fly that landed on her sleeve. She didn't kill it, but a red stain appeared there nonetheless. Her mind skittered to the watermelon rinds they'd seen outside Malachi's camp. She saw Malachi start slapping, and had a sinking feeling.

And so when they reached the tent and Malachi yanked open its flap to reveal an unmoving Max Brody, a broken whiskey bottle embedded in his neck, black flies swarming in his congealed blood, she couldn't say she was altogether surprised.

She calmly called the police, and then Liam. Only then did she have a meltdown.

First up was the morning's coffee. She had enough presence of mind to stagger away from the crime scene and those damn flies before heaving everything from her stomach. Then she remained on her knees, rocking in the silence, the buzzing, the silence, the buzzing. She was vaguely aware she was rocking as Demetrius had done. Was her mind breaking, like his?

Malachi looked stricken. "Miz Branigan, you all right? I thought you didn't know Max."

"I didn't!"

"Then what's the matter?"

"I got him killed. My stupid story got him killed!"

Malachi pulled away and went to sit on a tree stump near an empty fire ring. Police cars – two, then three, then four, sirens blaring – rocketed in on the dirt road. Figures from beyond the embankment popped onto the railroad tracks to see what was going on.

Liam rushed in, his SUV skidding to a stop beside a police car. He and Malachi had a hushed conversation, then he knelt beside Branigan, stopped her rocking. But he couldn't stop her shaking.

"The psychics were right," she whispered. "I woke him up. He thought he was safe and I woke him up. All my questions got Rita and Max killed."

At first Liam murmured soothing shushes, as if she were five years old. But then he sat back on his heels. "You know, I'm not sure about that, Brani G. Didn't Jess say Max was talking to him in mid-May about an old lady getting stabbed? You didn't start asking questions until June."

"Did you see his neck?" she moaned.

"And Rita," Liam continued, as if she hadn't spoken. "Rita was mouthing off for years, according to Dontegan. That's probably how Max found out."

"But Liam," she said softly. "That's just it. They were both talking all along. But they were *alive* until this week."

Her friend had no answer for that.

CHAPTER FORTY-THREE

Malachi and Branigan stayed at the police station, answering questions, until after dark. There was no holding back now from Detective Scovoy. Fortunately, the local TV reporters weren't terribly interested in one more violent death in a homeless camp. Max Brody got twenty seconds on the 6 o'clock news.

Despite Branigan's certainty – and guilt – the police were not convinced of a link between Mrs Resnick's murder and the deaths of Rita and Max.

"I hate to sound harsh," Detective Scovoy said, "but these people die all the time, in all kinds of ways. Traffic. Overdoses. Fights. Assaults. I hear what you're saying, Miss Powers, but I also hear that Max Brody was a first-class jerk. Lots of people hated him. It might be exactly what it looks like – a brawl that went bad."

Jody came by the station and had information on a more pressing angle of their story: Vesuvius's body had been cremated, but his mangled bike showed traces of paint from the church van's bumper. It looked as though both he and Rita were killed by the Jericho Road van.

"TV doesn't have it yet," he whispered, "but we'll have to run this. We can't sit on it until Sunday. The police lab has confirmed it, so I'm heading over to see Liam now."

By the time Branigan left the station, her guilt had turned to numbness.

"Maybe the police are right," Malachi offered. "Max was a jackass. He's come purty close to gettin' killed before today."

"Thank you, Malachi," she said. "And thank you for going with me. Where can I drop you?"

230

"Jericho Road," he said. "I want to talk to Pastor Liam about somethin'."

"Me too," she said, and turned toward the mission church.

It didn't take Malachi or Branigan long to realize they weren't getting in to see Liam. He was in an emergency meeting with his church deacons. A police officer was with them too, apparently informing them that their church van had run over two homeless people in the past two weeks.

Jody waited with Chan and Dontegan in the dining hall, glasses of iced tea untouched in front of them. Jody had his laptop out, typing. Branigan knew he was constructing his story and would have it ready to file as soon as he got comments from Liam and the deacon chair.

"Are you putting Max Brody in the same story?" she asked.

"No. There's nothing to connect them yet," he said. "I filed six inches on the Max Brody death. It's the hit-and-runs connected to a homeless church that's the zinger."

"I hope it doesn't shut this place down," she said.

Chan looked up in alarm. "Could that happen?"

"I would think. Not that anyone from outside would do it. But Liam's deacons might. This is terrible publicity. They might shut down for awhile to show the community they're taking it seriously."

"But the van is gone," Chan said. "The police impounded it."

"The van is gone," she agreed. "But the driver's not."

Halfway down the hall, the conference room door opened. Liam came out first, his face strained so that every freckle stood out. He introduced an attractive, middle-aged woman as chair of Jericho Road's deacons, as the other church leaders stepped away.

Liam and the chairwoman pulled out seats across from Jody. Jody read to them from the police report findings about the paint on Vesuvius's bike and from Liam's own information about Rita's deathbed remarks. Then he asked for comment.

"Obviously, we are devastated," Liam said, reading from a prepared statement. "Everything we have built over the past five years has been designed to provide our homeless parishioners with a safe space and transformational opportunities. We do not understand how or why our van has been used to kill two of those parishioners. We are inviting the Grambling Police Department to set up an office right here at Jericho Road to get to the bottom of this matter. We will cooperate fully with their investigation."

"Meanwhile," added the chairwoman, "we, as a church, express our confidence in Pastor Delaney. We have asked him to keep Jericho Road open during the investigation so as not to harm the people its closing would hurt."

Branigan glanced at Chan. His shoulders relaxed slightly.

"Jody, you got any more questions?" Liam asked.

Jody double-checked the make, model, year and color of the church van. He asked what it was used for, and who usually drove it. Then he asked who had access to the key.

Liam stood and led him to the reception desk, and pulled out the drawer that held the key. Branigan trailed behind, and saw a frown pass over his face. Jody's head was bent, scribbling, and he missed it.

Liam explained that Dontegan or another staff member or a volunteer oversaw the reception desk from nine to five every day. During that time, volunteers, interns, staff members, board members and shelter residents were in and out. In addition, Jericho Road allowed Grambling's homeless to use its address for mail; thus, street dwellers were frequently in the office as well.

"We try to lock the room when no one's at the desk," Liam said. "But I can guarantee you there are times when the receptionist is called to the kitchen or to the door for a donation and it doesn't get locked." He held his hands out. "It's the nature of a place like this. It will never be fully secure."

Jody looked up, satisfied. "Thanks for your help," he told Liam. Then turning to Branigan: "I'm so close to the office, I'll go there to file."

"See you tomorrow," she said.

Liam looked at her tiredly. "You staying?"

"Oh, yeah," she said. "I'll wait for you to get all these people out."

It was another forty-five minutes before Liam got his deacons out of the building. They were understandably anxious and wanted to talk to him and each other. Malachi melted into the darkness without Branigan noticing.

She took the opportunity to make three calls to the Resnick heirs, telling them she had more information on their mother's murder and asking them to meet her at Ramsey's drug store the next morning. She reached only Amanda, who agreed to drive over from the lake. She left the brothers voice mails, hoping they'd come as well.

Finally, only Liam, Dontegan, Chan and Branigan were left in the Jericho Road dining hall.

Branigan wanted to know what Liam had seen in the reception office, but didn't know if he could talk in front of Dontegan and Chan. But apparently, it was her presence that made him hesitate.

"Can we go off the record?" he asked.

"Sure," she said.

He turned to Dontegan. "The money box is missing."

Dontegan looked confused. "You took it weeks ago, Pastuh. Don' you 'member?"

"I didn't take it," Liam said, his mouth tight.

"I come in one mornin' and the box was gone, and they's a note from you, sayin' you moved it to your office. I didn' think nothin' 'bout it."

"Did you keep the note?" Liam asked.

"No, suh, Pastuh. If I keep every Post-It note you write, wouldn' be no room in our files."

Liam laughed in spite of himself. "That's true." He rubbed his eyes.

Branigan jumped in. "So Dontegan, did this note look like Liam's writing?"

"It mus' have. Sometimes they's be three, four notes in one mornin'. It look like the rest of 'em."

"In other words," she said, looking at Liam, "it would be easy to forge one of your notes."

His eyes flicked to Chan, then quickly away.

"Oh, no, Dad, that was just the one time! I learned my lesson." Chan turned to Branigan and Dontegan. "In ninth grade, I signed his name on my report card. All hel– All heck broke loose at our house. I never did it again."

"I wasn't accusing you, Chan," Liam said.

"Tell me about the money box," Branigan said. "Locked, unlocked? Petty cash? What?"

"Locked," said Liam. "It was for donations that came in the door. Several times a week, someone drops by with a cash or check donation. We give them a receipt on the spot, but the receptionist can't always bring it to the safe in my office right then. So I bought a lock box to keep money in until Dontegan could get it to me."

He turned to Dontegan. "That's why you've been shoving envelopes under my door," he said. "I wondered why you weren't waiting until the end of the week like you used to, but I kept forgetting to ask."

"Yes, suh," Dontegan nodded. Branigan could tell he was relieved.

"Is there any way of telling how much money was in the box?" she asked.

"Maybe. I'll give Libby – that's our office manager – the receipt book, and she can compare it against deposits she made. That should tell us what's unaccounted for. Dontegan, do you know how long the box has been gone?"

"Maybe three weeks?"

"So we're looking at a week's worth of receipts sometime in May. There's just no telling. Sometimes people leave fifty dollars, but they've been known to leave thousand-dollar checks or hundreds in cash. And since they already received the receipt for their taxes, they'd have no way of knowing anything was wrong on our end."

Liam thought for a moment. "I'll need to call the police back," he said. "Man, when things go south, they really go south."

"You know, Liam, I hate to say this, but it may be your cost of doing business," Branigan said. "You're trying to help people most churches won't touch. I've heard Chief Warren say that criminals are mixed in with the homeless. And you don't differentiate. Criminals are as welcome here as anyone else. Occasionally, that's gonna bite you."

"You're right," he said, standing. "It doesn't make the betrayal hurt any less."

"Seems I've heard you preach that."

She was rewarded with a smile. "Yeah, someone we're quite fond of here was once betrayed, wasn't He?" He sighed heavily. "Let me make that call."

CHAPTER FORTY-FOUR

Branigan admitted it: she was afraid to be alone. On one hand, she was consumed by the fear that she had lured a killer back into action. Rita and Max, possibly even Vesuvius, were dead because of her story. On the other hand, she was scared for her own safety.

She drove to the farmhouse. It was well after dark, so she didn't get out of the car, but simply opened the passenger door for Cleo. With the German shepherd's comforting bulk beside her, she swung the Civic around to shine the headlights on the cotton field. Even so, she couldn't see the barn in the blackness. She drove back to town, and pulled into her parents' driveway.

It was after 9 p.m., so she'd missed the chance to speak to Davison. She called anyway, and left a voice message.

Then she called her parents' number. In a moment, the front porch lights flicked on, and her mom, already in T-shirt and pajama pants, threw open the front door. She ran to Branigan's car and was waiting to envelop her daughter in a hug when she stepped out.

"I feel stupid..." Branigan started.

"Don't," said Mrs Powers. "I'm not sure I'd *ever* stay by myself at that farm with no close neighbors around. Tomorrow, I'll call about a security alarm. But for now, you come in and we'll make up your old room. Hey there, Cleo. Did you come to spend the night with Grandma?"

"I need something to sleep in," Branigan said.

"I'm sure Dad has a T-shirt he can spare. And I'll reheat the potato soup we had for supper."

"Thanks, Mom." She and Cleo gave themselves over to pampering.

* * *

A half-hour later, Branigan and her parents sat at their kitchen table over mugs of hot tea. They deserved to know the truth, whether Davison was ready or not. So she told them first about him – how well he'd done last week at the farmhouse, then at the beach. How he was safely checked into the gospel mission's rehab program. She told them it was, in fact, his fifth try at rehab.

Then she told them more details about the Resnick story she was working on for Sunday; about the hit-and-run deaths of Vesuvius Hightower and Rita Mae Jones, and the brutal slaying of Max Brody.

Her mother reacted to Rita Mae's name. "Wait a minute. That woman in yesterday's paper was Rita Mae Jones?" She turned to her husband. "You remember her. Her father was Arthur Jones. He worked with Hugh Resnick years ago, before he and his wife – Peggy, I think her name was – moved to Atlanta. Rita Mae came with them sometimes to Alberta's Fourth of July parties."

"Right," Branigan said. "The hit-and-run on Conestee was her."

Her mom went to get the paper from the recycling pile. "Rita Jones," she said, scanning the story again. "I didn't make the connection. She was living in Grambling, homeless? That's hard to believe." She passed the paper to her husband.

"Branigan, this sounds dangerous," he said.

"That's why I'm here. Cleo went crazy around 5 o'clock this morning. When it got light, we went running. And I found a water bottle in the barn from Jericho Road."

"You definitely need to stay here until things settle down," her father said.

"I think I will," she agreed. "Or at least until you install a security alarm at the farm. Thanks for being willing to do that."

They talked for awhile longer, then she and Cleo went to her old room. Her mom had replaced the curtains and spread from her teenage lavender period with fashionable Roman shades and a comforter in blue and gold. But the four-poster bed felt exactly as she remembered. She wriggled deep into its embrace and fell into an exhausted sleep.

She was walking to the barn at twilight, her hand in Pa's. She was an adult, but glanced over to see a four-year-old Davison holding Pa's other hand. Davison was skipping in excitement.

"Are we gonna see the cows and the chicks, Pa?" he shouted.

"Yes, son," Pa chuckled. "But we need to be quiet so we don't scare them, okay?"

They heard a low moo. "She knows we're coming, doesn't she?" Pa asked.

Davison answered with a gleeful laugh.

They reached the heavy barn door, and Pa let go of their hands in order to swing it open. She turned to look back toward the farmhouse and was alarmed to see two raggedy people limping toward them. Looking closer, she recognized them: Rita and Max. What were they doing on the farm? She didn't want them here. She turned to tell Pa about the interlopers, but he had already ducked into the barn's dim interior.

"I want to show you something," he whispered, beckoning Davison and her to the closest stall. "Miss Moselle had a calf last night."

He grabbed Davison by the waist and held him aloft so he could see through the slats.

"A baby cow!" Davison shouted. "Brani, look! It's a baby cow!"

She wanted to share Davison's delight, but was too anxious. Rita and Max were coming, and they didn't belong on the farm. They didn't belong in their lives.

Pa pulled a baby bottle from inside his shirt. "Unfortunately," he said, "Mosie's having trouble feeding her calf. We need to help her."

He stepped inside the stall and upended the bottle into the calf's eager mouth. She greedily sucked down the milk.

Pa tossed the bottle to one side and went to check on the calf's mother. He and Davison seemed unaware of Rita and Max. It was up to her to protect them. Her eyes darted to the barn door, where the two suddenly appeared, outlined against a shaft of dying sunlight.

"Help him!" screeched Rita drunkenly. And then she saw Max's face, and the steak knife protruding from his forehead. Spurting blood, he pitched forward.

She tried to scream, tried to warn Pa about the intruders. But nothing came from her throat.

She grabbed the baby bottle, thinking she'd throw it to grab Pa's attention.

"God loves you," read the blue and white label on its side. "And so does Jericho Road."

238

Branigan jerked awake, heart hammering, choked screams in her throat. Cleo placed her head on the mattress, whining softly.

At first it had been so nice to see Pa again, and Davison, before the currents of adulthood pulled him under. But then the guilt flooded in over Rita and Max.

Who were these homeless people to encroach upon her life? And why had she invited them in?

CHAPTER FORTY-FIVE

Malachi sat alone in the Jericho Road dining room, his eggs, toast and bacon eaten but untasted. He'd wanted to return to where he'd first seen Vesuvius's moonscape, and if possible to ask Pastor Liam about its purchase.

He sipped his coffee, liberally sweetened. And he thought.

He had arrived in Grambling on a Greyhound bus a little more than ten years ago. He remembered the story of the downtown lady who got stabbed that July 5. How could he not? It was in the newspaper every day for three months.

He had stayed two nights right about where he sat now, he recalled, glancing around him. It'd been an abandoned grocery store then, a real mess, with dog and human excrement in one corner. Two nights had been enough, and he'd fled to the outdoors.

Malachi tried to remember the three men who'd been staying in the vacant building at the time. People came and went so freely out here. "Homelessness is fluid," he'd heard Pastor Liam say, and it was true. From motel room to boarding house to a cousin's home to a friend's couch to a car to a tent in the woods to a shelter to a blanket under the bridge. When there was no movement toward getting clean or permanently employed, the cycle of living arrangements was endless.

So, the men in the grocery store. Were they still in Grambling? Did they see who ditched the old lady's Thunderbird in the parking lot?

It was inconceivable that someone didn't know something. *Lot of double negatives there*, he chuckled to himself. Okay, someone knew something. He agreed with the police on little, but he thought they were right about that maxim: someone always knew something. About the old lady's murder, about V, about Rita, about Max.

He needed to know who they were and what they knew.

Malachi had been startled yesterday when Demetrius spun around and called him an invisible man. *Out of the mouths of the insane…*

Then Miz Branigan leaped in with what nearly amounted to an accusation: that the second dweller in Mrs Resnick's pool house was black and homeless. "Like you," she'd said.

That's why it was so unexpected to find himself caring – worrying even – that something might happen to the newspaper lady. She tried to be all tough and professional, but he'd seen her throwing up after they found Max's body. He'd seen the guilt racking her. He knew something about guilt.

Malachi stretched his legs, settled his cap more firmly over his braids. He'd lived in Grambling's shadows long enough to know about its underside; to know how the rich and poor, the sophisticated and the raw, the proper and the dangerous, merged after dark.

Rita, for instance, had once had some pretty well-to-do clients. Not recently. But once.

And he knew things about some of Grambling's *la-de-da* families. The executive who picked up male prostitutes. The high school cheerleader who scored crack. The community theater director who was convinced his creativity depended on cocaine.

When no one saw you, they had nothing to hide.

He knew some things, too, about the Resnicks. He knew, for instance, that Ramsey had a soft spot for the homeless. His name appeared frequently on Pastor's Liam's newsletter donor list. He taught a class on budgeting here at the shelter. He prayed with people who came for groceries. He quietly gave feminine products and toiletry items to Rita. And Malachi knew for a fact he had given Rita a bottle of cheap vodka from time to time.

And then there was Heath, nastier on the surface than his brother. Those Westside mill condos he'd bought had gone bust. Some street people, including Max Brody, had broken in afterward and stayed there. Sure, they had no running water or electricity. But the units were dry and relatively warm.

Malachi saw Pastor Liam walk through the sliding doors and head for the coffee urn, speaking briefly to the shelter residents serving breakfast. The man seldom took time to eat in the morning. Malachi stood and followed him to his office; he knocked, despite the artsy, hand-crafted sign that read "Come on in".

"Come on in!" Pastor Liam's voice echoed his sign. "G'morning, Malachi. I hope you slept better than I did."

"I imagine so."

"What's on your mind?"

"V," Malachi said, taking a rocking chair as Pastor Liam came around his desk to do the same. "I wanted to ask you 'bout a pitcher he did of a pond in the moonlight. You 'member that one?"

"I sure do. It was beautiful. I used it during worship with a sermon on John's prologue. Darkness and light and all that."

"Well, V sold that pitcher to another homeless dude. He told me you said he could take it off the dining room wall. Do you know who he sold it to?"

Pastor Liam thought for a moment. "No, I don't. There wasn't anyone with him when we talked. Vesuvius said someone offered to buy it, so I told him to take it. Why?"

"You don't think it's funny that a homeless dude bought his pitcher?"

"I didn't know a homeless dude *did* buy it. I assumed he was commissioning it to one of the downtown galleries."

"He told me it was a homeless dude, and he got at least $130 for it," said Malachi.

"Wow." Pastor Liam frowned. "And you think that's tied to what's been happening?"

"Aw, I don't know what I think. They's just a lot of unexplained money and a lot of unexplained homeless dudes turnin' up dead."

Pastor Liam couldn't help smiling at Malachi's turn of phrase.

"One more thing, Pastor. Did you find out how much money was in your lock box?"

"Yeah, I talked to our office manager this morning: $650 in cash."

A small fortune, Malachi thought. *Enough to buy a painting, bottles of liquor, maybe even crack rocks.* But apparently not enough to buy silence.

242

CHAPTER FORTY-SIX

After a quick cup of coffee with her parents, Branigan hustled Cleo into the Civic and drove to the farm. At the last minute, she decided to get in a brief run; the wisps of last night's dream lingered and she wanted it out of her head.

She changed into shorts and running shoes, and she and Cleo set off. The morning was deliciously cool, calling to mind a poem she'd memorized in fifth grade.

> *And what is so rare as a day in June*
> *Then, if ever, come perfect days.*

James Russell Lowell was a New Englander, but he could have summered happily on a Georgia farm. She longed for that fifth-grade Branigan who knew nothing of guilt.

Branigan's Uncle Bobby had already let his cows out to join another fifty head; they watched with mild interest as she and Cleo circled their pasture. Her lungs filled with clean air. This was home, and she wondered how she'd been scared of it the night before.

A half-hour later, sides heaving, she walked toward the barn. Cleo began barking and charged inside. Branigan hesitated until she heard the dog's bark switch to an excited whine. A familiar voice called, "Branigan? That you?"

"Uncle Bobby!" He held open his arms and she stepped in, warning, "I'm sweaty."

Her mom's younger brother was solidly built, his gray hair in a brush cut, his jeans and work shirt and lace-up boots identical to what Pa had worn every day. He had his own 200 acres adjoining Pa's land on one side, and the two had always shared their lakes and pastures.

"Your mama called this morning and told me about your visitor," he said. "I wanted to take a look around."

She peered into the last stall, where the water bottle remained where she'd found it. "See that?" She pointed. "It's a water bottle that Liam Delaney gives out to the homeless at Jericho Road. But I can't imagine one of them coming this far out. Can you?"

Uncle Bobby looked as if he wanted to say something, but stopped.

"What?" she asked.

"What about your brother?"

"Davison's in rehab at the Grambling Rescue Mission. He was here all last week, but in the house, of course."

"Could he have left the bottle then?"

A light dawned as she realized that, until yesterday, she hadn't been inside the barn for weeks. "You know, he could have! I'm sure he was walking around while I was at work." She breathed a long sigh. "You have no idea what a relief that is. My imagination was running wild."

She thought for a minute. "But what about you?" she asked. "You use this barn a lot, don't you? Had you noticed the bottle?"

"No, but that doesn't mean anything," he said. "I haven't used that stall since winter, so I really haven't been paying attention. Anyway, your mama and I still want to install an alarm. You and Cleo are kind of isolated out here by yourselves."

"I do appreciate it. But you've already helped more than you know."

They chatted for another minute, then Branigan headed to the house to shower, dress and get to Resnick Drugs.

The roped bells clanged as she walked in. A clerk and a pharmacist were working in the store and pointed her to Ramsey's closed office. She knocked. Ramsey opened it, and she was gratified to see Amanda and Heath seated inside. Ramsey wore his usual suit and looked puzzled as he took his place behind his desk. Amanda wore a gaily printed sundress and matching red sandals, but her body language was anything but casual. Her spine was ramrod straight, and her legs were pressed tightly together. Heath wore khakis and a golf shirt; it occurred to Branigan she'd never seen him in anything else.

"What's this about, Branigan?" Ramsey asked.

"Mr Resnick, Mrs Brissey, Mr Resnick," she said formally, "we've moved the anniversary story of your mother's death up to this Sunday. A lot has been happening."

"Can you tell us?" Amanda asked.

"Did you see the story Tuesday about the homeless woman killed on your mother's street?"

Heath's lip curled, but he remained silent.

"Yes," Ramsey answered. "I was acquainted with Rita. I tried to help her from time to time. I believe you saw her in here one day."

"Did you know she was at the Fourth of July party the night before your mother was killed?"

"What?"

"That's impossible!"

"No way!"

All three wore looks of shock and disbelief. If they were acting, they were skilled at it.

"Apparently," Branigan said, "she was the daughter of friends of your family. Rita Mae Jones."

She watched the confusion pass over Ramsey's face.

"Rita Mae Jones? Arthur and Peggy's daughter? That wasn't the Rita who was homeless."

"Think about the things that don't change," Branigan said. "Height. Skin color. She'd been hard into crack and crystal meth for years. Lost her teeth. The sun bleached her hair, aged her skin. That changes a person's looks drastically."

Ramsey was still shaking his head, trying to reconcile the homeless addict he'd helped with a young woman he'd known years earlier.

Finally, he said, "Rita Mae would be in her forties. I thought Rita was sixty or more."

Branigan nodded. "Liam assures me that crack and meth do that."

Heath and Amanda were looking lost.

"Wait a minute, Ramsey," said his sister. "You knew the homeless woman who was killed? How?"

"I volunteer at Jericho Road," he said. "I helped her with toiletries, things like that. I just never dreamed I knew her from before."

"And she never said anything about knowing you or being at your mother's house?" Branigan asked.

"Never," Ramsey said.

Heath spoke for the first time. "Do Arthur and Peggy Jones know all this? Did they know she was homeless?"

"They came in from Atlanta to identify the body," Branigan told him. "Whether they knew she was homeless before, I have no idea. Our cop reporter, Jody, is handling that part of the story."

"I'm speechless," Ramsey said, glancing at his brother and sister. "But what does this have to do with your story on Mother?"

"Apparently, when Rita Jones was drunk, which was quite often, she mentioned to several people that she knew something about an elderly lady who was stabbed. She even said that the rich family might pay to keep it quiet."

Ramsey, Heath and Amanda were staring at Branigan in open horror.

"Do the police know this?" Heath demanded.

"They do now. All the people Rita told – rather cryptically – over the years weren't the kind of people to go to the police. So this didn't surface until we had Liam Delaney at Jericho Road start asking questions among the homeless. In fact, I fear those questions may have gotten Rita and another homeless man killed."

"Are you saying Mother's murderer did turn out to be a hobo?" Amanda asked, her face ashen.

"Or more likely, that a transient saw who did it," Branigan replied. "Unfortunately, that could still be anyone."

She gave the trio a few moments to regain their composure before continuing. "We double-checked the guest list that the police compiled. Rita Mae Jones was on it. Furthermore, Ben Jr," she said, looking at Amanda, "told me he saw her at the party."

Amanda looked at her with stricken eyes. For the first time, Branigan felt she had hit up against something unexpected. The strain in Amanda's voice was unmistakable.

"What did Ben say?"

"That Rita Mae had joined him at the pool house. And that they had... um... smoked crack together."

Heath and Ramsey's eyes widened. Amanda bowed her head. "That doesn't surprise me. Ben Jr had quite a wild period, as we all know. I'm happy to say that's behind him."

"He was quite helpful," Branigan told her. "He was the one who told us about Rita Mae being at the party. What we now believe happened was that Rita Jones talked a great deal about something she saw – either that night or the next day. And that ultimately got her killed."

She watched the three closely. Heath looked disgusted, Ramsey thoughtful. But Amanda appeared to be breathing so shallowly Branigan feared she might hyperventilate.

What are you hiding, lady? she thought.

CHAPTER FORTY-SEVEN

JULY 5, TEN YEARS AGO

After dropping her nieces at the Peach Orchard Country Club, Amanda drove to the hotel near the interstate where her family was staying. She needed to think about what her mother had told her that morning – about Heath's youthful stealing and sexual assault, about his Prodigal-Son-like run through his portion of the inheritance, about her mother's upcoming visit to her lawyer to cut Heath from the will.

It was a lot to take in. Plus, she was hungry, having had her fruit-bowl breakfast interrupted. So instead of pulling into the hotel parking lot, she drove past it and entered a fast-food outlet. She parked her car in the only space she could find that provided shade from the Georgia sun.

Once inside, she rather mindlessly ordered a grilled chicken sandwich and a bottle of water. Her mind was whirling. *Heath. Boy, what have you gotten yourself into?*

She'd always been closer to Ramsey, two years her senior. She'd looked rather benignly upon Heath, five years younger. Maybe that was the problem, she now contemplated. Maybe he had manipulated them all into being – what was her mother's word? – indulgent. But stealing? And sexual assault? She hadn't heard a whisper of that. Did Ramsey know? Like her, he had been out of Grambling during Heath's late teens. Had their father covered it up so thoroughly that even Ramsey didn't hear about it?

That part of the story shook her. But upon reflection, she was more intrigued by the money. How much had Heath gone through? What was her mother's estate worth? Amanda thought it was sizeable. She appreciated her mother's sense of fairness. But was Mother being completely honest, even now? Or had Heath gone through, perhaps, more than a third? Was he broke? And how would he react when he found out he was being disinherited?

Amanda stood and tossed half her sandwich into the trash, then drove to the hotel. Bennett, she knew, was playing golf with clients from the region. He had already told her to drive home to Atlanta in one car with the boys; he'd keep the other and catch up with them tonight.

She expected to find Ben Jr and Drew at the pool, and sure enough, she found Drew under an umbrella, reading.

"Where's your brother?" she asked.

"He dropped Dad at the golf course, then took the car," he said. "He went to breakfast, I guess. When are we leaving?"

"A little later than I'd thought. I need to run one more errand for your grandmother. Do you want to wait for me at her house, or stay here? I can ask for an extension or even pay for another night if we need to."

"I'll stay here." He returned to his book. "Call me fifteen minutes before we need to leave."

Amanda walked to the front desk and added another night for the boys' room to Bennett's credit card. It was easier than trying to pack their clothes and stow the luggage.

She wanted to talk to Ramsey, but he was accompanying Mother to Dr Arnott's office. That conversation would have to wait. Restless, Amanda walked to the shopping strip next door and got a pedicure she didn't need.

That took up the remaining time. Her nails were blood red – and dry – by 1:40. She walked back to the hotel, and breaking into a sweat, hopped into her blue Mercedes and drove to her mother's house.

Amanda turned off North Main Street, cutting her speed automatically, watching for children to dart into the street. It occurred to her that she'd been in Grambling longer than her usual twenty-four hours. Another couple of hours in the lawyer's office, and she'd be on the road to Atlanta. Thank goodness.

The duskiness of her mother's driveway was a welcome relief from the mid-day brightness. No other cars were there, so Ramsey must have already dropped her off after the doctor's appointment.

Amanda got out of the car, careful not to let her newly polished toes touch anything. There was nothing worse than smearing a fresh pedicure.

She saw the broken panes of the back door and stopped. Oh, no. Someone at last night's party had broken the door. It was always something. But wait. This was the door she exited two hours ago. It wasn't broken then.

The door was standing ajar too. She pushed it, and saw a sack of dirty clothes on the floor. But Tabitha had left when they did. She wouldn't leave laundry in the middle of the floor. She blinked, trying to adjust her eyes to the gloom of her mother's kitchen.

The clothes moved.

Mother's dog, Dollie, whimpered and limped toward Amanda. And that's when her brain caught up with her eyes. Amanda fell to her knees, staring, trying to comprehend the incomprehensible. She reached blindly for the dog. She wasn't tempted to go to her mother, wasn't tempted to hold the body that had once held hers. She felt only revulsion. And then fear. She looked around wildly. Heath! Was Heath still here?

She scrambled in her purse for her phone, and started to hit 9-1-1. Then her eyes fell on the open laundry room door. Something was lying on the floor, just beyond the doorjamb. *Something that shouldn't be there.*

Amanda's brain needed no time to make this leap. She snapped her phone shut and began to wail.

It took her only moments to pull her wits about her. She breathed deeply, gave Dollie a final pat, and stood. She walked to the laundry room, careful to avoid the blood puddles, and picked up the NYU Law baseball cap. She tucked it beneath her arm, then tiptoed back to her car. It wouldn't matter if she'd left fingerprints on the dog's collar, on the door, on the counter, anywhere. She'd been in the house all day and all night.

She opened her car trunk and found an old beach towel. She wrapped the baseball cap in it, then stowed it carefully as far back in the trunk as she could reach. She'd deal with it later.

Glancing about the property, she slipped into the Mercedes, and backed slowly out of the driveway. She turned in the direction of the hotel, scanning the yards lining Conestee to see if anyone was watching. Thank heavens, no neighbors were outside.

Okay, who knew what? Only Drew knew she was doing an errand for her mother. She would make it an errand that didn't require going back to the house. She could say she picked up dry cleaning. No, that made no sense. The girls. Caroline and Ashley. Maybe she could buy something for them and say Mother had asked her to.

She turned onto South Main, headed to the interstate. A picture of a globe caught her eye – a globe as a head with a basket carried on top of it. *Ethnic Treasures*, read the sign below it.

Amanda wrenched her wheel to the right, and turned into the tiny parking lot beside the store. The glass door had bronze Indian bells that announced her entry. She glanced around at woven mats and rugs, pottery, paintings, baskets. Ordinarily, she'd love browsing in a place like this. But now, she turned abruptly to a side wall that featured jewelry, snatched two pairs of earrings and took them to the counter.

"I'd like to pay for these and have them gift-wrapped for pick-up later, please."

"Certainly," said a petite Asian woman, ringing up her purchase.

Amanda started to pay in cash, then switched to her credit card. She also asked for a piece of paper, and carefully wrote out *Caroline and Ashley Resnick*, then *Alberta Resnick*.

"I'm not sure which of these three will pick up the earrings," she said. "Alberta is the grandmother, and she asked me to buy them for her granddaughters."

"How sweet," murmured the woman.

Amanda carefully filed the credit card receipt in the section of her wallet that held cash. She concentrated on walking casually out of the store, though the screams in her head were telling her to run.

Drew probably wouldn't even remember she was going on an errand for her mother, but she was covered nonetheless. She glanced at her watch: 2:10.

What next? Mother's attorney would be wondering where they were. No, he was probably expecting only Mother. Mother was famously tight-lipped. She didn't know if Amanda would accompany her and wouldn't have presumed to tell the lawyer that she was.

Amanda gripped the steering wheel and forced herself to calm down. *I have to find Ben Jr and get Bennett's car to the golf course, then head back to Atlanta.* That was the important thing – getting Ben Jr far away from here and back to Atlanta.

Then they'd wait for the call. The inevitable call.

CHAPTER FORTY-EIGHT

B ranigan met up with Jody and Marjorie in the newsroom to compare notes.

"Jody, I always thought you were a little obsessed with Amanda Brissey," she told him. "But you're right. Something is up with her."

He looked surprised. "You think she killed her mother?"

"Hard to say. How closely did the police look at where Ben Sr, Ben Jr and Drew were on July 5?"

Jody leaned back in his office chair. Branigan knew he'd reviewed the files when they started reworking the story. She wanted to see if his take jibed with hers.

"Bennett Sr had a solid alibi from three other men on the golf course. Drew was in full view of waiters and hotel guests by the swimming pool until his mom and brother picked him up and left for Atlanta.

"Amanda and Ben Jr were a bit looser. They were alone, in separate cars. Apparently, the family had come up from Atlanta in two cars.

"Amanda dropped her nieces at the country club, had lunch, went by the hotel and paid for another day on one room, got a manicure or pedicure or whatever you call it, shopped at a store on Main Street, met the boys at the hotel, dropped Ben Sr's car in the golf course parking lot, and drove to Atlanta. They were literally pulling into their driveway when they got the call about her mother's murder."

"And Ben Jr?"

"Dropped his dad at the golf course, had breakfast at an International House of Pancakes, went shopping at one of those

253

stores that sell college gear, then back to the pool with Drew, dropped the car at the golf course for his dad, drove home with Mom and Drew."

"Okay," Branigan mused. "The police retraced their movements, driving and timing. But there's no way they could verify the exact amount of time they spent in each place."

"If you're asking *could* one of them have squeezed in a trip to kill Mrs Resnick," Jody said, "then yeah, probably."

"Tell me about these shopping expeditions," she said. "Why does someone from Atlanta come to Grambling and shop?"

"Well, police traced Amanda's purchase. She bought earrings for her nieces, Caroline and Ashley Resnick. Said they were from the grandmother and left them to be gift-wrapped. Police found all that exactly as she described."

"And Ben Jr's college gear?"

"He didn't buy anything, but a female clerk at the store identified his picture. He's a pretty handsome guy, so she remembered him."

Branigan went to her desk and looked up Ben Jr's cell phone number. He answered on the third ring.

"Mr Brissey, this is Branigan Powers again from *The Grambling Rambler*. I have one more question for you."

"Shoot, Miss Powers."

"The police files say you went to the University Shoppe on the Eastside on the morning of your grandmother's murder. Can you tell me why?"

"I was looking to replace my NYU Law School hat," he said promptly. "I lost it at the party."

"How did that happen?"

"Like I told you before, I was drinking pretty heavily. But I remember my Uncle Heath kind of kidding around and taking it. When I woke up at the hotel the next morning, I didn't have it. I figured it'd be easier to buy another one than track him down. But the Grambling store didn't have one. I got one a couple of weeks later in Atlanta."

"I see. You know, Mr Brissey, what you told us about Rita Mae

Jones turned out to be helpful. Is there anything else you can remember? Anything that struck you as odd, even if it didn't seem to relate to your grandmother's murder?"

"Well, yeah, since you were asking about that baseball cap. A couple of years later, I was in my parents' attic, looking for an old baseball mitt I wanted in New York. I found the mitt in a trunk. And it was with my old NYU Law hat."

"The one you lost at the party?"

"I presume so. Sure looked like it anyway."

"Did you ask your parents about it?"

"I asked Dad. He didn't know anything. So I took it with me. Didn't hurt to have two."

"Okay. Thank you so much, Mr Brissey. I hope I won't have to bother you again."

"No bother at all."

Branigan hung up and tried to make sense of the conversation. A hat that Heath had taken from Ben Jr later showed up in Amanda's attic. Heath was getting cut from his mother's will. Amanda was hiding something. Was she protecting Heath? She'd been pretty open about revealing her mother's intention to cut him from the will, but equally insistent that he didn't know.

I'd make a lousy detective, Branigan realized. Amanda had probably seen the hat at her mother's house the morning after the party and tossed it in her suitcase.

She picked up the phone again, feeling like some insane Lieutenant Columbo. "I really apologize. One last question."

Ben Jr was clearly puzzled. "Okay."

"Did you tell your mom that you'd lost the NYU hat?"

"Yeah, on our ride back to Atlanta. I told her I'd been at the college store in Grambling trying to buy one."

"What'd she say?"

"She reminded me of the place in Atlanta where I could replace it."

"Okay, thank you."

"Do you mind telling me what my hat has to do with your story?"

"Probably nothing," she told him honestly. "Thanks again."

So Amanda had the NYU hat and chose not to give it back to Ben Jr. There could be a logical explanation for such behavior. Or illogical and uninteresting. But it had occurred in a house that was the scene of a brutal murder. That's when illogical became interesting.

Amanda didn't return the cap to the son who was looking for it. Instead, she hid it in her attic.

Like she was hiding something else.

CHAPTER FORTY-NINE

"**D**ad?"

Liam waved his son into his office as he finished a phone conversation with Detective Scovoy. The detective checked in several times a day from an office down the hall. Liam couldn't tell if he was making progress, but his officers had interviewed the entire staff and were now talking to volunteers.

He turned to his son with relief. "I'm glad to see you." He took a chair across from Chan. "What brings you in?"

"Mom said you might not get home 'til late, with the police here and all."

"She's right about that."

Chan looked troubled – in fact, to Liam's mind, had looked troubled for weeks. At first Liam thought it was nervousness about going off to college. Now he wasn't sure. The boy was acting strange, alternately distant and needy. Liam and Liz had discussed it before everything blew up with this morning's *Rambler* story about the church van running down Vesuvius and Rita. He'd been on the phone much of the morning with fellow clergy and friends from sister agencies. Rather than the suspicion he'd expected, he'd received everything from prayers to offers of vehicle loans from other churches. He was in the middle of organizing a prayer service for the weekend.

But seeing Chan's worried face banished everything else from his mind.

"I don't know how to ask you this," Chan started. "Because I don't want you and Mom to think I'm anything but grateful for sending me to Furman. For everything really."

Liam had a sinking feeling. But he tried to mask it. "You know you can ask me anything."

"It's about my adoption."

"I wondered if that might be it."

"Might be what?"

"Well, Mom and I have noticed that you've not been yourself."

"Oh. Well, you know, I've never been... curious before." Chan looked at the floor, the wall, anywhere but at Liam. "But now that I'll be... living away, I thought maybe it's time for us to talk about it." He stopped and looked for a reaction.

"You're absolutely right," Liam said. "Past time. And that's my fault. I've wanted to protect you."

"Can we do it tonight?"

"The thing is, Chan, your biological father has gotten in touch with us. He wants to be in on the discussion, because there are... things he wants you to know. Things you *need* to know before going to Furman. Genetics and such. I think he can do it this weekend."

"He's in Grambling now?"

"Yes."

"And he told you he'd tell me this weekend?"

"Well, no, but I think we can push it up since you've brought it up."

Chan released a long sigh. "And you're not mad?"

"No! How could I be mad?"

"Maybe that's the wrong word. You're not... hurt? Is Mom?"

"No, Chandler. You are our son and nothing will ever, ever change that. Obviously your biological parents had problems, or they wouldn't have given you up. And it's time, it's *past* time, that you knew about it. It's you we've worried about hurting."

Chan smiled in relief. "I'm ready if you are."

Liam stood and grabbed him in a tight hug. "Deal."

Outside Liam's office a figure finished sweeping. He straightened his ball cap over his dreadlocks and glided away, unseen, unheard, unnoticed.

CHAPTER FIFTY

Tan offered to bring in sandwiches if the reporters didn't want to stop working.

"That would be great," Branigan told him. She needed to start writing so she could see where the holes were.

Marjorie was working on a story on homelessness in Grambling, and especially how street dwellers interacted with Jericho Road.

Jody was following the police investigation into the Jericho Road van that killed two of them.

Branigan was working on the anniversary story of Alberta Resnick's murder and how it intersected at several points with Grambling's homeless – with Vesuvius and Rita, certainly, but also with Max. All three of the reporters' stories needed to stand alone, but there would be cross-referencing. It was going to take an experienced editor to keep it all straight. Tan seemed disinclined to hand it over to an underling, so Branigan assumed he'd edit it with some serious fact-checking from Julie and the copy desk.

Branigan was creating a timeline of July 5, the last day of Mrs Resnick's life, when her cell phone buzzed. It was Liam.

"Branigan, when's the last time you talked to Davison?"

"Tuesday night. There was so much going on last night that I missed the window to call him."

"Chan is asking questions, so Liz and I want to move our conversation with Davison to this weekend. Can he do that?"

"I guess so. He has a twelve-hour pass on Saturday. You want me to call him?"

"No, that's okay. I'll do it."

"Do you want Mom and Dad there?"

"No, let's start with Liz and me and Davison. And maybe you and Charlie."

"I'll try, but I may be working on this story."

"Okay. I'm thinking I want you there to remind Chan that you and I have the same genes as Davison and Shauna. I want him to know that addiction's not a given."

"I understand. I'll do everything I can to be there. Call me back when you know what time you want me."

"Will do. And Brani G? Thanks for everything. I'm looking forward to getting this over with."

She set an alert on her laptop to signal her at 8 p.m. so she wouldn't forget to call Davison. Then she arranged the cardboard boxes of police files on the floor around her desk for easy access, and stacked her notebooks neatly beside her computer, with colored tabs marking the names of interviewees: Ramsey, Amanda, Heath, Caroline, Ashley, Ben Jr, Liam, Dontegan, Jess, Malachi, Detective Scovoy. At times like this her rigid organization paid off.

Julie brought her a cup of coffee from the canteen, with a whispered, "Looks like you can use this."

Branigan smiled her thanks. Then she dug in. The writing flowed more easily than she'd anticipated, probably because she'd lived inside the story for the past two weeks. By 5 p.m. she had a roughly sketched piece and a fresh list of questions on a pad.

The first one concerned that pesky NYU hat. She called Amanda's cell, figuring she'd be back at the lake house.

"No," Amanda said, "I took the opportunity to do some shopping. I've been at the mall all day."

"Can I meet you there?" Branigan asked. "I have a few more questions."

"I've already pulled out. What more can you possibly have to ask me?"

Branigan deliberately dodged the question. "A lot of times you have to start writing before you figure out what's missing. That's where I am now."

"Very well. I'm near downtown."

"Perfect. Let's meet at Bea's on Main in ten minutes."

* * *

Branigan took the opportunity to walk in the late afternoon heat. It felt good to get out of the chilly office, and even better to stretch her muscles after a day crouched over a laptop. As she walked, she called her mother, who said that Uncle Bobby had overseen the installation of an alarm system at the farmhouse and had already activated it. She gave Branigan the code she'd need to deactivate it when she got inside. Branigan thanked her and told her she would spend the night at the farm.

Amanda was already seated in a booth when Branigan arrived. She looked tired. Branigan ordered yet another coffee, and slid in across from her.

"This is going to sound strange," she began. "But I want to ask you about something Ben Jr said."

Amanda didn't move, but a muscle beneath her left eye twitched.

"In following the family's movements on July 5, the police knew that Ben drove to the University Shoppe on the Eastside around noon or so. A clerk identified his picture and Ben confirmed he was there."

Amanda merely nodded.

"He told me he went to replace an NYU Law School baseball cap." She watched Amanda closely. "He was headed to law school there."

"Anybody can buy one," Amanda said.

"Right. But as it turns out, Ben didn't need another one. He found his hat in your attic."

Amanda had a terrible poker face. She turned a water bottle round and round in her hands. "No," she said. "He bought another hat in Atlanta."

"Yes. *Another* hat. Because he lost one at your mother's house. And you took it and hid it in your attic. I want to know why."

"How could you possibly know that? Have you been in my attic?"

"I didn't have to. Ben said he found it there when he went looking for a baseball mitt, years later."

Amanda looked bewildered. "No, that's impossible. Why didn't Ben say anything?"

"I think he did. To your husband."

"Bennett never mentioned it to me."

"He probably didn't think it was important," Branigan pressed. "Only you did. Why did you think the hat was important enough to hide?"

Amanda's eyes skittered away. "You don't have children, do you, Branigan?"

"No."

"Things change when you're a mother. I don't believe I should answer any more questions."

"Where did you find the hat? Were you at the murder scene?"

"I don't believe I should answer any more questions," Amanda repeated.

"You do understand I have to give this information to the police, don't you?"

She looked at Branigan beseechingly. Then her eyes fell. "I suppose."

"Okay. But I think there's one more thing you should know."

"What is that?" she asked wearily.

"Ben Jr said that your brother Heath was kidding around and took his NYU hat the night of the party. That's how he lost it."

Amanda's head popped up. The weariness vanished from her face and shoulders as she looked at Branigan with widening eyes. And then she did something unexpected. She started to laugh, loud enough to draw glances from the diners behind them, long enough to unsettle Branigan. Her laughter had a shrill edge, veering toward hysteria.

"Mrs Brissey?"

"Heath was wearing Ben's hat? Oh, that is rich. All these years. All these years." Amanda was shaking her head and wiping her eyes.

Gradually, her laughter died away, though the tears still ran down her face. Her head shook from side to side, as if she couldn't quite take in this turn of events. "All these years," she whispered again.

She placed a hand over one of Branigan's.

"My dear girl," she said. "I think you've found your murderer."

CHAPTER FIFTY-ONE

B ranigan followed Amanda Brissey to the police station a few
blocks away, and waited with her while Detective Scovoy was
summoned from his makeshift office at Jericho Road. When he
arrived, he placed Amanda in a room for questioning, then guided
Branigan to his office. She filled him in on Amanda's evidence
tampering, pointing out that she was willing to confess, now that
she understood the evidence to point to her brother, not her son.

Branigan also told the detective about Ben Brissey Jr and Rita
Mae Jones smoking crack at the Fourth of July party. She added,
"When I told Heath Resnick that the homeless Rita killed by the
Jericho Road van was the same Rita Mae who'd been a party guest,
he seemed genuinely surprised. But you probably know when people
are lying better than I do."

"I'm beginning to wonder about that," Scovoy said. "Nice work
on the baseball cap. We knew Amanda Brissey was holding out on
us, but we had no idea about what."

"The question now," she said, "is whether Heath Resnick had
access to the church van. Was he trying to keep Rita and Vesuvius
quiet? And Max, for that matter?"

"That's the angle we'll be working tonight," the detective said.
"We questioned Ramsey Resnick today as a Jericho Road volunteer.
We'll backtrack to see if Heath could have obtained the van key
through him."

Branigan left, telling Detective Scovoy she'd swing by the next
morning to get the latest information on his inquiry into Heath
Resnick. If nothing else, it would provide the lead she needed for
the anniversary story.

She stopped by the newsroom to update Jody and Marjorie.

Resurrecting Heath as a suspect and introducing Amanda's presence at the murder scene wouldn't affect their stories, but she wanted to keep them in the loop. Luckily, Tan-4 had gone home, so she didn't have to tell him about his cousin's return to the suspect pool. Or maybe cousins, plural, if the police didn't entirely buy Amanda's story.

While Branigan was in the newsroom, she scrolled through her emails, discarding some, answering the rest. Julie asked her about a *Style* front for the Sunday after next. "Once I get past this anniversary story," she promised, "I'll do anything you need."

At 8 p.m. her laptop signaled it was time to call Davison. If she could get to the farm before dark, she planned to spend the night, so she hurried out into the last hour of daylight.

Halfway home, she called Davison and warbled the opening lines to "Rehab".

"You used that already," he replied.

"You sound tired."

"Tired of your singing."

"Ouch. What's up?"

He sighed. "Not a thing. Just learning why I got to say 'no, no, no' no matter what.

"'Nothing going to get better by putting dope on it.' 'Nothing so bad dope can't make it worse.' 'Sick and tired of being sick and tired.' More like sick and tired of all this recovery crap."

"You're in a mood."

"Aw, I'm fine. It's just that I've been through this so many times before. I *know* what I have to do to stay sober."

She held her tongue.

He said it for her. Sheepishly. "But obviously knowing and doing are two different things. I've got to lick this."

"That reminds me," she said. "Has Liam called you?"

"Why would he?"

"He wants you to meet with Chan and him and Liz this Saturday."

"What's the rush?"

"Chan is asking questions."

There was silence for a long moment. "I guess that'll work. Make sure Liam has my cell number, okay? Brani G, I better run. Another meeting."

He hung up before she had a chance to ask about the water bottle in the barn. The more she thought about it, the surer she was that he'd left it the week he'd stayed at the farm. She punched in his number again to ask. But this time it went to voice mail.

When she pulled into the driveway, it took Cleo a full minute to run out of the cotton field. Obviously she'd been beyond the patch – in the pasture, maybe. Or sniffing around the barn.

Branigan estimated there was another half-hour of light remaining, so she didn't even go inside to change clothes.

"Come on, Cleo," she said. "Let's see what you've been up to."

She kicked off her heels and left them in the driveway. The dirt path was hard-packed and relatively free of stones, warm on her bare feet. The barn door stood ajar, but that was not unusual, especially if Uncle Bobby had moved his cows earlier in the day. She pulled the door wide, to allow as much light in as possible. Keeping close to Cleo, she tiptoed to the stall closest to the door – the one with the Jericho Road bottle inside.

It was still there.

Only now there was a second one next to it.

Cleo barked, and Branigan jumped, letting out a shriek. The dog sniffed at the stall door, then ran up and down the line of empty stalls, whining and snuffling.

"Somebody slept here last night," she said to Cleo. "Even without us at home."

Branigan's skin was prickling, so she turned abruptly and headed for the house, checking to make sure Cleo was behind her.

Don't be a scaredy cat, she told herself. *Cleo would tear anybody apart for you.*

They hurried back to the house, slamming and locking the side door. Branigan heard the alarm beeping, but couldn't remember the code her mother had given her. As she clawed through her purse for the scrap of paper she'd written it on, the house phone rang.

"This is the alarm company. May I have your password, please?"

"I'm sorry! This is Branigan Powers. It was just installed today and I don't have the password yet."

"We'll send a deputy to this address immediately. Meantime, please see your paperwork for your code and password."

"Yes, yes. That's fine."

Branigan didn't try to talk the voice out of sending a deputy, because she wanted to report the barn intruder. She went to sit with Cleo on the steps leading to the side stoop, checking her watch. A Cannon County Sheriff's car pulled into the driveway in exactly eight minutes, a man and a woman inside. The woman took the lead, introducing herself as Deputy Mary Ann Hammond.

Branigan explained about the new alarm system. "But I was going to call you anyway. Someone has been spending the last few nights in my barn."

"How do you know?" Deputy Hammond asked.

"He – or she – left water bottles from Jericho Road. That's the homeless church downtown."

"The church under investigation for those hit-and-runs?" asked her partner.

"That's the one."

"Do you want to show us?" asked Deputy Hammond.

"If you've got flashlights."

The sky had turned from orange-red to dusky purple as she sat on the stoop, but Branigan could walk the cotton patch in her sleep. She led the deputies to the barn, explaining how Cleo had gone ballistic on Tuesday night and how she'd found a single water bottle the next morning. They'd spent last night in town and returned to find a second bottle.

The deputies poked around, but it was almost impossible for them to see anything in the murkiness of the barn's interior. With the darkness impairing Branigan's sight, she found her sense of smell sharpened. She smelled Uncle Bobby's hay on the wide shelf above the stalls, a faint lingering scent of manure from the stalls, but something else too – something pleasant. *Flowers,* she thought. *No, honeysuckle. Oh, of course...*

Deputy Hammond interrupted her thoughts. "You say you have a new security alarm?"

They left the barn and headed single-file toward the house. "Yes, installed today."

"And you haven't seen signs of anyone trying to break into the house?"

She shook her head.

The deputy handed Branigan a business card. "Lock yourself in," she advised, "with that dog. If you hear anything, you can call me directly in addition to having the alarm company alert the sheriff's office."

Branigan thanked them for coming and took the deputy's advice, checking all the exterior doors to make sure she and Cleo were securely bolted in.

Over a late supper of scrambled eggs, a toasted bagel and Aunt Jeanie's strawberry jam, Branigan pored over a folder on Heath Resnick she'd brought from the office.

Smug and arrogant, spoiled youngest child, perpetually dressed for a round of golf, he fit easily into her unschooled view of a murderer. She could picture him stabbing his mother in a rage after finding out she was cutting him from her will. She could picture him leaving his nephew's NYU Law cap, either by sheer accident or to implicate Ben Jr in the murder. (If the latter, he must have been surprised when the police never mentioned it!) She could picture him behind the wheel of the Jericho Road van, pressing his foot to the gas pedal to run down an unsuspecting Vesuvius Hightower, a drunkenly weaving Rita Jones. She could picture him lashing out at Max Brody with a broken whiskey bottle, angry that the drunk couldn't keep his mouth shut. She could even picture him calmly cutting her phone lines and creeping into the farmhouse, stabbing her as she slept.

What she couldn't picture was Heath Resnick sleeping in a cattle stall in her barn.

The first murder seemed spontaneous, a crime of fury and opportunity.

Vesuvius, on the other hand, took some planning. Did Heath buy a painting from him in order to strike up a conversation and find out what he knew? And then follow him to run him down?

And Rita. Did Heath know good and well that Rita Mae Jones was a family friend who had seen something on the weekend of the murder? Had she been blackmailing him? There was no obvious sign of money coming her way, but she could have smoked it.

And Max. Did Heath first try to buy his silence? And when that didn't work, did he bring a bottle to Max's tent? Things could have turned ugly, leading Heath to kill Max in the same rage in which he killed his mother.

Still, still, she couldn't picture Heath lying in wait in the barn for a chance to get at her. And she sure couldn't see him leaving two water bottles for her to find – unless, of course, he thought she never entered the barn.

She yawned. Despite her anxiety, she was getting sleepy.

She washed up the few dishes by hand, then walked around to check all the doors once more. She turned on the outside lights and closed the window shutters tight. She turned the television on at low volume, more for its welcoming murmur than an intention to watch it. Then she stretched out on the den sofa. Within minutes, she was asleep.

She was walking to the barn at twilight, her hand in Pa's. She was too old to be holding Pa's hand, at least seventeen or so, but it felt natural. She glanced over to see Chan right behind them, kicking a soccer ball down the cotton field path. No, that couldn't be Chan. It must be Davison.

"Are we gonna see the cows and chicks, Pa?" he shouted.

She giggled to hear the childish voice coming from his almost grown body.

"Yes, son," Pa chuckled. "But we need to be quiet so we don't scare them, okay?"

They heard a low moo. "She knows we're coming, doesn't she?" Pa asked. Davison answered by flipping the soccer ball from his foot into one hand. Only it wasn't a ball any more; it was a beer can. He popped it open, then flung the shiny metal tab deep into the cotton patch, glittering as it caught the setting sun.

"Don't litter," she said automatically.

They reached the heavy barn door, and Pa let go of her hand in order to swing it open. She turned to look back toward the farmhouse and was alarmed to see two raggedy people running toward them. One was Malachi, his faded camouflage clothes and dreadlocks instantly recognizable. Behind him was a man running awkwardly because of the large plyboard painting he carried. Vesuvius, she thought. But aren't you dead?

What were they doing on the farm? She didn't mind them being here, exactly, but she didn't understand their presence either.

Pa had entered the barn's dim interior, and beckoned them inside. "I want to show you something," he whispered. "Miss Moselle had a calf last night."

He grabbed Davison-who-looked-like-Chan by the waist and tried to hoist him, but of course he was too heavy.

"A baby cow!" Davison shouted. "Brani, look! It's a baby cow!"

Again she laughed at the incongruity of this boy's voice in a man's body, but she didn't share Davison's delight. She was too nervous: clearly Malachi and Vesuvius wanted to tell her something.

"Unfortunately," Pa said, "Mosie's having trouble feeding her calf. We need to help her."

"I'll do it, Pa," said Davison, and turned his beer can up for the calf to drink. She greedily sucked it down.

Her eyes darted to the barn door, where the two homeless men suddenly appeared, outlined against a shaft of dying sunlight. Vesuvius pulled out a hammer and nails, and began securing his painting to the wall facing the stalls. Malachi dashed forward and knocked the beer can out of Davison's hand.

"No!" he hollered. "She needs water." He took a baby bottle from his pants pocket and lifted it to the calf's mouth. She could see the blue and white label in the gloom. And even though she couldn't read it, she knew what it said.

"God loves you. And so does Jericho Road."

Cleo's yelping brought Branigan off the couch with a start, heart thumping. Her addled mind thought the alarm was going off again, but no, it was Cleo making all the noise. That meant that no one was trying to get into the house.

She turned off the television so that the side porch light provided the sole glimmer in the den. She tiptoed to the window, lifting a shutter slat to peer out. Cleo was on two legs, clawing at the door, barking frantically.

Branigan's body was on highest alert, heart hammering, nerves shrieking. She needed to look outside, but didn't want anyone to see her. A figure passed just beyond the porch globe's wide circle of light. A figure pushing a bike from the cotton patch down the driveway toward the road. Leaving.

A figure she knew.

A few moments later, Branigan flipped on the kitchen light and was surprised to find that it was 5 a.m. Little more than an hour to sun-up.

She made a pot of coffee and looked up *The New York Times* and *The Rambler* online. She wasn't quite brave enough to step outside to pick up the newspaper.

CHAPTER FIFTY-TWO

Chan Delaney hadn't had a decent night's sleep since school let out. Last night was no exception.

The sun was up, but no one in his house was stirring when he knocked on his sister's door. Nothing. He knocked again, stuck his head in. "You awake?"

Of course she wasn't. He'd have to be less subtle.

"Charlie! Charlie! You up?"

She began to stir, looked at him blearily. "What are you doing?" she hissed. Charlie was not a morning person. "If you want the car, take it." She pulled the covers up and turned her back to him.

"Charlie, it's not the car. Can we talk?"

She turned back, looked at him incredulously.

"I thought you've been wanting to talk," he said innocently.

"In daylight hours." But she sat up, shoved the red-gold hair out of her face. "What do you want?"

He pulled her desk chair over so that his knees touched her mattress. He didn't want to wake their parents.

"We're having a family meeting tomorrow to talk about my adoption," he said.

"Mom and Dad are getting rid of you? After all this time?"

"Very funny. I'm going to meet my real dad. Well, my biological dad."

That got her attention. "No kidding? Is this what's been going on, with all the whispering?"

He nodded. "I think so."

"Well, that's good, I guess. Are you excited?"

"The thing is, Charlie, I've already met him."

Her eyes widened, but she waited for him to speak.

"He's Davison Powers, Branigan's brother."

"*What?!*"

"Once you see him," Chan said, "you won't be too surprised. I'm not sure I look like him, but our coloring and build are the same."

"But isn't he a drug addict?"

Chan nodded. "Which explains what the big secret has been all these years. He wanted me to know before I go to Furman. How susceptible I'll be to drinking – and anything else. He's in rehab at the Grambling Rescue Mission right now."

"Wow." Charlie was shaking her head in wonder. "Did he say anything about your mother?"

"Yeah. It gets worse. Remember that picture we found that time at Grandma and Granddad's house? Grandma said it was their daughter Shauna, who'd gotten hooked on drugs as a teenager? That's my mom. Another drug addict."

Charlie covered her mouth. "Now we know why Mom and Dad didn't want to tell us." She thought for a minute. "Branigan knows."

Chan looked up. "She would. And Grandma and Granddad. And probably Mr and Mrs Powers too. Everybody but me."

"And me," she said. They sat in silence for a few minutes. "I know this is awful and a lot to take in all at once. But there's definitely a bright side. Look where you landed."

"Yeah, I'm not upset with Mom and Dad. It's just that…"

"What?"

"I'm not quite sure how to tell them I already know."

"How *do* you know, anyway? Where did this Davison guy find you?"

"At the library."

"I mean, did he just walk up and say, 'Hi, I'm your dad'? Or what?"

"To begin with, he wrote me a long letter and left it on a library table where my stuff was. He said he was getting ready to contact Dad and Branigan, but wanted to see me first. We've been talking for three weeks or so.

"It took me awhile to get used to the idea. But he's a really nice guy, Charlie, and he's honest. You'll like him. He told me all about himself – everything from messing up so bad at college to giving up a dream of law school to working carnivals and being homeless. He wants to get clean and buy a little cabin on Lake Hartwell where I can visit. You too. He really wants to meet you."

"Why didn't you tell Mom and Dad?"

"Davison didn't want me to until he could prove to Mom and Dad and Branigan that he was serious about getting sober. But that's been bothering me more and more – keeping it from them. That's why I told Dad I wanted to have this family meeting tomorrow. He actually brought up that my real dad – or my biological dad – would join us."

Charlie gave him the steady look he was accustomed to: the look he trusted, the look that led him to wake her.

"You know, Davison may be a great guy," she said. "I hope he is. But the fact is, he started off by asking you to lie to Mom and Dad."

"I don't think we should wait 'til tomorrow," she continued. "I think we need to tell them. Right now."

CHAPTER FIFTY-THREE

Malachi Martin waited across the street from the *Rambler* building, on a bench that faced its Main Street entrance. He would never sit on the sidewalk. That looked too much like begging, whether he held a cup or not. But he did allow himself to sit on a bench.

Miz Branigan had told him what Gerald Dubois looked like. Malachi hoped he would recognize the newspaper's arts writer.

A few women entered the building, then some men in suits. Then a man in chinos and a dress shirt, his black hair curling over his collar, walked down the street, a Bea's coffee cup in hand. Malachi stood, jaywalked, and approached him as he pulled open the heavy glass door bearing the *Grambling Rambler* logo, an entwined G and R. Gerald Dubois hadn't noticed him, so he spoke softly to avoid startling him.

It didn't work. Gerald jumped, came very near to screaming. It came out as something of a squeak. He skipped away from Malachi.

"Mr Dubois, I'm a friend of Branigan Powers. I'm helping her with a story."

The reporter relaxed. "Oh. Her story on homelessness?"

Malachi nodded. "Vesuvius Hightower, the man kilt by a hit-and-run driver, was an artist."

"Yeah, that was in Branigan's story," Gerald said. "Interesting."

"I've got one of his pieces I'd like to show you. Over at the bench."

Gerald's apprehension seemed to return, but the bench was sitting in broad daylight, a piece of plywood propped against it. He followed Malachi across Main Street. When he looked at the moonscape, the last of his unease vanished.

"My word!" he said. "What a gorgeous example of outsider art!"

He checked his watch, then asked Malachi if he had time to accompany him to a folk art gallery. With a single phone call from Gerald, the owner came down from his apartment above the store and let them in. He propped Vesuvius's painting on an easel, studied it closely, then from across the room, then up close again. Malachi was glad to see that the moonlit pond mesmerized these men as thoroughly as it had him.

The gallery owner offered Malachi $2,000 on the spot, provided he could prove he owned the painting.

"I could get Pastor Liam at Jericho Road to vouch for me," Malachi said. "But I'm not sure I'm sellin'."

Gerald stepped in and told the gallery owner that Malachi most assuredly wasn't ready to sell. He wanted to take the piece to some Atlanta galleries to make sure Malachi got top price. The man upped his offer to $3,000.

"No," Gerald told him. "This painting is part of an ongoing story *The Rambler* is doing. I just wanted your take on it."

He thanked the man and pulled Malachi away, whispering about getting an appraisal from a national folk art museum too. Malachi wasn't terribly concerned about that. Anything he got, he intended to donate to Jericho Road anyway. But he did want two things: recognition for his friend V, and confirmation that discarding this painting was as strange as he thought it was.

He was no art critic, but throwing this work away seemed to cry out against anyone with education or breeding or… *what*, exactly, Malachi wondered?

Then he had it: *heart*.

No one with heart would throw this painting away.

CHAPTER FIFTY-FOUR

Chan needn't have worried about waking his parents. His mom was sitting at the breakfast table when he and Charlie came down, but his dad was already at the church.

"With the police there, he left early," Liz said. "What do you need to talk about?"

Chan hesitated. "I'd rather tell you together. Could we all have dinner tonight?"

"Of course," said Liz. "We'll skip pizza at the church and I'll whip up something. How's that sound?"

"Thanks, Mom. That'll be great."

"So can I go back to sleep now?" Charlie asked.

Liz looked mystified.

Liam poured himself a cup of coffee when he entered Jericho Road, but the men had only just started cooking breakfast. He could smell muffins baking. "Save me one of those," he called as he passed the serving window.

"Sure thing, Pastor," Jess answered.

Liam deposited his briefcase in his office, then continued down the hall to the latest addition he'd requested from a partner church's mission team – a prayer room. The room was small, pieced together from remnants of a renovation at Jericho's mother church. A floor-to-ceiling stained-glass window of Jesus in Gethsemane took up an entire wall. Because it was an interior wall, the construction team had installed lighting behind it. Liam flipped the switch, causing Jesus' robe to glow ruby red, his tormented face bronze. Behind a rock, almost comically out of proportion, huddled three tiny figures: Peter, James and John.

Rows of pew segments, wide enough to seat three abreast, faced the window. The staff used the space for weekly devotions, but more often for individual contemplation and prayer.

Liam sat on the front pew, head bowed, hands hanging between his legs.

"God," he said helplessly. "Chandler. Please help Chan when he gets this news. God, he is such a good boy. Don't let this destroy him. I pray for Davison and Shauna, but as you know, my heart is not right about them."

He paused a moment, regrouped his thoughts. "And God, this church. You have been with us every step of the way, blessing, protecting, loving this place. Help me know how to deal with this evil, Lord, to understand how and why evil has crept into this place. Help me know, Lord, the right way to respond to the police and the media. Give me wisdom and courage, as You had during Your time in the garden."

Liam was silent for awhile, trying to listen for a word, but aware his mind was ricocheting from Chan to Vesuvius to Rita to Max.

"I'm sorry I failed them," he whispered. "All of them. Help me make it right."

CHAPTER FIFTY-FIVE

Branigan drove past the *Rambler* building and straight to Jericho Road. Heaven knew she didn't need more coffee, but she took a cup anyway. She was too upset to eat, even though the banana-walnut muffins smelled delicious.

Dontegan greeted her as she turned from the urn. "You gettin' to be a regulah, Miz Branigan." He smiled. "I think Pastuh Liam back there in the prayin' room. Or with the po-lice."

"That's okay. I'm looking for someone else."

She spotted Malachi's distinctive dreadlocks and headed for his table.

"I brought you something," she said coldly, pulling a cantaloupe out of her purse and rolling it across the table to him. "Do you want to tell me why you've been sleeping in my barn?"

He didn't answer.

"Malachi, what's up? I know Liam has offered you a room here a dozen times. Why would you bike ten miles out of town to eat my cantaloupes and sleep in a cattle stall?"

"I can assure you, Miz Branigan, your cattle stall holds no attraction for me."

She was too angry to be amused at his language. "So what's up? Clearly you haven't tried to break in and kill me. Yet."

Malachi looked startled. His next words were so low she had to lean in to hear. "Maybe that's what I'm tryin' to prevent."

At least, that's what she thought he said.

She stomped out of the Jericho Road dining hall, and turned her car toward the police station. She needed to get the latest from Detective Scovoy on the interrogation of Heath Resnick. As she pulled into the parking lot in front of the station, she saw Heath slam through the front door. She slunk down in her seat, hoping to avoid him. He jumped into a black Range Rover and squealed out of the parking lot, raising eyebrows among the police officers reporting for work.

Detective Scovoy met her in the hallway, dark circles under his eyes.

"You didn't hold him," she said.

"Couldn't," he said, rubbing his face. "We went at it all night. I called Ben Brissey Jr and their stories matched up. They both say Heath took the hat from Ben Jr at the pool house. Heath says he wore it, as a joke, for the next hour or so at the party. Then he doesn't remember what he did with it – probably just laid it on a chair.

"When I told him Amanda found it on the laundry room floor, he didn't blink. Said he could have left it on a kitchen counter and it got tossed into the laundry room. He just doesn't remember. And Tabitha, Mrs Resnick's maid, died last year, so we don't know if she could back up his story."

"So after that huge web of lies by Amanda, nothing's different?"

"We're not stopping," he said. "The investigation is officially re-opened. Amanda Brissey also told us more about her mother's plan to revise her will. She said it wasn't simply a case of cutting Heath out. She claimed that Heath had already spent his portion of the inheritance in the form of unpaid loans from Mr Resnick.

"We looked into Heath's finances at the time, but loans from his father didn't surface. Now we know what we're looking for."

Branigan pulled out her recorder and took the quotes Detective Scovoy was willing to give on the record. At least she could write that the investigation was being reopened on the basis of new information from Amanda Brissey.

"One other thing, off the record," Scovoy said, as she was packing to leave. "We're also looking into any relationship Heath Resnick had with the homeless community. You've been right about a lot. If you're convinced his mother's death provoked these homeless murders, I'm willing to listen. I suppose it's even possible Heath Resnick paid a transient to do his work for him."

That was something Branigan hadn't considered. "Heath owns a lot of property. If some of it is abandoned, I guess he could have run into homeless folks."

As she left the police station, she had another thought – one that explained the switch from vehicular homicide to Max's cutting death. What if Heath had paid Max to kill his mother, then run down Vesuvius and Rita? Then the two conspirators could have got into an argument that ended in Max's murder. She wished she had more time before the story ran.

But waiting, she reminded herself, hadn't worked so far.

Branigan drove to the newsroom and spent a couple of hours putting the final touches on the anniversary story. She gave it to Tan to read, with the understanding she might make changes as she got more information from Detective Scovoy.

A lot of the story was color and rehashing. Unlike Branigan, readers hadn't been thinking of this murder every moment for the last few weeks. They needed to be brought up to speed on the players and the places. The facts alone made a compelling read, whether reporters had anything new or not. Add the reopening of the investigation, Amanda's tampering with the crime scene and the possible ancillary murders of three homeless people, and it became a real news piece.

Normally at this point in a big story, Branigan felt exhilaration. Now there was none, and she knew why. Her nosing around might have led to important new information, but it had also led to the deaths of two people, possibly three.

She abruptly left the office. It was almost time for Rita's memorial service.

Branigan slipped quietly into a back row in Jericho Road's dining hall, rearranged for a funeral service. About eighty people were present, the majority of them homeless, but others drawn because of the newspaper coverage. An older man, two women and three children in the front row appeared to be Jones family members, presumably from Atlanta. Detective Scovoy and two other homicide detectives were intentionally scattered among the crowd, undoubtedly to see if they could glean anything new on the murder.

A robed gospel quartet opened with an a cappella version of "I'll Fly Away", followed by "May the Circle Be Unbroken". Branigan recognized the singers from Jericho Road's Sunday services, their voices sweet and clear.

The woman she assumed was Rita's sister read next from the fourteenth chapter of John's Gospel. Then Liam stood and launched his remarks from that passage: "In My Father's house there are many dwelling places... I go to prepare a place for you."

Liam spoke for awhile about the Christian understanding of death as the beginning of a new time with the Lord. He read from Romans that "neither death nor life nor angels nor rulers nor things present nor things to come... will be able to separate us from the love of God in Christ Jesus".

Then he paused. "I hardly know how to continue," he said finally. "This is one of those situations when an earthly life was filled with unbearable pain. And while I truly believe that Rita is in a better place now, I also carry a burden that this church failed her while she lived, that we were unable to ease that pain."

Branigan heard several "amens". The older woman in the first row began to cry into a handkerchief.

"The fact is Rita had a monkey on her back," Liam said. "I know we don't always like to talk about addiction at a memorial service, but to deny it is ludicrous. Her body and mind were racked with this disease of addiction. But even that is no explanation for the fact that she was killed by a van from this church. This church charged with living out the gospel somehow failed to do that. That is the nature of things on this side of the cross.

"And so I urge any of you who have information about Rita's death to please share that information with police officers who have set up an office here. We want justice for our friend. We want to honor her in death in a way we failed to do during her life."

The quartet rose and, singing "Amazing Grace", led mourners from the dining hall.

After the service, Branigan drove to an inner-city park built around a waterfall. It was a small place, bursting with day lilies and hostas and waterside ferns. For awhile, she simply sat on the grass, images crowding her mind – how confused Vesuvius must have felt when headlights bore down on him. What Rita's frightened face must have looked like in her last moments. What Max must have felt as the life drained from him.

She knew she needed to get back to the newsroom, but her stomach was clinched and her throat sore from unshed tears. She sat another few minutes, then rose on leaden legs.

In the newsroom, she looked over Tan's questions and comments, expanding some sections, shifting and tightening others as he suggested. She planned to return Saturday morning to deal with any final edits.

She then took a look at Jody's story, which was basically a recounting of the investigation into the hit-and-runs of Vesuvius and Rita by the Jericho Road van. Detective Scovoy had assigned two detectives to conduct interviews at the shelter, while he delved into the reopened Resnick case. Tips from the public were also streaming in to the police hotline. Branigan offered Jody a paragraph on Rita's memorial service, and he wove it into his story.

Then she read Marjorie's story, which was an insightful piece on homelessness in Grambling. She touched on the deaths of Vesuvius, Rita and Max, but talked more about the people no one else was talking about – the people still living under the Garner Bridge, in abandoned Randall Mill houses, in Eastside encampments. The impression the story gave was of disposable lives. You wouldn't expect it in the United States, but here it was. Every society, Branigan supposed, had its throwaways.

She stared for awhile at the photographs that would accompany their articles, including one of Rita's shack on the ledge under the Michael Garner Bridge.

She remembered finding her brother there, and shuddered to think of the things he'd seen during twelve years of homelessness. *But all that's over,* she told herself. *He's getting sober. He'll meet Chan tomorrow. Maybe he'll stay at the farm for awhile after rehab. Maybe we'll go back to the beach before summer's over.*

She pushed Marjorie's story from her mind, and drove toward home.

On an impulse, she turned into Uncle Bobby and Aunt Jeanie's driveway. Visitors were rare in the country, so Jeanie heard the car and was waiting at her kitchen door.

"Where've you been?" she greeted Branigan. "Your mama said Davison left on Monday."

"He did, but I've been too busy to get by. Let me get my wine out of your way."

Jeanie helped load one box into the trunk, and Branigan realized she didn't feel like going home. "Aunt Jeanie, would you like to have a glass of wine?"

"Hon, I'd love to, but your uncle and I are going to the Grambling Little Theatre tonight. You have no idea how long it took me to talk him into it."

Branigan laughed. "Oh yes, I do. Next time, invite me. I love live theater."

"You better believe I will. Bobby will be whining to leave at intermission."

Branigan packed the second box of wine and liquor into the Civic trunk and pulled out of the driveway. A quarter-mile down the road, she turned into her own.

For one of the few times since she'd moved back to the farm, she felt lonely. A long Friday evening stretched before her. She'd always loved these long days, the march to the summer solstice. But with no one to share them with, they were just that: long days.

At the sound of the car, Cleo ambled from the back porch, undoubtedly having been sleeping in its shade. That gave Branigan an idea.

After bringing in the boxes, she pulled on her running clothes and tied her hair into a ponytail. But instead of running, she retrieved an old CD/radio/cassette player out of the guest room closet. This boom box had traveled with her from Grambling to Athens to Detroit and back. She rifled through a canvas tote filled with CDs, and came up with the beach music she and Davison had heard last weekend at the Isle of Palms: The Tams, Drifters, Chairmen of the Board.

Carrying them to the back porch, she plugged the player in and turned it up loud. No one to disturb out here.

She'd thought to pour a glass of pinot noir, but at the sight of her newly returned rum, she had a better idea. She rummaged through the freezer and found a can of pina colada mix she'd purchased as soon as the weather warmed in April. She located her well-used blender and added the mix, rum and crushed ice from the freezer door. The final touch was a straw and a paper umbrella in pink and yellow and green. Soon she was sitting on the porch, feet up, listening to "Be Young, Be Foolish, Be Happy" and gazing across the cotton field, the pasture, the lakes – her favorite view in the world.

She was doing her best to release the ache in her chest.

CHAPTER FIFTY-SIX

The Delaneys were gathered in their funky black and white tiled kitchen with the red appliances and cabinet pulls. The 1930s feel ran throughout the house, but this room had been the most fun for Liz. Visitors often requested that she recreate the color scheme in their homes.

Remnants of salad, spaghetti and garlic bread littered the table. Liam had left Dontegan in charge of the church's pizza night.

"I'm only sorry," Liz was telling her son again, "that you went through this alone for the past month. We never intended that."

"If family is nothing else," Liam added, "we're the people who have your back. Always."

"I know," said Chan. "That's why these past few weeks have been hard. It was exciting to meet Davison, but it didn't feel right – you not knowing. Charlie convinced me of that."

"I wonder why he didn't want us to know," Liz said. "Do you think he was worried about being ganged up on? I mean, with all four of us staring at him?"

"I think he wanted some clean time behind him," Chan answered. "He wanted you to know he was serious."

"Could be." Liam shrugged. "Who knows? Maybe the whole thing will be easier now. I'll call him to set up a time for tomorrow."

"I have his cell number, if you need it," said Chan.

"Branigan said he can only answer between eight and nine at night," Liam said. "But I know the   director and counselors at the mission. They may let me talk to him."

Liam scanned his cell phone directory. He nodded to Chan when the assistant director came on the line. He explained that he needed to talk to a client in the rehab program, or at least to leave a message: for Davison Powers.

"Liam, we don't have a Davison Powers," said his colleague.

"His sister, Branigan Powers, checked him in Monday morning."

"Hold on. I can look at Monday's check-ins."

He was back in less than a minute. "You're right. We did check a Davison Powers in Monday at 8 a.m. But he walked out before lunch the same day."

Liam put his phone down on the table. "He's not in the mission," he said tonelessly.

"Sure he is," Chan said. "I talked to him every night this week."

"On his cell?"

"Oh," Chan said, the color draining from his face. "Yeah."

"You mean, he didn't even try?" asked Charlie, looking from Chan to her father. "He didn't even try to get sober?"

Liz shot a look at her daughter.

"No, it's okay, Mom," said Chan, though the look on his face belied it. "He lied about getting clean."

He shook his head, trying to understand this new information, trying to understand how everything he'd learned over the past few weeks was shifting beneath his feet. "He lied about getting clean," he repeated.

He drew in a ragged breath. "There's one more thing I need to tell you."

CHAPTER FIFTY-SEVEN

Two strong pina coladas later, Branigan was feeling fine. She didn't want to run, but the thought of Cleo pacing through the night, unexercised, persuaded her.

"Okay, girl, let's do it," she said. "Though I'm not sure why you can't run during the day without me."

Cleo thumped her tail.

They set off down the path through the cotton field, avoiding the barn and rolling under the barbed wire and into the pasture, vacant now of Uncle Bobby's cattle. Branigan guessed he'd moved them onto his adjoining land. She never could keep up with their coming and going, and suspected there wasn't a lot of science behind it. Maybe more to do with keeping out of Aunt Jeanie's hair.

She giggled. They trotted past the lake and woods where she and Jason Hornay had enjoyed more than one wine-soaked picnic and make-out session, back when her grandparents were living here. She turned maudlin. "Hey, Jason!" she yelled. "Whatever happened to you? I hope it was worth losing me!"

Cleo stopped and looked at her mistress, cocking her head. "That's right, Cleo! You heard me!"

She finally stopped her chortling and began to run. The pina coladas sloshed in her empty stomach, but the fresh air sobered her up a bit. They ran about three-quarters of their regular course, which was all Branigan could manage. On the way back, they passed the barn. That's when she got the idea.

At the house, she ate a bagel and shredded cheese, as much to convince herself she was sober as because she was hungry. She didn't bother showering, but did change clothes – into a black T-shirt, black sweat pants and gray tennis shoes. After a few moments in front of a mirror, she covered her blond hair with a navy scarf.

She saw a message from Liam on her phone, but didn't take the time to return it. She'd be back in plenty of time to call him tonight.

Branigan's only moment of doubt came when she turned on the outside lights and left the house – locking Cleo inside. The dog didn't like that one bit. Her indignant bark followed Branigan halfway through the cotton patch before dissolving into the dusk. She slipped into the barn, which was already fully dark inside, and used a flashlight to locate the ladder at the far end. This took her to a broad shelf that provided a ceiling for the cattle stalls. It was Uncle Bobby's area for hay storage, and there was plenty of it up here. She shifted several bales around until she could see through the cracks to the floor below while remaining unseen.

Branigan settled down to wait for a homeless man who, for some unfathomable reason, was biking ten miles out of town to sleep in her barn and, from the luscious smell in here, eat her cantaloupes.

It was a measure of Branigan's lack of fear of Malachi that she fell asleep. She hadn't intended to. But she jerked awake when she heard the loud screech of the barn door opening, followed by the softer squeak of bicycle tires. Malachi left the door wide open – she could see the farmhouse off in the distance, lights glowing inside and out. She couldn't see him in the stall below, but she heard him humming.

For the next half-hour, he puttered, going to the barn door every ten minutes or so to look across the field at the farmhouse. *What is he waiting for? For me to turn out the lights?*

He lit a candle in the stall. She still couldn't see him, but could see the ring of light that flickered outside the stall. Then she heard more squeaking of bicycle tires.

The squeaking grew louder, and suddenly another figure stood in the doorway, dark against dark.

She squinted to see him, but couldn't. Then the newly arrived figure spoke.

"So you finally shown up. You gonna kill your sistah now too?"

What? If Malachi was in the doorway, who was in the stall?

And then she heard the voice she'd heard every childhood day on this farm; the voice that she loved above all others. *But he's in the gospel mission,* her mind clamored. *He can't be here.*

"Of course I'm not going to kill my sister."

"But you kilt them others," said Malachi.

"What others?"

"Vesuvius. Rita. Max."

"It wasn't me. I read in the paper they were killed by the church van. How would I get the church van?"

"I 'spect you talk Mr Chan into tellin' you where the key was. You is his daddy, ain't you?"

This new information was coming so fast, so discordantly, that Branigan refused to take it in. She wondered wildly, disconnectedly, why Malachi was letting his grammar slip.

"Malachi, you're letting your imagination run away with you."

"I don' think so. You bought you a pitcher from Vesuvius, but then you threw it away. That's what made me start thinkin' of you."

"I did buy a painting from Vesuvius. But I planned to give it to Branigan. She's a big art lover."

"Why din't you give it to her then? Why you throw it away?"

"I don't have to explain anything to you. In fact, you're trespassing on my family's property."

Malachi didn't back down. "I figures you kilt some rich lady a long time ago. Then you comes back to town and hear Rita yappin' 'bout it. She done tole Vesuvius and me and Max and Dontegan and who knows who else? An' you start spreadin' money 'round tryin' to stop the talkin'. But there's too much talkin'.

"What I din't unnerstan at first was why you come back. Then I saw you at the li-bree with Mr Chan. And it make sense.

"What I don' unnerstan is why you gots to kill V. He done stop talkin' when you buy his pitcher. Why you gots to kill him?"

This was obviously another bad dream set in Pa's barn. Branigan's mind skittered away from Malachi's outlandish accusations and settled on his speech patterns. So country. So uneducated.

And suddenly she knew what Malachi was doing. He was luring Davison into confessing to an ignorant, uneducated man who didn't matter. The confession wouldn't matter because Malachi didn't matter. She wanted to scream a warning to Davison. But she didn't.

"I had to kill Vesuvius because he was 'touched in the head', as we used to say," Davison said. "How could I trust him to keep quiet?"

"How you got him outta Jericho Road after dark?"

"I called his cell phone and told him I wanted to meet about commissioning a painting. The fact that street people have free cell phones is enormously helpful."

Malachi's voice turned chillier. "Why you move in Rita's shack under the bridge? You plan to kill her there?"

"Hell, I didn't know who she was. And I sure didn't know she'd seen me at Mrs Resnick's. I only put that together when I heard Branigan and Liam talking."

There it was: her worst fear. Her meddling had gotten Rita killed. She felt the pina coladas coming back up, but forced herself to swallow and keep quiet.

"And the 'rich-ass family' she talk about payin' to keep quiet, that's yo' family, right?"

"Yeah, except that shows how little she knew my family. You see them paying to keep me anywhere? And Branigan's trying her hardest to send my butt to prison."

Branigan hugged herself and clinched her eyes. If she'd thought there was nothing worse than getting Rita and Max killed, she'd been badly mistaken.

"Why you not run Max down with the church van?" Malachi was relentless. "Why change your MO?"

She had a mad desire to laugh at Malachi's use of police lingo.

"My MO?" Davison said mockingly. "My MO changed because I was afraid that damn Liam would connect the church van to Chan. That's how I got it. Chan told me where the key was and I made a copy."

Branigan clamped a hand over her mouth, repulsed that Chan had been pulled into this ugliness.

Malachi didn't let up. "You give Max money?"

"I gave the old drunk $100, but he used it to get drunker and keep talking. So I went to his tent. Took another bottle and offered it to him. He went off on me, demanded $200. Where am I going to get that kind of money?"

"From the Jericho Road box?" Malachi guessed.

"It was only good the one time," Davison said.

"So what you doin' here in the barn?"

"You tell me. Obviously you expected me."

"I think you come to kill your sistah 'fore she figure ever'thin' out."

Branigan didn't know who was more horrified – her or Davison. He let out a roar and rushed Malachi. Too late, she saw the gleam of a knife in his hand.

She wanted to scream a warning to Davison, to tell him Malachi was military-trained, street-smart. You didn't survive fourteen years on the streets without knowing your way around weapons.

But another part of her brain knew a deeper reality – knew that Malachi's words, as crazily painful as they were, were true. And so she screamed something quite different.

"Malachi! He's got a knife!"

The disembodied shriek coming from the barn rafters startled Davison and gave Malachi the time he needed to swing around and grab Davison's wrist. The knife scuttled into the darkness.

Malachi twisted Davison's arm behind him as her brother sank to his knees.

"Branigan," he cried. "I caught this guy waiting to break into the farmhouse."

She clambered down the ladder and stood over him, her breath breaking unevenly.

"He was waiting for your lights to go off," said the voice of her dreams, the voice of her nightmares. "I've seen him before. He's homeless."

"Yeah, he is," she said. "But he's so much more."

CHAPTER FIFTY-EIGHT

B ranigan supposed she could have called the Cannon County Sheriff's Office. It was their jurisdiction should anyone want to charge Davison with the attempted murder of Malachi Martin. Or, for that matter, the attempted murder of Branigan Powers. Davison swore he'd never planned to do that. She chose to believe him.

The truth was bad enough without that.

Instead, she called the Grambling Police Department, and she and Malachi waited in the barn for the nine minutes it took Detective Scovoy and his colleagues to arrive, blue lights flashing, sirens screaming. They charged Davison with four counts of murder: Alberta Resnick, Vesuvius Hightower, Rita Mae Jones, Max Brody.

During the interminable wait, as Malachi kept Davison on his knees, his arm locked securely behind him, Branigan tried to clear her head. "I believed you when you said you'd never been homeless in Grambling," she said. "But you lived in Mrs Resnick's pool house the spring before her murder, didn't you? Those were your books."

"Yeah, but I didn't move in until after Billy did," Davison said. "When he attracted so much attention, I left."

"And did you come to the farm before contacting Liam? That footprint outside my window before I knew you were back. . ."

In the candlelight, she saw a look pass over his face – a look she'd seen in the past week and identified as embarrassment, or even shame. Now she recognized it as cunning.

"I wanted to see where you were living, Brani G. I wanted to see if we couldn't get back to the way things used to be."

It was that look that sealed things. Things she wanted to believe slipped away. She felt the dark weight in her chest crack and shift.

"I thought you loved Mrs Resnick."

"I did, I guess, when we were kids. She bought us ice cream, remember? From the ice cream truck." He shrugged. "I guess I loved crack more."

He must have seen the look of horror on his sister's face, because he grew defensive. "You just don't understand, Branigan. You never have."

"What's to understand? You let drugs rule you. You let drugs ruin everything." She checked her anger. There was so much more she needed to know. She took a breath. "Rita. She was killed the night we got back from the beach. You sneaked out?"

Davison pointed to her bike. "After what you told me on the way down, I knew she was a ticking bomb. All I had to do was bike to town, pick her up in the church van and offer her crack. Then I put her out and, well... you know the rest."

"But why'd you put her out on Mrs Resnick's street?"

"I wanted to know what she'd seen all those years ago, how she knew me. She said she knew me – and you – from when we shopped at the mall. It was her idea to drive to Mrs Resnick's so she could point out where she'd been hiding. She thought I wanted to talk about paying to keep her quiet, so she was plenty talkative. Right up 'til the end."

Branigan was too numb to ask anything else, so Malachi took over. "What happen to you, man? You had everythin'."

Davison sighed. "You've been out there. You know what this life can do to you. I knew the old lady had money. All I needed was enough to get high, and she wouldn't give it to me. Slammed the door in my face.

"I got away with it too. Would've gotten away with it forever if I hadn't come back to see Chan." He shrugged, turned his face toward Branigan.

She couldn't see him clearly – could see only the angle of that face so like her own. That's why his next words cut so deep.

"Would've gotten away with it if I didn't have you for a sister."

For the first time, her tears began to flow. They flowed for a gentle disabled artist named Vesuvius. For a horribly damaged woman named Rita Mae. For a mean drunk named Max, who undoubtedly had his own demons. For a brother so lost to her he would wish away their kinship.

"That's something I'll have to live with," she whispered. "I just wish Chan didn't have to live with it too."

Branigan and Malachi followed Detective Scovoy's convoy back to Grambling, Malachi's bicycle in her trunk.

"I owe you an apology," she told him. "You've been sleeping in my barn to protect me. And you left those bottles to let me know." She was too ashamed to tell him she'd misread his signal, taken it as a threat rather than a promise. In her own way, she was as bad as all those people who looked through Malachi.

"No problem, Miz Branigan." He'd dropped his slang; was mirroring her speech patterns again.

As devastated as she was, she still had a job to do. "How did you know it was Davison?" she asked. "I thought it was Heath Resnick and we'd never be able to prove it."

"The main thing," he said, "was V's paintin'. It didn't make sense to spend money on a paintin', then throw it away. The fact that it ended up in the trash under the bridge pointed to a homeless dude.

"The other thin' was Mr Chan. He seemed awfully unhappy for a young man headin' off to college. Somethin' bad had a-hold of him. I think he suspected his real daddy had taken the church van after he got him to tell where the key was. But he didn't know 'bout the old lady's murder, so nothin' made sense. Why would a homeless dude go out and run down other homeless dudes?

"The third thing was there was a lot of talk goin' on in the homeless camps. A lot of what you hear you got to take with a grain of salt. But everybody knows when somebody comes into money. So V and Max kind of stuck out. Rita, not so much. If your brother gave her money, she smoked it up."

"I had all the same information and didn't put it together," she said.

"Without living out here, you couldn't know these folks," said Malachi. "And you loved your brother. Ain't nothin' wrong with that."

Malachi asked to be dropped off on North Main. She watched him wheel his bike through the glow of the streetlights, then disappear into the trees on the courthouse lawn, donning his familiar cloak of invisibility.

She drove down Main Street to *The Rambler*.

The newsroom was as crowded as it got these days, alerted by Jody who, along with a swarm of TV reporters, was at the police station. Tan-4 and Marjorie and Julie were compiling and editing his remotely filed pieces for the website.

Tan greeted Branigan with uncharacteristic gentleness. "We're breaking the story online and in Saturday's paper," he said. "But it'll only be enough to whet readers' appetites for Sunday. I want Jody and Marjorie taking the lead. Branigan, feed 'em what you've got."

"No," she said, not loudly or belligerently. "I'm writing this."

"No way. It's about your brother."

"I'm writing this."

Tan stood over her desk, glowering.

"She's right," Julie said.

Marjorie nodded. "It's her story, Tan."

Tan thought it over for another few seconds. "Fine. But I okay every word. What are you waiting for? Go!"

She slipped on the ugly maroon sweater to stop her shivering.

And she began to write. She had so little else.

CHAPTER FIFTY-NINE

TWO MONTHS LATER

Liz called Branigan to say they were running late. Liam's SUV was packed, and he'd borrowed her car to run by the church. Now it was sputtering, so he planned to leave it and deal with it later.

She asked if Branigan could pick him up on her way to their house.

Branigan and Liz planned to follow Liam and Chan to Furman University. Between the Beetle and the SUV, his belongings fit easily, his mom said. Charlie's trip to the University of Georgia the previous week had required Branigan's car as well.

Branigan was already downtown when Liz called, so she pulled into Jericho Road within minutes. Dontegan was directing the breakfast clean-up, and Malachi was sweeping. He nodded and gave her a shy smile. "Miz Branigan."

She ignored his reticence and gave him a long hug. "Mr Malachi." When she released him, she added, "By the way, I've got too many cantaloupes ripening. May I bring you some?"

He nodded. "That'd be just fine. You grow a decent 'loupe."

She laughed. "Is Liam in his office?"

"Or in the prayer room."

She passed Liam's empty office and approached the only door that was painted on – "… for my house shall be called a house of prayer", it read in beautiful blue script.

The door was ajar, and she could hear Liam's voice, mid-sentence. His voice was unlike she'd ever heard it, choked, raspy. Was he crying?

"… how he's going to make it. I beg of You, I beg of You, to heal his heart. Lord, what is going to become of him? Will he be like them?"

Then all she heard was ragged breathing.

She tiptoed to Liam's office to wait.

He came in a few minutes later, eyes red. "Liz called you, huh?"

She nodded, waited for him to say something. When he didn't, she asked, "Want to tell me?"

He sighed. "Not a thing to tell that you don't know."

"I know you've had him in counseling. I know you wanted him to stay home for a year to continue it. I know he said no, he wanted to start college."

"But what chance does he have?" said Liam, sitting heavily in the navy rocker. "It was one thing to have two druggies for parents. It's another to have a serial killer for a dad."

She flinched.

"I'm sorry, Brani G. You know I love you. But God help me, I wish Davison were dead. As long as he's alive, Chan's going to have to deal with him."

"I know."

He asked his question again. "What chance does he have?"

"A good one, Liam. He may have been born to two druggie parents and even a killer, but he never spent a day – not one single day – with them. You and Liz and Charlie and your parents have loved that boy and made him yours. And now he's got Mom and Dad and me. He's got a good chance, Liam. I swear to you he's got a good chance."

He wiped his eyes and drew a deep breath. "I hope you're right. Okay, let's go to Greenville."

They drove to his house in silence. When she pulled into the Delaney driveway, Chan was stuffing the last of his cardboard boxes, guitar, soccer ball and desk lamp into the bright blue Beetle he and Liam had restored.

"Aunt Branigan, Mom says it's okay if you ride with me. Is that all right, Dad?"

She looked at Liam. He nodded, though she could tell it pained him.

Liz and Liam climbed into the SUV and led the way. She and Chan followed. She had been over this ground with her nephew, every childhood memory of Davison she could remember, every lovely, loving part of him.

This boy knew every horrid detail about his father from the guilty plea, from the newspaper stories, the TV broadcasts, the whispers everywhere he went in Grambling.

The story he could get from no one else was the one she didn't write for *The Rambler:* the story of a gentle and protective brother, a beach dancer, a cotton picker, a boy who ate cinnamon toast and listened for long-distance trucks in the night.

And so, once more, she told his son about that boy.

THE JAZZ FILES

POPPY DENBY INVESTIGATES

"What a delight to escape into the world of the irrepressible Poppy Denby in this cleverly-plotted debut."

– Ruth Downie, author of the *Medicus* series

"It stands for Jazz Files," said Rollo. "It's what we call any story that has a whiff of high society scandal but can't yet be proven... you never know when a skeleton in the closet might prove useful."

Set in 1920, *The Jazz Files* introduces aspiring journalist Poppy Denby, who arrives in London to look after her ailing Aunt Dot, an infamous suffragette. Dot encourages Poppy to apply for a job at *The Daily Globe*, but on her first day a senior reporter is killed and Poppy is tasked with finishing his story. It involves the mysterious death of a suffragette seven years earlier, about which some powerful people would prefer that nothing be said...

Through her friend Delilah Marconi, Poppy is introduced to the giddy world of London in the Roaring Twenties, with its flappers, jazz clubs, and romance. Will she make it as an investigative journalist, in this fast-paced new city? And will she be able to unearth the truth before more people die?

ISBN: 978-1-78264-175-9 | e-ISBN: 978-1-78264-176-6

THE JAZZ FILES

POPPY DENBY
INVESTIGATES

series

ISBN 978-1-78264-192-6 ISBN 978-1782641926

THE RELUCTANT DETECTIVE

A FAITH MORGAN MYSTERY

"Couldn't resist touching the body, eh?" observed Ben.

Faith was defiant. "I had to check for a pulse."

Faith Morgan may have quit the world of crime, but crime won't let her go. The ex-policewoman has retrained as a priest, disillusioned with a tough police culture and convinced that she can do more good this way.

But now her worlds collide. Searching for the first posting of her new career, she witnesses a sudden and shocking death in a quiet Hampshire village. And of all people, Detective Inspector Ben Shorter, her former colleague and boyfriend, shows up to investigate the crime.

Persuaded to stay on in Little Worthy, she learns surprising details about the victim and starts to piece together a motive for his death. But is she now in danger herself? And what should she do about Ben?

Then a further horrifying event deepens the mystery...

ISBN: 978 1 78264 068 4 | e-ISBN: 978 1 78264 126 1

THE
CANTALOUPE
THIEF

A BRANIGAN POWERS MYSTERY

DEB RICHARDSON-MOORE

LION FICTION

Published by Lion Fiction
an imprint of
Lion Hudson plc
Wilkinson House, Jordan Hill Road
Oxford OX2 8DR, England
www.lionhudson.com/fiction

ISBN 978 1 78264 192 6
e-ISBN 978 1 78264 193 3

First edition 2016

Acknowledgments
Scripture quotations taken from The New Revised Standard Version of the Bible copyright © 1989 by the Division of Christian Education of the National Council of Churches in the USA. Used by permission. All Rights Reserved.

A catalogue record for this book is available from the British Library

Printed and bound in the UK, March 2016, LH26

To the late Vina and Durey Powers,
Georgia farmers.
And to Rick,
Ronald and Lori,
fellow cantaloupe eaters.

ACKNOWLEDGMENTS

Thanks to my writers' group: Susan Clary Simmons, Wanda Owings, Jeanne Brooks and Allison Greene, who demanded more tension, more menace. If it's not there, it's my fault, not theirs.

Thanks to later readers Elaine Nocks, Michelle McClendon, Lori Bradley, Taylor Moore, Lynne Lucas, Lynn Cusick, Doris Richardson, Rick and Candace Richardson, Madison Moore and Susan Stall.

Thanks to the Triune Mercy Center board and staff for allowing me a writing sabbatical to wrap things up. And a special thank you to the worshipers at Triune, who taught me that there are as many kinds of homeless people as there are housed people.

I appreciate Tony Collins, Jessica Tinker, Jessica Scott and their team at Lion Hudson in England, and their counterparts at Kregel Publications in the USA, including Noelle Pederson and Lori Alberda.

As always, thanks to Vince – for a quiet writing time in Crail and Edinburgh, and for everything else. And to Dustin, Taylor and Madison, who make it all worthwhile.